INNOCENT

The INNOCENT

A NOVEL

ANN H. GABHART

Revell

a division of Baker Publishing Group
Grand Rapids, Michigan

© 2015 by Ann H. Gabhart

Published by Revell
a division of Baker Publishing Group
P.O. Box 6287, Grand Rapids, MI 49516-6287
www.revellbooks.com

Printed in the United States of America

Library of Congress Cataloging-in-Publication Data
Gabhart, Ann H., 1947–
       The innocent : a novel / Ann H. Gabhart.
         pages cm
       ISBN 978-0-8007-2341-5 (pbk.)
       I. Title
       PS3607.A23I56 2015
       813'.6—dc23   2015005639

This book is a work of fiction. Names, characters, places, and incidents are the product of the author's imagination or are used fictitiously. Any resemblance to actual events, locales, or persons, living or dead, is coincidental.

Scripture used in this book, whether quoted or paraphrased by the characters, is taken from the King James Version of the Bible.

Page 268—"Come Dance and Sing"—Shaker Hymnal, recorded 1838.

Page 319—"Kindness and Love"—Shaker Hymnal, recorded at Enfield, Connecticut, 1852.

Page 350—"God Moves in Mysterious Ways"—words, William Cowper, 1774.

Published in association with the Books & Such Literary Agency.

15   16   17   18   19   20   21   7   6   5   4   3   2

To my family, and especially my son-in-law, Gary, who sparked the idea for this story by saying I should write about a sheriff and a Shaker.

1

SEPTEMBER 15, 1865

When she saw the two men riding down the lane toward her house, Carlyn Kearney lifted the shotgun down off the long nails that held it over her front door. One of the men was a stranger, but the other one was not. She needed to keep a gun between her and that man. Not that she intended to shoot anybody, but she wasn't about to let Curt Whitlow know that.

Beside her, Asher quivered as he watched the door with his gray-specked fur ruffed up on his neck and a low growl in his throat. The dog had barked once to alert her that the men were coming and now was ready for whatever she wanted to happen next. He was an uncommonly intelligent dog and the only reason she hadn't gone insane after she stopped getting letters from Ambrose two summers ago.

"Easy." She spoke softly to the dog, not wanting her voice to carry out to the porch. She gripped the gun tighter when she heard the tread of boots on her steps. The front door was

7

shut. A good thing. The windows were open to the warm September air, but unless the men poked their heads through them they couldn't see her. Maybe they'd knock and just go away if she stood silent.

That wasn't likely to happen. The door wasn't locked, and Curt Whitlow wouldn't let a closed door stop him. Not when he considered the house his. He wanted to consider her his, but she'd let him know plenty of times that he'd best reconsider on that score.

She kept the gun pointed toward the door with hands that trembled. The same tremble ran through the dog standing against her leg. She wanted to think she was like Asher, more ready than afraid, but not much use lying to herself. She could handle Curt with the gun between them, but two men might tip the scales against her even if she was willing to pull the trigger. She wished she'd gotten a better look at the other man before she stepped back from the window to get her gun. The set of his face might help her judge his purpose there with Curt. She pulled in a long breath to steady her hands and her resolve.

Even though she was prepared for it, the fist banging against the door made her jump. The dog tensed beside her, but didn't make a sound. It wasn't like they hadn't played out this scene time and time again. The only new actor was the stranger.

"Carlyn, open the door. I know you're in there." Curt banged on the door again, shaking it against the facing.

"Give the woman a chance to come to the door, Whitlow. You're apt to scare her beating on the door that way."

The other man's voice was calm with a sound of authority. Not what Carlyn expected from someone Curt would bring as reinforcements to put her out of her house. Carlyn shut her eyes a moment. What was it she'd just thought about not lying to herself? It wasn't her house. Not anymore. She hadn't been able to pay Curt Whitlow his due on it. He'd let her ride for almost a year because of Ambrose fighting for the Union, but when Ambrose didn't come home after the war ended, his patience ran out.

In the spring, he'd hinted she could find other ways to pay him. Through the summer the hints had become more like threats. It didn't seem to matter to him that he had a Mrs. Whitlow and a houseful of children back in town. He told Carlyn a woman alone had to make her way however she could. He said she could look through the Bible and see that was true. That was when she started keeping the shotgun over the door.

Now he was answering the man outside. "The Widow Kearney's not that easy to scare."

If only he knew how that word made her shake inside. Widow. It was harder and harder to believe it wasn't true. She hadn't heard from Ambrose since Vicksburg in June 1863. Over two years ago. But she had no proof he was dead. The army said missing. Missing wasn't dead. Ambrose might yet find his way home.

He could have been wounded or laid low by some sickness. In that last letter in 1863, he mentioned suffering fever chills, but he could even now be well enough to start home. It was a hope as fragile as the spun gossamer of a spider web. She knew that. Even so, she'd made Ambrose a promise till death do them part, and until she was sure death had parted them, she'd keep that promise. No matter how many people called her the Widow Kearney.

But vows of faithfulness didn't keep a roof over her head. Whether or not she was ready to admit being a widow, she was losing her home.

A rap on the door brought her back to the problem at hand. No banging this time. A polite knock.

"Mrs. Kearney, we want to talk to you. That's all. Mr. Whitlow has asked me to come see if we can work out the problem of the money you owe on the house."

"There's nothing to work out, Sheriff. She doesn't have any money and it's my house. It's your job to put her out," Curt said.

Sheriff. He'd brought the law. And the law was on his side. The man's voice was steady, calm as ever, when he answered Curt. "We're not putting anybody out today, Mr. Whitlow. You have to give the woman a chance to find another place."

"She's had chances. Plenty of chances." Curt's voice rose, his impatience plain.

"True or not, I suggest you tamp down your eagerness to bring trouble to a widow woman. We're not putting her out today."

"If she can't pay, she's out. That's the law and you're bound to uphold the law."

"I know my job, Mr. Whitlow." The sheriff didn't raise his voice, but his words had a cold edge to them.

"Then do it." Curt wasn't backing down. Not this time.

After a moment of silence, there was another sharp rap on the door. "Open the door, Mrs. Kearney. Please."

The fight drained out of her. She couldn't spit in the face of the law. She lowered the gun until she was holding it in the crook of her arm with the barrel pointing at the floor. Asher looked up at her with an uncertain wag of his tail.

She clicked her tongue at the dog and pushed a smile across her face. She didn't want to say the wrong thing and have the sheriff change his mind about setting her out in the road with night coming. At least with his promise, she'd have until morning, maybe longer, to figure out what to do. Or for Ambrose to make a miraculous appearance.

Miracles happened. The Bible was full of them. People coming back from the dead. That mother's son sitting up on his funeral pyre. Lazarus walking out of his tomb after four days. But even Lazarus hadn't been missing from the family circle for two years.

One day at a time. That had been her mother's constant refrain when Carlyn's preacher father went out evangelizing the world and left them to fend for themselves. Each day had worries enough of its own. No need adding on the ones coming on the morrow. Her mother had shown her where it said that in the Bible.

"He did say please." Carlyn whispered the words as she touched Asher's head.

The sheriff was ready to knock again when she pulled open the door. He lowered his hand and swept his eyes to the gun and back to her face. She was right about him being a stranger. He must be new to town, but that didn't seem right. The sheriff was elected, and it usually took a well-known person to win the votes. But then she hadn't been to town for months.

With no money to buy anything, she'd made do with what she could grow or barter for with the church folks. She did mending and made soap to exchange for salt, sugar, and tea. The church people felt sorry for her, and while she hated being the object of pity, the fact was her situation had declined to pitiful. She knew that. She just didn't know what to do about it. Her father had taken the rest of her family off to Texas before the start of the war. She had no way of getting there even if she could bear the thought of living under her father's roof again.

The stranger at her door was feeling sorry for her too. The pity in his eyes was even worse than that in the church people's eyes. Poor Carlyn Kearney. Won't admit she's a widow. The man, this sheriff, had probably never had anybody pitying him like that. He looked to be a man who took control and made things happen. Not someone buffeted by the winds of misfortune.

He was even taller than Ambrose and so broad across the shoulders that a lawbreaker would surely think twice before going up against him. Then again, here she was staring straight at him, a gun in her hands. The barrel was pointed at the floor, but that didn't mean she couldn't jerk it up if need be.

"See, I told you she'd have a gun, Sheriff." Curt looked even shorter and rounder than usual standing back in the man's shadow. His face was red as he pointed at Carlyn and took a step toward her.

Asher raised his hackles and growled. Curt stopped in his tracks.

"Make her call off her dog." Curt eased back.

Sometimes Carlyn thought he was more afraid of the dog than her gun, and he was probably right to feel that way. She didn't say anything, just held her ground the same as Asher. Her growl wasn't audible, but it was sounding inside her.

"Ma'am, you need to put down the gun and keep a hold on your dog," the sheriff said.

Carlyn found her voice. "The gun's pointed at the floor and the dog won't bother anybody who doesn't bother me." She flicked her eyes to Curt and back to the sheriff's face. "Mr. Whitlow knows that."

"I'd still feel more comfortable if you'd set the gun down. You wouldn't want Mr. Whitlow to suffer a heart attack here on your porch."

She could have told him that it wouldn't bother her one whit if Curt Whitlow fell down dead on her porch, but that might not be the best thing to tell a lawman. Might make her suspect if something untoward were to happen to Curt in the days ahead. She looked straight into the man's dark brown eyes. Without blinking, he met her gaze straight on. After a few seconds, she propped the gun against the door facing.

"And the dog," he said.

She touched Asher's head and made him sit. With an unhappy whine, he obeyed, but he stayed tense, ready to spring if the occasion called for it.

"Thank you, ma'am. That makes talking easier." He took off his felt hat, revealing wavy brown hair in need of scissors. "I'm Sheriff Brodie. Sorry to bother you today, but Mr. Whitlow claims you haven't paid what you owe on the house here."

He glanced around at the peeling paint and sagging porch as if he were assessing the house's value and finding it wanting. It wasn't a great house, but it was a house. A person learned to deal with leaky roofs and loose floorboards. Ambrose planned to fix it up when he got home from the war. They'd been so happy when he carried her over the threshold. Neither one of them had any money, so it had seemed a stroke of good fortune when Curt Whitlow offered to let them have the house and make a payment each year till they paid it off.

She scraped up enough money to pay him more than the old house was worth the first two years, but after Ambrose went missing, his army pay stopped. Now she couldn't scrape up anything except mud off her shoes. All she had were squatter's rights and that wouldn't hold up in front of a judge. Or a sheriff. Out west maybe, but not here where all the land had owners.

"My husband's been away fighting for the Union." Carlyn kept her voice steady, but then wondered if she should break down in tears. That had long ago lost any effect on Curt, but the sheriff might be moved by a woman's tears. Maybe moved enough to give her more time before he upheld the law and set her out of her house.

"The war is over, Carlyn." Curt practically shouted at her. "All the men have come home. Those that could. Ambrose Kearney is never coming home. He's dead. Can't you get that through your head? He's dead!"

She staggered back under the force of his words, and her eyes filled with tears. Not ones she had to pretend, but the true sorrowful tears that came to her nearly every night. While she couldn't be sure Ambrose was never coming home, it was true that he hadn't. His homecoming was way overdue.

2

The woman was not at all what Mitchell Brodie had expected. When Curt Whitlow had come in the office and demanded Mitchell make the Widow Kearney vacate his house, he'd ranted on and on about her recalcitrant ways. His complaints had made Mitchell think Carlyn Kearney would be older. Someone perhaps, if not soured on the world, at least hardened by it.

So the woman who opened the door surprised him. The dark brown curls escaping her tied-back hair made her look even younger than she surely was. Color burned in her cheeks, and with her mouth set in a grim line, she narrowed her eyes and stared out at them without a word. Those stormy blue eyes revealed plenty. Mitchell had learned to gauge the anger or fear of the people he confronted. In his job, if a man wasn't ready, he could be dead. The sheen of sweat on her brow and the throbbing pulse in her temple belied her calm exterior.

Plus there was the gun that maybe told more about

Whitlow than the woman holding it. He'd obviously been at the wrong end of her gun before and probably for cause. Mitchell didn't know Whitlow well, but he'd heard the gossip. The man beside him had a wandering eye and the means to make some women look past his unappealing looks and forget his marital status. Not this woman however. Else there'd be no gun and no need for him as sheriff to be standing at her door.

Carlyn Kearney was sad, scared, and angry all at the same time. He had to insist she put the gun down, but he took no pleasure in seeing her shoulders droop when she complied. She looked defeated. With reason. The law was on Whitlow's side. As much as Mitchell hated that being true, it was. He would have to carry out the distasteful task of putting her out of her home. He fervently hoped she had family to give her a spot under their roof. Her and her dog.

Mitchell looked down at the dog, its lips snarled back to reveal teeth. Whitlow had told him about her vicious beast. Claimed it was more wolf than dog. Now with the drone of Whitlow's demanding words playing back through his head, Mitchell almost wished the woman would set her dog on the man. It might be entertaining to watch the dog chase Whitlow out to his horse as he'd probably done on more than one occasion.

Mitchell was about to suggest Whitlow step off the porch so he could talk to the woman without interference when the man shouted out that the woman's husband was dead. True or not, Whitlow had no reason to throw the words at her like stones. Stones that found their mark.

The blood drained from the woman's face and she staggered back a step. Mitchell was so sure she was going to faint that he risked the dog's raised hackles and stepped across the threshold. The growl did make him think twice about touching the woman. Instead he grabbed a chair to push under her. She sank into it and dropped her head into her hands.

The dog's growls grew fiercer and Mitchell turned, prepared to grab it by the throat if it lunged at him. But the dog was paying him no mind. It was crouched, ready to spring at Whitlow. The woman, lost in her sorrow, didn't note the danger to her dog as Whitlow fumbled in his coat pocket for the pistol Mitchell guessed was there.

"Down, boy." Mitchell put force into his words. As sheriff, a voice of authority often worked with drunks and rabble-rousers, but he was more than a little surprised when it worked with the dog. The animal turned his head toward Mitchell and eased back to a sitting position.

When Whitlow started through the door into the house, Mitchell stepped between the man and the dog. "No need to pull that gun out of your pocket, Whitlow. Nobody's going to shoot anybody or anything."

"That dog needs shooting."

Behind him, the woman gasped. Without turning toward her, Mitchell addressed her worry. "That's not for you to decide. Now you need to wait out in the yard, sir." Mitchell used the word "sir" loosely. He had little use for men like Whitlow who thought they could order the world just because they'd managed to accumulate some land or money.

Whitlow didn't step back from the door. "I'm not the lawbreaker here, Sheriff. She is." He pointed around Mitchell and set the dog to growling again.

Mitchell locked eyes with the man. "I told you to wait in

the yard, Whitlow. Your presence here is upsetting the lady."
He paused for a heartbeat. "And her dog."

Whitlow narrowed his eyes on Mitchell. "You can't let a
pretty face keep you from doing your duty."

"My duty is to protect the people of this county from
harm. That includes this lady and it includes you. So do as
I say and step off the porch. You can rest assured I'll inform
Mrs. Kearney of the law."

Whitlow glared at him for another second, but when
Mitchell shifted his jacket back behind the holster he wore,
he backed across the porch to the steps.

"You tell her whatever you like as long as you get her out
of my house." His voice got louder as he stumbled down
the steps and almost fell out into the yard. He caught his
balance and straightened his jacket. "I've exercised saintly
patience. Nobody can say any different. But patience runs
out after a while."

Mitchell understood the truth of that. His own patience
had run out with Whitlow without a doubt. He stared the
man back from the porch before he turned to the woman. He
didn't close the door. He wanted to in order to shut Whitlow
away from them, but the woman might feel just as threatened
by Mitchell. After all, he was a stranger to her.

That the woman in front of him might fear him bothered
Mitchell. He wondered how she would look if she were to
smile. Really smile. He shied away from that thought. Carlyn
Kearney was still clinging to her marriage bonds. Besides,
whether the woman was a widow or not, Mitchell had no
desire to be charmed by her or any woman. He'd let that
happen once with no good coming from it. He had enough
sense to steer clear of that kind of hurt again. Better to stick

to the business at hand and not think about how her blue eyes might look with the warmth of a smile lighting them up.

That didn't keep him from feeling sympathy for her situation. If he could, he'd let her stay in the house and tell Whitlow to leave her alone, but he'd sworn to uphold the law. Charity wasn't part of the letter of the law.

With her hands gripped so tightly together her knuckles were white, she looked up at him. "Say whatever it is Curt Whitlow has told you to say and get it over with."

A little fire had returned to her eyes, but a cold fire without the warmth he'd wished for a moment ago. "I think you're misunderstanding the situation, Mrs. Kearney. I don't take orders from Whitlow." He met her stare straight on. "I enforce the law."

At the sound of their voices, the dog was up again, the low growl back in its throat. Mitchell kept his eyes on the woman. He wasn't afraid of the dog. He'd faced lots worse than that during the war.

She looked away first and called off her dog. "Asher." The dog gave Mitchell a look that seemed almost apologetic as it moved over to lay its head in the woman's lap. An apology the woman voiced as she stroked the dog's head. "I'm sorry, Sheriff. That was ill spoken of me."

"But understandable under the circumstances." He kept his voice emotionless. He needed to get the job done and be out of this woman's house. It wasn't his fault her husband had gone off to war and gotten himself killed. If indeed he had. Perhaps he'd just chosen not to come home, but Mitchell couldn't imagine that. Not with a wife like Carlyn Kearney waiting faithfully for him.

Not all women were so faithful. He turned from that

thought. No need making any comparisons between this woman and Hilda. The familiar stab of Hilda's desertion made him inwardly wince.

The woman raised her eyes back to his face and waited. She looked nothing like Hilda. Her hair was as dark as Hilda's had been light. Sunlight captured in hair, Mitchell had told Hilda once. She had laughed, surprised by his attempt at fancy words. She always said he lacked any claim to a silver tongue. A man ready to simply get the task done, whether that was unloading a wagon at her father's store or courting a woman.

She was right. He spoke truth straight out without dressing it up in pretty words. He'd thought she didn't mind that, but then a Boston dandy had sweet-talked her into running away with him while Mitchell was in Georgia fighting the Rebels. Her parents were still grieving over their only daughter marrying a man they considered wrong for her. They thought he was still grieving too. Maybe he was. It was just that some days he wasn't sure who or what he was grieving.

"Very well, Sheriff. What do you have to say to me?" The woman's question was direct and to the point. She'd obviously recovered from her earlier vapors.

He needed to be as direct. "Your husband bought this house from Mr. Whitlow. Is that right?"

"Yes. Before the war." Her words were clipped, as though she didn't want to say one syllable more than necessary to someone allied with Whitlow.

"Are you aware of the agreement your husband made with Curt Whitlow to pay a certain amount each year for the house?"

"I am aware of that. Very aware. Mr. Whitlow has made

sure of that." Her words left much unspoken as she slid her gaze past him toward the open door. Mitchell didn't look around to see if Whitlow was in sight.

She lifted her chin and seemed to brace for his next words, but it had to be said. "So have you paid the amount due? Mr. Whitlow claims you are in arrears."

"I paid some of what was owed in August last year, but had no money for any payment this year." She hurried out her next words. "But I have assured Mr. Whitlow that my husband will pay off the loan when he arrives home."

She stared at him as if daring him to doubt her words, but he noted a quaver in her voice when she spoke the word "home." "When do you expect that to happen, Mrs. Kearney?"

"That's hard to say. In times of war, much is uncertain." She lowered her eyes and stroked the dog's head in her lap. Her fingers were trembling.

He studied her bent head, and wished he could just go out the door and walk away. Let her continue her fantasy of her husband's return. He'd seen too much sorrow in the war. But perhaps Whitlow was right and it was time for Carlyn Kearney to face the truth. Right or wrong, whether he wanted to or not, he was going to have to push that truth at her.

"The war has been over for some time, Mrs. Kearney."

"I know that, Sheriff." She didn't look up at him.

Mitchell let the silence build in the room for a moment as he tried to come up with the least hurtful thing to say. He wouldn't be like Whitlow and throw words at her. "When did you last hear from your husband, ma'am?"

Her hand paused in mid-stroke on the dog's head. "It's been awhile, but Ambrose was never good at writing letters." She began stroking the dog again.

"I see." He did see, but it was plain she wasn't ready to face the truth that the husband wasn't coming home. They could tiptoe around that fact all day, but it wouldn't change a thing. Mitchell pulled in a breath and blew it out. Again silence built in the room.

Whitlow's shout from outside broke it. "Hurry it up, Sheriff! I haven't got all day."

Mitchell didn't look around as his hands tightened into fists. It was good the man wasn't standing beside him or he'd be sprawled on the ground. Mitchell didn't care how influential he was in the town.

The woman glanced out the door and then at Mitchell, who must not have been successful at hiding his irritation. She almost smiled as she said, "You can borrow my shotgun if you'd like, Sheriff."

A smile did crawl out on Mitchell's face as he uncurled his fists. "Sounds tempting. Or we could just turn your dog loose." The dog had raised its head and was staring out the door, looking eager for just that command.

She did smile now. "That would make Asher happy." She laid her hand atop the dog's head.

"Is he a hound? Those gray flecks in his fur make me think of a Blue Tick hound my father used to have."

"I don't know what he is." Her voice was easier now, talking about the dog instead of Whitlow and his demands. "He showed up a couple of months after Ambrose enlisted. Nothing but skin and bones and with a sore paw like maybe he'd been in a trap. Poor thing."

The dog seemed to know she was talking about him as he raised his nose toward her face and whined.

"He looks fine now," Mitchell said.

"He is fine."

When Whitlow shouted again, Mitchell shut away the sound of his voice and concentrated on Carlyn Kearney. He wanted her to talk more about the dog and keep smiling. Instead, she stared out the door and her smile faded.

To distract her from Whitlow, Mitchell held his hand out toward the dog. "Think he'd let me pet him?" He liked dogs. Had made friends with several that showed up in the army camps from time to time.

The dog turned his head toward Mitchell, but he didn't move to sniff his hand.

"Of course. He's not really vicious. It's only Curt he can't abide." Her smile came back when she looked down at the dog. "Asher, Sheriff Brodie is a friend."

It was foolish the way he let her words lift his heart. But wasn't that what he wanted all the people in his county to think? That he was their friend, ready to protect them. Then again, what kind of friend set people out of their houses? He kept his eyes on the dog and held his hand closer to its nose.

The dog looked from him to the woman. "Friend," she repeated.

The dog stood then and sniffed Mitchell's fingers. After a moment, Mitchell moved his hand to touch the dog's head. The dog stepped closer to sniff Mitchell's leg. If not for the animal's tail sweeping back and forth, Mitchell might have thought he was checking out the softest place to bite.

"Nice dog," he said.

"Do you have a dog, Sheriff?"

"Not since I was a boy." Mitchell glanced over at her and paused in rubbing the dog's ears. The dog bumped his nose against Mitchell's hand to get him to start up again.

"You must like dogs though," she said. "Ambrose doesn't like dogs much, not just as pets. Says hunting dogs are okay, but a dog needs to earn its keep. I don't know what he'll say when he comes home and sees Asher." Her words trailed off as though she knew that was a worry she'd probably never have to face.

Mitchell didn't say anything, just kept stroking the dog. He wasn't there to talk about her husband coming home or not. But he was going to have to tell her to leave her house. An uncomfortable silence replaced the easy talk about the dog. He pulled in a breath. He couldn't put it off any longer. Whitlow was right. The day was wasting and he needed to stop pussyfooting around.

"Do you have family nearby, Mrs. Kearney?"

"Nobody but Asher." At the sound of his name, the dog deserted Mitchell to go lean against her leg. "But I suppose a dog doesn't count as family."

"Somebody from your church then?"

This time she blew out a sigh and stood to face Mitchell. "It's no concern of yours whether I have friends and family, Sheriff. You must do your job. How long does the law give me to vacate my house?"

He wanted to say a month. A year. But instead he said, "A week."

"Very well." She squared her shoulders and looked back at him. "But you tell Curt Whitlow until that legally given time is up, I am within my rights to shoot any trespassers on my porch." Her eyes slid to the gun propped by the door.

"Yes, ma'am. I'll tell him."

Mitchell didn't look back as he went out the door and down off the porch. He wanted to, but he didn't.

3

Saturday dawned with enough chill in the air to warn of summer's end. Carlyn stirred the fire awake in the stove to fry eggs for her and Asher. Asher didn't care if his egg was cooked, but the skillet was hot. She did set his dish on the floor. She hadn't gone quite so crazy that she expected the dog to sit at the table. Not quite.

"But if you could, it would be company," she told Asher as she dumped half the eggs in his bowl. She put the other half on her plate on the table. She wasn't sure why she bothered with a plate for herself instead of eating out of the skillet, but it seemed she should.

She looked longingly at the teakettle beginning to sing, but it sang for naught. She had no tea and had never cared for the sassafras root her mother used to steep when her tea ran out. She scooted the teakettle to the back of the stove to keep it from taunting her and sat down at the table to bow her head over the egg on her plate. No bread or meat accompanied it. She had hoped to trade apples from her tree for some flour from her neighbor today. Now it hardly seemed worth the trek over to Mrs. Smith's house.

It was best to be grateful for what she had instead of wishing for what she didn't have. "Thank you, Lord, for the food you have supplied. Let it be used for the nourishment of my body and forgive me my sins. Amen."

From the time Carlyn could remember, her mother had spoken a prayer like that over their meals, no matter how scant those meals were. Always asking forgiveness when Carlyn saw no need for that request. Her mother was ever working, ever shouldering her load without complaint, ever thanking the Lord for whatever came her way.

Carlyn didn't feel thankful this morning. She looked out the back door left open to the morning air and resented the warmth the sun spread across the yard to offer a perfect workday. Carlyn had thought to drag fallen limbs in from the woods behind the house to add to her woodpile before the freezing winds began to blow. The late beans in the garden were ready to pick, and she needed to beat the varmints to the windfall under the apple tree. She wasn't afraid of work. Since Ambrose went off to war, she had diligently used every gift of the land to keep the wolf from the door.

But now the sunshine mocked her just as the teakettle had. The wolf had knocked down her door and claimed her house. She took a couple bites of her egg and then dumped the rest in Asher's dish. The dog looked at her for permission.

"Go ahead. I'm not hungry."

He tilted his head, but didn't put his nose to the bowl until she turned away. The bowl scooted on the floor as the dog emptied it with his tongue.

Carlyn wandered from the kitchen to the front room,

sliding her fingers across the wooden tables and chairs while memories assaulted her. Tears blurred her eyes as she touched the front door facing and heard the echo of Ambrose's laugh on that first day here when he carried her across the threshold. She'd felt almost as if she were floating on his love as they shut the door to the world outside and began their life together. A life interrupted by war.

A life ended by the war. *Ambrose Kearney is never coming home. He's dead.* Curt Whitlow's words slammed through her mind. Dead.

Curt had been telling her that for months, and while nobody else said it to her face, they thought it. The people at church. Mrs. Smith on the farm over the hill who was continually mentioning this or that unattached man. As if Carlyn could just declare Ambrose dead and pick a new man. Carlyn didn't want a new man. She wanted Ambrose striding up the lane, home. She had clung to that hope through two long winters.

When she was a girl, her mother often cautioned her about being too ready to wish and dream. "You can't dream up a fire in the cookstove or wish a pot on that stove full of beans. Men like your father can dream of paradise, but the women behind those men have to think more on the practical matters of empty stomachs to fill."

Carlyn raised her head and looked out the door. The grass was still green, the trees full with leaves, and yet summer was dying. The cardinal singing in the tree sounded almost frantic, as if it knew the hard times were coming when seeds wouldn't be plentiful. Carlyn stared out at the road. The empty road.

Never coming home.

When Ambrose strode away from her across their yard that

27

long ago January day, she'd grabbed the porch post to keep from running after him. He had already told her goodbye. His lips on hers were soft.

"'Twill only be for a little while, my Carly." He cupped her face in his broad hands and stared down into her eyes. "We'll beat those Rebels back and make our country whole again. Then I'll be running home to you."

He had kissed her one last time. "Nothing short of death can keep me from coming home. You can depend on that. You'll see me coming back across this yard, and when I see you in the door, I'll be shouting hallelujahs to the Lord for giving me the likes of you for a wife."

Nothing short of death.

Carlyn blinked her eyes to clear them of tears and imagined Ambrose coming across the yard toward her. He'd be smiling. Maybe slimmer than when he left due to the privations of army life. She smiled, seeing him in her imagination, but then her smile disappeared as the image shimmered and faded. Instead, in six days, it would be the sheriff striding across her yard to put her out of the house. Tall and strong like Ambrose but with a very different purpose. Not that he wanted to put her out. She'd seen his compassion when he asked if she had family. And seen his pity.

Why did that poke her so sorely? Did not her father forever preach that pride would bring a person down low?

She shook her head to rid it of the thought of the sheriff's pity and of her father's preaching. Her father could hardly accuse her of pride. The whole last year, she'd practically lived on the charity of her neighbors. Nothing prideful about that.

But her father's words wound through her mind from some long-ago sermon. Whether preached from a pulpit or from the head of the supper table, she did not remember. "Not accepting the lot the Lord assigns to you is sinful pride. You cannot think you know more than God of what your life should hold. A man does well to bend his head and accept the yoke the Lord has for him."

When her father was preaching, Carlyn always got shivers. Not holy ones that transported her into a glorious feeling the way her father said it should, but dreadful shivers that she would never be able to measure up to what a Christian should be. In her mind then, God was too much like her father. He took no excuses for failure and would be quick to dole out punishment.

The Lord chastises those he loves. Another of her father's oft-repeated verses. Her father was quick with punishment in the face of the smallest infraction. Carlyn had learned early to stay beyond his reach. To hide away from his sight. At times she wanted to do the same with God, even though she knew such was not possible.

But Ambrose had introduced her to a gentler faith. One where God was love. An ever-present help in trouble. She could embrace that vision of God when she was with Ambrose, but it leaked away without his strong presence beside her. If the Lord was a help in trouble, then why wasn't he helping her now? Why hadn't he let Ambrose come home?

Carlyn looked up at the sky, blue as Ambrose's eyes when he told her goodbye. Blue as the dresses of those odd Shaker women in the village a few miles down the road. Those women who never married. Her father had railed against them as heathens who rebelled against the natural order of life and God's instructions to go forth and be fruitful. Not only that, the Shakers danced in church.

The thought of that amazed Carlyn. What kind of church would encourage, even compel dancing? No church she'd ever sat in to hear a sermon. At those churches, dancing was roundly condemned as leading one down a sinful path to certain destruction. Akin to drunkenness, card playing, and other riotous living. And yet, the Shakers danced in their worship. Or so it was said.

When her father ranted about the Shakers' odd religious ways, Carlyn had tried to imagine the people in their church dancing. Wouldn't the pews be in the way? Did they dance on them? The very idea of that seemed too weird to consider. But the aisle would allow only a few jigging feet and surely no one would be so blasphemous as to dance around the pulpit. Yet, her father claimed even the Shaker preachers stomped and spun and shook.

Her father had been known to stomp his foot from time to time or pound on the pulpit to keep his listeners awake, but he declared in no uncertain terms that he'd never give his feet over to the devil for dancing. Feet were for walking the somber path of service and staying on the road of "thou shalt nots."

Once, while reading the Bible, Carlyn had come across the verses in Second Samuel that said King David danced as the Ark of the Covenant was carried into the City of David. He whirled and leaped, but nowhere did Carlyn see where the Lord condemned that. So could it be the Lord didn't mind holy dancing? Maybe that was the kind of dancing the Shakers did.

Carlyn mulled over that for weeks before she found the courage to ask her father about King David's dance. As soon as the words were out in the air between them, her father's face tightened into a thunderous frown. Carlyn's mouth went dry and her legs trembled. She could do nothing but stand and wait for judgment to fall down on her.

"It is sinful to search the Scripture to pull verses out of context in a vain attempt to excuse sin." Her father's voice was that of condemnation from the pulpit. "Is that what you have done, daughter?"

She inched back from him, but he reached out, gripped her shoulder with his bony fingers, and pulled her closer to him. His angry breath wrapped around her. His eyes demanded an answer.

"N-no," she stammered.

Across the room, her mother looked up from her sewing and surprised Carlyn by coming to her defense. "The child simply asked a question about something she read in the Bible, Joshua."

Her father's left eyelid twitched then, a signal that normally would send Carlyn running for a hiding place, but his hand still gripped her shoulder. He lifted his head to stare at his wife. Out of the corner of her eyes, Carlyn could see her mother looking back at him. Not with anger, but a resigned weariness.

"Wife, do not encourage wrong thinking in our offspring. There is much the female brain cannot comprehend. It is best to leave interpretation of the Scripture to those chosen by the Lord for understanding." He glared at Carlyn's mother until she looked back down at her sewing, her sigh audible across the room.

At the sound, her father's fingers tightened on Carlyn's shoulder and his eyes bored into her. "You have asked your question for wrong motives, but I will explain." His voice was stern. "King David was a sinful man, who gave into lustful desires and was punished for his sins."

A new question tickled through Carlyn's brain. How, if that was so, could King David be a man after God's own heart? She'd heard her father say that, and other preachers too. But didn't her father also say how much God hated sin? And what about all those psalms David wrote? Could that kind of praise be written by a man lusting after sin?

But she bit her lip and stayed silent. Her father's eyelid continued to twitch even as he narrowed his eyes on her and went on in a voice too calm. "You'd best copy out the Ten Commandments fifty times so that you can remember the way to act. Think hard on that one about honoring your father and mother."

Carlyn breathed a little easier then in hopes he would forget his anger at her mother speaking up. "Yes sir," she managed.

He shook her so hard she lost her balance and fell against the table next to him when he let go. The candle spilled over, the flame catching in her hair. She beat at her head while her father watched without moving to help. With a shriek, her mother dropped her sewing and raced across the room to smother the flames with her hands.

Her mother pulled Carlyn close then against her bosom and held her as she hadn't for years. "Would you sit there and let our child burn?" She seemed to almost strangle on the words.

"She lost naught but a bit of hair. It is well to remember that the fires of hell will be a thousand times hotter than any fire here on earth. Our daughter needs to learn not to reach beyond herself." He turned his eyes back to his Bible. "Now leave me to my studies. I must be prepared to save souls."

The next day after he rode away to yet another circuit of preaching, her mother sat Carlyn down in a chair on the porch to trim the burnt ends from her hair. After she trimmed a little here and there, she sighed. "Best just cut it short." She grabbed the hair that had escaped the flame and snipped it off to match that burnt away. "If it doesn't grow out before your father comes back from his journeys, you'd best stay out of his sight or wear a bonnet to hide your head. He won't be pleased. The Bible says a woman's hair is her glory."

"Yes, ma'am." Carlyn blinked back tears as she felt her mother cut off another hank of hair. The kids at church would be sure to make fun of her with hair cut like a boy's. Maybe it would be best to stay out of sight of everybody.

Her mother gently combed back her hair and then let her hand linger on Carlyn's head. She was not a woman given to affectionate gestures. Life was hard and had to be faced with steely determination. But now her voice gentled. "It would be best if you didn't question the Scripture to your father."

"Is it wrong to have questions?" Carlyn asked timidly.

"No. I think not. "

"Then who can I go to for answers?" Carlyn turned her head a bit to look at her mother. "You?"

"I have few answers." Her mother began combing Carlyn's hair again. "But there is one you can always ask."

"Who?"

"The Lord. He will supply every answer you need."

Whining softly, Asher bumped his cold nose against her hand to bring Carlyn away from her memory and back to the problem at hand. She would not willingly go back to live under her father's roof, even if his house were still just down the road instead of in Texas.

33

Carlyn stared out at the empty road and spoke aloud. "I'm asking, Lord. What am I to do?"

She stood very still as though she expected to hear a voice falling down from heaven, but all was silent. All but the thump of Asher's tail against the chair behind them. The chair the sheriff had pushed under her when she felt faint.

Carlyn let out a sigh and went out the door and around the house to the garden spot. Whether she would eat the beans or not, they needed picking. It was not good to let food go to waste. She could carry them to church in the morning. Perhaps someone there needed a servant. She almost smiled at the thought. No one in their church had that kind of money. Then again, they might give her a cot in the corner of the kitchen in exchange for her labor.

The Lord will supply every answer you need.

4

Sunday morning Carlyn woke early to be sure she got to church on time. The church house was only four miles down the road. An easy walk. The hard part was going without Asher. Always before, he went along and waited outside the church. Then last month, one of the boys had pulled his tail and gone crying to his mother when Asher rumbled a warning at him.

The preacher came to her house the next week to ban Asher from the churchyard.

"I realize he's probably harmless." Reverend Baskin looked at Asher, but made no move to pet him even though Asher was right beside him, wagging his tail, friendly as anything. "But he is a big dog, and seeing him there by the church steps makes folks nervous. We can't have people being nervous about coming to church."

She hadn't been to church since. Not because of Asher. She'd not felt well that one Sunday. Then it had rained the following Sunday. Four miles was a long way to walk in the rain. And after missing two Sundays, it just seemed easier to stay home the following Sunday too and read her Bible at the kitchen table with Asher stretched out on the floor beside her.

Not forsaking the assembling of ourselves together. That bit of Scripture from Hebrews had circled in her mind, but she wasn't forsaking going to church forever. Just for a few Sundays. Just until she figured out how to keep Asher from following her.

"We'll have to figure it out today." Carlyn looked at him in the mirror as she twisted her hair into a bun. "I won't be gone that long, but I can't not go."

Asher tilted his head as though asking why.

"You know why. Curt Whitlow is why." She shut her eyes and pulled in a breath. "No, that's not fair. Money is why. Our lack of it."

As if the dog had any pockets for money. But he knew when she was bothered. He whined and nudged his nose against her leg.

"You'll be fine here in the house." Carlyn glanced at the clock and settled her bonnet on her head. "I have to go. To see if the Lord will supply an answer to our dilemma."

She needed an answer and soon. The sheriff would be back. It was his duty. But even if he didn't come, Curt Whitlow would be there. He'd give her another chance to surrender herself to him or, failing that, vacate his house.

Asher's tail thumped against the washstand. He followed her to the door, but when she held her palm out toward him to stay, his ears flattened against his head as if she had struck him.

"You can't go. Stay here and pray."

She shook her head at her foolishness in suggesting Asher

pray. She should be the one praying, but she felt empty of prayers. Empty of faith that she would find an answer or at least an answer easy to accept. Besides, no matter how her father had preached on the sinfulness of pride and no matter how much she believed that preaching was backed up by Scripture, she still did not want to stand in front of the church and admit her dire straits.

She sighed and rubbed Asher's head. "Would that I could stay here with you, but what other choice do I have other than begging for help?"

She pulled the door shut on the dog's sad eyes. He would be fine. But how fine would she be?

At least the sun had come up bright, promising yet another day of summer before autumn appeared. But here and there leaves were going brown. No color yet. Not enough chill in the night air to begin that cycle.

Life was a series of cycles. Some good turns. Some not. But it went on. She had to go on too, putting one foot in front of the other even if despair trailed along with her on this day. If only Ambrose were there beside her.

She pushed away thoughts of Ambrose. While she couldn't desert her marriage vows until she knew for sure what had happened to him, neither could she deny the truth that he might never walk beside her again. The war was long over. Maybe she should quit fighting the title Widow Kearney and accept it, at least while she was appealing for charity. After all, the Bible did say helping widows and orphans was a Christian duty.

Even thinking that felt like a betrayal of Ambrose, as though keeping him alive in her mind insured he was still breathing somewhere in the South. She sighed. Wherever he was, the thing she could be surest about was that he was not there with her.

It was best to stop wishing for what wasn't and think about who might be at the church. Would the Lord point out one of them as her answer? She considered the Jacksons. Every Sunday one or another of the seven Jackson children sat in her lap or leaned against her shoulder. Mrs. Jackson might offer to take her in, but the family was barely getting by. Carlyn could not take their children's food.

There was the preacher, a man of God sworn to help his sheep. She thought of her own father. He'd had little time for temporal needs. Worry not about feeding the body. Feed the spirit. That would be his answer. Reverend Baskin seemed more understanding about physical needs, but even if he were of a mind to help Carlyn, his wife wouldn't allow it. She came from a big city to the north and didn't bother hiding her disdain for the country ways of the local women.

One by one, Carlyn went through the names of the people at church and mentally crossed off each and every one for some reason or other. It was useless. The Lord had no answer for her. She hadn't prayed enough. Hadn't had faith enough. Could this be the Lord's punishment on her? But Ambrose had always believed. He was forever pointing out the blessings of the Lord. His faith should have protected him.

She quickened her pace. If she kept dawdling, she wouldn't get to church until the preacher was ending his sermon. But that might be best. She wasn't sure she could sit through the worship hour as though this was a Sunday like any other.

Deep in thought, she failed to hear the horse behind her until it was almost upon her.

"Shouldn't you be packing?"

She spun around to see Curt Whitlow urging his horse toward Carlyn. She looked for an escape. But the ditch beside the road was deep, and she couldn't outrun his horse, even if it was overburdened with Curt's weight. So she kept her feet planted at the edge of the road. Curt turned the horse until he was looming directly over her, his bulk blocking the sunlight.

She backed up a step to the very lip of the ditch. That made her feel off balance. That and not having her gun or Asher with her.

"It's Sunday." She was relieved her voice came out without a tremble. "A day of rest and worship."

"So the preachers would have us believe."

"And the Bible. 'Remember the Sabbath day to keep it holy.'" She stared up at him and wished him gone. "You do read the Bible, don't you?"

"You have doubt of that?" He laughed and didn't wait for her answer. "Of course I do. It says when your ox is in the ditch you can break the Sabbath to rescue it."

"You have no ox in a ditch." Carlyn let her eyes drift from him for a second to seek an escape. She could leap into the ditch if necessary, but her dress would be the worse for it. She couldn't show up at church in a mud-covered dress. Perhaps it would be best to simply walk on in spite of the horse so near she could feel its warmth. She did not like thinking about being that close to Curt.

"Oh, but I do. A very lovely ox."

"Then I'll leave you to rescue it." She pretended not to know what he meant as she started on up the road.

He walked his horse beside her, pushing her closer to the ditch that was getting deeper the farther up the road they went. Suddenly Curt yanked the reins to turn his horse in front of Carlyn. She had no recourse but to stop.

"I really must get to church."

"I can give you a ride." He was a wall she couldn't get past.

"I prefer to walk." She stepped back to move around his horse, but Curt swung his leg over to dismount directly in front of her. He was more of an obstacle than his horse.

"I can give you so much, lovely Carlyn. A woman like you shouldn't be alone." He reached to touch her face.

Carlyn knocked his hand away. "Go home and take your wife and children to church."

He laughed then, entirely too sure of himself. "The missus knows I have many business opportunities that keep me occupied. She is accustomed to getting to church on her own."

Carlyn gave him a cold stare. "As am I. So please step aside."

Instead he moved closer. "You look a little desperate, my dear. Are you thinking if you can only get to the church house, you will find help for your problems?"

"The Lord is a present help in trouble." Carlyn held her ground even though everything in her was screaming to run.

"That is what the preachers tell us. But if you think I'm your trouble, you are so wrong. I am the answer to your troubles. I am your help, Carlyn."

The smile lingering on his face made her insides clinch. She would have to jump in the ditch to get away from him. Then again, surely he wouldn't attack her in broad daylight.

"I think not." She backed a step away from him. The ground on the lip of the ditch felt soft under her feet.

"You're not afraid of me, are you, Carlyn? I don't want to hurt you. Only help you. All you have to do is be nice to me."

"Shall I bake you an apple pie, then?"

"I was thinking of something a bit more interesting than that." His smile broadened into a leer. "A few favors. That's all I'm asking. No one else has to know. I'll tell the sheriff I was convicted that it was my Christian duty to be generous to a widow."

He reached toward her again. She leaned away from him. "Don't touch me." She put force behind the words.

"But I want to, and I get what I want. Always."

Carlyn looked at the road behind them in hopes of seeing someone coming. People should be making their way to church, but the road was empty. Even Curt Whitlow couldn't arrange an empty road.

"Do you dare attack me in broad daylight? Somebody might ride by and then what of your reputation."

"Money trumps reputations."

"Not in the Lord's eyes."

"You think he might be watching?" He laughed and snaked out a hand, faster than she thought possible, to grasp her shoulder.

"The Lord is always watching." She tried to shake off his hand, but couldn't.

"Do you think he might reach down to stop me? I think not." Curt tightened his fingers on her shoulder. "Besides, the Bible says a man is obliged to pay his debts. And since you have no man to pay your debts for you, the obligation is yours. Whatever happens next week in regard to the sheriff carrying out the law and removing you from my house, my dear Carlyn, you are still in arrears. I have a right to my proper due. Why would the good Lord interfere with that?"

"You are despicable." Carlyn spat the word at him.

He laughed. "Save your sweet talk for later, my dear. First things first. That barn across the road, we can arrange payment there out of the public eye since that seems to concern you."

She tried to jerk free, but he yanked her toward him and fastened his other hand around her upper arm. He was stronger than she expected. Always before she'd thought she could handle him, but that was with a gun and Asher between them. Now she was alone with no one to help her.

A verse her father often quoted in his sermons rose up in her mind, and she looked up and spoke it aloud. "'I will lift up mine eyes unto the hills, from whence cometh my help.'"

"I already told you, Carlyn." He leaned his face closer to her. "I am your help."

She screamed and kicked at him. His horse shied and took off up the road, but Curt's grip simply got tighter, bruising her arms.

She stopped fighting and tried to think. "I'll tell the sheriff."

"I wouldn't make threats, my dear. That could go badly for you."

She went limp then, pretending a faint that surprised him. His grip loosened enough that she twisted out of his grasp but lost her balance and slid down into the ditch. She landed on her back. He came after her, his boots slipping on the incline. Carlyn scooted backward away from him, but her foot caught in her skirt.

It would be a good time for that help, Lord. No sooner had she let the thought run through her mind than she heard the creak of a wagon and the sound of horses on the road. She started to cry out, but Curt fell on top of her and mashed his hand down over her mouth. The ditch was deep and the weeds tall. Whoever was in the wagon wouldn't see her.

Tears filled her eyes. If she hadn't fallen into the ditch, she would have been able to escape Curt. But now the wagon would pass them by and all would be lost. Curt was right. Nobody was going to help her.

Pray anyway. Her mother's words were in her head. She'd told Carlyn that, whenever Carlyn complained that her prayers weren't answered. "Pray anyway," she said again and again. "The Lord answers in ways we can't imagine."

Let them see us. But the steady clip-clop of the horses' hooves continued on.

When the sound of the wagon faded away, Curt raised up to look down at her. "How convenient. We can just finish our business here." He kept one hand tight against her mouth.

She pushed open her lips enough to bite him. He swore and jerked his hand away.

"Get off me," she demanded.

"Not yet, my dear." He put his injured finger in his mouth and sucked on it a moment, his eyes assaulting her.

She screamed then and fought against his weight holding her down. He grabbed her hands and fastened them against the ground over her head. She screamed again.

The dog leaping into the ditch was such a blur that it was a second before she knew it was Asher. He went straight for Curt's throat and only barely did Curt throw up his arm to keep the dog from his target. The dog clamped teeth down on Curt's arm and knocked the man backward. Carlyn scrambled to her feet. Asher turned loose of Curt's arm and made another lunge for his throat. When Curt huddled in the ditch to protect his head, Asher grabbed his arm again.

Curt let out a yowl. "Call him off."

"Why should I?" Asher was on top of Curt, growling and waiting for a chance at the man's throat.

"I'll leave you alone. I promise I'll never bother you again." His words were muffled against the ground.

"I don't believe you."

"Call him off," he shouted. "He kills me, they'll shoot him."

"Who will know?"

"You will. You'll be a murderer." He sounded desperate now. "Thou shalt not kill."

He was right. She had to call Asher off. Without a word and with a calm she didn't feel, she picked up her reticule and climbed out of the ditch. Curt looked to be trying to sink deeper into the ditch. Blood streamed from the ripped skin on his arm onto his head. Asher growled, waiting for her to say what next.

Carlyn took a deep breath. "If anything happens to my dog, I'll tell why he attacked you."

"I'll say it was a stray dog. I give you my word. Just call him off."

His word wasn't worth much, but she snapped her fingers and spoke the dog's name anyway. Asher looked up at her but didn't move. She had to call him twice. At last he jumped up beside Carlyn, the growl still evident in his throat and his muscles taut, ready to spring.

Curt sat up and put his hand over the wound on his arm. His hat was gone and the long hair he looped over his bald spot hung down across his face. It might have been funny except for the blood. "Help me get my horse."

"No." Carlyn backed away from him.

What was she going to do? She had thought the Lord's

answer might be at church, and then the devil had stepped between her and that chance. She considered going on to church. She might even look more convincing in her need for help, but then again, often as not, people blamed a woman for enticing a man into an attack. And while she knew the Lord looked more on right behavior than money, she was not entirely sure Reverend Baskin felt the same. Especially when it was the difference between a widow's mite and a landowner's plenty.

"Wait," Curt yelled at her. "I'm bleeding. You have to help me."

"No." She lifted her skirts and ran across the open field to the shelter of the trees. Asher loped alongside her.

Once out of sight of Curt, she was overcome with trembles and had to lean against a tree to stay on her feet. Asher shoved his head under her hand. Her crutch. Her help. Her answer to a desperate prayer. But then from whence would come the rest of her help? Church would be shuttered until next Sunday.

Pray anyway. Her mother's words again were in her head.

"I don't know what to pray," Carlyn said aloud. Her voice sounded lonely amid the trees with no one but Asher to hear.

Then the bell began to ring. Not at Carlyn's church. They had no church bell there. But the Shakers' bell calling them to worship. To dance and whirl. But the sisters there had no worry about men except as brothers.

The bell rang on. Clear. Strong. One toll after another. Her answer.

5

Carlyn walked toward the sound of the bell floating through the air. Each step felt surer as the toll of the bell pulled her toward the village. She didn't know what the Shakers might expect of her, but she'd heard they didn't turn potential converts away. She could live the Shaker life for a while. It wouldn't be forever. Just until Ambrose came home.

She wouldn't think about that not happening. Not today when she needed some hope to lean on. Not today when the Lord had saved her from Curt and given her an answer. She refused to be bitter about the answers she did not have. Better to concentrate on the answer she did have and keep walking toward the Shaker village.

Even after she came out of the trees, she didn't look back toward the road. Curt must have spotted her. She heard him yelling, but the sound was little more than the irritating whirr of a grasshopper in her ears. All she wanted to hear was the bell, the Lord speaking to her.

Then, the bell quit ringing. The silence assaulted her ears

and she stopped walking. Lost. Unsure which way to make her next step without the bell guiding her. Other sounds returned. Asher panting. Horses on the road. A crow cawing a warning. Of what Carlyn had no idea, but her heart pounded in her chest anyway.

She was suddenly aware of how she must look. Disheveled. Her bonnet gone, lost in the struggle in the ditch. Her hair no longer in a tidy bun but loose and flying in her eyes. Her dress streaked with dirt, grass stains, and worse. Dark smears where Asher had rubbed against her. She touched the damp spots on the dog's fur and stared at her hand. Curt Whitlow's blood.

The sight made her stomach lurch. She rubbed off the blood on a thick patch of grass. She had to get rid of it. Not only from her hand but from Asher as well. She couldn't show up at the Shaker village marked with blood. That was no way to step into a new world. An unknown world.

So even when the faint sound of singing replaced the toll of the bell, she did not move toward it. Instead she lifted her skirts and took off for home as though the devil himself was after her. Asher ran alongside, not bothered in the least by the blood on his fur. He couldn't know what that might make happen, for there was one thing Carlyn did know. She couldn't trust Curt Whitlow to keep his word.

Briefly, she thought of the sheriff with the compassionate eyes. She could go to him. Tell her story first. He might believe her. But then what? While Curt had attacked her, she had escaped without visible harm. Curt was the one in need of a doctor. It would be her word against his. A woman many in the community considered a bit unhinged against a man who owned half the county. Whether the sheriff believed her or not might not matter.

It would be better to rid her and Asher of evidence of the encounter. To pretend it had never happened. To hope that Curt would do the same. That his pride would make him say he'd been attacked by a stray dog. That might be too much to hope for, but Asher appearing out of nowhere to help her escape Curt's clutches had been more than she could hope for as well. An answer to prayer. And then the Shaker bell sounding. Dare she ask for more? Especially when she was running in the opposite direction of that answer.

Her mother's words were in her head again. *Pray anyway. The Lord's power is not made smaller by our limited faith. Trust the way the disciples in the Bible trusted.*

They had been having Bible study around the table during one of those times when her father had been gone for too many weeks and their cupboard was almost bare. At twelve, Carlyn no longer accepted whatever her mother said without question. She heard the church pray for this or that sick member and then watched them bury the very same person the next week. She'd read Job. She knew John the Baptist was beheaded. Stephen stoned.

"But didn't they all die martyrs' deaths?" She had stared across the table at her mother with some defiance. Sure of the answer, but at the same time wanting it to be different.

Her little brothers and sister had stared at her, dumbfounded, knowing even at their young age that it was bad enough to question their mother but even worse to doubt the Scripture. Carlyn didn't care. She was tired of praying and pretending to be thankful for mush for supper.

Her mother surprised them all by not reprimanding Carlyn. Instead she reached across the table to place her work-roughened hand over Carlyn's. "There are many ways to die, my daughter. The one way you do not want to die is without the Lord. The faith of those saints carried them through fearsome times to glory. That is what you must remember. We look upon death with worldly eyes, but our lives are as grass: as a flower of the field, so he flourisheth. For the wind passeth over it, and it is gone. But the mercy of the Lord is from everlasting to everlasting."

Carlyn had bowed her head in submission to her mother, but the Bible words had not sunk into her heart.

Her mother sighed softly and squeezed her hand. "You will understand more when you are older, my daughter. Meanwhile search out the stories of faith in your Bible and let go of your doubts."

Carlyn had muttered something. She didn't remember now what, and her mother had put a finger under her chin and raised her face up to look into her eyes. "Whatever else, even on the days you find it hard to believe, pray anyway. It will make you stronger and the Lord will hear and bless you."

Was any of that true or simply what her mother wanted to be true? That night and on many other nights, they still only had corn mush for supper. But they had not starved. She had met Ambrose and felt blessed in ways she couldn't imagine. At least until the war had torn them apart. Perhaps Ambrose had not come home because she didn't have the proper faith.

Yet she had been rescued this day by a dog that had somehow escaped a locked house to follow her and show up when she most needed him.

At the house, Asher's escape was easy to see. The kitchen window was open. She had not expected him to jump through that, but she was thankful he had. Thankful and worried at the same time.

It took the last of the water in the rain barrel to wash her dress and Asher. But what did that matter? Someone once told her the Shakers had running water and machines for washing clothes. She couldn't imagine such a machine and had wondered at the time if that could be true. Now, she supposed she'd find out.

She hung the dress in the kitchen by the open window. No need upsetting her neighbors by draping it on the line outside. A person shouldn't do laundry on Sunday. *Remember the Sabbath Day to keep it holy.*

There were things a person could do on the Sabbath. Tending a fire and cooking. Milking the cows and gathering in the eggs. Feeding the animals. Rescuing one's ox from the ditch.

Carlyn shivered. She didn't want to think about the ditch. Instead she lifted her gun off the nails above the door. She would not be caught unprepared again.

With the gun propped against the bed, she packed a few clothes in the same old carpet bag she'd carried away from her mother's house five years earlier. Best to take only what she needed most and then come back for the rest. She'd heard the Shakers took whatever possessions a person had when one joined their society. Land, buildings, tools, household plunder. Everything went into the society to be used by all.

The brother of a man in their church had joined with the Shakers some years before, and Carlyn remembered the man's anger and sorrow at seeing part of the family farm absorbed into the Shaker holdings. The father had gone with the men to the Shaker village to talk to his brother, but to no avail.

The brother had not come away with them. Instead he had tried to get them to accept the Shaker way.

"I could not bear his blasphemous words. As if he thought he knew more about the Lord's salvation than the Scriptures have revealed to me," her father had railed when he got back from the Shaker village. He paced up and down in the kitchen, his coattails flipping out when he made a turn. "They're the devil's leeches, sucking dry the weak and foolish for their own purposes."

The weak and foolish. If the Shakers sought such as that, she would fit their need, whatever that might be. They weren't of the devil. Her mother had assured her of that when they had crossed paths with the Shakers in town. Misguided, her mother said, but ever kind. After swearing Carlyn to secrecy, she revealed how some of the baskets of food they found on their porch from time to time weren't from their own church people but from the Shakers.

"Your father would not accept their charity, but while he is away doing the Lord's work, what the Lord supplies to feed you children, I will not refuse. Instead, I am thankful and pray the Lord's blessing on them for their generosity in sharing their plenty," her mother said.

Would they still be willing to share their plenty? Carlyn straightened up and caught sight of her face in the mirror across the room. Ambrose had been so proud when he brought the dresser home. He liked to watch her brush her hair in front of the mirror and often would wrap his arms around her to delay her pinning it up in the mornings. With his chin resting lightly on top her head, she would lean against him, wrapped in his love. Would she ever feel that safe again?

The wavy mirror bent her reflection out of shape, but that

seemed only right with the unknown future she faced on the morrow. She touched her hair and thought of the caps the Shaker women wore. Her hair would be tucked away all the time, hidden from the world. But then so would she, and after what happened today, she wanted to be hidden. Safely tucked away from danger. From Curt Whitlow. From starvation.

"Oh Ambrose, why didn't you come home?" Carlyn spoke aloud to the mirror, not paying any mind to Asher when he raised his head up off his paws to look at her. "We were going to have children, grow old together. And now if you don't come home to rescue me, I'll grow old alone."

Hardly alone. She'd be surrounded by people. Shakers, to be sure, but they were only people who had decided to walk a different path than most in the world. It would be like being a child again, sharing space with sisters and brothers. That would not be so bad. Like her mother, she would not look askance on the help the Lord sent her.

She wondered why her mother had been so much on her mind. Perhaps it was the Lord's doing, his way of helping Carlyn be brave enough to face the future with faith. Her mother's faith had never wavered even at those times when her path was obscured with difficulties.

Carlyn looked at the mirror again and wondered if her mother and father had shared love the way she and Ambrose had. They must have. Five children testified to their union as man and wife. Carlyn touched her flat stomach. Another regret. If Ambrose had given her a baby, the child would be at least three now. She imagined a little boy the image of Ambrose with laughter in his eyes, clinging to her skirts.

Her arms ached with emptiness at the thought. But it was just as well the child was no more than a yearning of her heart. The Shakers had a special house for the children who came into their society. Apart from their mothers. Carlyn couldn't have borne that, and hadn't her mother always assured her the Lord wouldn't test her beyond her endurance?

Funny how she remembered more of her mother's daily Bible teachings than she did her father's sermons from the church pulpits. His sermons always had a feeling of doom, while her mother told Carlyn about a compassionate Lord who knelt down to make mud to put on a blind man's eyes. Who healed lepers. Who offered living water to the woman at the well. Who knew the weaknesses in people but loved them anyway.

Her mother never doubted that love even when the cow went dry, the hens stopped laying, and the cupboard was bare. "God will provide," she would say. And he had. A few turnips overlooked in the garden. A rabbit in a snare. Fish from the nearby river. Walnuts in the woods. Those food gifts from the Shakers.

But Carlyn's father always made it home eventually from his preaching journeys. No one had ever called her mother Widow Wilson. No one had gone to the sheriff to put them out of their house. Carlyn sighed as she stared down at the few things packed in the bag. Her life stripped to the bare bones. Asher got up from his spot on the floor and leaned his head against her.

"I know." She put her hand on the dog. "If wishes and tears could bring him home, he'd have been here long ago. Now it's time to leave such behind and face an unhappy future."

Blessed are they that mourn: for they shall be comforted.

She pressed down the clothes in the bag to make room for her mother's Bible. Her mother had thrust it at Carlyn the day they left for Texas. Ambrose had already marched away to war and her mother wanted Carlyn to go with them to Texas. Carlyn had trembled at the thought of being under her father's roof again, but she also trembled at being left behind. Alone. But Ambrose had promised the war wouldn't last long. She had to stay and keep the house ready for his return. That's what she told her mother.

"Then keep this." Her mother had held the Bible out to Carlyn. Its cover was worn even then and some of the page edges tattered, showing the many trails of Scripture her mother had walked through it, searching for answers.

"I can't keep your Bible. You'll need it." Carlyn was unable to take the treasured book from her mother's hands.

But her mother had insisted. "It eases our parting for me to leave the comfort of God's Word with you. Each time you open it, I will be reading along with you. In my heart."

With her mother's words echoing in her head, Carlyn let the Bible fall open and smoothed her hand over the page, as though she could absorb the words through her skin. "Oh Mother, if you were only still near to help me find the answers."

Maybe she should try to find her way to Texas. But no. She had her answer. She would follow the toll of the bell in the morning.

6

Carlyn lay awake through the night, fearing footsteps on the porch. Each creak and groan of the house, usually so comfortably familiar, now seemed to warn of new threats. She had never felt so alone.

She told herself she was no more alone than she had been for the last few years, but the thought skittered away from her like water spiders on a pond. It wasn't just her fear of Curt Whitlow and what he might do to her or Asher. No, it was the thought of the morrow. The thought of going to the Shakers and what that meant. With the black of the night pushing down on her, she couldn't hold on to the whisper of belief that Ambrose might yet come home. Instead the name Widow Kearney echoed in her ears. Within these walls where she'd been so happy with Ambrose, she'd shunted aside common sense and held on to hope too long.

Come morning, she would leave this house forever and, along with it, that hope of Ambrose returning to her loving arms. A sadness beyond tears gripped her. She wouldn't pretend any longer, but neither would she forget the vow she'd made to him. *Till death do us part.* The army reported him missing. They had no proof of his death, and so she would stay faithful to her promise until she knew for sure he had gone to his eternal home.

Carlyn welcomed the first hint of pink in the eastern sky, glad to have reason to rise from her bed. The sky was clear, promising another day of sunshine, but Carlyn barely took notice of anything more than the daylight. She did her morning chores by rote. Smoothing the covers on the bed. Milking the cow. Mixing the leftover cornbread with a bit of milk for Asher. She didn't bother stirring up the fire in the stove. She thought it wise not to put anything in her queasy stomach.

Asher followed her every move as she shut all the windows and picked up the carpetbag and the gun.

"Don't worry," she told him. "I'm not leaving you behind."

He trailed her out of the house and then waited while she pulled the door firmly shut behind them. She considered pausing on the porch to say a prayer of thankfulness for the shelter and love she'd known there. Her mother had prayed each time they left a house or entered a new one, whatever the circumstance of their move. But Carlyn was not her mother. She went on down the steps to the ground. She felt too empty to summon up thankful words.

Pray anyway. She pushed her mother's words aside. She was weary of prayers. Weary of life. She just wanted to go and get it over with.

She cut across the fields away from the road. The going was harder, but fences could be climbed and creeks waded. She wasn't ready to talk about where she was going to any of her neighbors. Plus, it seemed wiser not to chance seeing Curt Whitlow. Best to keep the gun unfired.

Thou shalt not kill. She thought about the Bible in her bag. What did that mean when a man went to war? So many men had shot and killed each other. The Scripture didn't say "except when at war." It didn't say "except when provoked or in danger." It said "thou shalt not kill."

Why was she struggling with every thought? Why couldn't she just accept the words in the Bible and not look askance at them? Was it because she didn't want to think about the verse that said she could ask and it would be given, seek and find, when the prayer of her heart had not been given and what she sought most had not been found?

She squared her shoulders and kept walking. She needed no answers other than the one already given. She would be saying the Shaker prayers from this day forward. She had no idea what those prayers might be. If they were blasphemous as her father claimed, she'd find a way to speak them without meaning.

She wouldn't worry about beliefs on this day, only about a roof over her head and food for her and Asher.

Among the trees, she walked a ways in the wrong direction and had to retrace her steps. Asher with his nose for home was no use, for he had no idea where they were headed.

Eventually, on the edge of the woods she came upon the stone fences that marked the Shaker land. Men in straw hats flowed across the field, mowing down hay. Intent on their work, they paid her no mind as she stepped out of the trees and made her way across the field to the road. It didn't matter now who saw her. People would know soon enough that she had gone to the Shakers.

If they didn't know, it could be that some might think she'd come to a bad end. She smiled as she imagined them searching through the deserted house for evidence of wrong-doing. Perhaps the sheriff would suspect Curt Whitlow. But no, she had no desire to bear false witness against any person, even Curt. Another Bible "thou shalt not." Curt and his threat were behind her. She would soon be one of many sisters and no longer part of the world she'd always known.

The village buildings rose up in front of her. Sturdy, strong structures, severe in their plainness with no porches or covered entrance ways but impressive even so. She and Ambrose had ridden through the village once. When Ambrose found out she'd never seen a river, he took her down to the Shaker landing on the Kentucky River. The limestone cliffs and deep channel of greenish brown water had been amazing, but no more amazing than the Shaker town. That day, she felt as though the world was opening up before her. So much to see with Ambrose to guide her.

In the middle of the village, Ambrose pointed out the Meeting House where the Shakers sang and danced their worship. Obviously with great enthusiasm. At times, Carlyn could hear them singing a few miles away at her house, although no words were ever plain.

But it was the white stone building across from the frame Meeting House that had captured Carlyn's eyes and admiration. With the midday sun bathing it in light, the stones practically glowed.

Ambrose noticed her awe. "That's where the faithful Shakers live. The house for those who have been here longest."

"Are you sure it's a house?" She had seen large plantation

houses, but never anything like this square building with its stark exterior and rows of windows.

"A house for many." Ambrose laughed. Eventually they rode on past brick buildings as big as the stone house. Dark yellow frame buildings were scattered in and around the houses. Their workshops, Ambrose explained. The pounding of hammers, the clank of washtubs, and other sounds not so easily identified, but clearly the noise of industry, drifted out the open windows of the shops.

That day the Shaker people had moved along the paths from building to building, each intent on his or her own journey and not at all concerned that Carlyn and Ambrose watched them with curious eyes.

A few people were in sight on this day too, moving with purpose the same as then. Everybody but her.

Carlyn felt as lost here as she had when she strayed in the wrong direction in the woods. Even more so. In the woods she could retrace her steps. Here, her next steps were a mystery.

She continued hesitantly through the village. Asher stayed close by her side, as uneasy in this strange place as she was. It was all Carlyn could do to keep from running back the way they had come, but where could she go?

A small building next to a three-story brick house had a sign indicating it was a post office. She might find help there. Or maybe she should go into the meetinghouse to seek a preacher to guide her.

She jumped when the bell began to toll from the top of the white stone house. Men and women spilled out of the workshops and headed toward the stone building, answering the summons of the bell. Others moved down paths toward other houses. With the sun high overhead, the bell must be calling them to the midday meal.

Carlyn stepped off the path, set her carpetbag down, and kept her hand on Asher's head when the rumble of a growl sounded in this throat. The men all kept their eyes away from Carlyn, but several stole a peek at Asher or maybe the gun she was pointing down at the ground. Worried the gun might make them uneasy, she laid it down next to her bag.

She didn't know whether the sight of it bothered the women or not, since most of them kept their heads bent, their caps sliding forward to hide their faces. Here and there one glanced her way, but it was as if Carlyn were no more interesting than a fence post. She considered calling to them for help, but they were so like sheep following after their leader she hesitated to disturb their order.

The caps were all white and the skirts of their blue, gray, and rust red dresses were covered with aprons. The generous white collars draped around their shoulders concealed evidence of their feminine shape. Most kept their hands hidden under the aprons. They not only didn't speak to Carlyn, they exchanged no talk at all as they glided past with only the rustle of their skirts and the soft patter of their shoes on the rock walkways.

Then one sister stepped out of line toward Carlyn. She was plumper than most of the others, the neckerchief not completely hiding her abundant figure. Her round face was flushed, perhaps from the warmth of the day or perhaps from daring to break from the ranks to speak to Carlyn. Her light brown eyes shone with kindness and made up for the lack of a smile on her lips.

"My sister, are you in need?" The woman's eyes skittered

to the gun on the ground and then back to Carlyn's face. "A plate of food can be brought to you."

"I have come—" Carlyn started, but another sister called out from the pathway to cut off her words.

"Sister Annie, you will miss the midday meal if you tarry."

The woman beside Carlyn looked over her shoulder toward the one on the walkway. "Nay, I will hurry," she assured her.

"It is best to give oneself time without the need for haste." The Shaker sister frowned at Carlyn, then scurried past them toward the stone house without waiting for a reply.

"Yea, Sister Benita is no doubt right." Sister Annie looked back at Carlyn with a smile now. "Even so, it would not hurt me to miss a meal, as you can tell by looking, although all the afternoon, my stomach might grumble in complaint like your dog here rumbles. He won't bite me, will he?" She looked down at Asher, still smiling.

"No. He just feels anxious around so many strangers."

"Oh dear, I suppose I do seem a stranger without telling you my name. I'm Sister Annie and it has been ages since I rubbed a dog's ears. Do you think he'd let me pet him?" She held her hand out toward Asher's nose.

As if Asher knew what she wanted, he bumped his head up under her hand. The sister laughed out loud before she slapped her other hand over her mouth. "For a surety, I will have to confess this pleasure to the eldress."

"Can you not have pleasure here?" Unease filled Carlyn at that thought.

"Oh yea, we find much pleasure in work well done and the laboring of the dances. The love of my sisters is reason for happiness and, of course, Shakering one's plate. That is eating the fine food at our dining tables." She looked toward where the men and women were disappearing inside the stone house and her smile faded.

"Don't miss your meal on my account," Carlyn said. "Just direct me to where I might speak to someone about your society."

"Are you coming among us?" Sister Annie's face lit up. Then her eyes went to Asher and a shadow crossed her face.

"Is something wrong?" Carlyn asked, worried again about the gun on the ground.

"Nay. Well, there are rules, but I am not the one to explain such to you. Wait here, and I will bring you food, for although you may deny it, I can see you have been too long without a proper meal. I'll find a bit of sustenance for your handsome dog too." With a last tousle of Asher's ears, she started toward the stone house.

"Eat your own meal first," Carlyn called after her.

"Yea, if I'm not too late." She hurried her step and disappeared into the building.

Carlyn picked up her things and moved back into the shade of an oak tree. Suddenly too tired to stand, she sank to the ground and leaned against the tree trunk. Asher settled beside her, his head in her lap.

A peace she hadn't expected settled over her as Carlyn rubbed the dog's head. "She was nice, wasn't she, Asher? And she liked you too. Perhaps the Lord's answer will not be so hard to bear."

She kept her voice low, but it still sounded loud in the blanket of silence that had fallen over the village after the people all disappeared into the houses. A horseman rode past on the road, but he paid no notice of her there under the tree and continued on his way through the village. A bee buzzed past her head. A hen cackled. Her ears welcomed those familiar sounds in the quiet village.

She had not expected silence, but she was used to such from living alone so many months. "Not entirely alone," she said, as though Asher might know her thoughts. "But you are a dog of few words. Or barks." She almost laughed then. Her mother was right. The Lord did at times supply answers when most needed.

But not about Ambrose. That was it. She just needed an answer. A sure answer so she could know where she stood. Married or widowed. She blew out her breath. It wouldn't matter here. None were married in this place. All were merely sisters. She could be a sister.

"A sister with a dog," she whispered. "Wonder where your brother dogs are?"

She looked around. No dog had barked a warning of their arrival in the town. That was not common. Dogs generally raised a ruckus when new people came calling, and even more so when a strange dog invaded their territory. Perhaps they kept their dogs somewhere away from the road that went through their village, or could be they were inside under the table hoping for a scrap of food to be dropped. What had Sister Annie said? That they found pleasure in Shakering their plates. The dogs might Shaker the floor.

A smile pulled at Carlyn's lips again. The village must be good for her to find reason to smile twice in such a short time. Smiles had been too rare lately.

She was nodding off when the men and women began coming out of the stone building, the men through the door closest to her and the women through the other door. Carlyn remembered Ambrose saying the Shakers strictly separated the sexes and that was the reason for two doors. Men stayed on one side of the buildings with their own stairways and women on the other. It had to do with their religion, he said.

That she could understand. After all, their church was the same with the separate doors for the men and women and the men's side of the church so they wouldn't be distracted from the gospel by unruly children. Carlyn's father said it was only proper to take extra measures to be sure the men of the church were fed spiritual food. Then, the men, properly fed, could explain the Scripture to their families.

But Ambrose said it wasn't that way among the Shakers. He claimed women were church leaders in the sect, as strange as that sounded. Everyone knew it wasn't proper for women to speak up in church, much less attempt to lead men in spiritual matters.

When Carlyn had asked Ambrose how he knew so much about the Shakers, he told her his mother lived with the Shakers for a couple of years after her mother had died of the consumption. Then her father had remarried and she'd gone home again, but Ambrose said she never had a harsh word to say about the Shakers.

Funny that Carlyn hadn't remembered that until just now here in the Shaker village. Or perhaps that buried memory had pulled her to the village as surely as the tolling of the bell.

Carlyn left the gun on the ground and got to her feet when she saw Sister Annie coming across the road. A tall, slender woman glided sedately alongside Sister Annie's more labored pace. But then Sister Annie was balancing a plate of food as she walked. She handed it over to Carlyn, who hadn't seen so much food since Ambrose marched away to war. Meat, boiled potatoes and green beans with stewed apples and a biscuit to boot. Asher looked up at the plate with hopeful eyes, but Carlyn thought it best not to drop the biscuit his way with the sisters watching her.

"This is Eldress Lilith. She will guide you once you have eaten." Sister Annie was obviously not comfortable next to the eldress. "Eldress, this is . . . Oh my, I neglected to ask your name." She looked even more discomfited as she rubbed her hands on her apron.

"Worry not, Sister Annie. Names are easy to come by, are they not, my young sister?" A smile touched the older woman's lips.

Carlyn pushed an answering smile out on her lips even though the other woman's smile did not tarry on her face. "I'm Carlyn Kearney. I live not far down the road. At least I did live there."

The eldress lowered her eyelids for a second as though considering her answer before she asked, "And did you live there alone? Or have you come here to escape the marital snares of the world?"

"My husband has not come home from the war."

The woman sighed. "The sins of the world fall on the innocent. We have no use for war here. Peace is what we ever seek."

Carlyn didn't know exactly what she was expected to say. She was beginning to feel as discomfited as Sister Annie by the eldress. "Peace sounds good."

"So you seek the same? Peace?" The woman swept her eyes across the gun beside Carlyn's bag and frowned. "With a firearm?"

"It's a h-hunting gun," Carlyn stammered in the face of the woman's obvious disapproval. She had no idea what the woman would say if she revealed who she worried might be hunting her.

"A weapon, nonetheless."

"Yes." Carlyn tried to think of what else to say, but the eldress held up her hand to stop her.

Her face smoothed back into calm lines. "But it is wrong of me to question you while you hold your meal. After you have eaten, I will take you to Sister Muriel. She will find you a place should you decide to stay with us. And then we can deal with the gun and the dog." The woman peered over at Sister Annie. "Go ahead and give the animal the biscuits you secreted in your apron pocket, Sister Annie, and then be about your duties."

A guilty flush spread across Sister Annie's cheeks as she pulled the biscuits from her pocket. "Yea, forgive me, Eldress, but the dog looked as hungry as his mistress."

Asher took the offered food politely and settled down at Carlyn's feet to eat. Sister Annie didn't attempt to rub him with the eldress watching, but instead shoved her hands under her apron as she turned away.

"Thank you, Sister Annie." Carlyn lifted the plate a bit. "For your kindness and the food."

"'Tis a small thing." Sister Annie shot a little smile over her shoulder. "Best eat it before it gets cold."

Carlyn ate standing up. It was awkward, but she couldn't very well sit on the ground beside Asher with the unsmiling eldress towering over her, even though the woman suggested she do so. It was all Carlyn could do to swallow the food. While the taste was fine, her throat was tight and her stomach still uneasy. She didn't want to appear ungrateful, but there was no way she could eat all the food piled on the plate.

She sneaked a look at the woman in hopes she'd be looking away so that Carlyn could slip some of the meat to Asher. But the woman's eyes were locked on her with too much understanding.

"Sister Annie was perhaps too generous with her dippings for you," the eldress said.

"It is very good, but I am not accustomed to eating so much." Carlyn ate the last of the apples and nibbled on the biscuit. "My stomach cannot hold it all."

"While it is our custom here not to waste food by taking more than one can eat, since you did not dip out the food, I cannot fault you for not eating it all. So what you cannot eat it, you may spill out for your dog. I assume the animal is yours."

Asher was eyeing the eldress with none of the friendliness he'd shown Sister Annie. To forestall a growl at the woman, Carlyn dropped her biscuit for him.

"Yes." Carlyn touched the dog's back. "He's a very good dog." She finished off the green beans and eyed the roast meat.

The woman looked from Asher straight at Carlyn. "He very well may be, but a Shaker animal must earn his keep and be useful. We keep no pets."

"No dogs?" Carlyn stared at the woman, sure she misunderstood. She'd never once thought about Asher not being allowed to stay in the Shaker village. Not inside with her as he did at the house, but surely in the village under a porch or in a barn. Her stomach turned over and she willed herself not to be sick even as her hands began shaking so much that she could barely keep the plate from spilling. She'd thought the Shaker village was the Lord's answer, but perhaps she was wrong. What was she going to do?

With a concerned frown, Eldress Lilith took the plate from Carlyn. "My sister, do you feel faint?"

"I can't stay here without Asher."

"Asher?" Her frown darkened.

With despair choking her, Carlyn couldn't speak. She looked down and laid her hand on Asher, who moved closer until she could lean against him.

"It is only a dog," the eldress said.

"But my dog." Carlyn met her eyes with some defiance.

"I see." The woman studied her a moment before she let out the whisper of a sigh. "Do you have someplace else you can go, my child?"

Carlyn shut her eyes and lowered her head. After a moment, she forced out her answer. "No." Another of her mother's lessons rose in her mind. Sometimes following the Lord's will required sacrifice.

The woman laid her hand on Carlyn's shoulder and her voice was not unkind. "Then is there someone in the world who will take the dog?"

7

Every morning that Mitchell Brodie woke up in the comfortable bed at Mrs. Snowden's boardinghouse felt like a gift. The first thing he did, even before he splashed water on his face from the bowl on the washstand, was look out the window to watch daylight ease over the street below his second-story window. The town looked so peaceful with only a few people out and about.

He wanted to keep it that way. Peaceful. His town. His county. He'd spent too many months in the middle of everything but peace, with cannons booming and men who might have been his neighbors before the war shooting at him. He shot back. God help him. He shot at men across the divide between the armies. Men just like him, only fighting for the South while he fought for the North. At times, he'd wondered if anybody knew why they were shooting at one another. What were they fighting for?

"The Union." That was what his captain said. With great conviction.

But then what were the Confederates fighting for? Captain Trowbridge had no trouble answering that question either. "Because they're idiots."

"And we're not?" Mitchell looked across the pathetic fire toward the other man. It was freezing. They barely had anything to eat and the coffee had run out the day before. From the looks of the sky, it was going to snow and they faced another miserable winter in camp instead of being home with their families.

"Nobody ever likes to think he's an idiot, Brodie. In our case, it's the generals who are the idiots." He laughed then and threw a few sticks on the fire. "At least the best of them. A man starts doing too much thinking, he makes a sorry soldier. We can't be sorry soldiers. The fate of the Union depends on us."

Mitchell had liked Captain Trowbridge. A man who could smile in any type of weather and who never asked his men to do anything he wasn't willing to do first, including dying. He'd done that in a skirmish in the spring of 1864 at a bridge over a creek a long-legged man could almost jump across. They'd won the skirmish, but lost the heart of their unit.

But they'd finally won the war. Saved the Union. Captain Trowbridge would say it was worth it, and when Mitchell looked out at his town coming to life every morning, he could believe it.

Across the street, Billy Hogan came outside to lean against the door to his barbershop and give everybody walking past the once-over, sizing them up for haircuts and shaves.

Mitchell could use a haircut. The blasted curls were lapping his collar again. While he was in the army, he'd just sawed them off with his knife. It didn't much matter how his hair looked, marching out to face cannon fire, but now he needed to consider his appearance. The people in the county expected their sheriff to look like an upstanding citizen. Especially the older ladies. The younger ladies weren't too worried about the length of his hair. They were more concerned with his marital status. Eligible bachelors had been thinned out by the war.

With a sigh, Mitchell turned away from the window to begin his day. He never knew what might be waiting for him. Besides those anxious young women. Thinking about them brought to mind the young widow. He still had a bad taste in his mouth from the trip out to her house with Curt Whitlow. It wasn't a good thing putting a person out of their home, especially a young woman with no family nearby.

On Friday night, Mrs. Snowden had been glad to tell him all about Carlyn Kearney. Mrs. Snowden was anything but tight-lipped about the citizens of Mercer County. Her loquaciousness was helpful at times. Not that he needed to know more about Carlyn Kearney. He didn't. If he had to put her out of her house, the less he knew the better. But he kept seeing her facing them off, a gun in her hands and the dog by her side.

"Poor girl." The corners of Mrs. Snowden's mouth had turned down. She wiped a bit of sweat from her face with her apron tail after retrieving Mitchell's supper from the stove's warming oven. She saved his meals for him if he was delayed for supper with the stipulation he had to eat in the kitchen. She didn't want the other boarders to see him eating at all hours and expect like treatment. She had strict meal times, but she also had an unmarried niece she managed to mention every time Mitchell took a late supper.

He had met the niece. Mrs. Snowden had seen to that. Florence. She came every Monday to help her aunt with the laundry. She wasn't a beauty, but her face was pleasant enough. At least what he managed to see of it. The timid creature kept her head bent and her eyes away from him whenever he happened across her path. He couldn't decide if she was embarrassed about her aunt's matchmaking attempts or if the very sight of him terrified her.

Mitchell had no desire to coax her out of her timidity. He liked a girl with spirit, but after Hilda, he was in no hurry to bare his heart to any girl, spirited or not. And yet Carlyn Kearney kept coming into his thoughts, both the girl with the gun and the girl in tears.

So he had purposely dropped her name in front of Mrs. Snowden.

"I'm not one to gossip about folks, but that poor child has known her share of problems."

"Oh? You mean because of her husband not coming home?" Mitchell looked up from the hash on his plate. Mrs. Snowden's cooking might not compare to his mother's, but it beat the army rations by a long sight. And she did make a fine apple cobbler. A generous helping of that awaited him when he finished off the hash.

"Well, that too, of course." Mrs. Snowden poured him a cup of coffee and one for herself. That meant she had plenty to tell. She pulled another serving of the cobbler out of the warming oven and settled down across the table from him.

Mitchell waited while Mrs. Snowden took a noisy sip of her coffee. Then she surprised him by not saying anything as she stared off at the wall. She didn't even pick up her fork to dig into her cobbler.

"Are you all right, Mrs. Snowden?" It was unlike her to be so quiet, and her face was extra red even for her. She was a heavyset woman and the heat of the kitchen kept her flushed.

She shook herself a little and turned back to him. "Oh, sorry about that, Mitchell. You speaking of Carlyn's husband just sent my thoughts back to losing my Quentin. It's a hard thing being a widow. Never having been married, you likely can't understand, but when you love somebody, them being gone slices you in two."

He had thought he was in love, but Mrs. Snowden knew nothing about that. It could be he knew nothing about that either. Even if he'd been in love, Hilda hadn't shared those feelings.

Mrs. Snowden sighed and picked up her fork. "But a person has to go on. When my Quentin died, our boys were already grown and on their own. They might have opened their doors to me, but two women in one kitchen is nothing but a recipe for trouble. I didn't want that for my boys' wives. Or for me." She laughed a little then and took a bite of the cobbler.

Mitchell dug into his dessert too. "Delicious, Mrs. Snowden. You've outdone yourself."

"It's the apples that make the pie. Florence brought me these. She picked them herself." The woman gave him a pointed look.

"I'll have to thank her when next I see her." Mitchell shoveled in another bite.

"We had some fine trees on our farm, but after Quentin passed I traded the farm for this boardinghouse. Had to make my way. The one thing I knew how to do was cook and clean. And I've learned to put up with a bit of noise and bother from the likes of you." With a smile, she pointed her fork toward Mitchell. Then her smile faded. "Of course, I had to leave Quentin out there on the farm, but I go now and again to tend his grave. Such can be a comfort to a widow woman, you know."

"I'm sorry, Mrs. Snowden." Mitchell put down his fork and reached across the table to touch her hand.

"Now, don't let my sorrowful talk ruin your appetite. You go on and eat that cobbler. I was just thinking it has to be different for poor Carlyn. Not knowing, you know. Ambrose Kearney didn't come home, but nobody knows what became of him either. They say he's missing. What kind of word is that? Missing." Mrs. Snowden shook her head. "What's a woman supposed to do with that? No body. No grave. It's like he walked away to the army and just vanished in thin air. It's no wonder the girl is confused about whether she's a widow or not."

"Do you think she is?" Mitchell dug into his cobbler again.

"Well, of course she is. Ambrose Kearney was a good man and he loved his pretty little wife. The only thing that would have kept him away from her was dying. But you can understand why she hangs onto hope that, well, I don't know what. It's right pitiful when you think about it. She can't go on with her life for wondering. I mean, I'm sure she wouldn't have any trouble finding another man eager to step into Ambrose Kearney's shoes." Mrs. Snowden gave Mitchell a curious look. "You say you saw her today?"

"Right." Mitchell wanted to avoid saying why.

But Mrs. Snowden guessed. "That Curt Whitlow is bothering her, ain't he? That man. I don't know why his wife puts up with him. But then I suppose you make your bed, you have to lie in it. Comfortable or not. And Gladys never has to count her pennies when she goes to the general store."

Mitchell took a drink of his coffee and waited for whatever else Mrs. Snowden had to say. Once rolling, she generally kept talking until she told everything she knew about a person. This time was no different.

"Carlyn was a Wilson before she married, you know. Daughter of Reverend Wilson. Now there was a man bent on doing the Lord's work, come what may. Went all over the countryside preaching and down in Tennessee too, I'm told. Just left his family and went. Claimed if he was doing the Lord's work, then the Lord would take care of the rest. But I'm telling you, pretty words, spiritual or not, don't make a very good supper. I have as much religion as the next fellow, but it appears to me the Lord gives a man a family, he expects that man to provide for them."

"Sounds reasonable." Mitchell finished off his cobbler and picked up his cup. "So do they live around here?"

"No, the Reverend heard there were sinners in Texas. They packed up and headed west a few years back."

"No other family around these parts?"

"Not that I ever heard of. They showed up here after they married. Guess the Reverend heard about sinners here then." She laughed a little at that. "Why are you asking? Is that Curt Whitlow putting her out of her house?"

"She owes him money on it," Mitchell allowed. He'd probably already said too much, but he wanted to know about Carlyn Kearney.

"Money she ain't got no way of getting." Mrs. Snowden shook her head. "She still have that dog?"

"She has a dog."

75

"I've heard tell it's a vicious thing. As apt to bite you as not."

"It didn't bite me, but it wasn't overly fond of Mr. Whitlow."

Mrs. Snowden snorted. "Dog must be smarter than people say."

Mitchell peered over the top of his coffee cup at the woman. She rarely had an ill thing to say about anyone. "Has Mr. Whitlow given you trouble?"

"Curt Whitlow gives everybody trouble. The man would sell his grandmother for a pittance to put coin in his pocket." She stood and began gathering up the dirty dishes. "Praise the Lord, I never had to have any dealings with the man. He's quick to loan to a person when hard times come to call."

"But that's good, isn't it? To give a man a hand when he needs it?"

"I doubt he's ever given the first man nothing. Or woman either. He just sits back and waits till things get harder and then calls in his loan. When the money's not there, he takes over the property." She dropped the dishes down in her dishpan with a clatter. "It's all legal, I'm guessing. But everything that's legal ain't right. You know that's true, Sheriff Brodie. At least in the Lord's eyes."

Mitchell took a sip of the tepid coffee. "Could be, but I better stick with the law and let the preachers figure out the rest."

"Some things can't none of us down here on earth figure out." Mrs. Snowden sighed. "I'm glad I took my pappy's advice. Neither a lender nor a borrower be. Then can't nobody own your next dollar or leave you wanting their last dollar."

Now Mitchell turned away from the window and tried to push thoughts of the young widow out of his mind. But he couldn't. At the end of the week, he'd have to make another visit to be sure she'd vacated Whitlow's house. And if she hadn't? He didn't want to think about that.

Maybe he could ask around town and see if there were any positions open for a young woman. It wasn't his job to find her a place, but he'd feel a lot better about putting her out of her house if he knew she had somewhere to go. He took another look out the window at the barbershop. After breakfast, he'd get that haircut. Billy Hogan had his ear to the ground. He might know if anybody was looking for help.

An hour later, Mitchell took off his hat and settled in the barber's chair.

"Wondered when you'd get around to coming by." Billy draped the cape around Mitchell's shoulders. "Been needing a cut for a while."

"Things have been busy," Mitchell said.

"Yeah, I heard Curt Whitlow made you go with him to that poor Kearney girl's house out near Oak Spring Church." Billy combed and clipped.

Mitchell made a sound that could mean yes or no. Billy was like Mrs. Snowden. He didn't need much encouragement to keep talking.

"Ambrose Kearney was a fine young man. You never knew him, did you?" He looked at Mitchell in the mirror across from the chair.

"No, can't say as I did," Mitchell said.

"He made a bad deal on that house, but guess he didn't know better than to borrow money from Curt."

"Lots of people have."

"And lived to regret it." Billy pushed Mitchell's head forward to trim the hair along his neckline.

"You one of those?" Mitchell peeked up at the barber in the mirror.

"Naw. I paid the man what I owed him. I don't have to give him free haircuts no more. He sits in my chair, he pays these days."

"Sounds reasonable."

"You see him last night or this morning?" Billy paused, his scissors still in the air behind Mitchell's head.

"No, not since Friday."

"You don't say." Billy began snipping Mitchell's hair again. "I figured he'd be knocking down your door."

"Why's that?"

"Got a nasty dog bite, according to Doc Baker. Said it looked like the man had been in quite some tussle when he showed up at his door yesterday afternoon to get his arm stitched up. Mud and blood all over his clothes."

"Doc Baker been to get a haircut this morning?" Mitchell asked.

Billy laughed a little. "Not today, but word gets around."

"He say what dog got Curt?" Mitchell knew which dog he was suspecting, but he didn't have much sympathy for the man. He told him to stay away from the Kearney woman.

"Haven't heard if he did. Thought maybe you had. I figured Curt would be after you to do something about it."

"I haven't been to the office yet."

"Could be he'll hunt you up yet."

"Could be." Mitchell hoped not.

Billy was quiet a minute as he combed and cut. Then

without raising his eyes from Mitchell's head, he said, "I hear that Kearney widow has a dog."

"Lots of people have dogs. The town's full of them." Mitchell kept his eyes away from Billy's mirror.

"True enough," Billy agreed. "I used to have an old dog here in the shop with me. Fine company on slow days, but then he wasn't vicious. Couldn't have had him if that had been the case."

Mitchell didn't bother saying Carlyn Kearney's dog wasn't vicious as long as nobody bothered his mistress. He'd worry about taking up for the dog once he heard Whitlow's story. It might not have been her dog. He sincerely hoped not.

When Mitchell asked about jobs in the town that a woman might be able to do, Billy shook his head. "Can't think of anything offhand, but I'll keep an eye out. Who's it for? That Mrs. Kearney?"

He hadn't wanted to mention Carlyn Kearney's name, but Billy had a way of figuring out more than a man said. "Right. I hear she doesn't have any family around here to help her out."

Billy unwrapped the cape from around Mitchell and swept the hairs off Mitchell's neck with his shaving soap brush. "I haven't seen her for a spell, but best I remember, she's a pretty thing. I'm surprised she's not already married again."

"She's not as sure she's a widow as everybody else seems to be." Mitchell got out of the chair. "Her husband's listed as missing, not dead."

"Yeah. She'd be better off knowing for sure she was a widow, but she's not the only woman in that boat. I read in the papers that there are thousands of soldiers unaccounted for. War's a sorry thing."

Mitchell walked down to his office, glad Curt Whitlow wasn't there waiting for him. Then, that bothered him too. If Whitlow wasn't demanding something be done about the dog attack, there had to be a reason. One Whitlow wasn't ready to admit.

Later, for his peace of mind, Mitchell would ride out to Carlyn Kearney's house to check on her. It didn't have anything to do with how pretty she was. It was his job.

But then, that afternoon before he found time to make that trip, she came to him. Riding in a Shaker wagon. With a rope around her dog's neck.

8

~

The Shakers were kind, even Eldress Lilith with her somber face, but that didn't mean they would bend their rules. Not for a newcomer. Certainly not for a dog.

Carlyn followed the eldress to the imposing brick building beside the post office. She left Carlyn on the walkway while she went to the door to summon this Sister Muriel. Then she came back to stand beside Carlyn to await the sister who would have the necessary answers. Carlyn kept her hand on Asher, as silent as the eldress. She bent her head and considered prayer. To perhaps remind the Lord she had a dog. But he already knew that.

At last a Shaker sister came out the large double doors. She was dressed much the same as the other Shaker women, in a faded blue dress with the wide white neckerchief lapped over her chest and a long checked apron practically covering the front of her skirt. She looked to be near the same age as the woman beside Carlyn, but instead of the stern stoniness of Eldress Lilith's face, this new sister's face was soft and gentle. Even so, she hesitated on the broad stoop and visibly shuddered when she noticed the gun Carlyn had once more tucked under her arm and pointed at the ground. Then she looked even more distressed when Eldress Lilith nodded toward Asher.

"Sister Muriel, the young sister has sought us out for help," Eldress Lilith said.

The woman came down the steps, a concerned smile hovering around her lips. "My dear sister, you do bring problems with you."

"I didn't know about your rules against dogs." Tears jumped to Carlyn's eyes as she was all too aware of the familiar comfort of Asher leaning against her. "I can leave."

"Nay, let's not be hasty," the sister said.

"She has not told me her trouble." Eldress Lilith spoke up. "Only that she has nowhere else to go."

"Yea, those in the world suffer many trials." Sister Muriel answered the eldress but kept her eyes on Carlyn, who was beginning to feel like the lost soul they obviously thought she was. The lost soul perhaps she was.

But no, her mother had assured her, once in the Lord's hand, he didn't drop any of his children. Not unless they willfully pushed away from his love and ran from him. Even then, he kept his hand outstretched for his child to return. Just as the prodigal son's father had in the Bible story.

"Is that true, my sister?" Sister Muriel's voice was as gentle as her face, as she reached toward Carlyn but stayed her hand short of touching her.

Carlyn drew in a breath. "I thought the Lord was pointing me toward your village as the answer to my need. But he knows I have a dog."

"Yea, the Lord knows everything and Mother Ann is ever ready to help those who desire to follow the Shaker way." Sister Muriel looked over at the eldress. "Is that not true, Eldress Lilith?"

"Yea," the eldress said. "If the Lord sent you here in answer to your prayers, young sister, then he will give you an answer for your distress over your dog."

Sister Muriel smiled fully all across her face. "If you ask with faith."

"And the willingness to accept the answer," Eldress Lilith added without a smile.

"Why can't he stay here in one of your sheds or barns?" Carlyn looked around. There were buildings everywhere.

"We have no dogs." Sister Muriel's voice was kind but also firm. "It is not the Shaker way. But there are many such dogs in the town. One more can surely find a place there."

"He won't leave me to go into the town," Carlyn said.

"The animal does seem attached to you." Sister Muriel studied Asher, then raised her hands up toward the heavens. "Let us ask for an answer."

Eldress Lilith lifted her hands too, but neither of the women spoke a word aloud. Carlyn lifted her free hand high alongside them. It wasn't the attitude of prayer she was used to, but it didn't feel wrong. Hadn't her mother sat at the table with her hands open in front of her to receive the Lord's answers? Answers she received time and again. And accepted without wishing for different ones. At least not as far as Carlyn knew.

Carlyn closed her eyes even though the other two women did not. The sound of horses' hooves and the creak of a harness interrupted her attempt to pray.

Sister Muriel dropped her hands down with a sound of victory. "There's Brother Thomas on the way to the town. The Lord has supplied our answer."

"Or Mother Ann," Eldress Lilith said.

Carlyn wanted to ask who this mother was, but bit back the question. She looked to her mother for answers. Why shouldn't they? Perhaps they were actual sisters instead of merely Shaker sisters, even though they shared no family resemblance other than their like dress.

Sister Muriel stepped out to the fence to flag down the wagon. The Shaker man pulled back on the reins to stop his horses.

"Are you on the way to the town, Brother?"

"Yea, have you a need for something there?" the man answered.

"Nay. We have a dog that needs to be carried to the town," Sister Muriel said.

Carlyn opened her mouth to protest when the memory of the sheriff asking to pet Asher popped into her mind. Another answer, perhaps. Not the one she would most like, for it made her heart hurt to think of giving up Asher, but the dog would be safe with the sheriff. If he would take him in. More need of prayer.

The brother studied the dog for a moment. Then he climbed down from the wagon and rummaged under the seat until he found a rope. "Best tie this around his neck." He made a loop in one end of the rope and handed it across the fence toward Carlyn.

"He's never been tied." Carlyn took it with reluctance.

The brother looked straight at her. "I doubt he'd stay in the wagon without a rope to hold him there."

"I'll go with him," Carlyn said.

"Do you mean to find new answers in the town, my sister?" Sister Muriel asked.

"Only for my dog. The sheriff there. I met him last week. He might know of a place for Asher."

The two women looked doubtful, but Brother Thomas spoke up. "Sheriff Brodie is a good man for one of the world. The young sister may be right to count on his help."

"And then what?" Eldress Lilith's eyes bore into Carlyn.

Carlyn pulled in a deep breath and faced her future. "Then I'll return and find a place here if you have one for me."

"We turn no sister in need away," Sister Muriel said. "Brother Thomas can bring you to me after you are rid of the dog."

Brother Thomas nodded toward the rope. "Best put it around his neck, young sister, to be sure nothing along the road entices him away from us. A squirrel. Another dog. Dogs are prone to be off on a chase, and I must be about my errands with no time for running down dogs."

The three Shakers stared at her with impassive faces that expected her to do as they said. With a murmur of apology to Asher, she slipped the loop over the dog's head. If the Shakers heard her, they gave no indication.

Then the brother pointed at the gun. "You will have no need of a weapon."

"I have needed it in the past." Carlyn's hand tightened on the gun. Curt Whitlow lived in town.

"But you are beginning a new life now. One where, engaged in your duty, you will have nothing to fear." Brother Thomas gently lifted the gun away from her and propped it against the fence. "Sister Muriel will have a brother fetch the gun."

"But—" Carlyn looked at the gun, "I'm not a Shaker yet."

The brother paid her words no mind as he turned back to the wagon. "Climb in and call your dog up after you. He might use his teeth on me if I try to put him there."

After Asher jumped up in the wagon, Carlyn settled on a box toward the front of the wagon. Asher leaned against her, trembling at the strangeness of it all. Or perhaps because he sensed her own tremble. She was losing everything. Even her carpetbag. She'd left it there on the ground beside the two Shaker sisters.

As the wagon began moving, Carlyn wanted to ask Brother Thomas to stop so she could retrieve it. Perhaps in the town another way would open to her. But she didn't call out. She needed to accept the answer already given.

She leaned close to the dog and spoke to him in whispers Brother Thomas couldn't hear over the creaking of the wagon wheels. "You will make Sheriff Brodie a wonderful dog." She would not let herself think about the sheriff turning the dog away. "You remember him. You wagged your tail when he rubbed your head. It will be good." She stroked down his head and back. "It will. You'll have food. I'll have food and a roof. Each day it is given unto us that which we need."

Something like that was one of her mother's oft-quoted Scriptures. Needs and wants were not the same. She wanted Ambrose home months ago. She wanted flowers around her house and chickens in her yard. She wanted Asher on the front porch guarding the door. But she needed food and shelter. That would be supplied by the Shakers who did not embrace the gift of a dog. So her second need was food for him.

She stared into Asher's dog eyes. He stared back, trying to figure out why they weren't at their house going about their daily chores. Even so, he didn't bark or pull against the rope around his neck. He trusted her. She stroked his fur and leaned her head against his. He had survived before showing up at her house. He would survive again. She would as well. As one of the odd Shaker sisters.

When they finally reached the town, Carlyn kept her head bent as they rode down Main Street. She didn't want to chance Curt seeing her and pointing an accusing finger at Asher. She was glad when Brother Thomas stopped in front of the sheriff's office first thing.

He looked back at her. "I ask you to be ready when I return, for I would not like darkness to overtake us on the way back to the village."

"I will be ready."

Carlyn climbed out of the wagon and Asher jumped down after her. His legs were shaking and his tail curled under him. She knew how he felt as she turned toward the sheriff's office. The door was closed. What would she do if he wasn't there? She gripped the rope around Asher's neck and stared at the door, willing the sheriff to appear as the Shaker brother flicked the reins and started his horses away.

"Mrs. Kearney, are you looking for me?" Sheriff Brodie didn't come out of the office but down the street instead.

She turned toward him. "Yes." That seemed to be the only word she could force out. What she really wanted to do was sit down right there on the walkway and give way to tears, but she'd already dissolved in tears in front of this man once. She would not do so again.

"Come inside." He gestured toward his office. "It will be cooler there and you can tell me what you need."

The sun was warm for September, but she'd hardly noticed

once she got to the Shaker village. She hesitated, her free hand on Asher's head.

He noticed and added, "Your dog is welcome inside too if that's your worry."

As if Asher knew he spoke about him, his tail eased away from his body to flap back and forth. He took a step toward the sheriff. That good sign unfroze Carlyn's tongue. "I have come to ask a favor from you."

9

She looked so unsure that yes was on Mitchell's tongue even before hearing what she had come to ask him. When he noted her hand trembling as she held the dog's rope, he wanted to put his hand over hers to calm her. He put the brakes on his feelings. She hadn't come looking for a man. She was looking for a sheriff.

"I'm here to help." He hoped his words would be true and he could help her. But it would be best to hear what she had to say before making promises, no matter how the sight of her weary eyes touched him. She had sweat stains on the bodice of her dress, beggar mites lining the hem of her skirt, and the trace of tears on her cheek.

He pointed toward his office again. When her feet still seemed attached to the walk, he put his hand under her elbow to guide her to the door. Her dog didn't growl. That was a good sign. His heart speeding up at her nearness was not.

She perched in the chair in front of his desk as he took the chair behind it. He needed to keep some distance between them. After giving her a moment to gather herself, he asked, "What can I do for you today?"

"It's about Asher." She stroked the dog's head with a hand that was definitely trembling. At the sound of his name, the dog eased closer to her.

Mitchell prodded her to continue. "What about him?" Whatever it was, it couldn't be good. Not if her face was any indication. He wished he hadn't gone for that haircut this morning. Then he might not know about a dog biting Curt Whitlow.

She pushed out the words in a rush. "You know I don't have the money to pay Mr. Whitlow for the house and no family near who might take me in until . . ." Her voice faltered. She moistened her lips and went on. "Well, since Ambrose didn't come home. The Shakers will take me in."

"The Shakers?" He shouldn't have been surprised, since she'd climbed down out of a Shaker wagon, but he was. Carlyn Kearney didn't seem the type to go to the Shakers. But then other young women were there, turning their backs on the more common pursuits of marriage and children.

She lifted her chin a bit. "It is the answer to my problem. They will supply my physical needs in return for my labor."

"They have strange beliefs." Mitchell should have stayed silent, but the words slipped out.

"None of which I have to believe to live among them," she said, then sighed. "But they also have many rules."

"So I've heard. Like no marriages. Separating men and women." Again he should have been silent.

"Those rules present no difficulty for me." When she twisted the rope in her hands, the dog licked her arm. She shut her eyes a moment and pulled in a breath, as though summoning courage for her next words. "But they have a rule against dogs. I can stay with them, but Asher cannot."

"They don't have dogs?" That surprised Mitchell. "I didn't know that."

"Nor did I." She glanced up at Mitchell, then back down at the dog. "But that is what they tell me."

"So you're hoping I know someone who might give him a home?"

"No." She looked straight at him then. "I want you to take him."

Mitchell searched for the right words. He had no place for a dog.

She spoke again first, her voice not much above a whisper. "I realize Mrs. Brodie might not want a dog, but Asher likes you. So I was hoping."

"There's no Mrs. Brodie." A flush climbed into her cheeks at his words. "But I can't have a dog. I live in a boardinghouse."

"Mrs. Snowden's?" When he nodded, she hurried out her next words. "I think she's fond of dogs and Asher is a very good dog. Or he could stay here at your office." She leaned toward him. "Please."

He wanted to say no. He had to say no, but he couldn't bring the word to his lips while staring into her eyes. Instead he said, "I hear a dog bit Curt Whitlow."

"Is that so?" She sat back and stared down at her lap. The dog's ears came up at the sound of Whitlow's name and she stroked his head. Her hand was trembling again. "Was he badly hurt?"

"I don't know. I haven't seen him."

"Dog bites can be painful, I'm told." She kept her eyes on the dog.

After a moment's silence, he said, "I don't think the two of us need to play games about this, Mrs. Kearney. Did your dog attack Curt Whitlow?"

She looked up at him boldly then, the way she had at her house with the gun in her hands. "Yes."

"With cause?"

"Yes." Her eyes stayed steady on his.

He clenched his hands at the thought of what her yes might mean. "Would you like to elaborate on that cause?"

"No." She shut her mouth tightly as if determined not to let any other words out.

"I won't be able to take the dog if you don't tell me what happened. Not knowing what made him bite the man."

"Asher was protecting me." She moistened her lips and seemed to need to summon courage to continue. "I think you can guess the reason."

Mitchell clamped down on the anger surging through him. "Did Whitlow injure you or violate you in any way?"

Her face stiffened. "When Asher attacked him, I managed to escape the man's clutches before anything untoward occurred."

"That's good to hear." Mitchell forced his voice to stay calm. What was it about this woman that made him want to protect her? He pushed the thought aside. He wanted to protect every woman in his county. That was his job. "I can arrest him for accosting you."

"I'd rather you didn't. It would be my word against his. And I will be gone from his influence with the Shakers. It's just Asher I worry about." Her face softened as she pleaded. "Please take him. I beg of you."

"All right." He could hardly believe he'd said those words.

He couldn't have a dog. Especially a dog that had attacked one of the town's leading citizens. Whether it was with cause or not.

A smile exploded across her face. She jumped to her feet and leaned across the desk to brush her lips across his cheek. "Thank you, Sheriff. I know Asher will be safe with you. I feel so much easier about going to the Shakers now."

He had to bite back the words telling her he could find her a better place than one with the Shakers, but it was crazy to even imagine saying that to a woman he barely knew. He couldn't let pity make him do something even more foolish than taking her dog.

Her face turned sad again as she crouched in front of the dog and talked to him as though he could understand every word she said. Perhaps he could, for when she handed Mitchell the rope around the dog's neck, he didn't pull against it to follow her out to the waiting Shaker wagon. He did whimper when the wagon began moving away.

Mitchell watched her out of sight before he shut the door. "Well, Asher, you better hope she was right about Mrs. Snowden."

The dog paid no attention as he settled down in front of the door.

"She's not coming back. No matter how much we wish she would." He only wished that, because having the dog was going to cause problems and plenty of them.

The dog turned to him for just a second, then stared back at the door.

Night was falling by the time Mitchell walked through town to the boardinghouse. He kept the rope on Asher, even though the dog showed no sign of running away. But Mitchell didn't want to take any chances. At least until after he saw Curt Whitlow.

If the man thought he was above the law because of his money, he'd find out differently while Mitchell was sheriff. The very thought of the man touching Carlyn with violent intent was enough to make Mitchell ready to throw him in jail and lose the key. Without benefit of a judge and jury. But he couldn't do that. She had left too much of what happened to Mitchell's imagination. He didn't like what he was imagining.

He didn't like anything about it all. Not the thought of Curt Whitlow forcing his attentions on the young woman. Not the fact that Mitchell might never see her again after she joined up with the Shakers. The dog wasn't reason enough to chase her out to the Shaker town. Maybe if he could find out what happened to her husband, that would be cause to see her again.

He pushed that thought away. He needed to block Carlyn Kearney completely from his mind. She was no longer his concern. Her dog was, but not her.

When he got to the boardinghouse, he tied the dog to one of the back porch posts, but Carlyn was right about Mrs. Snowden.

She peered out the back door at the dog. "You can't tie the poor thing out there. He'll be howling the whole night through and all my boarders will start looking for other rooms." As though the dog heard her, he let out his first howl since Carlyn had left him.

"But I can't leave him loose. Not yet. He might run away."

She gave him a curious look. "I didn't know sheriff duties included taking in stray dogs?"

"He's not a stray. I promised his owner I'd take care of him for a while."

The dog let out another howl, more pitiful than the last. Mrs. Snowden grabbed a biscuit out of her warming oven and headed for the back door. "I'd better take a look at this critter."

Asher stood up and flapped his tail back and forth as soon as Mrs. Snowden stepped out on the porch. The dog was uncannily smart.

So was Mrs. Snowden, who shot Mitchell a sharp look in the fading daylight. "What are you doing with Carlyn Kearney's dog?"

"She needed somebody to take him. It's just until I find him another place." That wasn't exactly true. He'd promised to keep the dog. Finding the dog another place was a promise he made to himself because he couldn't keep a dog. Not even Carlyn Kearney's dog. Especially not her dog. The sooner he put her out of his mind, the better. "Right now I just need to figure out what to do with him tonight."

"Where's Carlyn? Headed to Texas?" Mrs. Snowden gave the dog the biscuit. He took it from her politely with another sweeping wag of his tail.

"No. Gone to the Shakers."

Mrs. Snowden clucked her tongue at that. "Poor child. Trouble can end a body in some sorry places."

"The Shaker town isn't a bad place."

"Maybe not, but it's no place for a young woman like Carlyn. Those old women out there aren't much better than dried-up prunes."

"She's not old." Mitchell tried not to think of how very young she'd looked sitting in his office earlier that day. And how lovely. Or how her lips had felt brushing his cheek.

95

"Indeed." She sent him another look.

"I've heard they're very kind to those in need." He kept his eyes on the dog. The last thing he needed was for Mrs. Snowden to guess how Carlyn Kearney had awakened feelings inside him best left sleeping.

"So they say, but I've been hearing that some strange things are going on out there."

"They do worship some different than the average church-goer."

"Not their worship. Other things." Mrs. Snowden screwed up her face as though trying to remember the gossip she'd heard.

"What things?"

"Can't rightly remember. Maybe something Billy across the street said. He hears all sorts of things. Not that none of the Shaker men would come to him for a haircut. They do their own barbering. They do their own most everything. Hard workers."

"That doesn't sound like any kind of problem. A man should work."

"True enough. The Good Book is clear on a man working if he wants to eat. That surely goes for a woman too, and I've heard those Shakers set a fine table." Mrs. Snowden sighed. "Guess I shouldn't be gossiping about them, but it just ain't right them dancing in church. Can't be nothing proper about that. I don't care if they do claim holiness. But then the Good Book also says a person should leave the judging of others up to the Lord, so who am I to say? 'Cept it just can't be right, can it?"

"It's not illegal. I'll leave whether it's right or not up to the Lord. All I need to figure out is what to do with this dog tonight."

"Hmm." She tapped her finger against her chin for a moment. "He appears to be a nice enough dog, and he does look extra clean. I can't smell him the least bit. Carlyn must have given him a bath before she brought him to you. Now, that was nice of her, wasn't it?"

"I guess." She didn't really need encouragement to keep talking, but Mitchell stuck the words in anyway.

"I do hate knowing she's out there with those Shakers. The least I can do is let her dog have a place." She pointed her finger at Mitchell. "As long as he doesn't bark."

"It'll just be until I can find somebody to take him."

"No need to hurry." She patted Asher's head and untied the rope from the post.

The dog stayed beside Mrs. Snowden as they went in the kitchen as if he knew who was going to fill his plate.

"Florence will be excited to see him." Mrs. Snowden smiled back at Mitchell. "She's fond of dogs, you know."

Mitchell managed to hang on to his smile. He hadn't had his supper yet either.

10

⤜⟡⤛

Back at the Shaker village, Sister Muriel made no mention of Asher or the evidence of tears on Carlyn's cheeks. That was just as well, for it was surely foolish to weep over a dog when she had so many other things to mourn. Ambrose missing, her home gone, her dreams being whipped away by the winds of reality. Losing Asher seemed the final blow.

With her face hidden in her hands, she had given in to the sadness ripping through her after she crawled into the wagon in front of the sheriff's office.

Brother Thomas must have heard her sobs, for when he helped Carlyn down from the wagon, he said, "Don't be in such distress, little sister. There are many sisters in our village. Sisters are far better than dogs. You will see."

Carlyn wanted to tell him Asher was no ordinary dog, but instead, she managed to turn up the corners of her lips into what might pass as a smile to one with so solemn a face as Brother Thomas.

Sister Muriel escorted Carlyn inside the large brick

building to a quiet room where she made it clear Carlyn had much to learn to become a Shaker sister. Her voice was soft, kind, but just as with Asher, there was no bend in her words. Carlyn would be expected to abide by the Shaker way. Unity of spirit and action was greatly to be desired, and that unity came from the discipline of following the Society's rules.

"Must I learn the rules this night?" Carlyn was so tired she could barely stand. She looked longingly at one of the chairs hanging upside down on the pegs of the blue railing that circled around the room. The chair legs pointing up toward the ceiling looked so odd that Carlyn wondered if she was seeing things that weren't there.

"Nay, my sister. That would not be possible, but worry not. The Ministry will assign a sister to guide you into our ways. Here at Harmony Hill, you will have many sisters to love."

"I loved my husband." Carlyn didn't know why she said that. These people didn't have husbands.

"But now you are putting that love aside for a greater love. A purer love. You can pick up your cross, and in time, the burden will seem light. Your brothers and sisters here will help you."

"And the Lord. My mother would say he will help me." Carlyn swayed a little on her feet. If only she could sit down.

"Yea, and Mother Ann will lend you courage and strength."

"Who is this Mother Ann?"

"My dear little sister, you are a true innocent, are you not?"

"Innocent? No. That is for children. I am not a child."

"Are we not all children of God?" Sister Muriel raised her eyebrows at Carlyn.

"Yes," Carlyn whispered the expected answer as tears

popped into her eyes. She did want to be a child of God, but she felt so alone. And so tired.

A frown flickered across Sister Muriel's face as though Carlyn's answer was somehow lacking. "You need to surrender your worries to the Lord and then you can find peace."

"Peace," Carlyn echoed.

"Yea, peace. But forgive me, my sister, for concerning you with things that can wait until you have rested." Sister Muriel touched Carlyn's shoulder. "Follow me."

Sister Muriel led Carlyn down the entrance hall to two staircases that seemed to nearly float in the air as they spiraled upward. Clinging to the railing, Carlyn fought the vertigo that staring at the steps above her brought on. She was thankful when Sister Muriel stopped on the second floor and ushered her into a room with a bed that was little more than a cot. Here, the same as in the room below, a ladder-back chair hung on a blue railing that circled the room. What good was a chair hanging upside down when she desperately needed to sit down?

"Tonight, you will rest here," Sister Muriel said. "Tomorrow you will be given a bed at the Gathering Family House as a new convert."

The word "convert" banged into Carlyn's ears. She had no desire to convert to their religion. She was there for the bed however uncomfortable it looked and to put her feet under their table. After hearing her father rail against the Shakers' blasphemous ways, she could not imagine accepting what they believed, but it was not necessary for them to know that. A bed was a bed and Carlyn was determined to be thankful for whatever food she found on their table.

In everything give thanks. She had struggled with that since the letters from Ambrose stopped coming. How could she give thanks when Ambrose was missing from her life? But she could give thanks for a roof over her head. For the sheriff keeping Asher. For food to eat. For Curt Whitlow no longer able to bang on her door and make demands.

A young sister with a shy smile brought Carlyn warm water to wash and a plate of food. Sister Muriel pulled a plain white cotton nightgown from a chest drawer and laid it on the bed.

"I have a gown in my bag." Carlyn pointed to the carpet-bag someone must have carried up to the room before she returned to the Shaker village.

"Nay." Sister Muriel waved her hand in dismissal. "You will no longer have need of worldly clothes, my sister, but if you wish to cling to the bag for a while, such will be allowed. Come morning, we ask you to wear the clothes supplied in the top drawer of the chest. You will find the Shaker dress quite comfortable and serviceable." Sister Muriel pointed at her own plain dress. "It is good to have unity of dress with your sisters."

"If that is what you want." Carlyn didn't care what she wore.

"It is also good to have an attitude of cooperation, my sister. Such a mind-set will serve you well here."

"I will work at whatever tasks you ask to earn my keep."

"There is nothing to earn. We labor with our hands for the good of all." Sister Muriel held her hands out toward Carlyn. "Work is worship."

Carlyn had no idea what to say to that. How could work be worship?

Sister Muriel must have noted her puzzled look. "With rest, things will be easier to understand."

"Yes," Carlyn murmured.

After Sister Muriel opened the door into the hallway, she turned back for a last bit of instruction. "Remember, if you have need to leave the room, use the staircase on this side of the hall. This is the sisters' side. The opposite side is for the brethren."

With a smile, Sister Muriel was gone. Carlyn stared at the closed door. She had the strangest urge to pull open the door and flee down the proper stairway and out of the Shaker village before it was too late. Too late for what, she wasn't sure, but she was filled with a sudden dread of the days ahead.

She shook away the foolish thought. Her weariness clouded her thinking. In the morning the future would not look so drear.

She shed her clothes and pulled the Shaker gown over her head. The material was soft and smelled of sunshine. The Shaker ways seemed strange, but if all the Shaker sisters were like Sister Annie and Sister Muriel, there would be comfort living among such kindness.

She missed Asher beside her, but summoned up an image of him keeping guard in the sheriff's office as she crawled into bed. While it had been obvious the sheriff was reluctant to take the dog, she had no doubt he would keep his word and care for Asher. Not as she would, but Asher would have food and protection from any who might wish to do him harm.

Carlyn moved uneasily in the narrow bed, sorry she had revealed to Sheriff Brodie so much of what had happened on the road. She had hoped to avoid saying anything about Curt's attack, but he had asked so directly. Perhaps that was part of being a lawman. Getting to the truth. She wanted to forget what had happened. To block it from her mind. She had been rescued from the unthinkable, and here among the Shakers, she would be safe.

She had no reason to feel so bereft. Instead she should be on her knees thanking the Lord for supplying her with an answer whether she felt properly thankful or not.

Pray anyway. She was too tired. How many times had her mother refused to accept weariness as an excuse to skip her prayers? But her mother wasn't standing over her now. Carlyn could do as she wished. At least until morning when she would be the same as indentured to the Shakers. With shaking hands, she pulled the woven cover up over her and sought the escape of sleep.

The bell began tolling the next morning at daylight. For a few minutes, Carlyn didn't know where she was. She reached down to touch Asher, but when her hand felt only the floor, she came fully awake. The Shaker bell. She pushed back the cover and sat up to face her new life.

By the time Sister Muriel rapped softly on her door, Carlyn had on the Shaker dress. It was too large, but that didn't matter with the apron tied around her waist. She struggled with the neckerchief, but at last got it pinned in place over her bosom. She wasn't sure it looked right, for she could find no mirror in the room to check.

"Oh good," Sister Muriel said when Carlyn opened the door. "You must have heard the rising bell."

"Yes." Carlyn stepped back to let Sister Muriel in the room. Only then did she notice another sister with her.

"Not yes. Yea," the other woman said without a smile. "A Believer says yea."

"Have patience, Sister Edna." Sister Muriel put a hand

on the other sister's arm. "I have not instructed her in the proper speech of a Believer."

"What instructions have you given her?" A frown wrinkled the other sister's forehead.

Sister Muriel's smile stiffened a little. "On how to rest her first night among us and the proper stairway for a sister to use." But her smile came back full as she turned to Carlyn. "Sister Edna will be your instructor in the Shaker way. She has been a Believer for years and has ushered many young sisters into the Society."

No smile touched Sister Edna's face, so Carlyn stopped trying to force her own lips to turn up. The new sister did not have a gentle face. Deep lines cut into her face and the corners of her mouth bent downward, but that could be merely evidence of many years of living. She looked even older than Sister Muriel.

"I will do my best," Carlyn said.

"We know you will," Sister Muriel said. "Don't we, Sister Edna?"

"Yea." Sister Edna's mouth spoke the agreement but her eyes showed little warmth.

"I'll leave you then to be about my morning duties." Sister Muriel touched Carlyn's hand. "It is good here. There is much love to be shared."

With a last gentle smile at Carlyn and a worried glance toward Sister Edna, Sister Muriel left them alone. Carlyn didn't know why she was surprised at Sister Edna's lack of smiles. She had been naïve to think all the sisters here would have the sweet spirits of Sister Muriel or Sister Annie. Hadn't she noted Eldress Lilith's solemnity? Just as there were diverse members in Carlyn's church family, the same would be true here.

Besides, it was wrong to judge the kindness of Sister Edna's spirit without knowing her better. Looks could be deceiving. Still, the sister's first words after Sister Muriel left did sound a warning as clear as the Shaker bell.

"Sister Carlyn, it is good that you have left the wicked ways of the world to come among us. My duty will be to teach you the proper behavior of a Believer." She leveled an unsmiling gaze on Carlyn. "I take my duties very seriously."

"I am willing to work at whatever tasks are given me." Carlyn could be meek. After all, she'd come begging to them.

"There is much more than work."

"What more?"

"It is not good to have a questioning spirit." A frown settled on Sister Edna's face that got darker when Carlyn asked yet another question.

"How can I know what I should do without asking?"

"Answers will be given to you at the proper times. You merely have to ready your mind and spirit to receive them."

Carlyn wanted to say she couldn't ready her mind for the Shaker way without asking questions, but the look on Sister Edna's face discouraged argument. So she said, "I will try."

"Yea, and I will see that you do." Sister Edna looked her up and down. "Your cap is crooked." She reached over and tugged one corner of Carlyn's cap down with a scowl. "You have a pretty face."

Carlyn didn't know whether to thank her or apologize. "The Lord gifts us with our looks."

"Outer looks mean nothing and a face such as yours generally leads only to troubles. Inner beauty is what we strive for as Believers."

"My father often said the same."

"Did he?" Sister Edna adjusted Carlyn's neckerchief. "A wise man then. Did you commit some grievous sin to make him turn you out of his house? Is that why you've come to us?"

It was on the tip of Carlyn's tongue to tell Sister Edna that a questioning spirit wasn't good, but she thought it prudent not to speak those words. Better to do whatever needed to be done to get along with the sister. "No. My husband hasn't returned from the war and I had a debt on my house with no way to pay."

"Ahh," Sister Edna said. "And if your husband does return, will you be running back to the world?"

"He may not return." The words tore a hole in her heart, but it was time she said them.

"Good. That will make it easier for you to overcome the sin of matrimony. We are all brothers and sisters here."

"Why?" The question slipped out before Carlyn could stop it. She had felt nothing sinful about being married to Ambrose. Their love had been a blessing rained down on her by the Lord.

"In heaven there are no marriages, only children of God. We, here in Harmony Hill and at the other Believer villages across the country, have brought heaven down to us in order to live a perfect life and shut out worldly things."

"Nobody can be perfect. For all have sinned and fallen short of the glory of God." Even her father had preached that. Carlyn wasn't sure he believed it in regard to himself, but he certainly had not believed his children perfect, or his neighbors, the Shakers.

"So you are familiar with the Bible. A good guide to a sin-less life." Sister Edna gave an approving nod. "That should make it easier for you to accept the true way when such is shown to you. Those of the world often look but refuse to see."

"Those of the world." Carlyn dared another question. "Aren't we all of the world?"

"Nay. Here in our Society of Believers, we have left the trappings of the world for a higher, nobler life. One where we put our hands to work for the Lord and give our hearts to God."

"Hands to work." Sister Muriel had said the same. "I can work."

"And hearts to God."

"I gave my heart to God many years ago," Carlyn said.

"And now you will have a chance to do so properly with full confidence that you are living a godly life. Our testimony is for peace, now and always. We oppose wars of households, and wars of nations. All wars are the result of lusts for lands and for women." The woman frowned at Carlyn. "And the lusts are often greater for women fair of face. Our mother taught us the truth that those who marry will fight."

"My husband and I didn't fight." Carlyn should have stayed silent.

Sister Edna let out an exaggerated sigh and turned toward the door. "Come, the day is wasting. The bell for the morning meal will sound soon and there are instructions for you to hear before eating."

When Carlyn picked up the carpetbag, another frown darkened Sister Edna's face. "You have no need of that now."

"Then what shall I do with it?"

"Pitch it aside like so much trash." Sister Edna made a

dismissal gesture with her hands. "That's all worldly trappings are to a Believer. Trash."

"I have a Bible. That's not trash."

"Nay, the Bible is a book to be valued as are the books you will soon have the opportunity to read about our Mother Ann."

"Mother Ann? Sister Muriel and Eldress Lilith spoke of her too. Who is she?"

"Deliver me from the ignorance of those from the world," Sister Edna muttered as she led the way to the stairs. She stopped halfway down to turn back toward Carlyn with her frown firmly in place. "Those of the world refuse to see the truth that Mother Ann was the second coming of Christ. That the Christ spirit lived within her was proven over and over by visions given to her and by the miracles she performed."

A faint memory of her father's anger at the Shakers surfaced in Carlyn's mind. He'd abhorred the very mention of Shakers and had railed against a woman named Ann Lee. Carlyn had paid little attention at the time, since it wasn't unusual for her father to call down judgment on those he thought were straying into sinful paths.

Was that what she was doing now? Straying into a sinful path? She had been so sure the Shaker village was the answer the Lord had given her, but perhaps she was wrong. Perhaps even now she was on a treacherous road that would require vigilance to avoid the kind of condemnation her father had said would surely come upon those who chose the wide paths to destruction.

Sister Edna was staring at her, waiting for her to say something, but Carlyn knew nothing to say. She was here. She would stay. It was only Sister Edna's unhappy attitude that made her doubt the answer she'd heard with the ringing of the Shaker bell.

The bell began to ring again, causing Sister Edna to look even more distressed. "Come. Follow without lagging and listen without questions. I do not want to miss breakfast."

She turned and swept down the winding stairway with sure tread. Carlyn grabbed the railing and hurried after her. She kept her eyes on Sister Edna's back and didn't look down at the floor below. Prayers and silence, Sister Edna was telling her. Both of those Carlyn could handle. She was to sit when the rest of the sisters sat. Stand when they stood. Pray when they prayed. Eat when they ate.

"You must Shaker your plate. Eat whatever you dip out. Waste is sinful." Sister Edna instructed Carlyn as they rushed along the walkway to another brick house.

By the time they entered the dining area, Carlyn was glad for the silence.

11

Sister Muriel was waiting for her after the morning meal. "Elder Derron wants to speak to Sister Carlyn," she told Sister Edna. "When he has determined the information he needs, I'll return our new sister to your care. Will you be in the garden today?"

"Yea, the butterbean seeds are ready," Sister Edna said.

A ripple of relief went through Carlyn. She liked garden work, but even if they told her to wash dishes or scrub floors, she would not complain. That she could also do.

"Don't dawdle on your return, Sister Carlyn," Sister Edna said.

"Yes, ma'am," Carlyn said.

"Yea." Impatience was plainly evident in Sister Edna's voice. "Remember you are striving to become a Believer now."

"Yea." The word sat oddly on her tongue, but she could get used to that. Yea. Yes. The words were little different, and if it put Sister Edna in a better humor, that would be good.

Sister Muriel waited until they were out of earshot. "Sister

Edna does fervently desire our converts to embrace being a Believer as quickly as possible. That explains her impatience at times."

Carlyn wasn't sure who Sister Muriel was trying to convince most. Herself or Carlyn. Either way, Carlyn had no answer. She was stuck with the nettlesome Sister Edna, but she had not come to the Shaker village to be happy. She had come for a roof over her head and to be safe from Curt Whitlow. If that meant saying yea and working to please Sister Edna, so be it.

Sister Muriel led the way back to the building where Carlyn had spent the night. As they stepped inside, Sister Muriel told her about the elder she would be meeting. "While we keep the world from our village, we do, of a necessity, have business dealings with those outside our village. The Ministry chooses brethren who are trustworthy and industrious to oversee such matters. Elder Derron has the burden of such duty."

"Why does he want to talk to me?" Carlyn asked.

"It is customary whenever one joins our Society for that person to turn over any property for the good of the community at large."

"But I have little of worth. I lost my house for lack of ability to pay what I owed on it."

"We will see, my sister. Don't fret over things. Keep your spirit true and the other matters will be easily handled."

Carlyn bent her head and did not answer. How easy it was to read that verse in the Bible about taking no thought for the morrow. Sufficient are the evils of the day. But how could one not worry about evils to come on the day at hand or the morrow? Blessings. She needed to look for the blessings.

When they entered Elder Derron's office, he continued

writing in the account book on his desk a moment before he carefully positioned his pen on a blotter and turned to greet them. He did not smile. "Come sit down, Sisters, so that we can determine what must be done."

He motioned toward the chairs hanging on the wall. When Sister Muriel took down one of the chairs, Carlyn did the same. She wanted to ask why the chairs were hung on the railing, but she feared Elder Derron might have the same dislike of questions as Sister Edna. He did appear to favor silence, since he let several moments pass without speaking even after she and Sister Muriel settled into their chairs. Sister Muriel seemed unbothered by the lack of words as she folded her hands in her lap and waited.

The elder's steady gaze made Carlyn want to shift uneasily in her chair, but instead she sat very still. He looked to be in his middle years, with few lines on his solemn face to reveal fondness for either smiling or frowning. He wore a white cotton shirt with suspenders to hold up his dark trousers, his outfit no different from that of the other Shaker brothers she'd seen. While he was not a large man, he had a sturdy look. Yet he seemed to fit at the desk, ready to handle whatever business concerns came his way.

His eyes narrowed a bit as though trying to determine what her looks might reveal about her. She wondered if she might yet be turned away in spite of Sister Muriel's assurance that no sister in need was ever refused a place in their society.

She was relieved when at last he spoke. "Sister Muriel tells me you seek to live among us."

"Yes." Carlyn remembered Sister Edna's yea too late, but the elder didn't seem bothered by her lapse.

"Here in our Society, all things are held in common with

no individual ownership. The needs of all are met and each member contributes to the whole. So new converts are asked to give over their property when they join with us."

"I brought little with me. My mother's Bible and a few baubles. Nothing of worth except to me."

The shadow of a frown chased across his face. "One should not put worth in things, my sister. Only in deeds and actions."

"Yea." This time Carlyn remembered the Shaker yes.

"Why have you come among us?"

"I told Sister Muriel."

"Now you must tell me." His voice was insistent, a man accustomed to being obeyed. "Things spoken directly into our ears are better understood."

"Very well." Carlyn clasped her hands in her lap. "My husband bought a house before the war and we were paying for it by the year. We lacked four payments when he joined the army."

"On which side did his sympathies lie?"

"He fought for the Union."

"Did he give his life for the Northern cause?" The man studied Carlyn's face as though probing for answers beyond those she was speaking.

"The army says Ambrose, my husband, is missing. His fate is unknown." Carlyn forced out the words. Perhaps it was good she had to say them so often in the last few days. She needed to look straight at the truth and accept it.

"According to the news reports, many are reported such. War is a grievous affair and one all men should abhor, as we do here at Harmony Hill." His expression didn't change as he ran his hands up and down his thighs.

Silence fell over the room again. Carlyn didn't know

whether to speak or not. She peeked over at Sister Muriel, serenely waiting for the elder's next words.

Then, as if he'd just remembered her name, he said, "Ambrose? Ambrose Kearney was your husband in the world?"

"Yes." She forgot the Shaker yea again in her eagerness. "You knew him?"

"Yea. A fine young man. I once thought to convince him to join our number here, but he was not ready to give up worldly pleasures." The elder stared at her as though realizing she might be the worldly reason Ambrose had not become a Shaker. "Is not your house the one a few miles down the road from here?"

"It is." Carlyn looked down at her hands. "Or it was."

"I see." The elder tapped his fingers on the edge of his desk. "And whom did you owe on the house?"

"Curt Whitlow."

The elder's fingers stilled in the air above the desk for a moment. "Ah, Mr. Whitlow." If his face had seemed devoid of expression before, now it was even more so as he spread his hand flat on the desk. "Have you given over the house to him already?"

"The sheriff gave me until Friday to surrender the property."

The elder almost smiled. "Then it is not too late to perhaps save what is yours. We will make payment of what is owed and then you can sign over the property to our Society. I assume you also had furniture and other household plunder."

"A few things."

"And livestock?"

"A cow and some chickens."

"Did you make arrangements for their care before you came to our village?"

"I did not. I don't know what I was thinking." Guilt stabbed her. How could she have forgotten to ask Mrs. Smith to come get the cow and chickens? At least the cow had almost gone dry and wouldn't be suffering from a full udder. "I guess I wasn't thinking."

"Don't be distressed, my sister. We will collect them and bring them here." He looked pleased for the first time, perhaps because now he knew she had not joined them empty-handed. "Would you like to accompany us to the house to gather your belongings?"

"Not unless it is necessary." Carlyn had no desire to go through the sorrow of seeing her lost home again.

"Nay, I know the house. I will take care of arrangements and make the necessary payment to Mr. Whitlow. Or to the sheriff." His lips turned up in a slight smile. "You made a good choice coming among us, my sister. Once we have assessed the value of your property, I will draw up a paper for you to sign. Then you will no longer have to concern yourself with anything of the world."

"And if I should ever leave here?" She couldn't believe she was thinking about what she might own, when the day before she had felt stripped of all possessions except her mother's Bible.

"We would hope you are not considering a return to the sinful world when you only just put your feet on the proper path here." His eyes bored into Carlyn, but she didn't look away from him. After a moment, he went on. "But if such a sorrow were to happen, you would be given the value of your property minus whatever must be paid on your behalf. Is that acceptable?"

"Yea." And with that word she stepped fully onto the Shaker path.

12

Tuesday morning, Asher sniffed the scraps Mrs. Snowden put in a pan for him, then lay down with his head on his paws without taking the first bite.

"Poor thing must be missing his mistress," Mrs. Snowden said. "Maybe you can bring him by later to see if he will eat then. Florence is coming today to help with the cleaning. Seeing her might cheer up the dog. You know, since she's young like Carlyn. You'd like that, wouldn't you, boy?" Mrs. Snowden patted the dog even as she gave Mitchell the eye.

Mitchell planned to find plenty to keep him too busy to make it by the boardinghouse. He could get the dog something to eat, but he couldn't take Asher everywhere with him. So after they got to the office, he led the dog into one of the cells. The dog turned sad eyes on him, but that wasn't any different from how he'd looked all morning.

"It'll be all right, boy." Mitchell scratched the dog behind the ears. "You'll forget her after a while. We both will."

Asher turned his back to him and lay down with a huff

of breath. Mitchell blew out a sigh to match the dog's as he pulled the cell door closed. "Then again, maybe not."

Before the day was over, everybody in town knew he had a dog. Mrs. Snowden must have told Billy Hogan. So Mitchell wasn't surprised when Curt Whitlow waylaid him as he headed to the office that afternoon to get Asher. Nor was he surprised to hear a volley of barking coming from the jail. Decidedly unfriendly barking.

"Somebody told me you had a dog." Whitlow cradled his heavily bandaged arm against his chest.

"I do." Mitchell stopped in front of the door. "Sounds like he's going to be a great watchdog."

"Are you out of your mind, Brodie? You're hired to protect the citizens, not terrorize them with a vicious dog."

"What makes you think he's vicious?"

"You have ears. Listen to it." When Mitchell turned the doorknob, Whitlow went pale and stepped backward. "Don't let him out."

"Don't worry. He's locked up." Mitchell stuck his head inside the door and yelled. "Down, Asher!" The dog hushed barking at once. Mitchell turned back to Whitlow. "He seems an intelligent animal."

"Asher?" Whitlow fished a handkerchief out of his pocket and wiped the sweat off his face. "Did you call it Asher?"

The way Whitlow's hand was shaking made Mitchell remember how Carlyn's hands had trembled as she danced around answering his questions the day before. He balled up his fists and considered how much pleasure it would give him to punch Whitlow right in the face, but he couldn't dole out punishment himself. That was for judges and juries. He couldn't even arrest the man and throw him in jail. Not without Carlyn doing more than merely hinting the man had assaulted her.

"Yes, Asher." He uncurled his fists. "Not a common name for a dog. It's from the Bible, if I remember right. One of Jacob's sons." Mitchell pushed the door all the way open. "You want to go in?"

Whitlow didn't move. "So you do have her dog."

"If you mean Mrs. Kearney, yes, I do. She asked me to take the dog since she was losing her house and had no way to keep him." Mitchell leveled his eyes on Whitlow. "Now, is there something I can do for you today, Curt?"

"You can get rid of that dog before it kills somebody."

"I wouldn't worry about him. His bark is worse than his bite." Mitchell kept his eyes on Whitlow's face and let the silence build between them for a moment. "What happened to your arm?"

The man slid his eyes away from Mitchell's face. "Dog bite."

"No wonder you're so nervous. What dog got you?"

"A stray. Out on the road. I shot it. Dead." Whitlow pointed toward the office. "I'll shoot that one too if it bothers me."

"That would make Mrs. Kearney very unhappy." Mitchell watched Whitlow's face. "I think you've made her unhappy enough already."

"All I did was ask her to pay what was legally due me." Whitlow's voice was a little too loud. "Where is she?"

"Out of your house. That's all that matters to you."

"Well, no. She still owes me money." A frown darkened the man's face.

"You have the house. I think you'd best forget trying to

118

get any other payment from her." The man was despicable. "Of any kind."

"What'd she tell you?" Whitlow's face was flushed and sweating again. It was warm, but not that warm.

"That she wanted me to keep her dog."

"That's all?" Whitlow's eyes narrowed.

"No, that wasn't all." Mitchell met his stare.

"You can't believe everything a woman tells you. Especially one who owes money." Whitlow looked down and fiddled with a loose edge on his bandage.

"She doesn't owe me money."

"No, but you've obviously been taken in by her looks." Whitlow glared at him. "Agreeing to take in that dog. Mark my words, Sheriff. You'll come to regret that."

"Could be." Mitchell just wanted the man gone. The very sight of him made him sick.

"Billy Hogan says she's gone to the Shakers."

"Billy sometimes knows."

"Well, if that's true, I better head out to my house to make sure they don't strip it clean. Those Shakers take everything that's not nailed down when somebody joins up with them."

"You have to stay away from Carlyn Kearney's place until the agreed-on week is up." Mitchell put iron in his words.

"They'll rob me blind." Whitlow was almost shouting.

"The things in the house belonged to her, didn't they?"

"I don't know what she had in the house," Whitlow said. "But those Shakers, they're liable to tear the planks off the shed if they decide they want them. I have the right to protect my property."

"The Shakers abide by the law. They won't take what's not hers."

"You can't know that for sure, Sheriff. I've had dealings with those men out there. They're a strange lot and not above doing whatever suits their purposes." Whitlow yanked out his handkerchief again and then stuffed it back in his pocket without using it.

"All right. I'll ride out there tomorrow to check the house for you."

The man stalked away without another word.

Inside, Asher stood with his nose between the bars, a growl rumbling in his throat.

"I know, buddy. He deserves every tooth mark you gave him, but you can't go after him now. Not if you want to stick with me."

Asher stopped growling, stepped back, and waited for him to open the cell.

"You're one odd dog." Mitchell wrapped the rope around the collar he'd fashioned out of an old belt that morning. "It's almost as if you understand everything I say."

The dog lifted one of his ears.

"We'll go out to her place tomorrow. Could be she'll be out there helping the Shakers pack up her stuff."

The next morning, the dog ran alongside Mitchell's horse. Mitchell was getting used to the dog's company, and Asher had completely won over Mrs. Snowden, who enticed the dog to eat by feeding him bacon from her hand.

"You shouldn't lock the poor thing up in jail." She had looked distressed when she found out that's where Mitchell had left him yesterday. "Let him stay here with me in the kitchen."

120

But the dog was eager to be along on this morning trip. His ears were up and his tail ready to wag.

Mitchell felt some of the same anticipation. He was fighting it, but Whitlow was right. Mitchell had let a pretty face turn his head. Not that he planned to do anything about it. He didn't. The woman was not available. She was in love with her husband. It didn't matter if the man was dead. He was alive in Carlyn Kearney's heart. On top of that, she was a Shaker now. That closed every door to romance even if she did find out her husband being missing in the war meant he had moved on up to his heavenly home.

Maybe it wasn't all bad. He hadn't thought of Hilda once in three days. It was good to be ready to move on with his life. To imagine a house with a picket fence around the yard where kids could play with a good dog. He would have to be careful not to let Mrs. Snowden know that, because Florence wasn't part of those dreams. But he could imagine Carlyn Kearney there, whether it was reasonable or not.

The place looked deserted when he rode up to the house. No chickens scratched in the yard. No cow grazed in the pasture. No pretty widow stood in the door with a gun in her hands. Even so, he got off his horse and went up the steps. Asher trailed along behind him, his ears flat against his head now. The dog didn't have to go in the empty house to know she wasn't there. His nose had already told him.

When Mitchell knocked on the door, it creaked open like a ghost was inviting him in. The house was stripped of any sign of the woman living there. No chairs or tables. No dishes and pans. Everything was gone. They must have moved her out the day before. Still, somehow her presence lingered. A faint odor of lavender water. Or perhaps that was simply his imagination.

The dog pushed past him to sniff through the empty rooms. Mitchell followed him into the kitchen. A fine dusting of ashes showed where the cookstove had been. Asher padded away to a different room, but Mitchell stayed there. He could almost hear the echo of the happy times Carlyn and her husband might have had before the war tore them apart.

Asher came back in the kitchen to pull Mitchell away from his imaginings with a whine. When Mitchell looked down at the dog, he dropped something at his feet.

"What'd you find, boy?" Mitchell reached down to pick up a handkerchief that must have been missed by the Shakers. He held it to his nose. Definitely lavender water.

The dog raised his nose toward the ceiling and let out a mournful howl.

"Poor boy." Mitchell stuffed the hankie in his coat pocket and touched Asher's head.

He went out the back door and around the house to his horse. He'd seen all he needed to see, including Whitlow's shed with all the planks intact. He started to mount up when he noticed the dog had taken up position by the front door like a sentry on watch.

Mitchell whistled. The dog didn't move.

"Come on, Asher. Let's go." Mitchell clapped his hands.

The dog turned his head away, as though listening for a different call.

"You can't stay here, you crazy dog."

The dog looked back at him but didn't budge.

Mitchell sighed. At least he'd been smart enough to bring the dog's rope with him, because he couldn't leave him here. Asher cowered at the sight of the rope, but once Mitchell had it tied to his collar, he reluctantly came off the porch.

"She's gone from here, Asher." Mitchell stroked the dog's back. "She won't be back. But Whitlow will be out here checking on his planks, and he'd shoot you in a minute. Then what would I tell her if she ever does come back for you?"

Sometimes people left the Shakers. Shaker leaders came to town from time to time looking for members who'd slipped away in the night. Usually a couple tempted away from the celibate life. Mitchell touched the handkerchief in his pocket. If only he could figure out a way to tempt Carlyn away from the Shakers.

When Mitchell rode back into town, two Shaker men were waiting in front of the sheriff's office. Mitchell slid off his horse and attached the rope to Asher's collar again. He'd taken the rope off after he'd walked his horse and the dog a little ways up the road. He expected the dog to run back toward the house, but he didn't. With his ears down and his tail low, the picture of dejection, he nevertheless stayed with Mitchell.

The Shakers climbed down from their wagon. Only one of them, the younger man, gave Asher a glance. The older Shaker completely ignored the dog. He was all business as he stepped toward Mitchell.

"Sheriff Brodie, we meet again. We spoke concerning one of our converts some weeks ago." As though he didn't expect Mitchell to remember, he spoke his name. "Elder Derron and this is Brother Mark."

"Of course, Elder Derron." Mitchell reached his hand out and the elder shook it without enthusiasm. The other Shaker stayed a few steps behind the elder. "What can I do for you? Have you had more trouble with Mr. Jefferson?"

Jefferson had been distraught and sure his daughter was

being coerced to join the Shakers, but Mitchell had seen no evidence of that. She was of age and had seemed content there in the village.

"Nay, Sister Willene's worldly father has at last accepted that Sister Willene has made her decision to live a Believer's life."

Elder Derron lifted the corners of his mouth in a slight smile. Something about the man had bothered Mitchell when he met him that first time at the Shaker village, and the same feeling was poking him now. The man's face was too solemn, almost stony, but the inability to smile was hardly a crime.

"That's good to hear." Mitchell didn't think it was all that good. The woman had been young and with much of life before her, but if she wanted that life to be in a Shaker village, who was he to say that was wrong? For her anyway. He was readier to judge the right and wrong of Carlyn Kearney spending her life at their village.

As if the man read his thought, he said, "We come on behalf of a different sister. Sister Carlyn Kearney who joined with us this week. I understand you gave her until Friday to pay the amount she is indebted to Curt Whitlow." The elder stared straight at Mitchell. "Is that what you told her?"

"I said she had until Friday to vacate the property."

"It seems reasonable that, whether it was spoken or not, it could be assumed that if payment is made before that time, the property will not have to be surrendered. We are prepared to pay off the loan on the house with the going rate of interest added to the overdue amount." There was no give in his voice or posture.

"That is reasonable." Mitchell didn't smile, but he felt like it. While he hated the thought of Carlyn becoming a Shaker, he wasn't sorry Curt Whitlow was going to be bested in this transaction.

The elder looked at the dog for the first time. "I was told our young sister came to the village with a dog. Is that the one?"

"Yes, she asked me to keep him for her. He's a fine dog. He would have been a good addition to your village."

"Nay, we have no use for pets there. Only animals that earn their feed."

Mitchell laid his hand on Asher's head. "This fellow has done that and more, but he's not particularly fond of Mr. Whitlow."

"Yea. Some say dogs are good at reading a man's character." The Shaker's face didn't change, as if he had done no more than comment on the sun shining down on their shoulders.

"So I've heard."

"Now if you have a few moments to accompany us, we can complete our transaction and return to our village." It was more an order than a request. "We feel it best serves our interests to have a witness of the payment."

The Shaker man had obviously had dealings with Whitlow before.

13

The Shaker village wasn't a bad place. Carlyn told herself that each morning when she knelt by her bed to offer her morning prayers. Sister Edna told her she must pray but did not tell her what to pray. Even if she had, she couldn't have known if Carlyn followed her directions since the prayers were offered up silently.

Carlyn had no idea what Sister Edna or the other sisters around her were praying or even if they were. They assumed a posture of prayer just as Carlyn did, and so it seemed only reasonable they were thanking the Lord for the blessing of a new day. Carlyn needed to be doing the same instead of letting her thoughts swirl around like autumn leaves caught in a whirlwind.

But if she came up short of proper prayer thoughts in the morning, she had more opportunities at meals and during designated times for rest and contemplation as the day went by. All in silence. At mealtimes, they marched into the eating rooms and stood at their seats. When all were at their places, everyone knelt to silently offer thanks for the provision of food. Then they stood again with their right hands on the chair backs. At the chosen moment, like a giant centipede whose legs all worked in unison they pulled out their chairs and sat down at the tables.

No one talked. Eating was serious business and silence necessary for good digestion, according to Sister Edna. Serving bowls were put in front of each group of four diners to eliminate the necessity of asking for something to be passed. The silence was broken by the clang of forks on plates or spoons scraping the bowls when a new portion was dipped. A cough, a slurp of water from a glass, even her own chewing sounded loud in the odd silence.

But it wasn't only during meals that silence ruled. Idle chatter was discouraged except at something called Union Meetings. There a few sisters and brothers sat in chairs a proper distance apart in one of the sleeping rooms and talked about whatever they wanted, even things happening in the world.

Sister Edna told Carlyn she could not take part in such meetings until she'd been at the village longer. That was just as well. Carlyn was having enough trouble figuring out proper behavior around the sisters. So it seemed wisest to lower her head and hide beneath her bonnet whenever any brethren were near. Sister Edna warned her often enough not to be a temptation to brothers new to the village.

"A pretty face can cause a man to fall off the proper path and slide into sin. It would be well to remember true beauty rises from the soul intent on doing good with a mind dwelling on heavenly thoughts. That is the beauty Mother Ann sees and rewards with bushels of love."

"Yea." Carlyn had learned it was best to agree with whatever Sister Edna said and not give voice to the questions circling in her head. The question she wanted most to ask, but dared not, was how long she had to suffer Sister Edna by her side. The sister had a way of making Carlyn long for the silent moments of prayer just so her ears would be free of the woman's voice.

Silence didn't bother Carlyn. At her house, she had lived with silence except for the sounds of nature and the words she spoke to Asher. She missed how he ever had his ears up ready to hear whatever she had to say. She liked to imagine Sheriff Brodie talking to him now. The sheriff wasn't married, so perhaps he appreciated a listening ear, albeit a furry one.

Of course, not everyone talked to dogs as though they could understand. Her father would condemn the practice as worse than foolish. Her mother, on the other hand, would simply shake her head and remind Carlyn that the best listener was the Lord, a mighty help in times of trouble. Not that Carlyn was in trouble now. She was safe among the Shakers.

She'd get used to sleeping in a room with seven other women. She wouldn't always feel hemmed in on every side and that she had to grab for fresh air to breathe. She'd get used to how the Shakers talked and her tongue would stop stumbling over saying yea and nay. She could hide her hair under the Shaker cap and properly pin the neckerchief to cover her figure.

In time, the odd Shaker songs of worship wouldn't sound so jarring to her ears and she might even enjoy the marching dances, strange though it seemed to dance in church. It was a simple matter to step up with the proper foot when climbing stairs and remember to kneel on her right knee and not her left. She could learn their ways without changing her beliefs.

Until she demonstrated the proper behavior, Sister Edna would watch and guide her. Carlyn tried to remember Sister Muriel's assurances that Sister Edna was a good teacher in spite of her prickly ways, but Carlyn seemed unable to please the woman. She couldn't even confess her sins properly.

"Do you think you're perfect, Sister Carlyn?" Sister Edna asked when Carlyn struggled to think of sins to confess during her second week at the Shaker village.

"Nay, I am far from perfect." Carlyn tried to look sorrowful. That wasn't difficult.

"Then you must have need to confess." Sister Edna glared at Carlyn across the table in the small room where she heard the confessions of the novitiates she was guiding into the Shaker way.

In the chair beside Carlyn, Sister Berdine, who had come to live with the Shakers two weeks before Carlyn, stared down at her hands. They had been paired to work under Sister Edna's watchful eye and thus shared confession time. Sister Berdine always quickly numbered her lapses to satisfy Sister Edna's need to hear wrongs. This day she confessed sweeping dirt under the table instead of in the dust pan. She hid a biscuit in her apron pocket because she had taken too much on her plate and was unable to eat it all as she should to Shaker her plate. She had grumbled about the duty of picking beans. She entertained an uncharitable thought.

Carlyn couldn't imagine the Lord being upset over such small wrongs, but she tried to follow Sister Berdine's example just to get the confession time over. "I lost my patience with one of my sisters," she said when Sister Edna continued to stare at her.

"Did you go to that sister and ask forgiveness?"

Carlyn moistened her lips. She couldn't very well admit the sister she had lost patience with was Sister Edna. Sister Berdine came to her rescue.

"Yea, Sister Edna. Sister Carlyn asked my forgiveness and I gave it without hesitation. I know I can be slow at times when I am working in the garden and Sister Carlyn is very quick with her hands." Sister Berdine looked over at Carlyn with a slight smile, but her face was solemn when she turned back to Sister Edna.

"Very well, Sisters. It is good to speak honestly about our faults so that we can be forgiven."

"Yea." Carlyn and Sister Berdine answered in unison.

"It is also good to be in agreement." Sister Edna's eyes narrowed on them. "Sister Berdine, you may return to your duties in the garden, but I have more to say to Sister Carlyn."

Carlyn managed to hold in her sigh as Sister Berdine stood to leave. With her back to Sister Edna, Sister Berdine let her hand brush Carlyn's arm as if by accident. But there was nothing accidental about the way she rolled her eyes at Carlyn. Sister Berdine was into her thirties, but seemed younger. She'd never been married and told Carlyn she came to the Shakers because she was tired of shifting between her siblings' houses as the poor maiden aunt.

"Better to be stuck here with a bunch of maiden sisters. At least maiden after they came to the Shakers," she said.

She loved to talk and grabbed every chance to do so. Working to harvest the butterbean seeds gave them many opportunities, as Sister Edna was too advanced in years to bend and pick the seeds. Instead, she sat at the end of the garden and hulled the beans while keeping a watchful eye on her charges. With their heads down and their hands busy, Sister Edna couldn't tell they were talking. Other sisters working in the garden did the same. Carlyn heard softly voiced snippets of conversations whenever she stood for a moment to stretch her back.

Now, Carlyn wished she could return to the gardens and work in the sunshine instead of being stuck in the small room with the impossible-to-satisfy Sister Edna. Indian summer weather was lingering outdoors. Carlyn looked past Sister Edna toward the open window behind her. Oh, to be walking with Asher in that sunshine to search out walnuts or hickory nuts.

She missed Asher. She missed having the freedom to spend each new day as she pleased. Here she was told what to do. And now Sister Edna would once more tell her what to believe. Carlyn was surely in for another sermon. While she found it easy to listen to the Shaker beliefs, she was not able to voice acceptance of them as Sister Edna wanted.

Carlyn would never accept the Shaker way. She did not believe marriage was wrong, and if she had been blessed with a child, she would have never wanted her child to live in one house while she lived among sisters in another house. Just thinking about having a child awakened a yearning inside her for what now seemed an impossible dream. Even if she did accept that Ambrose wasn't coming home, she was still bound to him with no proof of his passing.

She felt a flash of guilt, yet could not block out the thought that it would be better to know she was a widow. That way she could move on with her life. Perhaps marry again should a man show interest in her.

Unbidden, Sheriff Brodie's face popped into her thoughts, and a flush warmed her cheeks. He'd taken in her dog, but that didn't mean he would consider taking her in as well. It was best to wipe such thoughts out of her mind. Until she knew for sure what had happened to Ambrose, she was his wife. And even if proof did come her way as to Ambrose's fate, it would do her little good now. Not captured in this Shaker net of sisterhood.

Sister Edna kept her gaze steadily on Carlyn after Sister Berdine left the room, waiting for Carlyn to break the silence between them. Carlyn had no intention of doing that. If she had learned nothing else from the Shakers, she had learned the value of holding her tongue.

Finally Sister Edna spoke. "I worry about you, Sister Carlyn."

Carlyn lowered her eyes to her hands folded in her lap. She didn't know what Sister Edna wanted her to say, so once again she chose silence.

"Did you not hear me, Sister Carlyn? I said you worry me."

"I did hear you, Sister Edna, but it is not my aim to make you worry. I am trying hard to follow the rules here and ably do my duties." Carlyn held up her hands. "To work with my hands."

"But have you given your heart to God? Hands to work, heart to God."

"Yea." That was easy to answer. It mattered not how empty her prayers felt at times. She had no doubt she was a child of God. In time, she hoped to recapture the joy of that truth. But now she was in a valley with only shadows of sorrow.

"If that is true, then you need to examine your thoughts and motives. Clean away every wayward thought that has found harbor in your heart. For right thoughts, clean thoughts cannot exist alongside sinful thoughts. Praying and sinning will not work together. If you keep on sinning, you will quit praying. Mother Ann taught us so."

Carlyn folded the edge of her apron over and over. What sin did Sister Edna want her to confess? The sister couldn't be aware of Carlyn's wayward thoughts about the sheriff just now. But while Sister Edna might condemn her sinful thinking, Carlyn believed the Lord understood the need to be loved.

Carlyn unfolded the creases in her apron and smoothed them out. The rough skin on her fingers, dried out by the work in the garden, caught on the fabric.

"Have you nothing to say for yourself?" Sister Edna asked.

"Tell me what sin I am committing and I will strive to leave it behind."

"A person needs to recognize one's own faults. The sin of pride blinds a person." Sister Edna leaned across the small table between them.

Carlyn fought the urge to scoot her chair back. "I have no reason to be proud."

"Yea, you speak the truth. None of us do. Except in the gifts showered down on us by our Mother Ann."

"I will try harder to walk a righteous path," Carlyn said.

"Such paths are narrow with many obstacles."

"Surely not as many obstacles here in your Shaker village." Carlyn kept her eyes on her hands flat against her apron. "Here, where you endeavor to have no sin."

"We do block the sinful ways of the world from our borders. But sin is like a pesky housefly. It finds a way to sneak in. Worldly sins that tempt our brethren." Sister Edna's eyes narrowed on Carlyn. "You are a temptation to our brethren with your pretty face."

So that was it again. Sister Edna was forever harping on how Carlyn was too pretty. Carlyn didn't care how she looked. She would as soon be plain like Sister Berdine, whose upper teeth protruded a bit and robbed her of the chance for beauty. But then she had to admit that wasn't completely true. She had liked Ambrose thinking she was pretty, nor had she minded that the sheriff had seemed moved by her looks to give Asher a home.

But now in the Shaker cap and the shapeless dress, her appearance didn't seem to matter. Beauty of spirit was what was important here and what had ever been important. A fair face was a gift of nature, but the more important gift was a pure and innocent heart.

"It is not my desire to be a temptation to any, but I cannot hide my face." Carlyn looked straight at Sister Edna. "If there are those who look at me in the wrong way, then perhaps it is their sin and not mine." Just as Curt Whitlow's attack had not been her sin. She had not acted wantonly.

Sister Edna's mouth screwed up as though she'd bitten into a green persimmon. "Do you deny you entertain worldly thoughts when you feel the eyes of one of the brothers on you?"

"I have not noticed anything like that." Carlyn had barely looked at any of the men in the village outside of Brother Thomas and Elder Derron. Neither of them had given any indication of being affected by her looks.

"I notice. It is my duty to notice and to report wrong actions to the elders and eldresses."

"Have you noted wrong actions that I have done?"

Sister Edna looked down at the paper in front of her as though checking for wrongs that might be written there, but Carlyn could see that it was blank. That's how she felt. Blank. As though all that went before had been wiped away and now she was just a shell with nothing inside as she went through her days. That was why she couldn't find words in her mind to pray. She was too empty.

Pray anyway. Her mother's voice whispered through her mind. At least she hadn't lost that.

"Nay," Sister Edna said finally. "But I fear you are clinging to worldly thoughts instead of embracing the way of a Believer."

"I am listening. This way is much different than what I knew before. It takes time to change the habits of a lifetime." That was true, but not completely true. She had no intention of changing anything except how she said yes and no. But she would do her best to mollify Sister Edna. "Did you understand the Shaker way when you first joined?"

"That was long ago. Too long to remember."

"So did you grow up here among the Shakers?" Carlyn studied Sister Edna's face. Her wrinkles indicated she had to be well along in years, but she moved with ease other than claiming the inability to lean over to pick beans. Sister Berdine and Carlyn had tried to guess her age, but neither had been brave enough to ask.

"Nay. I was older than you when I came into the Society many years ago."

"So you had another life before this one."

"I died to that life when I put my feet on a better road."

"Were you married?" Carlyn couldn't quite keep the surprise from her voice.

"I told you I died to that life." Sister Edna frowned. "I put the sin of matrimony behind me long ago when I began walking the Shaker way. You have need to do the same."

"Yea." Carlyn let her eyes glide over Sister Edna's face. It was hard to imagine her married. Had her husband come into the village with her? Was it possible that she had children she'd surrendered to the Shaker way? The questions pushed against Carlyn's lips but she did not let them out. "I am trying to learn your way."

"I have to wonder if you merely speak those words you think will tickle my ears, Sister Carlyn. At times, I sense a lack of sincerity."

"Nay, I know it is a sin to be insincere in my words."

"Or prayers." Sister Edna's eyes bored into Carlyn as though she could read her thoughts.

"Yea." Carlyn met Sister Edna's stare. "The Lord recognizes the intent of our hearts over the sound of words. If you have noted wrongs that I am doing, please let me know what they are so I can correct my behavior."

That shouldn't be hard. Hadn't she done that all the time she was living with her father? Tried to please his idea of righteousness. It was only after she married Ambrose that she'd understood about grace. And now she had come back into a life where rules seemed to matter more than love.

Sister Edna lifted one of her fingers. "You are resistant to my instructions."

"I will try to listen with more openness." Carlyn felt a twinge of guilt knowing that she was lacking the sincerity Sister Edna had mentioned, but she didn't look away from the other woman's face. She did very sincerely want to be through with their meeting.

"You sway your hips when you walk." Sister Edna held up another finger.

For a moment, Carlyn was at a loss for words, sincere or otherwise. "I walk as I have always walked. Are there rules about walking as there are about kneeling and climbing stairs?"

Instead of answering, Sister Edna held up another finger. "You ask questions when you should be listening."

Carlyn spoke before she thought. "The Bible tells us to ask. That if we lack wisdom, we should ask and the Lord will liberally give answers." Her mother had always assured her of that, but Carlyn should have remembered how her father had resisted questions and kept quiet. It did little good to continually upset Sister Edna. When would she ever learn to say yea and bend her head in a posture of submission to whatever the woman said?

Sister Edna made an odd squawking noise. She planted her hands on the table and rose to her feet, glaring at Carlyn. "Young sister, you need to remember your place. It is not your duty to attempt to inform me of things I know much better than you. It is my duty to lead you to proper behavior. It is your duty to listen without question and without the sin of arrogance. Do you understand?"

This time Carlyn did consider her words. "Yea, Sister Edna. I beg your forgiveness." She looked down before the sister could see the insincerity that would surely be too evident in her face.

"Oh dear Mother Ann in heaven, what did I do to deserve such tedious duty?" Sister Edna breathed out a long exasperated sigh.

Carlyn dared not say a word for fear she'd not escape the room before nightfall.

Sister Edna sank back down in her chair. "Go on to your duties, Sister." She gave Carlyn a dismissal wave. "But it would be well for you to ponder why you have come among us and think upon the truths we are showering down upon you so generously."

"Yea." Carlyn spoke the word softly as she stood and backed toward the door.

She stepped into the hallway and hurried outside, thankful Sister Edna didn't follow her. She pulled in a deep breath of air. It was good to feel the sun on her face and to be blessedly alone and away from Sister Edna's probing eyes. But was she really? She peeked over her shoulder back at the house. She couldn't see Sister Edna watching from the window of the room she'd just left, but that didn't mean she wasn't. Or that even if she wasn't, someone else might not be watching.

Someone was always watching. On the first day in the village, Sister Edna had let Carlyn know people watched from rooftops or upper rooms. That was a duty to be carried out the same as the duty of sweeping away the dirt in the sleeping rooms. The rules must be kept.

Carlyn shook her shoulders slightly as though ridding the very thought of eyes watching her. She wasn't really free. Sister Edna would be coming to the garden. Her eyes would be following Carlyn's every movement, waiting to pounce on some wrong move.

Think on the truth, Sister Edna had advised. Carlyn could do that. If she only knew what the truth was. Ask and it would be given. It could be she should ask the Lord for a new answer for her life or to give her a new heart that could accept the Shaker life.

Carlyn thought she had answers, but maybe the answers

she'd been given were not the final answers. Each day was a new day with the Lord. A new day for answers. And whether her prayers felt empty or not, she did sincerely believe she was a child of God as she had told Sister Edna.

Pray anyway. At all times with belief that the Lord would send answers. But was it a sin to not want to accept the answer already given?

14

With so many thoughts whirling through her mind, Carlyn didn't pay the necessary attention to where she was going. When she did pause in her headlong rush away from Sister Edna to look around, she had no idea where she was. The stone pathway went between a corncrib and a chicken house with the garden nowhere in sight. She was about to retrace her steps when she spotted the barn roof on down the path. She'd seen that barn from the garden, so perhaps she could circle around the chicken house to reach the garden.

If Sister Edna made it to the garden before her, she would never believe Carlyn had not willfully dallied in returning to her duty there. Carlyn tried to remember if the Shakers had rules against running. Probably so, but since no one was in sight and surely no spying eyes watched from the crib or chicken house, she was ready to chance a dash for the garden when she heard men's voices.

She stepped into the shadow of the chicken house in hopes they would pass her by, unnoticed. It was not hard to imagine

Sister Edna's displeasure if Carlyn was seen on a pathway alone with Shaker men.

The men weren't speaking in the peaceful tones most of the Shakers used, but instead sounded agitated. Carlyn couldn't quite make out their words, but when one of the voices grew louder, she froze. She had to be hearing wrong. It couldn't be him.

She dared a peek around the corner of the chicken house. Two men faced each other on the path, one a Shaker brother, the other Curt Whitlow. A tremble swept through her. Had he come to demand more from her?

That couldn't be it. Elder Derron had made full payment to him for her house. When she signed the document giving the house over to the Shakers, she was certain she was done with Curt Whitlow. Yet, here he was. Right in front of her eyes. Angry the same as when he came to her house with the sheriff in tow. One arm was in a sling close to his chest, but he was jabbing the Shaker brother in the chest with his other hand.

The Shaker was short and so slight of build that Curt, with his broad girth, could make two of him. The man tried to step around Curt, but he stumbled on the edge of the walk and went down hard. His hat flew off to reveal his bald head. Curt stared down at him without moving to help the man up. Nor did the man reach a hand up toward Curt. Instead he scrambled to his feet as though afraid Curt might kick him while he was down.

The man snatched his hat off the ground and looked around. Carlyn jerked back out of sight and stood stock still, barely breathing. She had to hide, but where? To get to the door of the chicken house she would have to step around in plain sight. She couldn't do that and take the chance Curt might recognize her. She strained to hear if they were moving her way.

The Shaker brother was talking, his voice tense but so low she only heard scraps of his sentences. "You can't . . . He knows . . ." Then his voice rose and the words were clear. "You don't know what you're doing."

"I know exactly what I'm doing." Curt sounded angry. "We had a deal. And nobody goes back on a deal with Curt Whitlow without paying the price. Best not forget that, Brother."

"I can't—"

"Don't bother claiming a conscience now." Curt cut off the other man's words. "It's too late to hide under that Shaker hat and pretend to be all innocent. You tell him what I said."

"He won't like it."

"Then he shouldn't have made the deal."

"A deal with the devil, he says."

Curt laughed at that and Carlyn felt a new round of trembles, remembering the last time she'd heard that laugh.

"The devil, eh? Then you make sure he knows the devil expects his due on time or else." Curt sounded closer. Dare she chance staying where she was and hope he didn't look back?

"Wait, Mr. Whitlow—"

"The devil waits for no man." Curt laughed again.

He was definitely closer. She couldn't just stand there. Not and be caught by Curt here with no one around except the Shaker brother who sounded more afraid of Curt than she was.

She put her head down and walked as fast as she could toward the end of the chicken house. She didn't notice the two hens settled in the dust until they squawked and flapped away. Her heart bounded up in her throat. They had to hear that. She kept moving without looking back. Even after she knew for sure they saw her.

"Sister," the Shaker brother called.

She pretended not to hear. The hens were still squawking. That could keep her from hearing the Shaker brother's call. It didn't, but it could have.

"Who was that?" Curt asked.

"Just one of the sisters," the Shaker man answered. "Nobody to be concerned about."

"You think she heard . . ."

Carlyn was on the other side of the building and the voices faded away. She kept her head down, practically running now. She dared a peek over her shoulder. They weren't following her. Relief flooded through her. She didn't know why her heart was pounding so. They didn't know who she was. Curt wouldn't recognize her in the Shaker dress without seeing her face. She jerked her cap down tighter on her head as she rushed back up on the walkway directly into the path of Sister Edna.

"Watch where you are going, Sister!" Sister Edna threw out her arms to regain her balance as she tottered on the edge of the walk.

Carlyn was tempted to jerk back from her and keep going. Let the sister fall, the way Curt had let the Shaker man fall. But instead she grabbed Sister Edna and steadied her.

"I'm so sorry, Sister Edna. I should have been watching."

"Sister Carlyn?" Sister Edna voice was incredulous as she pulled loose from Carlyn and smoothed down her neckerchief. "Whatever are you doing here? I sent you back to the garden a half hour or more ago. Can I not trust you to do anything I say without my eyes on you continually?"

"Nay. I mean yea. I lost my way." Carlyn could not resist the urge to look over her shoulder again. The Shaker brother stood near the road watching them, but Curt was nowhere in sight.

Sister Edna's eyes narrowed on Carlyn. "How could you lose your way between the Gathering Family House and the garden?"

"I don't know, but I did. I ended up over there by the chicken house and then I heard some men talking. I thought of what you said about my swaying walk, so I hid to keep from being a temptation." Carlyn rushed out her words. "I'll hurry on to the garden now."

She started past the woman, but Sister Edna put a hand out to stop her. "What men?" She peered first at Carlyn and then beyond her toward the road. "Brother Henry?"

"Yea, if that is the man behind us."

"But you say men." Sister Edna's eyes probed Carlyn's face. "Why do you look so distressed? None of our brothers would ever do harm to one of their sisters."

"I was concerned because I went the wrong way and would be slow getting back to the garden."

Sister Edna shook Carlyn's arm. "Can you not tell the truth? Even once? Who was the other man? Had you arranged to sin by meeting someone from the world?"

"No. Never." Carlyn totally forgot to answer with the Shaker's nay.

Sister Edna frowned and gripped Carlyn's arm tighter. "Why, Sister, you are shaking. What has frightened you so? Surely not Brother Henry." She looked back out toward the road. "He is gone at any rate."

"Nay." This time Carlyn remembered. She pulled in a breath to calm herself. What could she tell Sister Edna that the woman would believe? Maybe it was best to be truthful. "Brother Henry did nothing to bother me. But I knew the other man from before I came here. He was the one I owed money for my house and I feared he had come here looking for me."

Wrinkles formed between Sister Edna's eyes as she considered what Carlyn said. "If the man from the world had come seeking you, he would not have started his search at the chicken house."

"Yea, I was not thinking clearly." Carlyn pulled in a long breath.

"Obviously. What is the man's name?"

"Why do you care? He is of the world."

"Yea, but he was here in our village and a concern to a sister in my charge. I, of necessity, need to report such to the Ministry."

"Curt Whitlow." Carlyn didn't care what Sister Edna reported to the Ministry about Curt. She never wanted to lay eyes on him again.

"I see. And what was he talking about with Brother Henry?"

"I could not hear them well." Carlyn couldn't see any point in telling Sister Edna the bits of conversation she'd heard. It would just prolong her questioning. The garden and Sister Berdine's cheerful conversation seemed akin to paradise at the moment.

"Come, Sister, are you saying you heard nothing they said?" Sister Edna raised her eyebrows in disbelief.

"Just bits and pieces. Nothing that made much sense."

"Why do I feel you are hiding something?" Sister Edna's fingers tightened on Carlyn's arm.

"I heard them mention the devil." Carlyn hoped that would be enough to feed Sister Edna's need to know.

"The devil?" Sister Edna's frown got darker.

"Yea. Perhaps Brother Henry was trying to convince Mr. Whitlow to consider the Shaker way." Carlyn knew that wasn't true, but she simply wanted Sister Edna to turn her loose. And it wasn't as though she were telling a lie. Brother Henry had definitely been trying to convince Curt of something. Perhaps he owed Curt money. Carlyn wasn't sure how that could be, since all here owned everything in common, but there could be hidden currents. Hidden sins.

"True." Sister Edna sounded thoughtful. At last, she let go of Carlyn's arm and looked toward where Brother Henry had been standing. "We are to generously share the blessing of belief." She looked back at Carlyn. "Did Mr. Whitlow seem to embrace Brother Henry's words?"

"Nay. They appeared to be at odds."

"Are you sure?"

"Yea. They were disagreeing over some sort of deal."

"A deal? How strange." Sister Edna rubbed her chin thoughtfully. "Perhaps it would be best if I spoke with Brother Henry to be certain I make the proper report to the Ministry." She turned back to Carlyn, her eyes mere slits of accusation. "I trust I will not find that you have peppered your story with falsehoods."

"Nay, Sister Edna. I was taught to tell the truth by my mother."

"That is good, but you need to think now on the teachings of Mother Ann."

"Yea." Carlyn was ready to agree with anything just to be finished with her questions.

"If only your spirit were as eager with yeas as your mouth." Sister Edna let out an exasperated sigh. "Go on with you. Sister Berdine will be full of curiosity about what has taken you so long to get back to the garden. And the bean seeds need gathering before the rains come."

"The sun is shining and there are no clouds." Carlyn looked up. The deep blue vastness of the sky gave her a feeling of freedom, even if she was hemmed in on all sides here in the Shaker village. But she was also protected as long as she stayed on the proper paths.

"The rains always come." Sister Edna studied the western horizon for a moment. "Clouds can come quickly when storms approach."

15

By the time Carlyn reached the garden, she had stopped shaking. She didn't think she lacked courage. After all, she had faced down Curt Whitlow time and time again, but it had been a shock to come upon him in the village. Not on the main road as one might expect, but hidden back in among the buildings and talking of being the devil. Brother Henry had appeared to believe it could be true.

As much as Carlyn disliked Curt, she had never thought him the devil. Wicked. Sinful. But he also had weaknesses. His fear of Asher. She smiled a little, thinking of his bandaged arm and then felt ashamed. *Pray for those who persecute you.* The Scripture poked her conscience. She forced herself to think a prayer for his arm to heal, but she felt as insincere as Sister Edna accused her of being.

"I am relieved to see you, Sister Carlyn." Sister Berdine looked up when Carlyn joined her in the garden. "I was beginning to think Sister Edna might have thought of a penance for you worse than picking these beans."

"I like working in the garden." Carlyn bent down and began filling her basket.

"It's all right for a few hours, but not all the livelong day, every day. My back is ready to break." Sister Berdine blew out a breath as she knelt down. She didn't even pretend to pick the beans. "Well, are you going to tell me why Sister Edna kept you so long?"

"She didn't. After she pointed out my usual lackings, she told me to come back here. But somehow I went the wrong way." Carlyn didn't want to talk about Curt Whitlow or think about the odd conversation she'd heard. It was enough that she'd told Sister Edna. She had no desire for his name to cross her lips again. "The Shaker pathways are like a labyrinth."

"And it is easier to wander around in the fall sunshine than to be forever bending over a bean plant." Sister Berdine pulled off a couple of bean pods.

"Nay, I did not tarry of a purpose," Carlyn insisted.

"Well, if you didn't, you should have." Sister Berdine dropped the beans in her basket, then stood to stretch her back. "Life is too short not to steal a few moments of joy now and again."

"Do you know joy, Sister Berdine? Here in Harmony Hill?" Carlyn didn't stop picking the bean pods, but she did slow her hands to keep from rattling the drying leaves so she could hear Sister Berdine's answer.

"Yea. More than I expected." Sister Berdine leaned down with her head close to Carlyn's. "Much more than I expected. In spite of a certain sister who is continually harping on this or that." Sister Berdine grinned over at Carlyn. "She seems even more ready to harp about your shortcomings than mine, though my faults are just as glaring. Unless I miss my guess, she envies your pretty face."

"You are not serious." Carlyn shook her head. "That certain sister worries only about beauty of the spirit."

"So she says, but I think there is more to that certain sister than she wants to reveal."

"Isn't that true for us all?"

"Perhaps for you, Sister Carlyn, but me, I am an open book." Sister Berdine sighed. "A very boring book without a colorful cover."

"Nay, nothing boring about you." Carlyn laughed softly. "But did you know that sister you're talking about was married when she came to the Shakers?"

Sister Berdine stopped picked beans and stared at Carlyn. "You jest."

"That is what she seemed to tell me. She said she was older than I am now when she came into the village and left her other life behind."

"Well, if she could find a man to marry with her sour face, perhaps I should not have given up so soon." Sister Berdine riffled through the leaves looking for beans. "Then again, it could be I have come to the perfect place. There are many brothers here. Unattached and available." She gave Carlyn a wicked smile.

"Brothers don't look at their sisters with such thoughts."

"Keep in mind, they are not really our brothers. Do you not note the brethren with their broad shoulders and strong arms?"

"I try to not look at the brothers at all."

"You must be an unusual woman, my sister, but then you have already tasted the joys of matrimony," Sister Berdine said.

"Or the sins of such, Sister Edna would say."

"Did you think it sinful to be married?"

"Not at all. Ambrose and I were very happy before the war."

"Do you think he will come back to you?" Sister Berdine peered over at Carlyn.

"I don't know. Probably not." Carlyn didn't meet her eyes. Instead, she studied the bean pod in her hand as though searching for an answer there.

"How long has he been missing?" Sister Berdine sounded sympathetic.

"Two years."

"That is a long time." Sister Berdine smoothed out the bean pods in her basket.

"Yea. A very long time."

"And in that time, have you never been tempted to look at another man with longing?"

"No, of course not." Carlyn jerked her head up to stare at Sister Berdine. "That would not be proper."

"Much happens that is not proper, dear sister."

"But I loved Ambrose." A shaft of sadness shot through her when she realized she'd spoken as if that love was in the past. She changed her words. "I do love him."

Sister Berdine reached across the row to touch her hand. "Of course you do. But if he does not return from the war—and don't you think he would have already if he were coming back to you—then you can open your heart to love another."

Sheriff Brodie's face popped into her mind. Carlyn looked down to hide the blush crawling up into her cheeks.

Sister Berdine bent low over the bean row to peer at

Carlyn's face. "It is good to know you have the natural feelings a woman was created by the Lord to have."

"The Shakers say such feelings are sinful."

"Words are easy to say. Feelings are not as easy to deny, and I haven't been convinced the Lord wants us to deny them." She picked a few beans. "Besides, we both know we aren't here because we have swallowed the Shaker idea of celibacy. We are here because we were penniless with no good way to change that. But perhaps you are considering a better way open to you and that is what colors your face." She bent to look directly at Carlyn again with a questioning look.

"Nay, I have no other way. I am married still."

"Odd to cling to the idea of being married here where such unions are condemned," Sister Berdine murmured. "Although some of the sisters I've talked to seem quite content to have their husbands as brothers instead of bedmates now. They tell me the union of matrimony can get tedious as the years pass. That I would not know, but would not mind finding out."

"I did not find marriage tedious."

"Then it is no wonder that you might wish to return to that happiness."

"That is not a choice open to me." With only a second's hesitation, she added, "Which I have not once considered."

And she had not. While it was true she had thought of the sheriff often since she'd come to the Shaker village, that was simply because of his kindness in taking Asher. It was Asher that made her wonder about the sheriff. Asher she wished to see.

Can you not be truthful? Sister Edna's question echoed in her head. Perhaps the sister was right. She couldn't even be truthful in her own thoughts. But that didn't mean she was going to be unfaithful to Ambrose. Not as long as she did not know whether he lived or died. She shut her eyes to pull up the memory of his face. He seemed more distant from her since she'd come into the Shaker village. But that had nothing to do with Sheriff Brodie. It had only to do with her giving up her former life and embracing a future without the love she'd known with Ambrose.

"Not once?" Sister Berdine didn't wait for her to answer. "I think your face tells another story. Is it one of the brothers here that has attracted your eye?"

"Nay. I told you I've barely noticed the brothers here."

"I am not so good. I notice everything. And there is this one brother I've noted who seems to let his eyes drift my way and linger there whenever we are in the same room." Sister Berdine touched her bonnet. "I think he likes the way I look in my cap and apron."

Carlyn couldn't keep from smiling then, partly with relief that Sister Berdine was not probing for answers Carlyn did not know. "But do you like the way he looks in a Shaker hat?"

"I am not concerned with his hat. As long as he wears trousers I like the way he looks."

Carlyn laughed. "Don't you dare run away in the middle of the night with some brother without telling me."

"Worry not. Should that happen, I'll be asking you to pinch me to be sure I'm not dreaming." Sister Berdine began stripping off the bean pods with quicker fingers. "But now we'd best be busy. That certain sister is giving us the eye. She does not look happy."

"Have you ever seen her happy?" Carlyn bent to her task.

"Nay, but then I have only been here a few months."

Carlyn hid her smile as she pulled the dried pods from

the bean vines. It was good to have Sister Berdine working beside her. Carlyn stood to move up the row. Other sisters were bent to the task of picking the beans. It was not a bad thing to be surrounded by sisters ready with smiles and helping hands. She let her eyes drift out to the road. Whatever Curt Whitlow was talking about with Brother Henry, he couldn't touch her here. She was safe as long as she stayed among her sisters.

She looked toward the end of the garden expecting to see Sister Edna frowning at Carlyn for taking such a long pause from her labors, but instead she too was peering out toward the road, her hands in her lap while beans waited to be hulled in the basket beside her. Carlyn wondered what questions she might be pondering. It was strange thinking of Sister Edna as someone with her own worries and perhaps sorrows, instead of simply an impossible-to-please taskmaster. Perhaps Carlyn should try to think of her as a sister the same as Sister Berdine and the others around her.

But then Sister Edna turned her eyes back to the garden. When she saw Carlyn watching her, a frown darkened her face. Carlyn bent back to her task as the woman started up off the bench under the tree, no doubt ready to scold Carlyn's lack of industry. She was not a sister easy to love.

One of her mother's Scripture lessons came to Carlyn. Something about there being nothing special about loving those who loved you. The true test of Christian love was to offer love freely to those who were hard to love. She was surely being tested with Sister Edna.

By the time they finished the last row, dark ominous clouds lined the western horizon.

Perhaps Sister Edna was right. Clouds did always come

in life, and no matter how one hid, the storms still came. Thunder rumbled nearer while they were eating the evening meal, and when they went to the upper room to practice the worship songs and dances, lightning flashed eerie shadows on the wall.

Sister Edna had not yet allowed Carlyn to join in with the dances. A wrong step by a novitiate messed up everything, as the dances were often intricate patterns of back-and-forth movements with lines of the men and women passing each other but not touching.

Sister Berdine was sometimes allowed to participate, but this evening, she claimed a sore back and stood with the watchers. It was not the back that was her problem, but the storm raging outside. With each crack of thunder, she clutched Carlyn's arm a bit tighter.

"Do they not hear that?" Sister Berdine's eyes were wide. "We would be safer hidden under our bedcovers."

Sister Edna stepped up beside them in time to hear her last words. "Worry not. You have no reason to be frightened. Mother Ann will watch over us as long as we are engaged in our proper duties."

"Yea." Sister Berdine waited until Sister Edna moved away to whisper. "But we would be safer in our beds." She let out a little shriek when a crash of thunder shook the windows.

"She is right." Carlyn patted her hand. "In here, we are safe from the storm."

Sister Berdine gave her a wondering look. "Are you not afraid, Sister Carlyn?"

"Not of nature's storms." Carlyn watched the lightning flash outside the window and thought of Asher. "But the thunder bothered my dog. He was afraid of little else, but storms made him tremble." She hoped the sheriff was letting him sleep by his bed on this night and hadn't fastened him somewhere out in the storm.

The thunder had let up by the time they went down to their retiring room, but Sister Berdine barely let her knees touch the floor for her night prayers before she was burrowing down in her bed. The Shaker beds were narrow with little softness, and Sister Edna insisted the proper Shaker slept on her back with her legs and arms stretched out straight like a corpse. Another of the Shaker rules that made little sense to Carlyn. All that did was make for plentiful snoring in the room, the loudest of which came from Sister Edna. That was not all bad, for as soon as they heard Sister Edna snoring, they were able to turn and curl however they pleased under their covers.

This night Carlyn was slow to go to sleep in spite of the weariness of her muscles. Thoughts flashed through her mind like the lightning outside the window. Curt Whitlow in the village. Sister Edna demanding she confess sin. Sister Berdine's talk in the garden. The storm. Asher, and yes, the man he was with.

"Oh Ambrose, if I only knew where you were." She whispered the words into the dark air over her bed. "I loved you so much."

Once again, just as in the garden, she realized she'd spoken of her love for Ambrose as in the past. Her heart could no longer keep him alive in her mind. He had been gone too long. Missing. What a dreadful word. Not alive. Not dead. Missing.

Just as Sister Berdine had done earlier, Carlyn pulled the cover up over her head. While she was not frightened by the thunder and lightning outside, she did want to hide from the storms in her heart. At last, she slept.

In the midnight hours, the Centre House bell began to clang. Again and again. Rousing them with warning in the sound.

16

Sister Alice was first out of bed to push up the window to see why the bell was ringing. "Fire!" she shouted as smoke swept in on the wind.

"What burns?" Sister Edna demanded from her bed on the other side of the room.

"The barn."

Carlyn and several other sisters squeezed in around Sister Alice to peer out the window with her. Flames leaped up through the roof of the barn behind their house. The barn visible from the garden where they'd been working.

"Why won't those of the world stop tormenting us?" Sister Edna said.

"You think someone set the fire on purpose?" Carlyn turned to Sister Edna.

"Yea." Sister Edna was on her feet now.

"Why? Couldn't it have been the storm?"

"It is not time for questions, Sister Carlyn. It is time for action, but be assured this is not the first barn torched by those of the world who envy the peace we have here." Sister Edna reached for her dress. "Now stop gawking out the window and get dressed. We will be needed to fight the fire."

"That fire is past fighting." Sister Alice leaned back out the window as though pulled by the sight of the flames. She had been a Shaker longer than any of the others in the room besides Sister Edna. "The seeds we've been harvesting weren't stored in that barn, were they?"

The sisters who'd worked alongside Carlyn and Sister Berdine in the garden groaned at the thought.

"Think not about seeds, Sisters." Sister Edna said. "Think more of stopping the fire before it spreads."

"Our house won't burn, will it?" Sister Marie, the youngest sister in their sleeping room, sounded ready to cry.

"Nay, the brothers will put out the fire." Sister Alice put a comforting hand on the girl's cheek. "With our help."

The bell ceased tolling, but there was no silence. The night was filled with the crackle of flames and shouts as Shakers spilled out of the houses. Carlyn pulled her dress over her head. The panicked whinnies of a horse sent a chill through her.

"Are horses stabled in that barn?" she asked no one in particular.

"Yea," Sister Alice answered. "In my time here, I have often seen Brother Henry taking them in and out of the barn."

"Brother Henry?" Carlyn paused in tying her apron around her waist. That name. The Shaker brother who'd been arguing with Curt Whitlow on the pathways earlier that day. When she looked up, Sister Edna was staring across the room at her.

Sister Alice spoke first. "Brother Henry is very devoted to

his horses. He will be sorrowful if all of them do not escape the fire."

"There is much to be sorrowful about," Sister Edna spoke up. "The devil is loose amongst us tonight." Her eyes bored into Carlyn before she turned to lead them outside.

The devil. The words echoed in Carlyn's thoughts along with Curt's laugh. But Sister Edna hadn't heard Brother Henry accuse Curt of being the devil. And when she remembered what Brother Henry said, he was repeating someone else's words and not his own. None of this could have anything to do with her. It couldn't. Not the fire. Not Curt's harsh words to Brother Henry. It was nothing more than happenstance that she had overheard them.

A hot wind full of ash and smoke met them on the pathway. Sister Marie began whimpering again and even a stern word from Sister Edna couldn't stop her. Sister Berdine put her arm around the young sister and whispered something that helped Sister Marie swallow her tears and keep following after Sister Edna. She wasn't the only one bothered by the fire. Many of the faces looked fearful as they formed a bucket brigade.

Sister Alice was right. There was no saving the barn. A few brethren led some horses away from the fire. One of them reared up and pawed the air when an unearthly scream came from within the barn. More horses must be inside.

Carlyn's stomach turned over. A young Shaker brother ran toward the barn, but older, wiser men held him back. It would be suicide to go into those flames. Finally the animal's screams stopped and Carlyn was glad even though she knew what that meant.

They passed bucket after bucket of water forward to douse

the flames. It was no longer raining, but it was impossible to know if the clouds were gone. Smoke billowed up into the sky and dropped down around the workers. Carlyn stood in line with the other sisters and tried to think of nothing except taking hold of each bucket of water and passing it to the next person in line, over and over. The back of her dress was wet with sweat and her skirt soaked from water splashing from the buckets. But she couldn't keep her eyes away from the flames dancing greedily as they ate the barn.

Then as the fire began to die back, they stopped passing the buckets of water and Sister Edna gathered her charges around her like a mother hen seeing to her chicks. "There are men from the world among us."

"You mean those you think set the fire?" Carlyn asked.

"Perhaps." Sister Edna looked grim. "That is hard to know without a witness to see. But our neighbors have been attracted by the flames and come to gloat."

"They may have come to help."

"We need no help from the likes of them." Sister Edna turned her eyes from the fire to Carlyn. "You are too soon from the world. You carry the smell of it on you yet, even as we will carry the smell of smoke back to our houses. It is not a pleasant odor."

"I have nothing to do with the fire." Carlyn looked from Sister Edna to where the flames seemed content now to slowly devour the remaining wood in the barn. Black smoke settled around them and Carlyn lifted her apron up over her nose to filter the air.

Sister Edna seemed unbothered. "How long have you been among us, Sister?"

"Two weeks."

"And in that time, we have had strangers in our midst causing unrest, and now this." Sister Edna looked back at the barn.

Carlyn was speechless. Sister Edna was determined to find fault with her. No words were going to change that on this night while the fire licked up the remains of the barn. If only Carlyn could go back to their room, fall down on her bed, and pull the cover over her head again. Shut it all away.

But there would be no more rest this night. Dawn was spreading a gray light across the village, revealing the buildings beyond the reach of the fire's glow. Daylight made it easier to see those watching the fire and to pick out the ones who did not belong in the Shaker village.

"Do you see him here?" Sister Edna swept her arm out toward the men nearer the fire.

"Who?" Carlyn asked, although she knew the person the sister meant.

"The man you saw speaking to Brother Henry yesterday." Sister Edna's eyes came back to Carlyn.

Carlyn started to say he wouldn't be here, but then she hadn't thought he would be there yesterday either. She looked at the men, but none carried Curt's girth. "Nay, I do not see him."

"Nor do I see Brother Henry," Sister Edna said. "That is odd. As Sister Alice said, our brother does treasure his horses."

"Perhaps he is with those horses," Sister Berdine said.

"That is my worry." Sister Edna's frown grew darker. "Stay here and pray while I find out."

They were silent until Sister Edna was several steps away,

but then several sisters spoke at once. Sister Berdine held up her hand to stop them as she kept her voice low. "We'd best whisper to avoid trouble. Sister Edna's ears are sharp."

"Yea," Sister Alice agreed as she stepped closer to Sister Berdine. "But she can't think Brother Henry is . . ." She stopped as though unable to finish the thought.

"In there?" Sister Marie's eyes widened as she looked toward what was left of the barn.

"Nay, she cannot know that," Sister Berdine said. "It is more likely as I said—that he is with the horses they rescued from the fire."

"But they didn't rescue all of them," one of the other sisters said. "I've never heard anything like that sound. That horse."

Carlyn shuddered as they all fell silent.

"We should pray as Sister Edna said." Sister Alice reached for the hands of the sisters nearest her.

They joined hands then and bent their heads in silent prayer. Carlyn held Sister Berdine's and Sister Hallie's hands and bent her head like them, but she couldn't still the questions in her mind enough to pray.

Was Sister Edna right? Could Curt Whitlow be the reason for their trouble? And could that be because of her?

After Sister Alice signaled the end of their prayer time with a quiet amen, Carlyn moved away from the others to look around again. She wasn't sure she would be able to pick out Brother Henry among the Shaker men. The brothers looked so alike with their hats on. He'd been slim and not as tall as Curt, but that was a description that fit many men.

"Who was Sister Edna talking about?" Sister Berdine stepped up beside Carlyn. "A man from the world?"

"The man I owed on my house was in the village yesterday

talking to Brother Henry." She had no reason to keep that secret. "I happened up on them when I was coming back to the garden and heard them arguing."

"Do you think that has anything to do with this?" Sister Berdine gestured toward the barn.

"Nay. That man would not be sneaking around in the night setting fires." Carlyn was sure of that. However, he might slip around and try to do other things just as wrong. Carlyn pulled in her breath. She had no reason to worry about him. Not here surrounded by sisters. "Sister Edna must be wrong. It surely was a lightning strike."

Sister Alice stepped up behind them in time to hear Carlyn. "Sister Edna may be wrong about many things." The sister took a quick look around as though worried what ears might be listening. "But she is rarely wrong about troubles. She has her eye out for such. At one time, she was a watcher for the Ministry to catch those doing wrong. But now she merely watches to know."

"To know what?" Carlyn asked.

"I'm not sure, but I would not want to be on the wrong side of Sister Edna," Sister Alice said.

"Is there a right side?" Sister Berdine asked.

"It does not seem so for our Sister Carlyn." Sister Alice smiled a little as she reached over to squeeze Carlyn's hand. "But we do not all think like Sister Edna. I and the others in our sleeping room are glad you have come among us. We know you could have nothing to do with this. No matter the fate of poor Brother Henry."

Sister Alice's and Sister Berdine's eyes drifted back to the fire, but Carlyn looked through all the men standing around instead. Curt Whitlow was not there. At least not in the open where he could be seen, but then he hadn't been in the open when she'd seen him with Brother Henry.

Sister Edna appeared to be searching for someone too. Perhaps Brother Henry. She did stop to talk to one of the brothers, but it wasn't Brother Henry. Instead it was Elder Derron, who had questioned Carlyn about the business of her house. Whatever Sister Edna said seemed to upset the elder since he stalked away from her. Sister Edna followed after him for a few steps before she stopped and put her hands on her hips. She did not look pleased.

A rooster crowed and the hens began coming out of their roosting house. Carlyn watched them ruffling their feathers and flapping their wings as they left sleep behind. This was just another day for them, with bugs to eat and eggs to lay. The fire meant nothing to them. That's the way she should be. Never mind Sister Edna's frowns and suspicions. While the fire was a sorrowful loss, it had absolutely nothing to do with Carlyn being at the Shaker village. Absolutely nothing.

Some of the Shakers began moving away from the fire. Breakfast had to be cooked. The animals fed. The beds made and the floors swept. There would be extra laundry with their soiled dresses and aprons too. It was going to be a long day for those working in the washhouse.

"Maybe we should go back to our room to clean up for the morning chores," Sister Berdine suggested. "Sister Edna appears to have forgotten us."

"But she told us to wait here." Sister Marie's voice trembled. Poor girl was frightened of everything.

"And when she comes back, she may very well fuss because we did not go begin our duties for the day," Carlyn said.

"True enough, Sister." Sister Alice smiled a little. "We can always say it was Sister Carlyn's idea."

"You can. Then she will be upset that you followed the lead of one so recently of the world."

"True again." Sister Alice sighed. "We will all need to consider our confessions for speaking about our sister while she was too far from us to hear. She will be distressed that we allowed our tongues to tempt us into trouble."

"Trouble," Carlyn said. "I came here to get away from trouble."

"I suppose trouble is not so easy to escape." Sister Berdine pointed toward the smoke rising from the remains of the barn.

"Yea," Sister Alice agreed. "But come. The brethren can handle whatever remains to be done about the barn. Sister Edna will understand our desire to be about our duties, with the sun coming up in the east."

They were almost to their house when a lone man came riding up the road. Carlyn knew him at once and her heart bounded up into her throat. Sheriff Brodie. He must have heard about the fire. She looked to see if Asher might be following him, but there was no dog.

With a nod toward them, he dismounted and tied his horse to the fence. But then, as he started toward the barn, he looked back. "Carlyn?"

Sister Berdine put her hand on Carlyn's arm. "Is he the one you saw arguing with Brother Henry?"

"Nay. He is a friend." Carlyn's feet moved toward him of their own accord, even as she wondered if he was just another kind of trouble following her. Trouble she should shy away from, but she kept walking. She kept smiling. She wanted to talk to him. She had to ask him about Asher.

She would worry about Sister Edna and the rules later. She would worry about trouble when it came. But then her mother would say, what good did worry do. Prayer. That was always her mother's answer. Perhaps it should be hers as well.

17

"Mrs. Kearney, it's good to see you." Mitchell had let her given name slip past his lips when he first saw her in the cluster of Shaker sisters, but he wouldn't do so again. He had no right to speak so familiarly to her even if she was Carlyn in his thoughts. In too many of his thoughts.

She smiled but with a touch of sadness. "No one calls me that now, Sheriff. I'm simply Sister Carlyn here. My marriage is part of the past."

He did not want to think of her as a sister. "So have you heard news about your husband?"

"Nay."

The Shaker word surprised him. He hadn't thought she would be absorbed so quickly into their Society. But words were easy to say. He had to bite his lip to keep back words that might reveal feelings he shouldn't be having, but she was so lovely. Even with the smudge of soot on her cheek and strands of dark brown hair escaping her Shaker cap.

She did not seem to notice his surprise as she went on. "I have accepted the truth so many have pushed at me these last months that my husband is not apt to return from the war now. Leaving my home and coming here forced me to face that truth."

"I'm sorry." Mitchell was ashamed of how his heart lifted at her words.

"Yea, so am I." She lowered her head for a moment, then seemed to gather herself as she looked back at Mitchell. "But though I am still married since I do not know what happened to my Ambrose, the absence of a husband makes it easier to be a sister here. As odd as it seems, marriage is considered sinful in this place."

"Do you like it here?" He glanced over at the Shaker women behind her. One of them edged a bit closer as though wanting to hear, but then another of the women held her back. From his previous visits to the village, he knew the leaders wanted the sisters to have nothing to do with a man of the world. Or any man, as far as that went. He let his eyes come back to Carlyn. "Are you happy?"

"Happy." She echoed his word and blinked a few times. "Happiness is not a necessity for life. Food and shelter are what matter." She sounded as though she were trying to convince herself the same as him. "Both are plentiful here. And many of the sisters claim happiness as well."

What was it about her deep blue eyes that made him want to take her hand and convince her that happiness might be possible with him? His army discipline saved him from making a fool of himself. "Then perhaps in time you will find happiness here too."

"In time perhaps. On days when barns are not burning

and horses dying." She turned her head to look back toward where smoke rose between the buildings.

He looked that way too. "So the men couldn't get the horses out?"

"Not all of them." She shuddered.

"But no people were hurt?"

"I cannot be sure of that. You will have to ask the elders." A shadow crossed her face. She looked over her shoulder at the other women, then back toward the smoke. "I shouldn't be talking to you."

"Why not?" He wanted her to keep talking to him. He wanted to know her better, to find out why he'd allowed her to move into his dreams. He'd been in love with the wrong woman once. Best not to let that happen again no matter how he was drawn to her.

"I will be in trouble with the sister helping me learn their ways here."

"Where is she?" He looked back at the other women. "I can tell her I approached you."

"But that wouldn't be true."

"I called out to you."

"I didn't have to listen." A corner of her mouth turned up in a very small smile.

His fingers itched to push the lock of hair straying out on her cheek back from her face. "Why did you then?"

"I wanted to ask about Asher. Is he all right? Curt hasn't—" She hesitated. "He hasn't hurt him, has he?"

So the dog had drawn her to him. Of course. If not for the seriousness of the fire that had pulled him to the Shaker village, Mitchell would have laughed out loud at himself. Here he had imagined her eyes glad to see him when she simply wanted to know about her dog. As Whitlow had told him on that first day at her house, he was letting a pretty face turn his head. The truth was he knew more about her dog than he knew about her, and that wasn't likely to change now that she was a Shaker with her yeas and nays. He should put her out of his mind, but how could he with her standing right in front of him, making his heart thump as if he'd just charged up a hill into enemy fire? He forced himself to think about her dog instead of her beautiful eyes.

"Asher's fine. He's back at the boardinghouse." Mitchell managed a smile. "You were right about Mrs. Snowden. That dog. He's a charmer. He went right to work on her the very first day I had him and found a place in her kitchen."

Carlyn finally smiled fully. "I'm glad."

"He still misses you though."

"You won't let Curt do anything to him? About the bite?"

"What bite?" Mitchell raised his eyebrows a little. "Whitlow claims a stray dog attacked him. And that he killed the dog."

She looked relieved even as she said, "Poor dog."

"You don't have to worry about Asher. I'm keeping him close for the time being. If I let him run free, he'd run right back to your house."

"Not my house now. I signed it over to the Shakers. One of the elders here says they will sell it to buy more land. That's their way." Saying that seemed to make her remember other ways of the Shakers. With an uneasy glance around, she backed away from him. "Thank you, Sheriff. You can't imagine how much I appreciate you taking Asher in. And thank Mrs. Snowden for me too."

When she started to turn away, he reached for her as though

his hand had a mind of its own. He so wanted to keep her there. The fire could wait. The Shaker women behind her could wait. She looked down at his hand on her arm, then back at his face, a question in her eyes. A question he couldn't answer. Not yet.

Instead he stammered out some words. "If you ever need anything, Mrs. Kearney, you let me know." When she didn't say anything, he rushed on. "It's my job, ma'am. To take care of the people in the county. That includes the people here in the Shaker village." He knew he was sounding like a fool. He was a fool to let himself be carried away by a pretty widow. He dropped his hand away from her arm.

"Yea, Sheriff, then you best be about your work. Sister Edna said fires like this are often the work of people intent on making trouble for the Shakers." She whirled away from him to rejoin the women at the bottom of the steps going into the big brick house.

One of the younger ones had her hand over her mouth with her eyes big circles in her face. Eyes that got even bigger when a strident voice called out Carlyn's name.

"Sister Carlyn." An older sister strode toward them, anger in every step. "Whatever are you doing?"

The other young women all scurried on into the house, but Carlyn stayed where she was on the walkway and seemed to brace herself for combat.

The woman turned her frown on Mitchell even though she directed her words at Carlyn. "Is this the man from the world who was bothering poor Brother Henry yesterday? The one you fear?"

"Nay, Sister Edna. Sheriff Brodie has come to investigate the fire."

"A man of the law." The woman's eyes narrowed on Mitchell. "Then I fear you are too late. The barn is burned. A team of horses lost. Brother Henry nowhere to be found."

"Do you suspect this brother of setting the fire and then running away?" Mitchell gave the woman his complete attention.

"Nay. Brother Henry was a good and faithful Believer and would never injure an animal in his care." The lines in the woman's face deepened as her voice faltered. "I suspect something much worse. The work of the devil. Those of the world determined to rob us of our peace."

"If the fire was intentionally set, I'll find who did it."

"Will you, Sheriff? How? By delaying one of our young sisters from her duties?" Her eyes narrowed until they were mere slits. "By forgetting your own duties at the sight of a pretty face? Such puts your feet on a slippery slope and our young sister's as well."

"I meant no harm." Mitchell looked past the old sister to where Carlyn stood, her head still bowed. Where was the woman who had met him at the door of her house, gun in hand?

"Men of the world make that claim often, but look what is the result of those like you." Sister Edna threw her hand out toward the fire, almost hitting Mitchell.

"Nay, Sister Edna." Carlyn looked up and stepped toward them. "Sheriff Brodie is here to help. Not harm."

The older woman's face went rigid as she peered over her shoulder at Carlyn. "You speak out of turn, Sister. And with the taint of worldly sin clinging to you. You need to push the devil from your mind."

Carlyn stopped in her tracks, but dared more words. "He is not the devil."

"The devil shows up in many guises, Sister Carlyn." She pointed toward the house. "Now be about your duties to keep yourself from further sin."

Carlyn's face was devoid of expression as she met the older woman's stare. After a long moment, she turned and went up the steps. She looked back at Mitchell before she went inside, but he still had no inkling of her thoughts.

The face of the older Shaker sister wasn't as hard to read. It had been awhile since anyone had looked at Mitchell with such distaste. She began stomping the ground and pushing her hands against the air in front of Mitchell. "Get thee from me, Satan."

Mitchell stared at her. "Calm yourself, Sister."

His words seemed to only upset her more, so he left her there to go search out one of the elders. Men he could talk to. Men he could understand. Even if they were Shakers with their odd beliefs. At least none of the Shaker brethren he'd dealt with had ever called him the devil.

That the old sister did bothered him. He wanted to be the good guy, the one on the side of right. All he'd done was talk to Carlyn. He couldn't understand how the Shaker woman could think that was so wrong. Mitchell sighed. Perhaps the old woman was right. Perhaps he was doing nothing but making trouble. For himself. For Carlyn too.

He hoped Carlyn wouldn't be chastised for her attempt to defend him to the older woman. Perhaps if he apologized to the leaders here and took the blame for the contact between them, then Carlyn would not suffer. But whatever happened, Mitchell knew Carlyn would have dared speaking with him anyway. Not because she wanted to talk to him, but because of Asher. He wondered what the old Shaker woman would think about Carlyn breaking the rules to learn about a dog.

Mitchell smiled a little at the thought of playing second fiddle to a dog. And a missing husband. Foolish to even imagine himself in Carlyn's thoughts at all. His smile faded as he rounded one of the Shaker buildings and saw the smoldering fire. It was time to think business instead of hopeless romance. Time to find out if this was a tragic accident or something worse. He was hoping it was nothing more than a lightning strike from the storm that had gone through in the night, but something about the posture of the men standing around seemed to indicate nothing simple about it.

Elder Derron broke away from one of the groups when he saw Mitchell. "Sheriff, we were about to send for you."

The man's face was not marked with soot as Carlyn's had been but weariness cast a gray shadow over his features. "One of your neighbors sent his boy into town to let me know about your trouble here," Mitchell said.

"Yea, trouble." The elder sighed.

"I'm sorry about your barn. I hear you lost horses too."

"Yea. And we fear more."

"More?" Mitchell looked at the barn. The hay inside it could smolder for days. "What was inside the barn?"

"Not what. Who."

Mitchell sharpened his look on the elder and remembered the old sister's worry about one of her brethren. "What do you mean, who?"

"We are unable to account for Brother Henry Stratton. We fear he may have perished while trying to save his horses."

"Did someone see him go into the barn?"

"Nay. No one has seen him at all." Elder Derron coughed

175

into a handkerchief he pulled from his pocket. "The smoke," he explained.

"Perhaps your Brother Henry is just in another building or barn." Mitchell looked around.

"That is unlikely. Some of our brothers did manage to get a few of the horses out, but no one saw Brother Henry. No one. That is not like him. Brother Henry treated his animals with the greatest of care. Often if one was ailing in some way, he would sleep in the barn with them."

"Was he doing that this night?" Mitchell stared at what was left of the barn. If Brother Henry was there, his spirit had long since fled his body.

"I would not be surprised if it was so. Brother Henry could have been in the barn to calm his charges during the storm."

"Then it seems he would have been able to escape the fire with his horses," Mitchell said. "If lightning struck the barn, he would have known it."

"Yea, so it would seem. But the fire was not the result of lightning, Sheriff." Elder Derron looked directly at Mitchell, his face taut.

"Is there proof of that?"

"Yea." He drew in a ragged breath that set off his coughing again. When he was able to stop the coughs, he wiped his mouth with trembling fingers. "I do apologize, Sheriff, but this is a tragic morning. Anyway, to answer your question, the brethren found an empty can with the strong odor of kerosene just inside the doors when they went in to rescue the horses."

"And none of them saw Brother Henry? It seems they would have if he was in the barn."

"It could be that our poor brother had already been overcome by smoke."

"Or knocked in the head by whoever set the fire." Mitchell's voice was grim. He didn't like thinking he might be investigating a murder, but he couldn't ignore that possibility.

Elder Derron recoiled from Mitchell's words. "Surely those of the world would not be so cruel. To leave a man to die in a fire if they knew he was there." His voice grew faint and his face paled.

Mitchell should have guarded his words until he knew more. "Perhaps we are jumping to conclusions, Elder. It is best to wait for proof."

"Yea. But such proof has surely been lost to the flames." Elder Derron kept his eyes on the smoke rising from the fire.

Another Shaker man stepped up beside them in time to hear the elder's words. "The good Lord will know the truth. Whether the scoundrel escapes here on earth, he cannot escape final punishment."

Elder Derron started to answer, but instead was overcome by another fit of coughing. The new Shaker reached out a hand to support the elder. "Are you all right, Elder Derron? Perhaps you should rest before you try to talk more." The Shaker man gave Mitchell a hard look.

"I am distressed but able, Brother Thomas." Elder Derron held up a hand to reassure the other man. "Sheriff Brodie is here to investigate the fire and we must give him our cooperation."

"Ah, Sheriff Brodie, forgive me. I did not recognize you," Brother Thomas said. "We welcome your help if it stops such attacks as these from miscreants of the world."

Mitchell remembered the older sister's words when she first saw him. "I spoke with a sister named Edna when I got here. She said something about a man of the world bothering

Brother Henry yesterday. She had suspicions that I might be that man."

"I'm sure you disavowed her of that wrong idea. But yea, we have a new sister among us who saw such and reported it to Sister Edna." Elder Derron stuffed his handkerchief in his pocket. "Sister Carlyn. The one who owed Mr. Whitlow that debt we paid on her behalf last week."

"The sheriff knows Sister Carlyn." Brother Thomas spoke up. "She took her dog to him. An unusual-looking animal but our sister was quite concerned with its welfare and thought Sheriff Brodie could help her. Did you?" Brother Thomas peered at Mitchell.

"I kept her dog," Mitchell said.

Elder Derron frowned. "We have more worries than a dog now."

"Yes." Mitchell looked at the pile of smoldering wood and hay. Here and there a flame licked up out of the debris into the air.

"The Lord and Mother Ann will supply every answer needed," Elder Derron said. "Already we can note the Lord's blessing of the rain-dampened ground that kept the fire from spreading."

"It would have been better for the rain to keep the barn from burning." Brother Thomas frowned a bit. "And Brother Henry from perishing with his horses."

"It is not our place to question the ways of the Lord. He makes all work for the good of his plan." The elder gave Brother Thomas a stern look as though to remind him to speak with care in Mitchell's presence.

"Yea." It was easy to see Brother Thomas didn't feel as agreeable as he sounded.

If the elder noticed, he paid no attention as he turned to Mitchell. "Brother Thomas will take you to the men first at the fire. After that, if you want, I will arrange for you to speak with Sister Edna."

"And Sister Carlyn." It felt funny to call her sister.

"Is there need to talk directly to her?"

"If she was the one to see the men talking, it would be better to hear what she saw firsthand."

The elder nodded. "Very well. If you think it necessary."

"I do." What Mitchell didn't add was that any chance he had to see Carlyn felt very necessary.

18

By the time Mitchell talked to the men first to the fire who dared the smoke and flames to rescue four of the horses, the day was half gone and he didn't know much more than when he started. Flames had been licking up to the roof by the time the alarm was raised. A kerosene can was seen close to the door, but nobody knew where it was now. Destroyed by the fire, they assumed. Nobody saw Brother Henry. They had no way of knowing if he had been in the barn. By the time they got the horses out of the stalls nearest the doors, more men were there, but the fire was too hot to attempt to reach the other horses.

They told their stories plainly and quickly with nothing hidden in any of their words. They knew nothing about who might have set the fire. If men from the world were skulking around in the shadows, they didn't see them. They saw only the fire and all their hard work being lost to the flames. The grief of losing a brother came later.

The Shakers hadn't wasted the morning. They'd rigged up

pipes and used horsepower to pump water from one of their ponds to douse the fire. If they could have gotten that apparatus working in the night, they might have saved some of the barn, but it probably wouldn't have saved Brother Henry.

They found the man's charred remains under smoldering hay in one of the middle stalls. A young brother who helped Brother Henry said that stall had been empty ever since Brother Henry's favorite workhorse died last winter. As yet Brother Henry hadn't found a horse he considered worthy of getting the honored stall.

"Some of the brothers thought that odd, but Brother Henry loved his horses." The young Shaker looked around as though worried one of those brothers might be listening and think he was speaking out of turn. "He'd do anything for them."

Brother Carson looked to be on the young side of sixteen. Just a boy. So when tears welled up in his eyes, Mitchell wasn't surprised.

Growing up among the Shakers who preached peace hadn't prepared the young Shaker for violent death. Even the war had passed the Shakers by when the president exempted them from the army draft. So while other men marched off to war, the Shakers stayed in their isolated villages and claimed peace in spite of the world blowing up around them.

Now somebody had disturbed that peace. Even if Brother Henry was simply in the wrong place at the wrong time, he was still dead. Because of the fire.

None of the Shakers thought Brother Henry's death was intended. While they were sure the fire wasn't an accident, they did think Brother Henry being in the fire was. Mitchell didn't like thinking the man's death was intentional either, but at the same time, he had to wonder why the man couldn't get out of the barn before he was overcome by smoke.

It made sense to say he died trying to save his horses. One Shaker even suggested a horse might have kicked him in a panic. But they found his body in the empty stall, the one with no horse to rescue, while just across the breezeway a horse had succumbed to the fire.

The more he heard about Brother Henry, the more suspicious it sounded. Not that the man had raised any suspicions among his brethren. When Mitchell mentioned the sister's report that he'd been seen arguing with someone from the world, most expressed doubt Brother Henry was the Shaker the sister had seen.

"Newcomers to our village are often confused regarding identities," one of the older men claimed. "The like clothes. Hats that shade our faces. The sister had to be mistaken. Brother Henry was not a man to argue with anyone. He was a true Shaker."

"What makes a true Shaker?" Mitchell asked.

"One who shuns worldly ways, works with his hands, and obeys the rules of unity. Brother Henry was such a man, favored with useful gifts from Mother Ann."

"What gifts?"

"Skill with horses and other spiritual gifts one of the world such as yourself could not understand." Brother Jonas settled his hat back on his head and straightened his suspenders. "I must get back to work."

Mitchell held up a hand to stop him. "Do you know anyone who might wish harm to Brother Henry?"

"Nay. Whoever did this meant harm to our barn." He pointed toward the burned barn. "Not harm to Brother Henry."

"But Brother Henry was harmed."

"Yea. Sin can bring about many tragedies." Brother Jonas turned away from Mitchell then and left without another word.

The man could be right. Whoever set the fire might have thought the barn empty except for the horses. Still there was that argument Carlyn had seen. Whether she was mistaken about who was involved, she had witnessed a disagreement. With the fire happening so soon afterward, a connection seemed a possibility. Besides, if it wasn't Brother Henry she saw, then some other Shaker knew more than he was telling.

Mitchell scanned the faces of the men who paused in their work to watch Brother Henry's remains being carried away. He saw nothing to arouse suspicion.

Brother Thomas said they'd bury their brother the next morning. "There will be no sadness." Brother Thomas had returned to Mitchell's side after the body was found. "Brother Henry has simply stepped over from our village here to the perfect village in heaven. We strive for the same perfection in our Society, but those of the world have ways of slipping into our midst to find ways to cause us trouble."

"But what do they gain from burning your barns?" Mitchell had no doubt the barn had been purposely set on fire, but he needed to know why.

"The wickedness of the world is difficult to understand, Sheriff." Brother Thomas gave him a direct look. "Don't you find that true as you endeavor to keep peace among the people of the world?"

"People are people wherever they are. Even here."

Mitchell's words brought a frown to the Shaker's face. "Nay, our brothers and sisters shut out worldly thinking and the sin such thinking causes. We work and worship with unity and treasure the peace that comes from brotherly love." Brother Thomas lifted his hands up toward the heavens. "Our Mother Ann showers down blessings on us when we shake free of the worldly shackles of sin."

"And yet you had no peace here last night and Brother Henry is dead."

"By reason of the world. You will discover that to be true." Brother Thomas set his mouth in a determined line. "I am sure of it."

"Whoever is responsible, I will find them." Mitchell wasn't as confident as he tried to sound. He didn't have much to go on. The one person who might know what happened was beyond telling. There was Carlyn. Odd that she had been the one to see the men arguing. He needed to get her story before he left the village. While he would have preferred to talk to her alone, he had to settle for a meeting in Elder Derron's office.

Brother Thomas escorted him to the Trustee House and left him there. "I must tend to my horses before darkness falls."

The man walked away with no hurry to his steps, sure of his path. Others moved through the village with the same single-minded purpose, to do their duty and shut away everything that might disturb the peace of their Society.

He hoped Brother Thomas was right and that the peace of the village would not be disturbed again, but Mitchell had a bad feeling about it all. The fire. Brother Henry. Whatever Carlyn had witnessed.

Surely she could have nothing to do with any of this, but she had been the one to see the men. He couldn't seem to get that out of his mind. Then again, he couldn't seem to get Carlyn out of his mind at any time.

She was already in the elder's office, the older sister beside her. No smile on that one's face. Mitchell had to wonder if she ever smiled, but then perhaps in their worship. While Mitchell had never witnessed a Shaker worship service, he'd heard others say the Shakers were often ecstatically happy while shaking and whirling. Whether that was so or not, she definitely wasn't happy now as she glared at him. He wouldn't have been surprised if she started calling him the devil again.

It could be she sensed his attraction to Carlyn and worried he'd tempt Carlyn away from the village. She'd probably seen many young women desert the Shaker way for a more normal life.

But if Carlyn was feeling any temptation to leave the Shakers, she didn't show it. She had washed her face and changed clothes since they talked that morning. Now he was the one with the black smudges on his face and the odor of smoke clinging to him.

She still wore a Shaker dress with the wide white kerchief draped around her shoulders and lapped across her front. No unruly strands of hair escaped her cap. With her head bent and her hands folded in her lap, she didn't look anything like the girl he carried in his thoughts. It was as if the Shakers had gathered her spirit and stuffed it out of sight somewhere the same as her hair hidden by her cap.

He wanted to reach across the space between them to lift up her chin and make her look at him, but he didn't. He couldn't. Even if the old Shaker sister and Elder Derron hadn't been there beside them, he couldn't. She was yearning after her missing husband, not him.

He needed to rein in his imagination. It could be he was simply moved by her admirable faithfulness after the way Hilda so quickly forgot her promise to wait for him when he marched off to war. His heart was bruised by Hilda's betrayal and by the war. Something about running toward death in battle after battle made a man dream of a wife and children around his supper table or sitting beside him on a church pew. He'd gone through the war certain that woman would be Hilda, but now when he thought about it, he couldn't imagine her being the wife he'd dreamed about in those army camps. If they had married, they would have both been miserable.

His foolish imaginings about Carlyn might be every bit as delusional. She had spirit. They both liked dogs. That was hardly enough reason for him to want to take her hand and lead her away from this place.

He needed to look for the answer to his dreams elsewhere. There were women who would welcome his attentions. Women other than Mrs. Snowden's Florence, who was definitely not in his dreams.

Did he reach for the unattainable on purpose? A way to protect his heart. He could stop that. He could put Carlyn out of his mind.

Then she raised her head and looked directly at him. While every inch of her posture suggested submission to the Shaker rules, her eyes were still that woman he'd first seen standing in her doorway, a gun hooked over her arm. And his heart beat a little faster.

Elder Derron cleared his throat and broke the odd silence in the room. "I believe you know Sister Carlyn and Sister Edna."

Mitchell pulled his eyes away from Carlyn but not before he caught the ghost of a smile on her lips. Strange how easy a man's hopes could be lifted.

He pushed that thought aside to turn toward the elder. The man's cough was gone. Also gone was the trembling weakness Mitchell had noted at the site of the fire. Here at his desk, the elder looked in control, very capable of attending to the business of the Shaker village.

"Yes. Mrs. Kearney brought me her dog when she found out she couldn't keep it here, and I talked with Sister Edna earlier today." He smiled over at the old sister. Her face tightened into a fiercer scowl. "I apologize, Sister Edna, if I upset you this morning."

Her face didn't soften. "It's my duty to protect the young sisters in my charge from those of the world."

"I meant no harm." Mitchell tried to look as sincere as possible, but there was no way he was going to win Sister Edna over. Not unless he joined the Shakers and began wearing their costume and probably not even then. She didn't seem much happier with Elder Derron than she was with him. In fact, her frown darkened when the elder spoke.

"I'm sure Sister Edna knows that." The elder turned toward Sister Edna.

The woman wasn't silenced by the elder's words. "Whether he did or not, someone meant us harm and our brother is dead because of it." She stared straight at Elder Derron until he looked down at his hands spread on his thighs.

"Yea, Sister, you speak truth." The elder pulled in a breath. "Sorrowful truth."

The old sister narrowed her eyes and stared at the elder's bent head. "The truth is what we need to discover."

Mitchell had heard the sisters had as much say in the Shaker Society as the men. Even so, he was surprised at how Sister Edna addressed the elder. Then again, that might be her usual manner of speaking. It was certainly how she'd spoken to him that morning when she'd accused him of being the devil.

He waited for the elder to speak, but instead another uncomfortable silence fell over them. Mitchell decided to take the bull by the horns. It was getting late in the day, and he needed to get back to town in case something there needed his attention. Problems didn't take turns. Instead they often came in bunches.

"I asked Elder Derron to let me speak to you about what you said this morning, Sister Edna. About Mrs. Kearney witnessing an argument between Brother Henry and someone." Mitchell let his gaze drift from Sister Edna to Carlyn. She was gripping her hands so tightly in her lap that her knuckles were white.

"Sister Carlyn reported such to me." Sister Edna stressed the Sister Carlyn as though Mitchell calling her Mrs. Kearney brought the idea of matrimony too much to mind.

Mitchell didn't care. Carlyn wasn't his sister. "Tell me what happened."

Carlyn looked up as though ready to answer, but Sister Edna pushed her words out first. "Our sister says she took a wrong turn yesterday on her way back to work in our Gathering Family gardens. She had been confessing her sins to me and was somewhat distraught due to her failure to conquer such wrong behavior. At least that is what she claimed. Is that not correct, Sister?"

"Yea," Carlyn murmured, but there was little conviction in her voice.

"It might be helpful if Mrs. Kearney speaks for herself, Sister Edna." Mitchell turned in his chair to face the women directly and used his most official voice. "Then once she has told her story, you can add what you feel necessary."

Sister Edna pursed her lips, refusal obvious in her frown, but Elder Derron intervened.

"Let the young sister tell the sheriff what she saw, Sister Edna."

Carlyn moistened her lips as she glanced toward the older woman and then at the elder. Mitchell worried he might be making trouble for her, but he did need to hear her story first-hand. She shot a look toward him and then stared back down at her hands. As though she suddenly realized she was gripping them too hard, she unfolded her hands and placed her palms flat on her apron. Her fingers danced up and down nervously.

Mitchell wanted to reach across the space between them and take those hands in his. Lend her some of his calmness. At the same time, he had to wonder what was making her so nervous. He didn't want to think she was involved in something wrong, but it was plain she wasn't eager to tell what it was she knew. At least to him.

Elder Derron leaned forward in his chair toward Carlyn. "Sister, it is getting late. It would be good for you to tell your story so that we can be about our duties and the sheriff can be about his."

A little of his earlier nerves sounded in the elder's voice. The fire had upset them all. Mitchell leaned back in his chair. He could wait. That generally brought out the story quicker than did peppering a reluctant witness with questions.

"Take your time," he told Carlyn.

She looked up then and lifted her chin a bit as she began

talking. "It is as Sister Edna said. I was meeting with her to confess my wrongs and Sister Edna suggested I give my behavior more thought. I know she didn't mean for me to do so if it meant not paying attention to my duties, but that is what happened. I let my thoughts blind me to my proper path back to the garden. Then I heard men talking, and because there was no one else around, I feared they would think I was doing something improper." She looked at the elder. "Sister Edna has impressed upon me that I should guard against being a temptation to the brethren."

"As is only proper." The elder nodded.

"What do you mean a temptation?" Mitchell knew what sort of temptation she was to him, but the Shakers didn't have normal ideas about such feelings.

Color rose in Carlyn's cheeks and she was so slow to speak that the other woman jumped in with the answer first. "She's pretty. That can be a problem for some among the brethren who have not fully embraced the Shaker way." Sister Edna glared at Mitchell. "I have no doubt that you, being of the world, understand exactly what I mean."

"Come, Sister Edna." Elder Derron held his hand out toward Sister Edna. "We are not here to judge the sheriff. We are merely here to let Sister Carlyn tell what she saw."

Sister Edna turned her frown on the elder, but he pretended not to notice as he said, "Please continue, Sister Carlyn."

Carlyn once more moistened her lips as though her mouth were too dry. "I stepped back against the chicken house out of sight of the men. I had already realized I was on the wrong path, but I hoped to find a way to the garden without backtracking. I had seen the barn and that's how I knew where I was."

"The barn that burned?" Mitchell asked.

"Yes."

It felt something like a victory to hear her answer without the Shaker yea, however foolish that was. "So then what happened?"

"The men's voices got closer." Suddenly the color that had been in her cheeks drained away. "They appeared to be arguing."

"And did you recognize Brother Henry as one of the men?"

"I did not know Brother Henry. I haven't been here long. But you know that." She flashed a look up at him and then at the elder. "Anyway, Sister Edna later said it was Brother Henry after I came back out on the main path and stumbled into her."

Mitchell looked at Sister Edna. "So you saw the men as well?"

"Nay, only Brother Henry. I did not see the man from the world." Sister Edna's voice carried distaste. "I feared Sister Carlyn had arranged to meet this man since she knew him, but when I said as much and she looked near to fainting, I realized that was not the case."

"What man?" Mitchell asked, but he knew before Carlyn answered. He knew from the way her hands trembled and she had to summon her voice from some place it had gone to hide.

"Curt. Curt Whitlow."

19

Carlyn hadn't wanted to say Curt Whitlow's name. She didn't want to even think his name. None of what happened had anything to do with her. It was a mere coincidence that she saw Curt arguing with Brother Henry. Nothing more.

Even so, speaking the man's name aloud to Sheriff Brodie made it sound too odd. Of all the people in the village, she was the one to stumble across Curt Whitlow. A coincidence, she reminded herself. But then her mother said coincidences were sometimes the Lord's invisible hand at work. Could it be that Carlyn was meant to be on the wrong path so she would overhear the argument?

But why? If it was to save Brother Henry, she had failed miserably in that. Or perhaps she wasn't the one who'd failed. She told Sister Edna about Curt. Sister Edna said she'd tell the Ministry, the two eldresses and two elders appointed leaders of the community. They lived in isolation with no contact with the rest of the village.

"That's so they can be impartial when they make judgments." Sister Berdine had pointed out the windows of their rooms one day when they passed the Meeting House. She kept her voice low as though worried she might be overheard. "They live up there over where we have church. They're supposed to be wiser and holier than everybody else."

"Have you ever seen them?"

"Only their eyes." When Carlyn looked puzzled, Sister Berdine explained. "In those peepholes above the doors in the Meeting House. They watch to be sure no one misbehaves during the worship."

"Misbehaves?"

"You know. Starts jigging to a different tune than the Shaker one. No waltzing around the rules allowed."

There was always someone watching. Even here, especially here in Elder Derron's office, eyes were staring at her. Sister Edna's. Elder Derron's. Sheriff Brodie's.

"The man you saw arguing with Brother Henry was Curt Whitlow?" Sheriff Brodie's voice held a measure of disbelief.

Carlyn pulled in a slow breath and raised her eyes to look at the sheriff. "I have no reason to lie about that."

Sister Edna spoke up. She lacked Sister Muriel's gift of silence. "The young sister has a propensity to bend the truth, but I have yet to know her to lie outright, Sheriff."

Carlyn ignored Sister Edna and kept looking at the sheriff. "I would not lie to you." She wanted him to believe her. With Sister Edna glaring at her and Elder Derron staring down at the floor as if the sight of her was painful, she needed to think the sheriff was a friend and not someone suspecting her of wrongdoing.

"Forgive me, Mrs. Kearney." Sheriff Brodie met her eyes.

"It wasn't that I doubted your word. I am just surprised that Whitlow was the man you saw."

"That is not so surprising," Elder Derron raised his head to say. "We have had dealings with Mr. Whitlow in regard to properties in the area and he has purchased things from us on occasion. He may have been asking Brother Henry about a horse." His voice turned somber. "Brother Henry was an excellent horseman. He will be sorely missed."

"Yea," Sister Edna added. "But let us get back to the business at hand. You have established that Curt Whitlow was the man Sister Carlyn saw talking with Brother Henry, Sheriff. You can question him about his purpose here." She started to stand.

"Leave if you want, Sister Edna, but Mrs. Kearney will have to stay. I have a few more questions for her." Sheriff Brodie's voice was calm but firm.

"Nay. Sister Carlyn is my duty. I will not leave until she leaves." Sister Edna huffed out a breath and lowered herself back down in her chair. "So get on with whatever you want to ask."

The sheriff didn't seem bothered by Sister Edna's irritation. Instead he smiled when he turned his eyes back to Carlyn. She had to bite the inside of her lip to keep from smiling back at him. She could not help liking the sheriff, but it would be better if Sister Edna did not guess that.

"Were you close enough to hear what the men were saying?"

Carlyn hesitated. The day before, she hadn't been completely truthful with Sister Edna about what she had heard. The woman would note that if Carlyn answered the sheriff honestly, but how could she do any differently? Carlyn managed to conceal her sigh. She would pay for what Sister Edna would consider bending the truth.

"I couldn't hear everything. Brother Henry's voice was so low I only heard some of his words." Carlyn stared down at her hands that she once again gripped so tightly her fingers ached.

They waited for her to go on, but when she stayed silent, Sister Edna poked her arm. "Get on with it and tell the man what you heard. Don't you remember?"

"I remember," Carlyn whispered.

"Take your time, Carlyn." Sheriff Brodie leaned forward in his chair and didn't seem to notice he'd spoken her given name again.

"Actually I don't remember every word exactly. But the Shaker—that is, Brother Henry—was talking about someone else who was going to be upset about whatever Curt wanted. Then he told Curt he didn't know what he was doing. But Curt said he knew exactly what he was doing and that they had a deal. He said nobody went back on a deal with him without paying a price." Carlyn hated the tremble she heard in her voice. She took a breath. She had no reason to fear Curt Whitlow now, but it had been obvious that Brother Henry feared him or perhaps the other man he mentioned.

"What did Brother Henry say then?" Elder Derron spoke up. "Be sure you answer rightly, Sister."

"He started to say something, but Curt cut him off and told him it was too late to claim a conscience." Carlyn looked up at the elder, who was obviously distressed by Carlyn's words casting suspicion on the brother he admired. A brother who was dead and could not defend himself or explain the words she'd heard. It could be they wouldn't believe her.

She let her eyes slide over to Sister Edna, but the sister wasn't looking at her. Instead she was watching Elder Derron, perhaps to see if he was going to allow Carlyn to continue speaking against their departed brother. The elder leaned his face in his hands as though suddenly weary.

"Did you hear more?" Sheriff Brodie asked.

Carlyn nodded and pulled in another breath. It seemed wrong to speak ill of the dead. "Curt told him to tell the other person what he said and Brother Henry said, 'He won't like it.'"

"He?" Elder Derron raised his head out of his hands. "Did he give a name?"

"Nay. Curt said he, whoever he was, shouldn't have made the deal and that's when Brother Henry said it was a deal with the devil." Carlyn looked at Sister Edna. "That's what I told you. That they spoke of the devil."

"But you heard much more you did not reveal to me." Sister Edna twisted her mouth in disapproval.

"Forgive me, Sister, but I didn't want to think about Curt Whitlow or talk about him."

"Wrong is wrong however you try to excuse it." Sister Edna narrowed her eyes on Carlyn, then the sheriff, and last the elder. She seemed to see wrong in them all.

"So what did Whitlow do then?" Sheriff Brodie asked.

"He laughed. I think he liked that the brother was afraid of him." A tremble was in her voice again. The sheriff would think she had no courage at all. She swallowed hard and went on. "I tried to slip around behind the chicken house without them seeing me, but two hens squawked and gave me away."

"Did he recognize you? Whitlow, I mean." The sheriff leaned toward her again.

Carlyn paused to think. "I don't think so. I kept my face turned away and my Shaker dress looks the same as any sister's. Brother Henry called to me, but I pretended not to hear. That's when I ran back to the other pathway and met Sister Edna."

"Met me? You almost knocked me over," Sister Edna said.

"Yea, I was not watching as I should." Carlyn breathed out a small sigh that brought a darker frown to Sister Edna's face. Carlyn didn't care. She was weary of Sister Edna and questions and all of it.

She'd come here to disappear among the sisters and find the peace they claimed in their village. She felt anything but peaceful now, but she had little choice except to continue along the Shaker path and do as they told her.

Work with her hands and give her heart to the Lord. That she could do. And answer their questions. That she must do as well to help the sheriff find those responsible for the fire and Brother Henry's death.

"So what did you tell Sister Edna?" Sheriff Brodie asked.

"I've already told you that," Sister Edna said.

"Please, Sister, allow Mrs. Kearney to answer." Again the sheriff held his hand out to silence Sister Edna.

Carlyn was sorry he didn't use her given name again. Calling her by her married name seemed to keep her at a distance when she so desperately needed a friend. Elder Derron and Sister Edna might claim to be her friends, even a sister and a brother, but she felt no warmth from them. Sister Edna made no attempt to hide her disapproval, while the elder's mind appeared to be miles away as he stared down at his fingers spread out on his knees. Carlyn was tired of being alone.

Carlyn's mother's words slipped into her mind. *I will*

always be with you, my daughter, whether I am near or far, but even better you can count on the Lord to ever be with you.

As a child she had no trouble believing that, but somewhere along the way, she had lost the freshness of her faith. She still believed in the Lord. Of course, she did. But she was no longer a child, innocently expecting her every prayer to be answered as she wanted.

But have you reached for the Lord in prayer? She blocked her mother's voice from her mind. She could pray later. Now she had to answer the sheriff's questions. It was expected of her no matter how weary she was.

"Sister Edna demanded I tell her where I'd been. As she said, she suspected that I had purposely strayed down the wrong path, but I had not. While it is true I didn't tell her every word I heard, I couldn't see what that mattered since the words were confusing."

"That was for me to judge. Not you," Sister Edna said.

"Yea, I realize my wrong now." Carlyn unclasped her hands and smoothed down her apron. "So I told her I heard them arguing and that Curt was the man I owed money to on my house and that I was surprised to see him there in the village. Very surprised and also concerned he might have come looking for me."

The elder roused himself from silence. "Why would he do that, Sister? We paid your debt."

"I wasn't thinking clearly," she said.

"It is true that Mr. Whitlow is a hard man with whom to deal." Elder Derron spoke almost as softly as Carlyn. "And then did you return to your duty in the gardens?"

"Yea, after I answered Sister Edna's questions. She said

she would need to report what I'd seen to the Ministry after she talked to Brother Henry."

Sheriff Brodie sat back in his chair, seemingly content to allow the elder to ask the questions.

"Did you do that, Sister Edna? Did you talk to Brother Henry?" The elder's eyes went to Sister Edna.

The woman lifted her chin and met his look directly. "I did."

"I see." Elder Derron stared back down at his hands.

The sheriff broke the odd silence between the elder and Sister Edna. "What did he tell you, Sister Edna?"

"He told me I had no reason to be concerned. He assured me he would take care of the problems the man from the world was bringing to the village. He wanted to know which sister had been upset by their words so that he could apologize to her."

"Did you tell him?" Sheriff Brodie asked.

"Nay. I thought it unnecessary, as I could tell Sister Carlyn myself that she had no reason to be concerned." Sister Edna shot a look at Carlyn. "I had not yet had the opportunity to talk with Sister Carlyn about the matter. The fire took precedence."

"And proved that thinking there was no reason to be concerned might have been premature," Sheriff Brodie said.

Sister Edna turned to the sheriff. "The words between Brother Henry and the man she knew had nothing to do with our sister. It is for you to discover if this man had anything to do with Brother Henry's unfortunate passing."

"So it is." Sheriff Brodie sat forward again. "You can be sure I will talk to Mr. Whitlow, but first, I need whatever answers I might discover here."

"You are here to question Sister Carlyn, not me," Sister Edna said.

The elder raised his head to look at Sister Edna. "We are none of us on trial, Sister Edna. The sheriff is simply trying to find out what happened. You have said you talked to Brother Henry. So has the Ministry been informed?"

"I'm sure they know all that's happened. That is their duty, but I have not offered them a report. As you know, Elder Derron, first I must speak of the matter with Eldress Lilith."

"As you should." Elder Derron shifted his eyes away from Sister Edna to stare toward the window while he rubbed his hands up and down his thighs. "But worry not. Mother Ann will watch over us and make it possible to continue our work for the good of our Society."

"Engaged in our duties we have no reason to fear," Sister Edna said. "In our assigned, proper duties."

Carlyn looked up to see if she pushed those words at her, but the woman watched the elder. Outside, the bell sounded to signal the time for the evening meal.

Sister Edna stood. "Come, Sister Carlyn. We have told the sheriff what we know."

Carlyn got to her feet. She had to do what the sister said, no matter how reluctant she was to follow Sister Edna. She had thought she could be happy here. Or if not happy, then at least content. And safe. But perhaps it had been wrong of her to expect the village to supply more than her physical needs. The Shakers couldn't give her peace. That had to come from within.

Sheriff Brodie stood too and stepped between Sister Edna and the door. "One more question, Sister."

Sister Edna screwed up her mouth as though she wanted to refuse him, but instead she nodded once. "Then ask it."

"Did Brother Henry tell you the name of the other man? The one who had made the deal with Curt Whitlow?"

"I knew nothing about that. Sister Carlyn neglected to tell me there was such a deal. She only spoke of the devil." Sister Edna narrowed her eyes on the sheriff. "But then anytime we have to deal with someone from the world, we are dealing with the devil."

When she pushed past him, Carlyn followed her but dared a look up at the sheriff.

The ghost of a smile crossed his face, and he put his hand on her arm to delay her leaving. "If you remember anything else, Mrs. Kearney, please let me know."

"I will," she murmured. She wished she could remember more right then to have a reason to keep talking with him. But instead she stepped away from his touch and hurried after Sister Edna down the hallway past the winding stairs and out the front door.

Sheriff Brodie followed them out. Carlyn chanced Sister Edna's disapproval by turning her head to watch him ride away from the village.

The road beckoned her too. A way to freedom, to life again, while the path back to the Gathering Family House seemed a return to bondage. Bondage she had chosen, she reminded herself. She had cast her lot with the Shakers and she would have to accept their ways, no matter how odd they seemed.

20

~∾~

The Shakers weren't sorry to see Mitchell on his way out of their village. That was obvious from how they had a man waiting with his horse when Mitchell followed Sister Edna and Carlyn outside. He didn't have a chance to say anything more to Carlyn. The old sister made sure of that.

The Shakers were tired of his questions and doubtful the answers would help him apprehend those responsible for the fire.

Brother Thomas had summed up the Shakers' thinking before he ushered him to the Trustee House to meet with Elder Derron. "Whether you determine who set the fire or not matters little. The damage is done and cannot be reversed. Nay, it is our duty to continue on, sorrowful for the loss of our brother but without anger in our hearts. Such is our way."

"It's my job to find the responsible party," Mitchell said.

Brother Thomas looked sorry for Mitchell as he shook his head. "You must seek answers since that is the way of the world. But Mother Ann will bless us with new barns as long as we work faithfully with our hands and give our hearts to the Lord. The world cannot defeat us."

Mitchell wanted to ask if he thought Brother Henry would feel the same way if he had a voice, but some words were best unspoken. And perhaps Brother Henry wouldn't disagree.

But whether they wanted him to investigate or not didn't matter. Somebody had set the barn on fire. A man had died in that fire. He couldn't ignore that, even if the Shakers seemed willing to do so. Nor could he ignore the argument Carlyn had overheard between the Shaker man and Curt Whitlow. That complicated things and could mean the fire was more than an act of vandalism. Perhaps even murder.

Carlyn was telling the truth. He was certain of that, but he wasn't as sure about the older sister. She was hiding something. He had the same uneasy feeling about Elder Derron. Tension had crackled the air between the elder and Sister Edna while Carlyn answered his questions. Whether that had anything to do with the fire, he couldn't say. Not without talking to them again and pressing for answers.

First he would find Curt Whitlow. He'd make him tell his part in all this, even if he had to throw him in jail until he was willing to talk. Or better yet, he could take Asher with him when he confronted the man. Mitchell smiled. Not that he would really do that. Still, the dog might scare the truth out of him.

He hoped Mrs. Snowden hadn't gotten tired of Asher in her kitchen. Mitchell had been at the Shaker village hours longer than he'd expected to be, but when he rode out that morning, all he'd known was there had been a fire. The problem was he knew little more now.

He gave his horse his head and tried to sort through what

he knew. The Shakers were sorrowful over their brother's death while resigned to the loss of the barn. It had happened before. It would probably happen again. They were persecuted for separating themselves from the world and living their beliefs.

They were different. Unnatural is what Mitchell heard most from the townspeople. Sinful, others insisted, sure that things went on in the village far worse than mere shaking and dancing in their worship services. But Mitchell had yet to see any signs of that. Nobody was forced to stay at Harmony Hill. They could leave.

Carlyn could leave. She had no reason to be there. Shut away from the world. Shut away from him. Mitchell sighed. That was nothing more than wishful thinking. She had chosen to go to the Shakers.

Because of Curt Whitlow. The words slipped through his mind. The man had taken more than Carlyn's home from her. He'd taken her peace of mind. Just saying the man's name had brought fear to her face. Mitchell wanted to assure her he could protect her. But he had no right to say anything to her. She was a widow with no proof of widowhood and now she was a Shaker with no reason to seek that proof to free her for a new life. She had a new life already at the Shaker village. A life that closed all doors to the love Mitchell was imagining.

Without thinking, he tightened his hands on the reins. His horse slowed and tossed his head back.

"Sorry, boy." Mitchell patted the horse's neck. "I'll pay more attention. It's just that right now I don't know up from down." Mitchell settled deeper in his saddle. "Good thing nobody's around to see their sheriff blabbering like an idiot to his horse. What a woman can do to a man."

Hilda had never had him talking to himself. But he'd thought she was his. That it was just a matter of coming home from the war and starting their life together. By the time he knew that wasn't so, it was too late to do anything about it. She was married to another man. Nothing at all he could do to change things.

With effort, he had slammed the door on any feeling in his heart and moved on. The war was over. He was alive and didn't have an empty sleeve or trouser leg. He was one of the fortunate ones. But maybe losing that dream he'd carried through the war had bothered him more than he was willing to admit.

Maybe that was why he couldn't get Carlyn out of his mind. She was his dream come back to life. He had her dog, but he wanted her. And she needed him. She didn't need to be hidden away among the Shakers. She didn't need to be afraid of Curt Whitlow. Mitchell was going to see to that.

Night was falling by the time he got back to town. The few people on the streets raised their hands in greeting when they saw him. His town. His people. But the Shakers were his people too. He caught a whiff of smoke from his shirt, evidence of the Shaker's fire.

His stomach growled as he thought of the supper in Mrs. Snowden's warming oven, but it would have to wait. First he'd talk to Curt Whitlow and see if his clothes carried the same odor of smoke.

Curt's house was an imposing two-story brick square with large windows looking out on the world. A white-columned front porch gave the house a stately air. A swing graced one end of the porch and a bench and chairs the other end, empty now. Children's voices drifted out the open windows.

A homey sound that took Mitchell back to his own childhood days. Their father hadn't been an easy man, but they'd learned to work together. Brothers and sisters. Maybe the Shakers were on to something after all.

Mitchell hesitated to knock on the door and bring a stop to the untroubled sounds inside. Curt had a couple of boys already taller than him and three or four younger kids. The gossip around town said Curt paid scant attention to his family, but they sounded happy enough tonight.

Whether he spoiled their happiness or not, he had to talk to Whitlow. He rapped on the door and the talk inside abruptly stopped. When nobody came to the door, Mitchell knocked again. The silence continued, as though they hoped he would just go away. But a sheriff couldn't walk away from what had to be done, whatever trouble it brought to a family.

"Mr. Whitlow, it's Sheriff Brodie," he called loudly.

The oldest boy, the one called Junior, pulled the door open. He didn't smile. "My father isn't here."

"Then can I speak with your mother?"

The boy, thirteen or fourteen, appeared to share nothing with his father other than his name. He shifted uneasily on his feet but stayed where he was, blocking Mitchell from the house. "Mother's not feeling well. Is it important?"

Mitchell had the feeling Mrs. Whitlow was sitting right inside at the kitchen table hearing every word, but he didn't insist. "Don't bother your mother. It's your father I need to see."

The boy looked relieved. "I told you. He's not here."

"When do you expect him?"

"Hard to say. Pa's business can keep him away for days at times." It was plain the boy knew what kind of business that was and that he didn't care when or if his father ever came home.

"How long has he been gone?"

"He left day before yesterday. Something about collecting some debts. I don't know where he was going."

"Would your mother know?"

"No." The boy stated the word flatly, staring straight at Mitchell, wishing him off the porch.

Mitchell seemed to be losing his welcome everywhere this day. "You're the oldest, aren't you, Junior?"

"I'll be fourteen in January." Even that seemed more than the boy wanted to tell.

"Does your father ever take you along on his business trips?"

He almost smiled then. "No."

"I see." Mitchell kept a steady gaze on the boy.

"He'll be back sooner or later. He always is." The boy didn't sound glad about that.

Mitchell saw no reason to push him for more. The boy might be covering for his mother who didn't want to talk to the law, but he was telling the truth about not knowing where his father was. "When he comes home, tell him I want to talk to him."

"Why? Is he in trouble?" For the first time, the boy sounded curious about why Mitchell was looking for his father.

"I need to ask him about some trouble out at the Shaker village."

"He won't know anything about those people."

"You sound sure of that," Mitchell said.

"I am. Pa has no use for Shakers. Says they're half crazy and the other half miserly. Talking people into joining up with them to grab their land."

"They do have a lot of land." Mitchell felt a little ashamed to be egging the boy on for information, but he did it anyway.

"Pa says some of it they the same as stole from him."

"Oh? What property was that?"

"That Widow Kearney's house. He already had a buyer for it."

"Do you know who that was? The buyer?"

Color climbed up into the boy's cheeks as if he realized he was talking too much. He shook his head and stepped back to close the door. "I'll tell him you were here, but he won't know anything about those Shakers. Mama doesn't either. None of us know anything."

Mitchell didn't try to keep the boy from shutting the door. The kid didn't know about the fire. Or his father. *None of us know anything.* Mitchell was right there with them. He didn't know anything either. He'd just have to wait until Whitlow came home.

It had been a long day and Mitchell was ready for it to be over. He led the horse to the livery stable and then headed to the boardinghouse.

Stars were popping out in the sky. He stopped and looked up at them for a long minute. Familiar old friends. He'd spent many nights under them during the war, not sure if he'd meet his Maker before they spread across the night sky again. His mother had loved the stars. She would point out the brightest ones and give them names she'd learned from her father.

Mitchell remembered once pointing at other stars and asking their names.

His mother had laughed softly and put her arm around his shoulders. "I don't know them all. Who could? There are

208

more than the eye can see or the mind can count." She had gazed up at the sky for a long moment then. When she spoke again, it was with wonder in her voice. "But our God knows them all. The Bible says so. My father taught me this verse in Psalm 147:4. Now it's your turn to learn it. 'He telleth the number of the stars; he calleth them all by their names.'"

Mitchell didn't remember exactly how old he was at the time. Still a boy, but that night there by his mother, he got his first inkling of God's power as he stared up at the stars spread across the black sky. Able to number and name every star. And so, during the war when the world was exploding around him, he studied the stars above him and remembered that verse. If the Lord knew every star's name, he knew his. Whatever happened, however much Mitchell didn't know, God did know. Every star. Every sparrow that fell. Every answer.

It was just up to Mitchell to search out some of those answers before anything else bad happened. He started to walk on, but then he looked back up at the stars. He hadn't exactly left the Lord behind, but once the war was over, prayer hadn't seemed as necessary. He could handle things now. But maybe that wasn't true.

What was it he had read in a book about George Washington a few weeks ago? *It is impossible to rightly govern a nation without God and the Bible.* If old George thought that about running the country, then it might be just as important in keeping law and order in a town. Tonight he felt like he needed all the help he could get. Not only with figuring out who was responsible for Brother Henry's death but also with what to do about his heart speeding up just at the sight of Carlyn.

And while his first prayer should have been about figuring out the crime, instead his heart jumped ahead. "Please, Lord, either help me forget her or let her find out what happened to her husband. That way I can be about the business of keeping the peace," Mitchell whispered. Almost as an afterthought, he added, "You can help me with that too, Lord. I'm little better than a fish lost in a new lake, swimming this way and that with not the foggiest idea which way leads to the answers I need."

He felt better then as he walked on toward the boarding-house. He still didn't know any answers, but he could believe that in time he would. The kitchen windows spilled out light, giving him hope for supper.

Mrs. Snowden pulled open the door the minute his boots hit the back porch. Light spilled out behind her so he couldn't see her face well, but there was no mistaking the tears in her voice. "I'm so sorry, Sheriff. I didn't aim for it to happen. I've been watching for you for hours. Florence wouldn't have done it on purpose for nothing."

"Done what on purpose?" Mitchell stepped across the porch and Mrs. Snowden backed up to let him in.

"Asher. She opened the door to dump the mop water and he was gone before we could say boo." She wrung her hands up in her apron while new tears streaked down her cheeks.

"How long ago?" Mitchell looked behind him out at the dark yard. The empty yard.

"This afternoon. We went out and called and called, but he must have took off running. Florence and me, we walked to both ends of the town, but we didn't see hide nor hair of him, and I had to get back to put out supper for the boarders. I couldn't very well keep them waiting. They'd all be moving to Mrs. Wallace's down the road."

"I understand, Mrs. Snowden."

"I'm sorry as I can be." She swiped the tears off her cheeks with her apron tail. "I know you didn't want him running loose. And he'd been laying right in the corner there on that old blanket I put out for him all the livelong day. I never thought about him up and shooting out the door like that."

"Don't let it upset you. Asher will be fine." Mitchell patted her shoulder. He couldn't blame her. He should have locked the dog up. Or then, maybe it was better this way. Let the dog take his chances. "Could be, he'll get hungry and find his way back."

"You could call him. He might come to you."

Mitchell stepped back on the porch and whistled, but all that did was set a dozen other dogs barking in the yards up and down the street. Asher wouldn't come. He'd be back out at Carlyn's house by now and then who knew where after that.

"I'll hunt him in the morning," he told Mrs. Snowden when he went back in the kitchen.

"You really think he'll be all right? I know he's just a dog, but I can't help worrying over him. That Curt Whitlow won't do nothing to him, will he?" She got his supper out of the warming oven.

Where moments before he'd been starving, now his appetite was gone, but he sat down at the table anyway. "You don't have to worry about that. I was just over at Curt's and his boy said he's out of town on business."

"Some business." Mrs. Snowden snorted. She handed him a napkin. "Land's sakes, you smell to high heaven. Smoke from that fire out there at Shakertown, I'm guessing. Wasn't one of their big buildings, was it?"

"No, a barn."

"Lightning?"

"It doesn't look like it."

She sat down across from him. "What's this world coming to? Guess that's why you were out there so long. Did you see Carlyn Kearney? Find out how she was doing?"

"I saw her. She looked like one of the sisters."

"Is that so?" Mrs. Snowden shook her head slowly. "I just can't hardly believe that. She never seemed the Shaker type. But I guess as long as she's happy."

"I don't know that anybody was happy out there today. One of the brothers died in the fire." There wasn't any reason not to tell her. That kind of news would travel fast. In fact, it was surprising she didn't already know. Plenty of people from the farms around Harmony Hill were at the village and knew about Brother Henry.

Mrs. Snowden looked stricken. "Dear heavens, and here I am worrying over a dog. The Lord won't know what to think of me."

Or me, Mitchell thought as he shoveled a spoonful of beans into his mouth. But he couldn't help worrying about what he'd tell Carlyn about her dog when he saw her next if he couldn't find Asher once the sun came up. And he did intend to see her again whether he found the dog or not.

21

⁂

Carlyn pushed open her eyes when she heard the bell. She jerked up, fearful the sound signaled another fire. It couldn't be morning already, but daylight crept through the windows to prove it was. The bell demanded she get out of bed, but all she wanted to do was lie back, pull the cover over her head, and block out the day.

The night before, she'd lain awake for too many hours with thoughts and wonderings bombarding her. Who was responsible for the fire? If the Ministry had known about the argument between Brother Henry and Curt, would Brother Henry still be alive? Why hadn't Sister Edna reported it to them? Who was the other man? The one regretting his deal with Curt.

If she had taken the other path, the proper path back to the garden, she would have heard nothing. Then the fire very well might still have been set. Brother Henry might very well have perished with his horses, but there wouldn't be the unsavory cloud of suspicions settling down over the village like the lingering smoke from the fire. No one would have known about the argument. And she would not have seen Curt.

That didn't mean she wouldn't still be tormented by the thought of Brother Henry trapped in the fire with those poor horses. If she lived to be a hundred she would never forget that sound. But Curt Whitlow would have never entered her mind. She would have had no reason to worry about her own safety there in the village.

Sheriff Brodie said she still did not, but Sheriff Brodie wasn't at the Shaker village. He was miles away in the town. With Asher. Oh, how nice it would be to have Asher here by the bed, nudging her with his nose. How nice to never have had a war to tear Ambrose away from her. How nice to know what to believe.

Believe in the Lord. That was what her mother would tell her. She'd remind Carlyn that the Lord was the beginning and the end. If she wanted answers, that was where to go. *But what if he won't answer?* She was a little child again at her mother's knee.

"He always answers," her mother had told her. "But sometimes we must wait for the answer and sometimes we refuse to hear the answer because it's not the answer we want."

"But doesn't he want to give us good answers?"

"Assuredly. God is love. But he sees the whole woven fabric of our lives and not simply the few threads we are trying to twine together at the moment. Good and bad weave into the pattern of our lives. Together they make us strong and able to endure whatever must be endured."

Carlyn didn't remember now what childish problem she might have had then, but she did remember her mother's hand soft on her head as she told her to pray about whatever it was. If she were with her on this day, she'd tell her the same. That was her mother's answer to any need. Pray until an answer comes. Continually pull the rope on the bell that prayer rings in the Lord's ear.

So when she heeded the Shaker bell to rise as she must, she knelt by her bed for the morning's prayer. Many mornings she knelt without purpose other than to satisfy the Shaker rules, but this morning a prayer rose from her heart.

Lord, if there be answers I need, supply them and open my ears to hear them.

She stayed perfectly still for a moment as though she expected the answers to whisper through her thoughts immediately. No answer came. Instead it was as if she were with Sister Edna demanding that she not whisper words just for the sake of making noise, but to pull from within her what she wanted most to know.

The other sisters in the room had finished their morning prayers and were getting dressed, but Carlyn continued to kneel by her bed as she opened her heart to the Lord. She'd prayed that way before, entreating the Lord on behalf of Ambrose. But then she'd never been able to surrender the answer to the Lord. She didn't want to listen to any answer other than the one she begged for, even demanded from the Lord. Perhaps he would have already sent her an answer if she had stopped making demands and simply listened.

"Forgive me, Lord. I will listen. Guide me to the answers I need." She whispered the words under her breath and got to her feet.

She stripped off her nightgown and jerked on her dress, sure that at any second Sister Edna would be haranguing her for being so slow with her prayers. Patience was not one of Sister Edna's gifts. She wanted things done promptly and on schedule. Prayers were to be said in the time allotted. Food eaten without dawdling. Work done well, but with efficiency. Any lapses were to be confessed with alacrity.

Carlyn's fingers fumbled with the tie of her apron. She took a deep breath to steady her hands. If she got an earful from Sister Edna, then she would simply endure it. She managed the proper bow with her apron strings and stuffed her barely combed hair up under her cap as she shoved her feet into her shoes. It wasn't until she turned to line up with the other sisters to begin their morning chores before the morning meal that she noted the odd silence in the room.

While Sister Edna continually cautioned them against idle chatter, they rarely stayed completely silent as they readied themselves for the coming day. But now they were not only quiet, but appeared discomfited as well.

Sister Berdine stepped to the side and pointed toward Sister Edna. The sister was still in her nightgown as she knelt beside her bed. Carlyn couldn't see her face, but there was no doubt she was in an attitude of prayer. And even less doubt that seeing her thus while those in her charge were dressed and ready for her to hurry them out the door to begin their chores had left those charges speechless.

Sister Alice recovered her voice first, but she kept it low. "Sisters, let us be about our chores before the morning meal and not disturb our sister in her prayers."

Sister Edna spoke then, but kept her eyes on the wall beside her bed. "Yea, do as Sister Alice instructs. I will join you in due time." Her voice carried a tone of irritation with their dawdling, the same as any other morning.

With a quick glance at Sister Edna, the two youngest sisters who had kitchen duty scooted out the door. The other sisters followed behind them to clean rooms on the brethren's side of the house. With a little shrug of her shoulders, Sister Berdine shot Carlyn a sympathetic look before she left.

Carlyn's morning duty was sweeping their own sleeping room, so she was stuck in the room with Sister Edna. Carlyn had no idea what Sister Edna's duty was. Perhaps to climb to the top of the stairs and keep watch for wrong actions. Carlyn had seen her at the top of the steep stairs to the upper storage rooms more than once. The attic windows gave a good view of the village paths. It appeared there was no place to hide in the Shaker village.

But then nobody had seen whoever set the fire in the night. Darkness had hidden that evil.

Carlyn straightened her bedcovers and gathered the dirty clothing to carry to the laundry room, but first she needed to sweep every inch of the sleeping room. Sister Edna was continually telling them that good spirits couldn't live where there was even an iota of dirt. Carlyn took down the broom from one of the wall pegs. She tried to keep her eyes from Sister Edna's bed, but it was impossible not to be aware of the woman kneeling there.

Carlyn began sweeping at the back of the room, shifting aside each bed equipped with rollers to make the job easier. The broom straws against the wooden floor, a natural sound she normally would not have even noticed, sounded loud this morning. Everything felt strange without Sister Edna pointing out each speck of dirt she missed.

The woman had to be sick or perhaps unable to rise from her knees after kneeling so long. Hadn't Carlyn's knees felt numb earlier? The woman's pride might keep her from asking for help. Carlyn shifted aside another bed, swept under it, and pushed it back into place. The rollers rumbled against the floor. But that didn't keep her from hearing Sister Edna's sorrowful sigh.

Carlyn smoothed the covers on Sister Berdine's bed. She never got all the wrinkles out of her top cover. Another sigh that was almost a groan. Perhaps the Holy Spirit was praying for Sister Edna with unuttered words. But then, what if she was in pain and simply too prideful to ask Carlyn's help?

The room was only half swept, but Carlyn hung the broom on a peg. She could hardly get in any worse graces with Sister Edna. So if the older sister chased Carlyn away with pointed words, naught would be different in their relationship.

Even so, Carlyn stopped a few paces from Sister Edna and wished the broom back in her hands. What could she say to her? But the woman still wore her nightgown and the bell signaling the morning meal would sound at any moment. With her shoulders hunched over the bed, Sister Edna looked a different woman. Not so formidable. Even so, Carlyn couldn't imagine her desiring help from one so newly from the world. At times, Sister Edna had acted as though merely being close to Carlyn was reason to ask forgiveness for worldliness.

Carlyn pulled in a deep breath for courage and forced out the words. "Sister Edna, it is almost time for the morning meal." She practically tiptoed the rest of the way to the end of the woman's bed and peered at her.

A tear rolled down one of Sister Edna's cheeks and fell off her chin to make a damp spot on her gown. She didn't turn her head to look at Carlyn. "Prayers take precedence over food."

"Yea." Carlyn didn't know what else to say as she fingered her apron. Sister Edna looked older and more fragile without the armor of her Shaker dress. Her gray hair, always covered with a bonnet, was wispy and barely covered her scalp, and the skin on her neck was creased with age.

"Prayer takes precedence over chores as well, but as you don't appear to be praying, you'd best be about finishing your morning work." Irritation was plain in Sister Edna's voice.

That put Carlyn more at ease. This Sister Edna she knew. So she stayed where she was. "I'm almost finished. Except for under your bed." When the woman didn't say anything, Carlyn went on. "Do you need help getting up? My knees sometimes go numb when I kneel too long."

"Then you should pray more to toughen them up." Sister Edna did look at Carlyn then. "My knees have prayer calluses. I could kneel this way all day."

"Yea, well . . ." Carlyn started to turn away, but hesitated. She didn't know why, but she couldn't simply finish her chores and go out of the room. Not and leave the woman alone. Something was wrong with her whether she would admit it or not. "But you know Sister Marie. She's bound to need some help finishing her chores. And I might miss a rumple in one of the beds. Your eyes are better at seeing the proper way of things."

Carlyn couldn't believe she was actually asking for Sister Edna's criticisms, but instead of her words encouraging the sister to be up and about her duties, Sister Edna dropped her head back down.

"I have seen too much." Her voice was low and sad.

Carlyn didn't know what to say. "Should I go get Eldress Lilith?"

"Nay." Sister Edna repeated the word with vehemence. "Nay. I can't talk to her or the Ministry until I am sure."

"If you think that best," Carlyn murmured even as she remembered wondering if Brother Henry would have died in the fire if Sister Edna had reported the argument Carlyn had witnessed to those leaders. She stepped between the beds and touched Sister Edna's shoulder, and even though Sister Edna was not being her normal self, it surprised Carlyn when she jumped. But then, Carlyn didn't know that she'd ever touched the woman. Sister Edna always seemed to stand apart, coming near only to jerk a collar straighter or point out a wisp of hair escaping a cap.

It was Carlyn's turn to be startled when Sister Edna reached up and grabbed her hand. Carlyn managed not to jerk her hand free.

"Perhaps I do need help," Sister Edna said as she moved to stand.

Carlyn pulled her up. When the woman wobbled as though her legs were giving way, Carlyn put an arm around her and helped her turn to sit on the bed. The woman was very thin, something else her Shaker dress concealed.

"I did not think to get so old so quickly." Sister Edna let out a sigh as she stared straight in front of her.

"You're just feeling bad this morning. You'll feel better soon."

Sister Edna turned her eyes on Carlyn. "Empty words that mean nothing. You cannot know what troubles me and so you offer words as useless as a velvet hammer."

"You are right, Sister Edna. I am useless. Let me go find

Eldress Lilith." Carlyn started to turn away from the bed, but Sister Edna grabbed her hand again.

"Nay. There are things I am not sure of as yet." She dropped Carlyn's hand and gripped her own hands in her lap. "I have ever been sure of things. Of the best way. But now I cannot know. I need to know."

The bell began to ring signaling the morning meal. Carlyn made no move toward the door, but Sister Edna must have sensed her urge to follow the demand of the bell. "Go. Eat."

"Nay, I am not hungry." Carlyn stayed beside the bed in spite of her stomach growling.

Sister Edna almost smiled. "You do have a loose attachment to the truth, Sister Carlyn."

"I have often skipped meals," Carlyn said.

"Yea, that is why you came to us, is it not? For sustenance and security. It is plain to see that you have little interest in the Shaker way."

"I listen."

"Or pretend to, but you do not want to believe."

Sister Edna didn't sound irritated as she usually did when pointing out Carlyn's lackings as a Shaker novitiate. Instead she sounded as though whether or not Carlyn accepted the Shaker beliefs no longer mattered to her. Still, Carlyn tried to explain. "Your worship is much different from what I always knew at church."

"Work is worship." Sister Edna nearly lapsed into one of her Shaker sermons, but then seemed to catch herself. "That you may learn someday, but now, if you are not going to eat, stop towering over me. Sit down."

Carlyn gingerly sat down on the bed beside Sister Edna.

She knew nothing to say, but Sister Edna didn't need Carlyn's words.

"I can barely remember the time before I came to the village and became a Believer," Sister Edna said.

"But you said you had a family. A husband."

"It is true. I did have the sin of matrimony to overcome."

"Why do you think of marriage as sin?" Carlyn wasn't sure she should ask that, but it was the part of the Shaker life she least understood. It didn't bother her that the Shakers danced and spun with the fire of the spirit. It didn't bother her that they shared all in common. That seemed to work well in their village. But she couldn't understand why they couldn't have families as Carlyn thought the Bible ordered. Go and be fruitful. Cleave unto your wife. Wasn't that what the Lord ordered? "I always thought it a blessing to find a person to share life with."

"Did you find it such? With your husband in the world?" Sister Edna stared at Carlyn.

"I did. We were going to grow old together."

"And now you have many sisters and brothers to share life with."

"It's not the same," Carlyn said. "Did you not love your husband?"

"I found marriage tedious."

"Even in the beginning days of your union together?" Carlyn asked.

"That was so long ago, I cannot remember."

"Had you no children?"

"Yea, that I do remember. With sadness. Three. One gone at birth, two buried before they were six. Fevers. God's way of turning me to the Shaker way, the same as with Mother

Ann. She lost four babies in England. That's when the Lord directed her to separate from the world and lead us to love all only as brethren and sisters. Such it is in heaven, and our villages are sweet spots of heaven on earth." Her voice trailed off.

Then after a weary sigh, she began talking again. "At least that is what I always thought. If everyone followed the rules and stayed united in spirit and purpose, all would be well. Over the years, I took on the duty of seeing, of watching to be sure the Shaker way stayed pure. Those who transgress have no place in our Society. Or so I thought . . ."

"Everybody makes mistakes," Carlyn said.

"Yea, and those sins are to be confessed. Forgiveness is possible. Correction is necessary. Perfection is possible when one follows the rules."

"I don't think I could ever be perfect."

"But a true Shaker can be. It is my duty to show sisters like you the Shaker path and then watch to be sure you do not slip back into the sinful ways of the world." Sister Edna grasped Carlyn's arm as though holding her away from sin even as they sat on the bed together. "And now those of the world have come among us, poisoning us with the vipers of sin."

"You mean those who set the fire?"

"That and all that followed. And went before. The argument you heard. The lawman coming with his questions. He is insistent on finding answers whether we want them found or not."

"Why wouldn't you want the answers found?"

"Some answers are hard for one's ears to hear. You found that true in the world before you came into the village, did you not?"

"Yea. But I think I'd rather know the answers than to forever wonder."

"You speak of your husband who went to war and didn't return." Sister Edna breathed out a sigh. "The sheriff would like for you to know that answer as well. Your good looks have tempted him."

"Nay," Carlyn said quickly, but she knew it was true. Sheriff Brodie did look at her with favor. "He is merely a friend."

"Again you skirt the truth, Sister Carlyn. Not only is he tempted by you, but I fear you are tempted by him."

"Nay," Carlyn said again.

"Time will tell if you will withstand the temptation and pick up your cross and become a proper Believer. Now fetch me my dress. Enough of shirking our duties of the day. We must put our hands to work." As Sister Edna stood up, she squared her shoulders as though preparing for combat. Perhaps to battle against sin. "The truth will out. Whatever the result, the truth will out."

22

Mitchell was up before daylight, but Mrs. Snowden was already rattling pans in the kitchen when he came down the stairs.

"Land's sakes, you're up early. I haven't even got the coffee started yet, but I can fry an egg fast as anything." Mrs. Snowden wiped her hands on her apron and reached for a skillet.

Mitchell held up a hand to stop her. "I need to get going, Mrs. Snowden. A piece of bread and cheese will do."

"Bothered about that dog, are you?" She pulled the bread out of the bread box and sliced a thick chunk. "I went out back first thing I got up. Thought he might show up for his breakfast, you know, but didn't see him. 'Course it is still dark out there and that dog's the same color as night." She sighed again and wiped her eyes with the tail of her apron.

"It's all right, Mrs. Snowden." Mitchell patted her shoulder. "No need to get so worked up over a dog."

"I suppose not. Not with the worse things that happened

out there in that Shaker village. The fire and all. And a man dead." She looked over at him as she unwrapped a block of cheese. "In the light of that, it seems past foolish to shed tears over a dog, but I can't help wondering what might come of the poor animal. He was a dear old dog, and I feel bad letting him get away like that."

"It wasn't your fault. Asher's a smart dog. He was waiting his chance."

"He's off hunting his mistress, I'm guessing." She put the cheese on the bread and handed it to him. "Not much of a breakfast. Eggs would be no trouble and wouldn't take five minutes. The stove's done heating up."

"No, no. This is fine." Mitchell took a bite to prove it.

"Do you think he'll find her? The dog, I mean." She poured him a glass of milk.

"I wouldn't be surprised if he headed out to her house. If he doesn't show up around here, I'll ride out that way to look for him."

"I'll say a prayer for you, Sheriff. That you find Asher and whoever made the trouble out there at the Shaker town too." She pulled her biscuit bowl out of the cabinet. "Florence will be here later. I could send her down to your office with your lunch." She smiled over her shoulder at him. "A man has to eat."

"Don't bother with that. If I'm close by, I'll come in and grab a bite."

"You do that. Florence will want to tell you how sorry she is about Asher getting away. That girl has a heart of gold. And she's a good worker too." She pulled out the flour bin and scooped some into her bowl. "She's going to make somebody a fine wife someday."

226

"I'm sure she will." Mitchell chugged down the milk and put the glass on the table. "But a sheriff does best single."

"Single is no account. A man needs a woman to take care of him. Even those Shakers out there have womenfolk taking care of them, cooking their meals and washing their clothes. Not the way most men would want to live, I'm thinking, if you get my drift. But guess as how it works for them." She plopped a big chunk of lard into the flour. "Not the way somebody like you would want to end up. An old man with no sons to carry on your name."

"Now, Mrs. Snowden, you'd best use your matchmaking talents on somebody else. I'm not ready for settling down."

"Humph." She plunged her hands into her biscuit bowl and began working the lard into the flour with her fingers. "A man sees the right girl, he's ready in a shake of a lamb's tail. I've heard tell that happens now and again out there at the Shaker village too." She sent Mitchell another look over her shoulder. "Could be, pretty Carlyn will be turning one of those Shaker men's eyes."

"Or a dozen of them." Mitchell managed a laugh as he went out the door, but it was forced. He didn't want to think about Carlyn turning any man's eyes, because the truth was, she'd already turned his. Mrs. Snowden was right. If Carlyn gave him any encouragement, he would be ready. More than ready.

That was why he had to find Asher. So she'd have a reason to talk to Mitchell. So he could hang on to hope that maybe someday, if she found out her husband had been killed in the war, then she might eventually look at Mitchell with favor. A lot of ifs and maybes, but he didn't want to deny their possibilities. Nor did he want to tell Carlyn he'd lost her dog.

He should have asked Mrs. Snowden for one of yesterday's biscuits in case he caught sight of Asher in the dawning light. Not that he really expected to.

Even so, his heart lifted a little as he headed down the last stretch of walkway to his office. But no dog was curled in front of the door or anywhere around the building. He went back up the street and down it again, searching through the shadows. He even walked around the Whitlow place as the sun came up, but while the dog next door raised a ruckus, Mitchell didn't see any sign of Asher.

On the way back to his office, a few men stopped him to ask about the fire. He told them what happened without elaborating, then noted what they had to say. A man could learn some unexpected things by listening even if what was said wasn't exactly backed up by fact. A wisp of smoke instead of a whole cloud of it still indicated a fire somewhere.

At the office again, he found a note to go see the judge about a case coming up. By the time he was finally free to ride out to Carlyn's place, the sun was high in the sky.

He was almost to the livery stable when Sam Duncan reined in his horses and called to him from the seat of his farm wagon. "Sheriff, glad I found you."

"What's got you in town on a Wednesday, Sam?" Mitchell shaded his eyes against the sun and looked up at him. The man's mouth was turned down and his eyes tight. "Something wrong?"

"Somebody made off with three of my cows. Stole them right out of my barn lot last night. Went to milk and they was gone. I come after you to track down the rustlers 'fore the trail gets cold."

"You sure they didn't just break down the fence and

wander off?" Mitchell had investigated several stolen cow cases that turned out to be nothing more than strayed cattle.

"They didn't break through my fences, Sheriff." The farmer's face tightened into an even fiercer frown. "Somebody took them, and we're wasting time sitting here talking."

There was nothing for it but to get his horse and follow the farmer out to his place clear on the other end of the county. Whether it turned out the cows were standing at the barn door when they got there or not, that was his job. Looking for dogs would have to wait.

Riding back to the Shaker village would have to wait too. He had crimes to solve there, but first he'd have to chase down Sam Duncan's cows.

What he really needed to be chasing down, or who, was Curt Whitlow. Mitchell was sure the man could give him some answers. But Mitchell would have to find him first. He had too much to find. Curt. The person or persons who burned down the Shaker barn. Asher. Maybe even his heart that he'd lost to the woman Asher was surely trying to track down.

All that would have to wait. Somebody had to go find Farmer Duncan's cows, and Mitchell was the only somebody available. Perhaps it was time to hire a deputy.

23

❧

The truth will out. Sister Edna's words kept circling in Carlyn's head all through the morning. After their garden duty ended, she and Sister Berdine had been assigned to the washhouse. Mountains of soiled sheets, towels, and clothing waited to be washed. At least the Shakers had wash mills, large water-powered wooden contraptions that did the scrubbing and saved the sisters' knuckles. Even so, the loads of wet clothes had to be transferred from tub to tub. The splash of the water and the slap of material gave little opportunity for talk among the workers.

But when they went outside to hang the clothing on lines strung behind the washhouse, Sister Berdine carried her basket to the line near Carlyn. After a look behind her to be sure no one was paying attention, she asked, "What happened? When you didn't show up for the morning meal, I feared Sister Edna might have locked you in the dressing room or something."

Carlyn draped a sheet across the line and smoothed out

the damp cloth before she pinned it. The wooden pins were another Shaker innovation, according to Sister Alice.

"I don't think there are locks on the inner doors," Carlyn said.

"Something delayed you."

"We were talking, so when the bell rang, I had not finished my chores."

"Talking?" Sister Berdine made a face. "You mean she was browbeating you."

"Nay. Sister Edna told me to go on to the eating room, but I didn't think I should leave her alone until she got off her knees. She is getting up in the years."

With a snap, Sister Berdine shook out a towel to pin on the line. "I can't believe you sound almost sorry for her." She reached for another towel. "That woman has done everything possible to make your life here miserable."

"She does cling to the rules." Carlyn pulled a pillowcase out of the basket. It was good to be outside. The sun was warm on her face and the fresh smell of the laundry filled her nose. Small, ordinary pleasures. Maybe that would be where she would find her happiness from now on. A piece of apple pie. The feel of dirt in her hands. Warm water for a bath. The smile of a friend. Simple things.

That was one of the Shaker songs she was learning in the practice sessions. *'Tis a gift to be simple. 'Tis a gift to be free.* Was that the truth she was supposed to find?

"So she was telling you the rules." Sister Berdine hung another towel on the line and turned back to Carlyn, doubt evident in every word.

"Nay. She was not herself. She was worried about something, but didn't say what." Carlyn shifted to the side to let

231

the wind blow the wet sheets away from her. "Perhaps we have misjudged her."

"Right. And Shakers don't whirl when they dance." Sister Berdine laughed. "That sister takes pleasure in every wrong she catches us doing because it makes her feel that much holier when she can point out how unholy we are. I can't imagine what she could have told you to make you miss breakfast and now defend her even when her ears aren't listening."

"I'm not defending her. Just telling you what happened."

"What I think must have happened is that you went back to bed and had a most interesting dream," Sister Berdine said.

"I did want to pull the covers up over my head when the rising bell rang this morning. Dream more." Carlyn looked over at Sister Berdine pinning a shirt to the line. "If you could dream whatever you wished, what would you dream?"

"That's easy. I'd dream a handsome man would ride through Harmony Hill, take one look at me, and decide he couldn't live without me." Sister Berdine sighed and held a handkerchief next to her cheek before she draped it over the line.

"Sounds like a fairy tale," Carlyn said.

"That it does." Sister Berdine grabbed another shirt out of her basket. "And one that's not likely to come true."

"What about that brother you said was watching you at the meetings?"

"That one?" A little color bloomed in Sister Berdine's cheeks. "He's not exactly Prince Charming, but he's not so bad."

"You sound like you've talked to him."

"We've met a few times."

"Met?" Carlyn stared over at her. "How?"

"There are ways if a person is determined." Sister Berdine wouldn't meet Carlyn's eyes.

"Are you thinking of leaving?"

"A girl can dream, can't she?" Sister Berdine sighed.

"But what would I do without you here to talk to?"

"Talk to Sister Edna, I suppose." Sister Berdine grinned across the line at her. "I think I have as much to worry about on that count as you. What with the way that sheriff was looking at you yesterday morning before Sister Edna messed things up. He has no problem filling the handsome prince role. Is he married?"

Now the color bloomed in Carlyn's cheeks. "He's not, but I was." Carlyn corrected herself. "I am." She pinned another pillowcase to the line. It was surely a betrayal of Ambrose to even think about the sheriff, and yet the thought was there. Sister Edna was right. She was entertaining sinful thoughts.

Sister Berdine reached between the lines to touch Carlyn's hand. "It is not wrong to be lonesome, my sister. I know the feeling well, and it must be doubly hard for you to have known love and lost it."

"But I can't be sure he's lost." Carlyn pulled her hand away from Sister Berdine and took another sheet from her basket.

"There are many things we cannot be sure of." Sister Berdine ran her hand along the wet clothes. "Whether we will be given breath to live through the day to bring in these clothes after they dry. Whether a rain cloud will appear to delay the drying."

Carlyn looked up at the blue sky. "There are no clouds."

"Yea, and we look to the promise of another day with the need for clean clothes, but do you not think Brother Henry was doing the same before the fire took his life? We face an unknown future." Sister Berdine gave her a sympathetic look. "And with your husband you are burdened with an unknown past as well."

"It would be easier to know. At least to be sure of what has already happened."

"Yea."

Carlyn smoothed out the sheet. "I prayed for answers."

"Then I will join my prayers to yours." Sister Berdine looked up with that smile that meant she was about to say something a Shaker sister should not say. "And you can join yours to mine that Brother Payton becomes more courageous and a bit, just a bit, better looking."

"Looks are not everything."

"Indeed." Sister Berdine reached for a clothespin. "So concentrate your prayers on the need for courage. For all of us." She nodded her head toward the washhouse. "We may need it posthaste. Sister Edna is headed our way. I fear we have been caught exchanging too many pleasantries."

They both snatched up something to hang on the line. By the time Sister Edna was near enough to speak to them, Carlyn's basket was empty and Sister Berdine's almost so. But that didn't change the frown darkening Sister Edna's face.

"The sun only shines for so many hours a day, Sisters. It is best to get the laundry hung on the lines with diligent efficiency to take advantage of those hours." Sister Edna appeared to be back to her normal self.

"Yea, Sister Edna." Sister Berdine managed to look contrite as she hung up the last shirt in her basket. "We will hasten our labor."

"Yea," Carlyn murmured in agreement as she started toward the washhouse.

"Give your basket to Sister Berdine, Sister Carlyn. She will have to work doubly quick. Elder Derron has need to speak with you," Sister Edna said. "Immediately."

"Has Sheriff Brodie returned with more questions about the fire?" Carlyn was ashamed at how her heart lifted at the thought of seeing the sheriff.

Sister Edna's eyes narrowed on Carlyn. "I am not privy to the elder's reasons for sending for you. I have been told to bring you to the Trustee House. So that is what I will do." Her words were clipped as if each cost her effort. Dark shadows lined her eyes and her hands were trembling. When she saw Carlyn looking at them, she thrust them out of sight under her apron and turned away. "Come. It is our duty to do as our leaders ask."

Carlyn handed her basket to Sister Berdine with a shrug and hurried after the other woman. When she caught up, she asked, "Elder Derron is not one of the Ministry, is he?"

"Nay, but they appointed him to oversee much of the financial workings we have with those of the world. It is a position of much import. And danger."

"Danger?" Carlyn asked.

"The ever necessary exposure to those of the world. Such worldliness can rub off on a person if he lets down his guard."

"Elder Derron seems very devout."

"I did not say he wasn't." Sister Edna slowed her pace to send Carlyn a pointed look. "I merely said worldly temptations might be stronger on a brother or sister who is continually exposed to such. You should understand that since you are struggling to give up your own worldly thinking."

"Yea." She should be like Sister Berdine and simply agree with whatever Sister Edna said, but then she went on. "I hope it's not Sheriff Brodie with more questions."

"Are you being truthful, Sister Carlyn?" Sister Edna turned to look at her again. "Moments ago you sounded eager at the thought the sheriff might be the reason you were called from your duties."

"Yea, I am telling the truth. It is better if I do not see the sheriff again." Carlyn ignored how that thought pushed tears toward her eyes. "Much better."

"I do not know the reason the elder wishes to see you, but temptations do fall into our paths at times even here in our heaven on earth. That is why one must be vigilant and why there are watchers to keep those tempted to stray away from the slippery paths of sin." She put her head down and began to walk faster. "Rules are good and necessary. Mother Ann rewards those who learn the rules and do not stray."

She sounded more as though she were trying to convince herself than Carlyn, so Carlyn followed along without speaking. It was plain the worries bothering the sister that morning were still trailing along after her.

No horse was tied to the hitching post in front of the Trustee House, and even while Carlyn breathed easier, a finger of regret poked her at the same time.

Sister Edna climbed the steps, pulled open the door, and hurried past the whirling stairways to Elder Derron's office as though the midday bell was already sounding and she feared they would miss another meal.

Carlyn wasn't sure of the time. Clocks were scarce in the village. The days were ruled by the ringing of the Centre House bell. A worker was not to be forever watching the time.

But she judged it was barely past ten. Unless the sheriff was there, they had little worry of being delayed long by Elder Derron. He would state his business with her and release them back to their duties. She had no idea what he could have to say of such import to interrupt their workday. Such was not the Shaker way.

Elder Derron turned from his writing desk when they entered the room. Sister Edna inclined her head, but said nothing. Two chairs were already down from the peg strip and placed a respectable distance from the elder.

Sister Edna sat down and pointed Carlyn to the other chair. At last she spoke. "We have come as you requested."

"Yea, I will not long keep you from your work."

"Does it concern the fire?" Sister Edna stared across the space at the elder, her impatience not quite concealed.

"Nay, this is a different matter." The elder shifted his eyes from Sister Edna to Carlyn as he picked up an envelope and held it in the air. "We have received a letter from Brother Josiah who is on a trading trip to the south."

"So what has that to do with Sister Carlyn?" Sister Edna demanded.

"Quite a lot actually." The elder leaned forward in his chair. "Quite a lot. Do you know Brother Josiah, Sister Carlyn? He has often been out in the world selling our products both near and far."

"Nay, I don't think so." Carlyn shook her head slightly.

"Even so, Brother Josiah remembered your husband."

Sister Edna spoke up. "Not her husband now. She forsook that union when she came among us."

"I fear he forsook it first." The elder waved the envelope. "I think you told us your husband—" he hesitated and adjusted his words—"your husband in the world was missing in the war. I have heard, oftentimes, the army considers that to mean a man deserted his company."

"Ambrose would not have deserted." Carlyn defended his good name.

"You are right." He indicated the letter in his hand again. "This letter proves that."

Carlyn barely kept from standing and snatching the letter from the elder. "Is it from the government?"

"Nay, it is from a woman Brother Josiah met on his trading trip. Ida Mae Watkins. She lives on a small plantation close to a battlefield. A couple of days after the battle there, her servants found your husband in her orchard, wounded and out of his head from a fever. In spite of his Yankee uniform, she took pity on him."

"Can I not read the letter for myself?" Carlyn felt as though her heart was being squeezed.

"Certainly." But the elder did not hold the letter out to her. "It merely seems expedient to tell you parts of it first."

"Then tell me the part I need most to hear. Whether my husband is alive." Carlyn was breathless at the thought.

"Nay, Sister. Mrs. Watkins claims to have done all she could for him, but just when she thought he was on the mend, he took a turn for worse and passed on to his eternal reward."

Carlyn bent her head, the sure truth of Ambrose's death like a knife twisting in her heart. "Why did she not let someone know?"

"She was afraid to post a letter to the North. She feared what her neighbors would think if they knew she had cared for one of the enemy, and then even after the war with her sons home from fighting with the Rebels, the secret seemed better kept." Elder Derron paused. "She didn't consider the pension she was denying you by not reporting your husband's death."

"Pension?" Sister Edna said.

"Yea, worldly money, but nevertheless useful in our society since it is not hoarded by one but used for the good of all." Elder Derron looked pleased as his eyes landed on Carlyn. "The Eternal Father gives us blessings in many ways when converts such as you, Sister Carlyn, join our society."

A pension. What the elder called worldly money could be a doorway for her to leave the Shaker village and return to that world, but Carlyn couldn't think about that now. Sorrow swamped her mind at the greater truth of Ambrose for a certainty never coming home.

"Please, let me see the letter." She needed to read the words with her own eyes.

At last he handed it to her. She stared down at the unfamiliar writing. The writing of this Ida Mae Watkins, she supposed. Carlyn had prayed for answers, and now hours later, she held them in her hands.

"Aren't you going to read it, Sister Carlyn?" Sister Edna asked.

"I would rather do so alone, even though Elder Derron has told me much of what it says already."

"Those in the Ministry examine all letters to be sure they are not damaging to our Shaker family," Sister Edna said.

"But can I not have a few moments alone?" The envelope seemed warm in her hands.

In spite of her evident curiosity, Sister Edna stood up. "Come, we will find a place."

Elder Derron also stood. "You may stay here. I have things to do outside. Sister Edna can wait for you in the hallway."

Sister Edna's face turned stony as she turned to the door. "As you wish, Elder." She looked back at Carlyn. "Do not take overlong, Sister. The sheets will not get dry without hands to put them on the line."

"But there are many hands, Sister Edna," Elder Derron said. "Many hands make the work easy."

"But each pair of hands must do their part," Sister Edna said. "Such is expected."

Carlyn was glad when the door closed behind them. The silence of the room wrapping around her was somehow comforting. She whispered a prayer of thanks for the answer the Lord had sent her in case she would be unable to summon up thankfulness after reading whatever words were there on the letter.

Her fingers trembled as she pulled out the top sheet of paper. Another letter, the paper yellowed with age, remained in the envelope.

> *Dear Mrs. Kearney,*
>
> *First I must beg your forgiveness for not sending this sooner. But it was wartime and I feared the repercussions that might come if it was discovered I had harbored a Union soldier. Compassion is in short supply in our town for those of the North, but I did feel compassion when I discovered your wounded husband in my orchard. His unit had moved on without him. Not intentionally, I am certain, but in battle, many soldiers are lost. I thought of my own sons, perhaps wounded and lost in some Northern state and I could do no less than*

open my heart and care for this unknown Yankee.

I washed and bandaged your husband's wounds and kept cool compresses on his head. Those first days he went from unconscious to delirious and I feared he would pass from life without ever opening his eyes and speaking his name. My servants searched the area, but could not find his knapsack or even his gun. All must have been lost on the battlefield.

After a week, his fever abated and he came back to consciousness. For three days he talked to me about his life. About you. He loved you very much. Then, in spite of my best efforts, the wound went septic. The fever returned and swept his life away in the dark of the night. I am truly sorry, Mrs. Kearney. My servants and I laid him to rest in a place we thought would not be discovered and watered his grave with many tears. Before he passed on to his heavenly reward, which I am sure was great as he told me how deeply he trusted the goodness of our Lord, he wrote a letter to you.

Again I apologize for being fearful to post the letter. First there was the war and then once it was over, my sons had such antagonism for anything Northern, I thought it best not to reveal my role in harboring one of their enemy. I shall have to beg our Creator for mercy for that lack of courage. That is why I was overjoyed to see the answer to my prayers

*when the Shaker trader came to our town. Your
Ambrose had told me the two of you lived near
a village of such people. I think the Lord let my
path cross Brother Josiah's just so that I could
finally forward this to you. Brother Josiah is
waiting in the town for my letter. One of my
faithful servants will deliver it to him and then I
will pray that it is delivered you.*

*May God bless you and comfort your grief.
A grief I understand all too well since I lost my
own husband in the war.*

Your sister in grief,
Ida Mae Watkins

Carlyn looked up from the woman's neat script and stared
across the room toward the window. She did not see the sunlight streaming through the glass. She didn't see the leaves
turning red on the trees outside. She saw Ambrose as she
had not been able to pull him out of her memory for many
weeks. Smiling. Ever joyful even when he was working to
clear ground to plant corn behind their house.

She very gently pulled Ambrose's letter from the envelope.
One of the last things he touched with the hands she loved.
The gold locket she had given him the day he left fell out of the
letter. With trembling fingers, she opened the catch. The locket
was empty. The strands of her hair she'd curled inside it gone.

She shut her eyes a moment. She did not want to weep.
Not yet. With a deep breath, she unfolded the letter to see
Ambrose's writing looping across the page. He could not
write small. He did everything large, even loving her.

My beautiful Carlyn. I am dying. Mrs. Watkins kindly tells me that is not so, but I see the truth in her eyes and feel the grip of death pulling me toward the grave. My only sorrow is the thought of never again holding you in my arms. But heaven awaits and someday I will see you again. Until then, live your life with joy. There is no limit to love so there is no need to be miserly with your feelings as your father is, but embrace the gifts the Lord offers so freely to his children. I mourn the family we will never have. But believe this through your tears. I release you to find another man to love and sire the children we dreamed of having. In some way, through the memory of the love we shared, those children will be mine as well.

My strength is ebbing. But know I loved you with every inch of my being. I have asked Mrs. Watkins to send you this letter and the locket, but she has promised to put the strands of your hair over my heart before I go into the grave. My last prayer will be for your happiness and your name will be on my last breath.

Your loving husband

She placed her fingers over those last words. Her husband. Tears spilled out of her eyes then. She was truly now the Widow Kearney.

24

❧

Carlyn read the letter again. Ambrose's last words of love to her. Such a good man. A man ruled by love. Of the Lord. Of her. Of country. He'd given his life for that country.

She could no longer deny the truth of that as she had tried to do for so long. He was buried on a plantation in the South. Carlyn would never plant flowers on his grave as a widow should. She held the locket up against her cheek and wet it with tears.

The bell signaling the noon meal jerked Carlyn back to the present. She stared around at Elder Derron's office as though seeing it for the first time. The tall windows. The desk with inkwell and pen waiting. The pegs on the railing circling the room. The chair hung on those pegs with the legs pointed toward the ceiling. Sister Edna must have hung her chair on its pegs before she left the room. Sister Edna. She would be waiting in the hallway, tapping her foot with impatience.

Carlyn carefully folded the letters and secreted them in

her pocket along with the locket. Whatever the rules, she would not part with Ambrose's last missive to her. Carlyn braced for battle over keeping the letters when she went out into the hallway. Sister Edna was at the foot of the sisters' winding stairway, holding to the railing, her head bent in an attitude of prayer.

Carlyn hesitated, reluctant to disturb her, but Sister Edna looked up. "The bell rings. We must hurry." She made no mention of the letters or of Carlyn's tearstained cheeks as she turned toward the door.

"May I return to my room instead of going to the eating room?" Carlyn followed after her.

Sister Edna paused with her hand on the door handle. She kept her eyes on the door as she answered. "Nay. You missed the morning meal. It would not be good to miss the midday meal as well. A Shaker has to take care of her body and continue to abide by the established schedules no matter how heartsick."

"But I—"

"Nothing is gained by resisting the rules that keep us ordered and in unity. Our duty is to eat the food prepared by our sisters. Such is necessary to keep up our strength." She pulled open the door and stepped out into the sunshine.

Carlyn stayed where she was. She could flee down the hallway. Find a different door. Find a place to be alone.

Sister Edna looked back at her. "Come, Sister Carlyn. We are sisters. We cannot run from our destinies." Sister Edna looked as sad as Carlyn felt. She reached a hand out toward Carlyn. "Without obedience, our Society will collapse. We must obey the rules."

"Perhaps the rules are wrong," Carlyn said.

"Nay." Sister Edna's voice was not much more than a whisper. "Nay. Our Mother Ann made the rules and Father Joseph who followed after her. I have ever clung to the rules and ensured others did as well by watching."

"But rules can be broken. It would seem better to be ruled instead by the love of God in our hearts." Carlyn put her hand over her pocket to feel Ambrose's letter. He had been ruled by the love of God.

"When rules are broken, confession can be made and atonement. One does not have to continue to slide down the slippery slope of sin to destruction." Sister Edna's face looked pale in the bright noon light. "They do not." As if she'd said the final word on the matter, she turned and went down the steps.

The Shaker sister was drawn by the bell. Controlled by the rules. Yet, she was not herself. Something seemed to be bearing down on her soul. Something more than her duty to see that Carlyn followed her to the eating room.

At the gate in the plank fence in front of the Trustee House, Sister Edna looked back and motioned with impatience for Carlyn to follow. Carlyn did. Her life too seemed bound by must-dos, for however much she did not want to entertain the thought of eating at this moment, she knew that would not last. Her stomach would demand food. She would need shelter from the winter cold. The pension the elder mentioned might change her ability to supply those for herself, but who knew how long it would be before she could do whatever necessary to receive that money? Weeks? Months?

Until then, the Shaker village supplied the necessities of life. Happiness was not a necessity of life. Had not her father lived many years without showing evidence of knowing one happy moment? At the same time, Ambrose had a way of cupping the glow of happiness in his hands and sharing it with those around him.

Now, he was gone. She'd known it must be so, but the surety of his words in the letter in her pocket awoke the sadness she had walled away from her heart. She could not follow after Sister Edna as though nothing had changed, yet that is what she did.

She lined up with the other sisters to go into the eating room. She knelt for the silent prayer. She stood with her hand on the back of her chair waiting for the moment when all sat down at the same instant. She stared at the bowls of food in front of her plate without making the first move to dip any portions out on her plate. She could not eat even if her stomach was empty. Instead she bowed her head and let the tears slide off her cheeks and drop on her hands folded in her lap. And she was glad for the silence of those sitting at the tables around her.

Some cast curious glances her way, but she doubted if it was the first time a sister sat at the Shaker table with tears wetting her face. A sister gave up much to live the Shaker life. Her spouse beside her. Her children nestled in her lap. Her own kitchen floor to sweep. Her freedom to choose her own way for even an hour of the day. Her dog.

Sister Berdine chanced Sister Edna's wrath by reaching over to touch Carlyn's arm. Carlyn gave her hand a fleeting squeeze as she peeked across the table at Sister Edna, expecting a look of daggers. But instead, Sister Edna was moving around the chunks of potato she had dipped out on her plate as if she had not figured out how to capture them with her fork. At last she did stick them in her mouth where she chewed with dogged determination but no sign of pleasure. She did not once look at Carlyn.

In the days to come, Carlyn would eat like that. She would satisfy her body's need for food. She would do what had to be done. Was that not why she was sitting at the Shaker table? Following rules.

At last the meal was over. They filed out as silently as they had come into the eating room. Sister Berdine stepped up beside her as they made their way outside to the privy before returning to their afternoon duty. More laundry to gather and fold. More tubs to fill. More tubs to empty. Was that life? An endless round of filling and emptying?

"What is wrong, Sister Carlyn?" Sister Berdine looked at her with concern.

Carlyn pulled in a breath and released it as they waited in the back of the line for their turn. "My husband is dead."

Sister Berdine wrinkled her forehead in puzzlement. "Didn't you already tell me that was so?"

"I did think it was probably so, but I had no proof. Now I do. A letter from him and one from the person with him when he died." Carlyn blinked to keep back new tears, but a few spilled from her eyes anyway. She squeezed Sister Berdine's hand. "Don't worry about me. The tears will stop. It's just that reading Ambrose's last words of love to me has put my feet on a path of sadness."

When at last they had their turn in the privy and came back outside, all the other sisters were gone to their assigned duties. Sister Berdine started off down the path toward the washhouse, but Carlyn didn't follow.

Sister Berdine looked back. "Aren't you coming?"

"I will beg forgiveness for my dawdling later, but I need time alone. I already told Sister Edna that."

"And she agreed?" Sister Berdine raised her eyebrows at Carlyn.

"Nay. She sees no excuse to shunt aside our duty."

"Then she'll be angry."

"That may be. But she is not herself today. She may hardly notice."

"That I would not depend on, but then what can she do other than browbeat us with her words?" A smile slid across Sister Berdine's face. "I will go with you."

Carlyn shook her head so quickly her cap slid sideways. She straightened it as she said, "You are a good friend, but this is a path I must walk alone."

Sister Berdine's smile faded. "I understand. I will do what I can to keep your absence hidden from Sister Edna. The washhouse has many corners and sundry duties."

"It's better not to lie. Sister Edna will know the truth anyway. There are probably watchers seeing us right now." Carlyn raised her eyes to the third-floor windows of the Gathering Family House up ahead of them. "The truth will out."

Those words echoed in her head once again as she left Sister Berdine on the path and moved away from the shadow of the buildings. When she crossed into the open field behind the Gathering Family House, she breathed easier. It was good to leave behind the Shaker rules and duties. She would have to go back, but at least for a few hours, she would shake free of the shackles of life's necessary bonds and think of nothing but what had been and what might have been.

On the far side of the field, she found a stile to climb over the fence and then was glad to step into the woods. The day was not hot, but even so, she needed the shadows. Some of the trees still held their leaves, while others had shaken them down to the ground to make a rustling carpet of red and gold. It felt right to walk through the leaves, stirring them as she went. They showed the cycle of life. Death now as the leaves dried and crumbled, but come spring, the trees would bring forth green again. Life would start afresh.

Ambrose had already begun his new eternal life. She was in a village that purported to be heaven on earth, but Ambrose had crossed the divide and was experiencing glory with no concern for rules and duties. His smile would be lighting up his corner of heaven just as it would always light up a special place in Carlyn's heart.

She sat down on a tree stump and read through both letters again. The words wrapped around her and comforted her. She had no idea how much time passed. It seemed the perfect amount. Then in the distance she heard a dog barking that made her think of Asher. It was only a short jump from Asher to Sheriff Brodie.

No guilt rose in her heart when the sheriff's face came into her thoughts. He was kind to take Asher, but in spite of what Sister Edna and Sister Berdine said, he had offered nothing more. She had not expected more.

The dog sounded so much like Asher that Carlyn looked toward the east, the direction of her house. No longer her house, but it didn't matter. Even if she did stand up and walk the miles back to that place, she would not find the happiness she longed for.

She had nothing. Not even the peace she had expected to find in the Shaker village. Instead, troubles found the Shakers in Harmony Hill the same as at any place, whether the rules were followed or not. Carlyn sighed at the thought of some of that trouble waiting for her when she returned to the village. Happiness seemed as fleeting as a butterfly on the wing. Something that might hover around a person and then without warning flutter away. But sadness seemed to soak into one like a cold rain that left shivers and the ague.

Pray anyway. That was her mother's answer to every part of life. Joy or sorrow. Peace or war. Plenty or want. And hadn't the Lord answered her prayer when she'd given herself over to accepting the truth?

The truth will out. Sister Edna had not been talking about Carlyn's wish to know about Ambrose. She had been troubled by other things. Unnamed things that she must not be able to control by obedience to the rules. Life could not always be ordered.

Pray anyway. Carlyn could almost feel her mother's hand on her shoulder and so she bent her head and prayed as the Shakers did. Without spoken words as she let the desires and sorrows of her heart rise up.

She was startled from those prayers by the sound of a horse and rider crashing through the woods. She leaped to her feet. She had no idea she was near any kind of trace, but she caught a glimpse of the horse through the trees. Her heart bounded up in her throat as she remembered the last time a horse and rider came up on her unaware. That didn't mean this rider was Curt Whitlow or anyone else who meant her harm, but it seemed wisest to slip out of sight behind a tree.

After the rider was gone, Carlyn leaned against the tree and waited until her breath came easy again. Then she turned back to the Shaker village. As she walked, she tried to come up with acceptable words to confess her dereliction of duty.

Once out of the trees, she could see the buildings of the Shaker village across the pasture. Sturdy. Strong against the winds of nature. But what of the winds of man?

She had to go back to the Shaker village at least for now, but each step was forced. Each step was taken with dread. She wasn't sure why, but it was as if she were carrying a shadow of worry back to Harmony Hill with her.

Pray anyway. There will be clouds and storms. But the Lord also gave us rainbows. Her mother's words echoed in her mind. And in the distance, the dog still barked.

25

By the time Mitchell rode back into town, the sun was going down. He'd found Sam Duncan's cows. Not stolen. But Sam was right about his fences too. No breaks or holes and the gates were fastened. After some investigating, Mitchell solved the mystery and the cows were back home. Mischief turned out to be the cause, and the culprits, two neighbor boys.

A few days ago, Sam had come in from the hayfield to catch the boys roughhousing around his pond. He lit in on them and chased them home.

"It'd been different if the rascals had been fishing, but they weren't even trying to catch their supper. Just acting up," Sam told Mitchell. "Besides, it was going on night and those boys needed to be home helping their ma with the chores. Poor woman lost her husband at Missionary Ridge. Fighting on the wrong side, but sorrowful anyway."

Mitchell hadn't asked which side because the war was over. Sides didn't matter now. Keeping the peace in his county, that was what mattered.

He was glad when Sam didn't want the boys arrested, though a night in jail might have thrown a scare into them. But they were just kids, and there was their mother to consider. Not that she asked Mitchell to go easy on the boys. The boys would pay for the trouble they'd caused by helping Sam get up his winter wood. They might live hard for a while, but they'd be better for it. And their mother too, because in spite of his gruff exterior, Sam had a generous heart. He'd no doubt haul the wood the boys sawed and chopped over to their woodshed.

Mitchell would ride back out that way next week to make sure the boys took their punishment seriously. That night in the county jail could still be arranged.

The afternoon had been well spent, but it was spent. He couldn't ride out to the Shaker village now. They wouldn't welcome his questions so late in the day. He wasn't sure he had any new questions to ask anyway. He could ride out to Carlyn's place to look for Asher, but by the time he got there it would be night. Mrs. Snowden was right about the dog being nearly impossible to see in the dark. If the dog decided not to come to him, it would be a wasted trip.

He'd go by there in the morning on the way to the Shaker village. By then, he might have some new questions. By then, Asher might have come back to the boardinghouse for something to eat. Mitchell wasn't looking forward to telling Carlyn he'd lost her dog. Plus, he still needed to talk to Curt Whitlow. That was where he might find some answers. Or at least, those new questions.

This time when he knocked on Whitlow's door, his wife opened it. A wide-eyed little girl peeked out from behind her mother's skirts and promptly stuck her thumb in her mouth.

"Sorry to bother you, ma'am, but I need to talk to Mr. Whitlow."

"He's not here." Dark smudges under her eyes made it look as though she'd been missing sleep. Could be lots of reasons for that. A sick child. A wayward husband. She met his eyes straight on. "Junior told you that last night."

"I thought maybe you'd heard from your husband today." Mitchell kept his voice calm. "It's important I talk to him."

"Is it about that girl?"

"What girl?" Mitchell asked.

The child switched her big-eyed stare from Mitchell to her mother. Mrs. Whitlow gave a bare shake of her head at Mitchell, then bent down to kiss the little girl on her forehead. "It's your bedtime, Thelma. Run upstairs and get into your nightie. I'll be up to tuck you in bed in a few minutes."

The little girl reluctantly let go of her mother's skirt and started toward the stairs rising up behind Mrs. Whitlow in the hall. The woman watched her all the way to the top before she stepped out on the porch and pulled the door shut behind her.

"Children don't always understand what they hear. That one's still young enough to miss her father coming home at night, though heaven knows why. He's not been here half the time since she was born."

Mitchell wasn't sure what to say. "She's a pretty child. Is she the youngest?"

"She is. A good one to end on. A sweet-natured child. She must have took back after my mother. Certainly not Curt or me." She blew out a breath. "I'm sorry, Sheriff. I know you didn't come here to talk about my children. So why have you come?" She tilted her head and stared up at Mitchell.

Night was coming on, but he could still see her face. She was an attractive woman, a bit on the plump side but pretty enough that most people wondered why she'd ended up married to Curt, who was some years older than her. Gossip claimed her father had pushed her into the marriage. That he owed Curt money.

"I told you, ma'am. I need to talk to your husband about his whereabouts day before yesterday. Was he here at the house with you that day?"

"Why do you want to know?" She frowned, and then as though fearing that might line her face, she smoothed away the creases between her eyes.

"There's been some trouble out at the Shaker village."

"You mean the fire?" She didn't wait for him to answer. "That has nothing to do with Curt. He can't stand those Shakers. Says they're out to steal the whole county." She shook her head a little and touched her lips with her fingertips. "I'm sorry, Sheriff. Curt's always telling me I talk too much. But you can't think Curt had anything to do with that fire. He wouldn't do anything like that. Even if he was angry over that widow woman's house."

"What widow woman's house?" Mitchell asked.

"I'm sure I don't know." She slid her hands down her skirt and looked away from Mitchell out into the yard. "Curt owns houses all over. That's his business. My business is taking care of the house and children."

"You mentioned a girl."

"Did I?" She gave a nervous little laugh while her fingers played over her skirt again. "I don't recall what I said."

Mitchell let the silence build between them, but her guard was up now. She wasn't going to say any more about any girl or anything else without weighing every word first. Finally he said, "I see. Well, I won't take up any more of your time, Mrs. Whitlow."

"I'm sorry I couldn't help you out, but Curt doesn't always tell me where he's going." She tried a smile, but it didn't quite work.

"I understand." Something was bothering the woman, but he couldn't force her to tell him whatever it was. "If you need anything while Curt's away, you send one of your boys after me."

He was halfway across the yard when she came out to the edge of the porch and stopped him. "Sheriff?"

"Yes, ma'am." He turned around. "Is there something I can do for you now?"

She hesitated, then pushed out the words. "There is something." In the dim light he could see her moistening her lips.

He stepped back toward her. "I'll help if I can."

She took hold of the porch post as though needing support. "The truth is, Sheriff, I am a little worried about Curt. I don't want the children to know, but Dr. Baker was by here earlier. He said Curt was supposed to let him treat his arm today. You know, where that dog bit him. Curt is away a lot on business." She swallowed as though the word "business" put a bad taste in her mouth she had to get rid of before she could say anything else. "But he was concerned about his arm. It's healing up, but I don't think he would have forgotten that he was supposed to see the doctor to check on it. I'm probably worried for no reason, but . . ."

"Yes, ma'am, but to be sure, I'll check around for you."

She rubbed her hands up and down the post. "You will be discreet, won't you?"

257

"Nobody will ever have to know about this conversation but the two of us. Not even Mr. Whitlow."

"Thank you, Sheriff Brodie." She let out a relieved breath. "I've heard you're a man a person can trust."

"I do what I can, ma'am."

That was what he had told the mother of the two boys earlier that afternoon. He'd said the same thing often during the war. But sometimes it hadn't been enough. The feeling was growing inside him that maybe it wouldn't be enough here either.

You can with the Lord's might. His mother used to tell him that whenever he complained about something being hard to do. His father's advice had been less holy and more down to earth. *If you come up on a rock too big to move, take a pickax to it. Break it down to a size you can move.*

As he headed toward the boardinghouse, he could see his mother smiling at his father and saying, "Sometimes the Lord helps you swing that pickax."

Mitchell looked up at the stars coming out. Two days in a row he was finishing the day with the stars and thinking about his mother. And for the second night in a row a prayer rose up from his heart for Carlyn. For himself. Even for the dog. Hadn't his mother always told him that no prayer was too small for God? Or too big.

He wondered when he'd stepped away from that little-boy belief in prayer. Maybe the war had caused that. Not that he didn't pray when the cannons started firing. Desperate prayers for courage in the face of battle. But then he'd left the prayers on the battlefield. He didn't need God once the guns went silent. He could handle the rest of the times. But maybe he couldn't. Maybe he did need the Lord's might behind his swing of the pickax to break up the rocks in his path.

"Just point me down the right road so I can find out the things I need to know." He whispered the words.

That little-boy hope was in his heart as he stepped up on Mrs. Snowden's back porch. But no Asher appeared out of the night or stood to meet him when he went through the door.

Mrs. Snowden looked around from washing dishes. Her face fell when she saw he was alone. "You didn't find him."

"Not yet."

She shook her head a little as she dried her hands on her apron and lifted his supper out of the warming oven. "You think it's wrong to pray for a dog, Sheriff?"

"I hope not, Mrs. Snowden. I sincerely hope not."

26

The confessions and apologies Carlyn rehearsed on the walk back from the woods became naught but a stuttering mumble when she faced Sister Edna at the Gathering Family House.

Without a word, Carlyn followed her into the room where the sister listened to confessions. Sister Edna settled behind her writing desk and waited for Carlyn to take down a chair from the pegs to sit across from her. Still she did not speak. The silence thumped against Carlyn's ears, but she saw no reason to step into more trouble with careless words.

At last Sister Edna broke the silence. "What have you to say for yourself?" In spite of the scowl that darkened the sister's face, her voice lacked its usual fire. She seemed weary of the continual necessity to upbraid Carlyn.

Carlyn answered with the truth instead of her practiced words. "I needed time alone. To mourn the true knowledge of the death of my husband."

"We have no marital ties here. Have you not read the book I gave you days ago?" She tapped the book on the desk, then held it up so Carlyn could see the title, *The Principles and Practices of a People Called the Shakers*. "On these pages you find the rules we must adhere to in order for our Society to prosper. The directives are written so even those of the world can understand."

"I am reading the book as you instructed, but I have not finished it."

"Or obviously paid attention to anything you have already read." Sister Edna let the book fall open. She didn't have to riffle through the pages to find the passage she sought. "Listen well while I read you principle number eight. 'A united interest in all things in their general order; but none are required to come into it, except as a matter of choice.'" Sister Edna peered up at Carlyn. "You did choose to come among us, did you not?"

"Yea," Carlyn answered weakly.

Sister Edna began reading again. "'For this order is not a principle; but is the result of mutual love and unity of spirits; and cannot be supported where the selfish relations of husband, wife, and children exist. This order is the greatest and clearest demonstration of practical love. "By this shall all men know that ye are my disciples, if ye have love one to another."'" Again she looked up. "That is the Christ speaking."

"I am familiar with that verse," Carlyn said.

"But the question is, do you practice it? Leaving your duty for your sisters to perform in your absence is not a demonstration of practical love. Item four states that 'to be a proper Shaker, one should be diligent in business serving the Lord. All—'" She poked the page and repeated, "'All labor with their hands according to their strength and abilities; all are industrious, but not slavish. Idleness is the parent of want.'"

"I will work tomorrow." Carlyn tried to speak with as much sincerity as she could muster, but the words lacked conviction even to her own ears. She would work. She did not mind working, but now her spirit was tired. Too much had happened in the last few days.

The same strain she was feeling seemed to be reflected on Sister Edna's face even though she was saying the expected Shaker words. The woman smoothed her hand over the book's page. "A proper Shaker knows her hands are to be devoted to work every day except the Sabbath."

"Yea, if one is able, but today sadness overwhelmed me. Such as was overcoming you this morning."

"A fleeting worry." Sister Edna threw out her hand in dismissal of Carlyn's words. "Mother Ann's teachings show us that happiness does not so much depend on circumstances as we think. Within our souls the foundations must abide."

"Do you have those foundations?" Carlyn asked.

"I did." She quickly changed her words. "I do." She stared down at the book. "I have kept the rules."

For a minute Carlyn thought Sister Edna was going to read more of those rules to point out Carlyn's wrongs, but instead she stared at the pages without speaking. Finally Carlyn said, "But others have not."

Sister Edna looked up. "You have not." Her voice regained its stern timbre.

"Yea, I have not." Carlyn knew what was expected. To bow her head and be repentant. At times she'd done that, but now an argument rose within her. "Rules do not open the gates of heaven, and following every rule in your book or anyone's book does not allow you through those gates. Faith in the Lord is what is needed."

"You dare to preach to me of faith?" Sister Edna's eyes flared open. "I am the one leading you. Not you leading me."

"Nay, I am not a preacher." She cringed at the thought of being like her father, but then in her quiet way, her mother had opened up the Scripture to Carlyn better than all her father's sermons. "You Shakers speak of the gift of being simple and yet you've written books of rules."

"To ensure we live a simple life with unity of spirit."

She told herself to bend her head and pretend to accept Sister Edna's rules. But words bubbled up inside her and she couldn't keep them in. "Is it not better to allow love to rule our spirits? The love of God and the love of one's neighbor."

"We have such love. Surely even you can see that such love is plentiful within our Society. Brotherly love. Sisterly love."

Again she told herself to be silent. Again the words would not be denied. "Do you have that love for me, Sister Edna?"

The sister's eyes snapped with anger and Carlyn thought the other woman was going to lie. Then a shadow passed over her face and she looked sad. "The truth is always better and necessary. You are not yet fully a Believer sister. Novitiates must earn their place in our Society."

"And love? Must we earn love when the Lord showers it down on us so freely, deserved or not?" Carlyn leaned toward Sister Edna, willing her to listen with an open mind.

Instead the woman put her fingertips on her forehead as though Carlyn's words pained her. "There is much you do not understand about the Shaker way."

"Yea, there is much I do not understand about many things."

Carlyn looked down at her hands then and gave in to the older sister. But in some deep, abiding way her words of

argument with Sister Edna put her own heart at ease. Whatever happened, she could lean on the Lord. Just as Ambrose,
while he still lived, had helped her feel the love of God, now
from the grave he was showing her that love was everlasting.
It didn't matter if she stepped up on the stairway with the
proper foot or neglected to hang out the last load of wash on
the clothesline. Such things had naught to do with the love
of God. That was available to her no matter where she was.

She ran her thumb over the back of her hand. Would
that be here? Would she turn from a confused novitiate to
a resigned Shaker sister living by their rules not because she
thought them necessary but for the more practical reasons of
obtaining food and shelter? Or dare she hope another way
would open? That she might once more have her own home
and perhaps find love different than that only for sisters and
brothers? The kind of love she'd known with Ambrose and
that he had released her to find again.

The thought of the sheriff's hand brushing her shoulder
came to mind. Her cheeks warmed. She shouldn't even be
thinking about Sheriff Brodie with her husband's last letter
in her pocket. But Ambrose wanted her to reach for joy in
her life. A joy she no longer believed she could find among
the Shakers.

She had no doubt Sister Edna was glaring at her bent head,
but the sister remained silent. Light-headed from her daylong
fast, Carlyn wanted nothing more than to be out of this room,
away from Sister Edna. She searched for words to appease
the woman. "Whatever the fitting punishment, I will accept
it and work harder in the days ahead to be a proper Shaker."

"Empty words can come from beneath any bonnet." Sister
Edna shut the book with a snap and let her fingertips dance

up and down on the book's cover. "Truth is what is necessary when one makes confession of one's wrongs."

"The truth will out." Carlyn repeated Sister Edna's words from that morning.

Sister Edna sniffed in a deep breath and touched her nose with her handkerchief. "Revelation of the truth is not in our hands, but Mother Ann will light our path and show us what we need to know. I fear you do not want to walk the Shaker way, Sister Carlyn."

"I am here."

"But will you stay?"

"The Lord gives us one day at a time. Tomorrow has not come. Who could have said on the Monday past the things that would happen before the week's end? The fire and the loss of Brother Henry. Nor would I have ever expected a letter from a woman I never met to put to rest the unknowns about my husband's fate in the war. We cannot know what tomorrow holds."

"The future is not fearful when one clearly sees the path Mother Ann has laid out for us."

Carlyn raised her head to look at Sister Edna. "Yet you seemed greatly concerned about facing the day when we awoke this morning."

The sister flinched back from her words. "I have confessed my lack of faith in the proper way to Eldress Lilith. I trust now that Mother Ann will continue to bless our community and those of the world won't be back to torment us."

Carlyn looked down again. "I will add my prayers to yours that there will be no more troubles here in the village."

"The responsible parties have not been apprehended." Sister Edna's voice sounded a warning. "And may never be.

Those of the world care little about what happens here in our village."

"Sheriff Brodie will search for answers."

"The answers he seeks will do little more than keep our Society in a state of upset. It would be best if he did not return with his questions." She narrowed her eyes on Carlyn. "For all concerned."

"Do you fear the answers he might find?"

"Nay." Sister Edna answered too quickly. "I have no reason to fear any truth. Things will turn out as they should. On Sunday, we will exercise a song to return peace to our Society." Sister Edna eyed Carlyn. "Perhaps you will be ready to labor the dances with us on that day."

"I fear my feet are too clumsy and I might miss a step." Carlyn had learned a few of the simpler dances in the practice times, but she still could not imagine taking part in dancing as worship in their Meeting House. Some of the dances on the Sabbath were ordered marches. Others seemed nothing but frenzied whirling. A few had the Shakers acting like children at play. None of what the Shakers called exercises had seemed any sort of worship to Carlyn, but at the same time, she did not doubt many of those who did dance felt a spirit of worship. Even Sister Edna's demeanor changed during the worship times. Her frowns disappeared to be replaced by a joyful quietude.

The woman exhibited none of that serenity now. Only the weariness that Carlyn had noted earlier. A weariness Carlyn shared.

"The proper spirit can make your feet float above the floor. Mother Ann will gift you with such feelings if you stop clinging to your worldly beliefs."

"Yea." Carlyn had no more energy for argument. "What would you have me do to make up for my lapses?"

"We do not dole out punishments here, but be warned. A person reaps what she sows. If you engage in wrong behavior, there will be sorrowful results."

"I am already sorrowful."

"But does your heart sorrow for the right reasons, Sister Carlyn, or because of your yearning for things of the world?"

"I will pray for right reasons." Carlyn avoided a direct answer. All she wanted was for their conversation to be ended. With the room seeming to close in on her, she fought the urge to gasp for air and dared stand even though Sister Edna had not indicated their time was finished. "I am very thirsty. May I get a drink of water?"

"Go." Sister Edna gave a wave of dismissal. "Make sure you put on a clean apron and cap before you come to practice. Good spirits will not abide where there is dirt. You must sweep all the filth of wrong thoughts from your heart to be a proper Believer."

Sister Edna followed Carlyn out of the room and hurried up the sisters' stairway. She would not want to be late to the practice time. Her life had long been ordered by the Shaker rules. Carlyn stood in the empty hall a moment. She could hear the others gathering in the room over her head. Could she become one of them?

The sound of singing drifted down the stairs to her. She couldn't quite make out the words, but the tune was lively, the voices strong, each sounding the same note to make even their voices stay in perfect union. Was it wrong to pretend to be in union with them when all she felt was disharmony?

Perhaps it was time to find a way to Texas to beg her

father for shelter. But even though it would be good to see her mother, dread at the thought of living under her father's roof again was like a heavy cloak weighing down her shoulders as she went down to the kitchen. She would wait. She had the promise of the pension. Elder Derron would eagerly seek the money to add to the Shaker coffers, but she could demand it be given to her instead. A few weeks would not be unbearable.

What was it Sister Edna had quoted the Shakers' Mother Ann saying about happiness? That it wasn't totally dependent on circumstances in life, but instead the foundation for it must rise from within. She had started building that foundation with Ambrose and now it was gone, blown away by the war.

The smell of ash drifted in through a window left open to cool the kitchen. The fire proved that fearsome things could happen anywhere, even in this village where the people claimed to desire peace above all. Sister Edna might wish for naught but goodness here, but Carlyn had felt safer alone in her house with Asher by her side and her gun over her door. Here, she was without defense.

Have you forgotten the armor of God? Her mother's voice whispered through her mind. *And take the helmet of salvation, and the sword of the Spirit, which is the word of God: praying always.* Her mother's answer for every problem, the Word of God and prayer.

Carlyn got a drink from the pipe that brought water to the kitchen. The sound of the Shakers singing was not as loud here, but enough of the tune drifted down that she recognized it as one she knew.

Softly she sang the words. "Come dance and sing around

the ring. Live in love and union. Sing with life, live with life. Sing with life and power."

She did the steps she'd practiced with the song, and there alone in the kitchen, she moved back and forth and twirled. It felt good to shake free of her grief and worries. Then the singing above her changed and the ceiling vibrated as the Shakers pounded their feet on the floor to chase away the devil.

Such a people of contradictions. Quiet and staid, serious-minded with peaceful calm except during their worship when they stomped and whirled. Spiritual joy in motion. Would that it was so easy to chase away the devil with stomps and shouts. But the lingering odor of the destroyed barn wafting in on the evening air proved it was not so easy to eliminate the threat of evil and make happiness shower down like flowers from heaven.

My last prayer will be for your happiness. Carlyn touched the letter in her pocket as Ambrose's words echoed in her thoughts.

Then even though her stomach growled in complaint of its emptiness, she didn't pilfer in the cabinets for bread, but went back up the stairs to join her voice and feet in the practice. Sister Edna noted her entrance in the room with a look of disapproval that made Carlyn remember she'd neglected to fetch a clean apron and cap.

27

❧

"Carlyn."

The sound of her name pulled at her, but Carlyn fought waking. She did not want to surrender her hard won slumber. With her stomach growling from hunger and her thoughts swamped with sorrow, she had almost given up on sleep after the retiring bell rang. Finally by repeating the Lord's Prayer over and over, she'd drifted off only to have someone demand she awaken what seemed like moments later.

"Sister Carlyn, wake up!" The voice was right in her ear, soft but insistent.

Carlyn gasped and a hand clamped over her mouth.

"Shh." Sister Berdine eased the pressure of her hand. "You'll awaken a certain sister."

Carlyn pushed away Sister Berdine's hand. "What are you doing?"

Sister Berdine's voice was so low Carlyn had to strain to hear her. "Exploring the pleasures of the world." The girl sighed. "Our Payton found that courage and I have decided he looks fine. His eyes are a crushing blue."

Carlyn sat up, sleep forgotten. She dared a look toward Sister Edna's bed. Enough moonlight drifted through the window to let Carlyn see the woman's shape under her blanket. Steady snores indicated she was sleeping soundly.

Carlyn turned back to Sister Berdine. "Are you running away?"

"Nay, not away." Sister Berdine's teeth shone in her smile. "Running to."

Sister Edna shifted a little in her bed and Sister Berdine held her finger to her lips as she stood and motioned Carlyn to follow her. When Carlyn hesitated, Sister Berdine leaned close to her ear again. "Please. I have more to tell you and I fear waking a certain sister."

Carlyn stood up. How could she refuse this sister, her friend? Sister Berdine pushed Carlyn's pillow around and bunched the cover over it so that it looked as if someone might still by lying there. Sister Berdine's bed showed the same lumps.

They tiptoed past Sister Edna's bed. It wasn't until they were through the door and out in the hallway that Carlyn realized Sister Berdine carried not only her own shoes but Carlyn's as well, along with a dress draped over her arm.

"I'm not going with you," Carlyn said.

"Shh." Sister Berdine handed Carlyn the dress. "Slip this on over your nightgown. It's safer to talk outside." She looked around. "If anywhere in this place is safe for recalcitrant novitiates such as us." She flashed another smile at Carlyn.

The house was silent except for the muted snores coming from behind the closed doors around them. In the deep of the night, the hallway was much darker than the sleeping room, with only the windows at the stair landings allowing in the spare moonlight. Carlyn pulled the dress over her head. It was better to do what Sister Berdine said than to chance waking the whole house.

Sister Berdine thrust the shoes at her but shook her head when Carlyn bent to put them on. She led the way down the steps to the kitchen and stopped by the open window.

"What's wrong with the door?" Carlyn whispered.

"Locked. But windows are as good as doors when a person is determined." She dropped her shoes out the window and then crawled through it herself. "There's a barrel to step on."

"You sound experienced in escape."

"Yea. It's time for freedom." She let go of the window and dropped down on the barrel and then to the ground. She grinned up at Carlyn. "Your turn."

"I'll never get back in."

"If one short as I can do it, then you surely can. Quit seeing obstacles and see opportunities."

"The opportunity for trouble," Carlyn muttered as she eased through the window. "Sister Edna will never forgive this." At the same time there was something exhilarating about sliding out the window and touching her feet to the barrel top, then the grass.

Sister Berdine was lacing up her shoes. "Best put your shoes on."

"I told you I'm not running away, although I won't have to after this. Sister Edna will escort me to the edge of the village herself." Carlyn stuck her feet down in her shoes.

"Nay, they're a forgiving lot. And I told you. I'm not running away. I'm running to." Sister Berdine stood up and clasped her hands under her chin with a happy sigh. "I have ever wanted a home of my own with children running about, and though I am a bit long in the tooth, I am not too old for babies. My mother had me when she was five years older than I am now. That's Payton's age."

"Are you sure about this? You barely know this man."

"Yea. But there are times when a person should run through the doors the Lord opens for her. This is such a time for me. Payton is a good man. He came to the Shakers when he was sixteen, over twenty years ago, and never until he saw me across the Meeting House did he feel the temptation to return to the world."

"Where is he?"

"By the corncrib. The shadows are deep there. He is sure about our leaving, but he worries some brother he has long known will see him and try to stop us."

"Then why are you here, taking that chance?"

"I couldn't leave without telling you goodbye, Sister Carlyn. While we may not have been cut out to be Shaker sisters, we are sisters of the spirit. When the day comes that you realize you cannot live among the Shakers, and I daresay it will, you can stay with us until your sheriff finds courage as my Payton did. That should not take long. He looked a courageous man. He will waste little time asking you to be his wife when he finds out you are truly a widow." She reached over and squeezed Carlyn's hand with a show of sympathy.

"It's not proper for me to even be thinking about such things." Carlyn pulled her hand free, ashamed of how the thought found welcome in her mind.

"You are wrong, my sister. You have long been grieving your husband and were faithful without fault to the love you shared. Now it is time to find a new life as I am doing. I have been praying for both of us and the Lord is good to answer our prayers." She was smiling again. "Be happy for me, Carlyn."

"I am." Carlyn gave her a hug. "But why did I have to follow you outside? You could have told me this in the kitchen and I might have avoided the trouble I will surely be in now."

"You are already in trouble thinking you can live the Shaker life, but fear not. You will be able to sneak back into the sleeping room without that certain sister awakening. She sleeps like the dead. And it will only be my bed empty in the morning."

"What will I tell her about you?"

"The truth. That I am gone. There will be far more consternation in the Centre House when they find Payton's bed empty. They will be ruing the day I came into the Society to lure their faithful brother into sin." Sister Berdine laughed, not at all upset by the thought.

"But where will you go?" A wave of sadness swept over Carlyn, knowing Sister Berdine would not be working beside her on the morrow.

"Payton has a sister who lives nearby. A natural sister instead of the Shaker kind. We will be fine." Sister Berdine tiptoed up to peer directly in Carlyn's face. "While the elders here will think this is of the devil, I think it is of the Lord. He brought me here to give me the desires of my heart by allowing Payton to look across their church house and invite me into his heart. A heart long closed to such thinking. Only the Lord could do that, so I will trust in his providence. As should you."

"I will miss you." Carlyn blinked to keep back tears as

she touched her cheek to Sister Berdine's. "And will pray for you and for Payton."

She turned to climb back up on the barrel, but Sister Berdine grabbed her sleeve. "Wait. There is more." Her face was serious in the moonlight. "We heard a dog in the shadows under the corncrib. We could not see it well, but it looks the size of the dog you told me you had. Payton thinks the poor creature may be hurt. He has a soft spot for animals."

"Asher? Hurt?"

"It may not be Asher, but a worry kept poking me that it might be. So I thought if it is your dog, it might crawl out to let you see if it is hurt or merely frightened."

"Asher would not cower." Carlyn started across the yard.

Sister Berdine jerked her back close to the house. "We must stay in the shadows."

"Surely there are no watchers at night." The windows of the house behind them were all dark, but then a watcher would want no lights inside to spoil the ability to see what moved in the moonlight.

"You cannot be sure with these people. They watch everything. Plus, I saw a brother moving across the road earlier headed toward the tanning sheds."

"Perhaps to meet another sister."

"Not there, I would hope. The smell near that place is dreadful." Sister Berdine shuddered at the thought before she began threading her way from shadow to shadow. "If I were the sister, I would wonder of the choice of rendezvous. Besides, he appeared to be carrying a shovel."

"Did you recognize who it was?"

"Nay. I only saw his back. I feared he might see me and spoil my meeting with Payton."

"But you took the chance to come back for me."

"For you, my sister, I would." Sister Berdine reached back to take Carlyn's hand. "But hurry now. Payton and I must be gone before the rising bell. I do not want to give these Shakers a chance to change his mind. The guilt might overwhelm his good sense."

The Shaker brother stepped away from the corncrib when they glided across the last patch of moonlight to melt into the shadows beside him.

"Is she coming with us?" A tremble sounded in his voice as he looked from Sister Berdine to Carlyn.

"Nay." Sister Berdine touched the man's cheek. He caught her hand in his and held it to his lips. For a moment, they seemed to forget Carlyn was there. Then Sister Berdine shook herself and said, "She came for the dog."

Carlyn was already on her knees beside the crib, which was built on poles above the ground to keep the corn dry. She peered back into the shadows. "Asher, is that you?"

The dog lifted his head and gave a soft bark. A bark Carlyn would have recognized anywhere. She started to crawl under the crib, but the Shaker brother stopped her.

"Best let him come to you if he can, Sister."

Carlyn nodded and brushed away the tears that had popped into her eyes. "Come, Asher." She spoke the words firmly and the dog limped out from under the crib, holding a back paw off the ground. Carlyn sat on the ground and let him crawl into her lap. "Poor boy, you're bleeding."

Asher licked her face and flapped his tail back and forth.

Brother Payton squatted down beside them. "Let me see his leg unless you think he might snap at me. I would much rather not start my new life with Berdine with a mangled hand."

Carlyn looked at the brother. She had seen him in the Meeting House. Not a handsome man, but his voice and manner bespoke gentleness. The gentleness of a longtime Shaker with none of Sister Edna's acerbity.

"Easy, Asher." Carlyn held the dog while Payton ran his fingers along his leg. Asher stayed still and didn't growl.

The brother gingerly put the dog's paw down. "It appears he has been shot, but the bone may not be damaged beyond healing." The man stood and looked at the sky. "We can help you take him to the West Family barn. Brother Willis there has a gift in healing animals."

Berdine grasped his arm. "Is there time before the rising bell?" Her voice was tight.

"Mayhap, if the dog lets me carry him."

"Nay, that is not necessary." Carlyn looked up at Sister Berdine. She gently moved the dog out of her lap to stand. "I can take him. He will walk with me."

"You will be in trouble with a certain sister if you do not go back before she wakes," Sister Berdine said.

Carlyn sighed. "Trouble has seemed to stalk me lately. She can do no more than make me leave the village. Now go."

"If you are sure." Brother Payton sounded uncertain.

Something Sister Berdine must have noted. She gave Carlyn a quick hug. "If that happens, come to us. Or better yet, take Asher back to the sheriff. Yea, that is exactly what you should do and ask him if he needs someone to make sure the dog does not escape his care again." She laughed, excitement bubbling out. "Better yet, I will tell him that for you. After we find a preacher." She hooked her arm through Brother Payton's to start him away from the village.

Brother Payton looked back over his shoulder. "Tell

Brother Willis I sent you. And tell him I am sorry to slip away in the night, but I could not bear breaking the Shaker ties with my brothers' eyes watching me and words of sorrow on their lips."

Sister Berdine stopped. "Do you want to stay?"

Carlyn knew how hard it must be for her to say those words.

"Nay. I will miss my brothers, but it is time for a new beginning. Together." He reached for her hand. "You are my life now."

"Then let us begin living it." Sister Berdine spoke over her shoulder to Carlyn. "Keep up your courage, Sister. In time, you will have a new beginning too."

Carlyn watched them disappear into the night. They were the ones with courage. To dare the unknown for love. She had done the same once with Ambrose. Would there be a new time for love for her? With Sheriff Brodie, as Sister Berdine hinted? He had been kind to her, but kindness did not equate love.

Stars still dotted the night sky, but soon it would be morning. An owl hooted from the woods and a cow bawled in the pasture. Then a different sound came to her ears. Not a natural one, but that of metal on rock. She remembered Sister Berdine speaking of seeing the Shaker man with a shovel. What could the man be digging in the dark before dawn?

Asher whined and leaned against her leg. His labored panting was evidence of his pain.

"We'd best get started, Asher. Pray Sister Berdine's Payton is right about this Brother Willis."

After Asher walked a little ways, he lay down as though he could go no farther. Carlyn tore a piece off the bottom of the nightgown under her dress. More reason for confession. She would have to make a list, although after tonight she doubted Sister Edna would even want to open her ears to hear Carlyn's wrongs. It could not be helped. She would not desert Asher.

She slipped the cloth strip under the dog's belly and used it like a sling to help him keep walking, but it was still slow. The rising bell was ringing when at last they reached the barn.

She stroked Asher's head and waited for Brother Willis to come down the path from the West Family House. When he did, the brother stopped as though unsure of whether to continue toward the barn if it meant coming near her. Then he saw Asher, and his compassion overpowered his worry about Shaker propriety.

He carried Asher inside to an empty stall and sent Carlyn after a bucket of water from the cistern beside the barn. When she brought it back, he looked her up and down in the dim light of the barn. His face, lined with age, had the solemn look of a devout Shaker.

"You do not wear the proper cap over your hair or the neckerchief, but you are nevertheless a novitiate sister, are you not?"

"Yea."

"And this is your dog?"

"He came here with me, but Eldress Lilith said he could not stay. I took him to town and gave him to the sheriff there. I suppose he tracked me down here. Brother Payton said someone has shot him."

"Brother Payton?"

"He said to tell you he is sorry."

"So he left with that sister." The brother sighed and slowly shook his head. "Such are the temptations of the world. Lust takes many a man down wrong paths."

Carlyn thought it best to stay silent.

"I have seen it happen many times, but I never thought to see it happen to Brother Payton. He has long been a faithful Believer." Brother Willis shook his head again, then seemed to remember the problem of Carlyn standing before him. "You must return to the Gathering Family House."

"But Asher—"

He held up his hand. "I will tend to your dog. Asher, you say?"

"Yea," Carlyn answered weakly. "Can't I stay while you treat him?"

"Nay, but worry not. I will fix his leg, but you must return to your proper place among us."

"Let me tell him goodbye."

"Very well. I will see to the horses." He moved past Carlyn out of the stall. "Do not tarry long. You will have been missed by now."

Carlyn knelt beside Asher and stroked her hand all the way down his back. She leaned close to his ear and promised to return whether it was allowed or not. He whimpered and licked her face. When Carlyn went out of the stall, the old brother was watching her with a frown.

"It is better to shower such love on your sisters and brethren, young sister, than on a dumb animal."

Carlyn wanted to tell him Asher was far from a dumb animal, but she bit back the words. He was helping her. For that she could be grateful and silent. So she only said, "Yea. Thank you, Brother Willis."

The walk back through the village to the Gathering Family House felt even longer than the walk in the night to the barn, for she knew who waited for her there. Sister Edna.

28

Still no Asher on Mrs. Snowden's back porch when Mitchell went down for breakfast the next day. He wasn't surprised the dog wasn't there, but he did look. His mother used to tell him that if a person prayed for rain, they ought to go outside expecting to get wet. But she also said sometimes it took the clouds awhile to gather.

Mitchell wanted to search for the dog. He wanted to have him in hand before he went back to the Shaker village and saw Carlyn again. But he didn't ride out to Carlyn's house. First, he had to hunt down Curt Whitlow. Men took precedence over dogs. Even a man like Curt Whitlow.

That Mrs. Whitlow had asked him to look for Curt meant something unusual was going on. Town gossip had it she didn't much care whether Curt ever came home, but gossip was ofttimes wrong. Either way, it was Mitchell's job to keep the people in his county safe. That included Curt Whitlow. What he thought of the man made no difference.

Whitlow wasn't at any of his usual haunts. Janie at the

hotel dining room said she hadn't seen him for a couple of days.

"I've been wondering where he's got to." She looked up from wiping off a table. "He's generally here about every other day. Says that wife of his hasn't ever learned how he likes his eggs." She straightened up and put her hands on her hips. "I figure she'd just as soon he found his eggs somewhere besides her kitchen. So I guess it's no surprise he's here a lot. A man don't find what he needs at home, he goes looking for it."

"He didn't happen to tell you anywhere he might go looking," Mitchell said.

"Money can make for plenty of places to look." She started cleaning the table again. "But he never had any reason to share none of those places with the likes of me. I'm lucky to get a nickel tip if the cook happens to get his eggs scrambled just so."

Billy Hogan was no help either. He looked up from cutting Harold Thompson's hair and shook his head. "Haven't seen Curt for a spell. Not since before he got dog bit. Figured he was laying low, taking it easy. They say he can't even use that arm."

Harold raised his head to add his two bits. "Doc said he had to put so many stitches in it that he lost count and Curt bellowed with every last one." Harold's shoulders shook with a silent laugh.

"Best sit still if you don't want me to take a chunk out of your ear, Harold." Billy pushed Harold's head down to trim the hair on the man's neck. He peered over at Mitchell. "You tracking down Curt for any special reason, Mitch?"

"Just need a little information he might have," Mitchell said.

"Don't have nothing to do with that fire out at the Shaker town, does it?" Billy looked back down at Harold's head and worked his comb and scissors.

"What makes you think that?" Mitchell had found that sometimes the best way to avoid answering a question was to ask one of his own.

"Oh, I don't know." Billy kept clipping Harold's hair. "Seems like I heard Curt was fussing about them people out there, but then Curt fusses about everybody. So it probably didn't mean nothing. Can't imagine him setting property on fire. He'd rather figure out a way to buy it for little of nothing and sell it for plenty more."

"I doubt if the Shakers would sell any property like that," Mitchell said. "They're pretty shrewd with their business dealings."

"Everybody can make a bad deal now and again. And those Shakers do like buying up land or taking it over when they get somebody to join up with them. I hear they're trying to sell that Widow Kearney's house now. That they paid off her debt on it." Billy brushed off Harold's neck with a shaving brush. "Don't imagine Curt was too happy about that. He thought he had that house in his pocket."

"Did he?" Mitchell pretended ignorance.

"So I heard." Billy looked up at him. "Heard you knew all about that."

"You can hear a lot around town. Some true. Some not." Mitchell would let Billy guess on how much was true of what he'd heard.

"I reckon you're right about that. Can't believe everything you hear, can you, Harold?"

"No, indeed." Harold looked at Mitchell in the mirror.

"Not around this place anyway." His shoulders did some more shaking as he laughed again.

"What do you hear about the Shakers and their deals?" Mitchell asked Billy.

"That they make plenty of them, but don't guess I ever heard anybody say they tried to cheat nobody out of nothing."

"Not much like Whitlow then." Harold spoke up from the barber's chair again. "Pity the poor Shaker what tried to deal with him."

"Why's that?" Mitchell asked.

"He'd do his best to cheat them." Harold twisted around in the chair to look at the barber. "Wouldn't he, Billy?"

Billy untied the cape from around Harold's neck and shook the hair off it onto the floor. "Could be, Harold. Personally I ain't got much use for Curt or them Shakers either. They make good brooms and the little woman likes their garden seeds, but it ain't natural the way they live. The good Lord intended folks to get married and have children. Says so right in his Word. Go forth and be fruitful. I don't think he meant growing apple trees."

Harold stood up and pulled a coin out of his pocket for Billy. "Me and the missus, we raised ten young'uns, so it's worked for us." He sneaked a look over at Mitchell. "But the sheriff here, he's still a bachelor. Maybe he's got Shaker leanings."

Billy laughed. "I think there's some in town trying to change that." He sat down in the barber chair Harold had vacated. "You find Widow Kearney's dog yet?"

"Not yet." Mitchell backed toward the door.

Harold's face perked up. "That widow woman is some looker."

"She is for a fact," Billy said. "A pure waste out there, in with those Shakers. A pure waste. I think you ought to do something about that, Sheriff."

"Don't think matchmaking is part of a sheriff's duties." Mitchell smiled as he opened the door. "Besides, she's not sure about being a widow woman. She never got any word from the government about her husband."

"That could be a problem," Billy said.

"But isn't that the kind of thing a sheriff is supposed to figure out?" Harold spoke up. "Whether somebody's dead or alive. Like that Shaker man in that fire out there. I've been wondering how anybody could be all that sure it was that Shaker man. Somebody was saying he was burned up pretty bad."

"The Shakers were sure it was him," Mitchell said.

"But maybe they were just covering something up. Like maybe it was Whitlow in the fire and now they're hiding out that Shaker brother." Harold hitched up his britches, enjoying the mystery he was imagining.

Billy joined in. "Wouldn't take much hiding. Not the way they all wear the same clothes and cut their hair the same. Hard to tell one from another."

Mitchell stopped in the door, all trace of a smile gone from his face as he looked back at the two men. "It was the Shaker in the fire. It wouldn't be good for a crazy story like that to get out. No need bringing unnecessary grief on Mrs. Whitlow."

"You're right there," Billy agreed. "The woman has grief enough putting up with Curt. We wouldn't start any rumors, would we, Harold?"

"Naw, Sheriff. We was just funning a little." Harold twisted his hat in his hands. "Not that the poor feller being burned up in a fire was anything to fun about. And I hear they lost horses too. Guess as how we should go back to talking about the widow woman."

"Yes sir." Billy shot a grin over at Mitchell. "She is a looker. A pure shame her being out there with those Shakers."

"A pure shame." Harold echoed as he followed Mitchell out of the barbershop.

Words that echoed in Mitchell's heart too as he headed toward the livery stable. A pure shame for sure. But there was nothing he could do about it. Except wait and hope that eventually she would know her husband's fate. Eventually she would be ready to give love another try. His job was to keep her safe until then.

Something about the fire and now Curt Whitlow being missing had the hairs on the back of his neck rising. He'd learned to pay attention to that feeling while he was fighting in the war. It didn't always mean something bad was about to happen, but then again, sometimes it did. Sometimes it gave him just enough warning to duck behind a tree or keep his head down. But this time the worry wasn't so much for himself as for Carlyn.

He shook his head. He was as bad as Billy and Harold, letting his imagination run away with him. Thinking bad things without the first bit of evidence. The fire was arson. No doubt of that. But he had absolutely no proof that anybody intended Brother Henry to die in the fire. Or any evidence that Curt Whitlow had anything to do with it.

The man had been in the Shaker village. He'd had an argument with Brother Henry. Those were the facts. Bare as they were.

He didn't have any facts about Carlyn either. None that he wanted to have. She was married to Ambrose Kearney. Whether he was alive or dead might never be discovered. Whether she would ever leave the Shakers and embrace a new life, a new love, was something he couldn't know. Wanting it didn't mean it would happen.

It was time to stop dreaming about what might be and think about what was. He was a sheriff charged with upholding the law. The law dealt in facts, not maybes. The facts were she had given him her dog, not her heart. And he hadn't even been able to hang on to the dog, but maybe he could find him.

Another one of those maybes. They seemed to be haunting his thoughts lately. Maybe the Shaker fire covered up a murder. Maybe Curt Whitlow was away on business, whatever business that was. Maybe Carlyn's husband had been killed in the war. Maybe the Shakers didn't want him to ask questions just because he was of the world. Maybe he was foolishly in love with a woman who had given him absolutely no indication that she might welcome his feelings. Could be that last wasn't a maybe, but a big mistake. Maybe he should just go dog hunting.

The house was deserted, sitting lonesome on its little bit of land. Leaves were drifted up on the porch against the door and a spiderweb draped down from the corner post. The dog was nowhere in sight. Mitchell got off his horse and walked around to the back, but if the dog had come here, he'd moved on when he didn't find Carlyn.

Mitchell stood in the yard and listened. Nothing disturbed the day's calm except the distant caw of a crow. A burst of wind rustled through the maple overhead and brought down a rush of yellow and red leaves. After the wind settled again, he whistled and called. It was a waste of breath.

The silence surrounded Mitchell again. The day was half over and so far he'd found out absolutely nothing. No trace of Curt Whitlow or of the dog. Could be he should go on back to town and wait for a lead to surface. It would eventually. Whitlow had to come home sometime. While Mitchell chased whispers in the wind that might or might not mean anything, his other duties were being neglected.

He mounted his horse and turned back toward town. The sound of the Shaker bell drifting across the fields stopped him. This close to their village, it would be a waste not to go see if the Shakers had discovered anything new that might help Mitchell figure out who had set the fire. Catching those who committed crimes was the most important part of his duties.

Besides, the dog might have tracked Carlyn down. If so, he needed to get the dog. If she would let him have Asher again. But what other choice would she have? The Shakers weren't rule benders. If they had a rule against dogs when she first went to the village, they still would. Carlyn would need him to take the dog.

He liked the thought of her needing him, even if it was only for the dog. It was a connection. A reason to talk. A reason to look into her beautiful eyes. He didn't know how he'd let himself be captivated so quickly by her when no other woman after Hilda had been able to penetrate his defenses. Carlyn hadn't even tried. She'd simply stood in her doorway, holding a gun, and stolen his heart. He needed to get to know her better to see if the way he felt was real or simply a fantasy.

The Shaker elders might not let him talk to her again, but that didn't mean he couldn't make sure their paths crossed in the village. He knew which house she was in. And the last time he was there, Elder Derron had sent a sister to the washhouse to summon her. He could watch for her there. Wait for a chance to talk to her without the old sister hovering around her.

Whether he got to talk to her or not, it would be good to see her, to ease his mind about her safety. He had no real reason to think she wasn't safe there. The Shakers were a peace-loving people. They spoke against any kind of strife or conflict with their fellow man. Yet, a man had died in a fire intentionally set. Only hours after Carlyn had seen him arguing with Curt Whitlow, and now he couldn't find Whitlow. Things didn't add up and Mitchell had the uneasy feeling more trouble was brewing.

He urged his horse into a faster trot.

29

By the time Carlyn got back to the Gathering Family House, her empty bed and that of Sister Berdine's had been discovered. The sleeping room was in an uproar. Sister Edna was demanding answers. Carlyn heard her strident voice before she reached the top of the stairs. Any semblance of peace had fled.

Carlyn pulled in a deep breath and turned the doorknob. Shocked silence greeted her. Even Sister Edna seemed at a loss for words.

Sister Alice recovered her voice first. "My sister, are you hurt?"

"Nay," Carlyn murmured, only then realizing how she must look with Asher's blood streaking her skirt and her hair uncombed and uncovered.

That's what Sister Edna noted first. "Where's your cap, Sister?"

Carlyn pushed her hair back from her face. "It is not lost.

I did not think to put it on after Sister Berdine woke me and asked me to go out in the night."

"Sister Berdine woke you?" Sister Edna's voice was disbelieving.

Sister Marie spoke up. "I told her that is what happened, but she would not believe I saw Sister Berdine kneeling by your bed to awaken you. She thought you had enticed Sister Berdine into wrongdoing."

"Nay." Carlyn wanted nothing more than to sink down on one of the beds, but such would not be allowed. "Sister Berdine has left for a new life."

"She went in the night by herself?" Sister Edna frowned over at Carlyn. "Our Sister Berdine?"

"She did not go by herself. A brother from one of the other houses went with her. Brother Payton."

"Nay. I do not believe it." Sister Edna recoiled from Carlyn's words. "Not Brother Payton. He has long been a devout Believer. Why would you lie about such a thing?"

"Why indeed?" Carlyn met her eyes. "Can we not wait for confession until after our morning duties and breakfast? I need something to eat since I missed the meals yesterday."

"Whose fault was that if not your own, Sister Carlyn?" Sister Edna said.

"It is my fault that I missed the meals, but that doesn't keep me from being in need of food today. I don't think I will be able to properly do my washhouse duties without eating first." Carlyn felt empty of food and of energy. "Haven't you told me that a complete Shaker needs to care for her body?"

Sister Edna's eyes narrowed on her. "It is not for you to quote Shaker truths at me. You would do well to remember your place as a novitiate."

"Yea." She had no energy for argument.

Sister Alice dared Sister Edna's wrath by asking again, "Are you sure you are not hurt, Sister Carlyn? That appears to be blood on your skirt."

Carlyn looked down at her dress. "Not my blood."

Before she could say more, Sister Edna gasped and put her hand over her mouth. "Mother Ann in heaven, protect us." All the color drained from her face and she looked faint even as she reached and grasped Carlyn's arm. "Pray, tell me no one else has died. If so, I will forever be sorrowful."

"Nay, Sister Edna. It is my dog that was injured." Carlyn spoke quickly to lessen the woman's distress. "Sister Berdine heard the dog and came back to get me. Asher was hurt. Shot, Brother Payton said. He told me to take him to Brother Willis in the West Family and so that is why I could not return before the rising bell."

Sister Edna's face went from distraught to disbelieving to angry while Carlyn talked. "You caused all this upset and ruined your dress over a dog?"

"I have done nothing but miss a night's sleep and soil a dress that can be put to rights with soap and water." Carlyn refused to bend her head and give in to Sister Edna's harsh words. "And perhaps saved a dog's life."

"Who cares about a dog?" Sister Edna's voice was rising again.

Sister Alice tried to deflect Sister Edna's anger. "It is not Sister Carlyn who left in the night."

Sister Edna glared at Sister Alice. "Would that she had. There has been nothing but trouble since she came into the village."

"You are not being fair, Sister Edna," Sister Alice insisted.

"Sister Carlyn did no more than help a dumb animal. It is Sister Berdine who has gone to the world."

"You best be silent, Sister Alice." Sister Edna's face was stiff and her eyes drawn as she stared around at the women watching her. "All of you. Go. Be about your duties if you want to be through in time for the morning meal." When none of them moved, she motioned them toward the door. "Be gone with you. Now."

The others scooted past Carlyn, but Sister Alice still hesitated. Carlyn spoke up before Sister Edna could lash out at her again. "I am all right, Sister Alice. Only weary."

Sister Alice stepped near to put her cheek to Carlyn's. "I am glad, Sister. I will do my chores as quickly as I can and come back to help you with the beds and sweeping here in our room."

"That will not be necessary, Sister Alice. I will assist Sister Carlyn." Sister Edna no longer sounded angry, but her voice was firm with the expectation of obedience.

"Yea," Sister Alice murmured without looking at the older sister.

After she left, Carlyn braced for a return of Sister Edna's anger, but instead her voice was almost too calm. "Make yourself presentable. I will begin on the beds."

"I will hurry," Carlyn said.

"Hurry does naught but cause more problems. Better to take your time and do things right." She began straightening the covers on the bed closest to her. "And don't neglect your prayers."

Carlyn did as she said, sinking to her knees by her bed to silently thank the Lord that anger seemed to be gone from the room and that Brother Willis was caring for Asher.

And I thank thee for Ida Mae. That she cared for Ambrose and kept his letter until she had the opportunity to send it to me. I asked thee for answers and thou answered that prayer. Show me what thou would have me do now and let Sister Berdine and Brother Payton find happiness in abundance.

She didn't ask for happiness for herself. But the Lord knew the desires of her heart even better than she did.

When she was in a clean dress with her hair combed and tucked under the cap, she turned to Sister Edna to confess her torn nightgown.

Sister Edna barely glanced at it. "Such is of no importance. It can be mended." She took the broom down from the peg and began sweeping. "Would that all could be mended as easily."

Carlyn stared at the sister carefully sweeping out the corner behind her bed. Could this be the same woman who only moments before had so fervently wished Carlyn had run away along with Sister Berdine?

"I am sorry to cause you distress and worry this morning." It seemed a good time to make confession.

"I was not worried. Worry is a sin against the providence of the Eternal Father. I was merely concerned." She didn't look up at Carlyn. "Now make up our former sister's bed. I do not want to touch the bedding of one so ready to sin and run down the path of destruction. It is a great sorrow that in her deviousness, she took one of our finest brothers with her."

Tears pricked Carlyn's eyes as she fluffed the pillows and pulled the covers straight. "I will miss her."

"You have other sisters. Loving sisters like Sister Alice." Sister Edna rolled one of the beds aside and swept under it and rolled it back.

They said no more then, with the only sounds the broom straws sweeping against the floor, the pillows being fluffed, and the beds shifting on their rollers as they chased down every last speck of dirt.

When the bell rang to signal the morning meal, Sister Edna hung up the broom.

Carlyn grabbed that opportunity to speak to her. "Thank you for helping me with my morning duties, Sister Edna."

"That is what sisters do. Help one another. Surely you have been among us long enough to note that." Sister Edna reached for the doorknob to go out in the hall, then hesitated. "I will expect to hear your confession tomorrow after you have had time to consider your wrongs."

"Yea," Carlyn murmured.

"And I will have need to confess my angry words earlier." Sister Edna turned and looked directly at Carlyn. She reached to adjust Carlyn's cap and straighten her neckerchief. She seemed to have to force out her next words. "Also, I would be remiss not to warn you, Sister. I fear there are forces of evil at work within our village."

"You mean Brother Henry's death?"

"Yea, that and other things. I would not want you wandering out in the night and being overtaken by that evil. So vow to me that you will wake me if you feel it necessary to leave the sleeping room prior to the rising bell."

"I don't think I will be slipping out in the night again. I only went last night at Sister Berdine's insistence."

Sister Edna winced at the sound of the Sister Berdine's name. "Do not avoid making the vow of obedience I ask of you. It is my duty to see to your well-being."

"Very well. I promise." It was easy to say the words, for

if she decided to leave the village, she would not wait until night, but leave in the light of the day.

"I trust you will keep your word even though there have been times when you have not had a close relationship with the truth." She didn't wait for Carlyn to respond but turned back to the door. "Now let us line up for the eating room and give our bodies the necessary nourishment."

Carlyn followed Sister Edna out into the hallway. The woman was a mystery. First angry and stern. Next weary and distraught. Then helpful and concerned. Odd as it was, Carlyn thought she preferred the stern Sister Edna. She knew her. She did not know this sister who warned her of evil in the night. Then again, should she remain in her kinder moments, she might allow Carlyn to slip away from her washroom duties to see how Asher was doing.

That didn't happen. The stern Sister Edna was back in control and would consider no departure from the duties of the day. "You have caused enough upsets for one day because of that dog. Best you should dwell on ways to show kindness to your sisters rather than a dog."

Carlyn didn't argue with her, but she did consider coming out of the Gathering Family House after the midday meal and walking to the West Family barn instead of back to the washhouse. But she didn't. Brother Willis had seemed kind. Asher would be all right in his care. Sister Edna was right. Carlyn had caused a great deal of consternation already. This day she could practice obedience to the Shaker way.

Even so, her feet wanted to escape the path of duty. She wouldn't be able to slip away after night to check on Asher, for she had made a promise to Sister Edna. Whether she wanted to follow all the Shaker rules or not, she did want to keep her word.

The morning had passed at a snail's pace with the drudgery of load after load of clothes to sort and wash and hang to dry. Inside the washhouse the noise of the machines and sloshing water closed out everything else as Carlyn pushed through the chores. Outside was better. The sun was shining and the gentle sounds of nature were like a salve on her weary soul. The cows out in the field. The cackle of the hens. The breeze in the trees and the music of the birds. Even the low murmur of the other sisters as they talked while they hung up the wet clothes and took down the dry ones was comforting though it made her miss Sister Berdine.

Why hadn't she told Carlyn she was leaving? Perhaps she would have if Carlyn had not disappeared into the woods after reading Ambrose's letter. She didn't have the letter with her now. She'd stuffed it in her mother's Bible for safekeeping. She didn't need to read it again. Ambrose's words of love were stored in her heart. Even before the letter came. Just as she had been grieving Ambrose long before she read the words of his death.

Was Sister Berdine right that Carlyn needed courage to reach for a new chance to love instead of burying herself here with the Shakers?

Out on the pathway, a group of children walked by. Several of the sisters around Carlyn stopped their labor to watch the children, perhaps with the same desire Carlyn was feeling to have one of those young hands clasped in her own. Or perhaps they were searching for sight of their own children they had given over to the Children's House when they came into the Shakers.

Sister Alice had children. She had pointed them out to

Carlyn once in the schoolyard. Two boys, seven and eight, and a girl, twelve.

"Wasn't it hard to give them up?" Carlyn had thought of how she had wept over Asher. She could not imagine the sorrow of turning a child over to someone else.

"Many things are hard." Sister Alice had breathed out a long sigh. "My husband came home from the war a changed man. He could no longer work the farm. The injury to him did not show, but the war damaged him nonetheless. He needed the peace of Harmony Hill."

"But your children," Carlyn said.

Sister Alice pressed her lips together for a moment before she answered. "I no longer have to see them hungry. They have warm clothes and sturdy shoes. They go to school. By giving up tucking them into their beds each night, I have given them more. A mother has to do what is best for her children." Sister Alice pulled her eyes away from the children. "As I am sure your mother did for you."

"She never had to give us over to others."

"Each person is faced with different challenges. Different hardships. Such is the way of the world. We must pray to have the courage to pick up whatever cross we are given and carry it with the help of our Lord."

"Do you believe as the Shakers do? That marriage is wrong." Carlyn looked around to be sure Sister Edna wasn't near. "That we can shake free of sin and live a perfect life?"

"Nay. But I do believe in peace and love and that working with my hands is a good way to show my love for the Lord and for my sisters and brothers." Sister Alice smiled at Carlyn then. "For me, that is enough. It is not enough for everyone. Do you think it will be enough for you?"

"I don't know," Carlyn answered honestly.

Sister Alice had touched her hand. "Then just consider this a good place to be while you decide what is enough."

It hadn't been enough for Sister Berdine. Carlyn was truly happy for her. Truly. But how she wished she'd waited a few more days. Or a few weeks. Carlyn needed someone she could talk to without worrying about every word. She needed someone to help her figure out what was enough.

Pray about it.

But Carlyn was too weary for prayer. She wanted to lean her arms over the clothesline and fall asleep standing up. The sun felt so good on her back. Maybe in time, the memory of the fire would fade. Maybe she would forget Curt Whitlow's threats. Maybe she would know if the feelings tickling awake inside her when she saw the sheriff would lead to anything. In time. But was there time?

The fresh air scent wafted off the sheet Carlyn pulled from the line. She deftly folded it to place in the basket at her feet.

"Carlyn." At first when she heard her name she thought it was just the memory of Sister Berdine waking her the night before. But this was a man's voice. She looked across the clothesline toward the cistern that was mounded up in front of the washhouse. And there as if she had summoned him with her thoughts was the sheriff.

30

Mitchell watched her a few minutes before he spoke her name. He didn't want to startle her. He thought she might notice him there the way some of the other women had. A few had frowned while others put their hands over their mouths to hide smiles.

He didn't see the old sister. It didn't matter if he did. He only wanted to talk to Carlyn. Surely that was allowed, and if the old sister claimed it was not, then he would pretend it had to do with his investigation.

It didn't. At least not his investigation of the barn fire. What he wanted to investigate was the way just looking at Carlyn made his heart do a stutter step inside his chest. He kept telling himself he barely knew her, but his heart kept whispering back how much he wanted to change that. Sometimes the heart could be unruly.

Her eyes widened when she turned toward him. She stared at him a moment, then glanced around, perhaps bracing for Sister Edna to descend on her. The old sister was no more than a clucky old hen trying to make sure her chicks stayed under her wings.

One must have gotten away already. The chatter among the women was about a couple running away in the night, but he hadn't heard any names. While he didn't think Carlyn would run away with one of the Shaker brothers, neither had he thought Hilda would run away with a Boston dandy while he was fighting the war. The very thought that he might lose any chance of winning Carlyn's affections made his heart freeze in his chest.

Then she appeared from between the sheets billowing in the breeze, and his heart began beating again. Hope was yet alive.

When she stayed rooted by the clothesline, he went to her. He would always be ready to go to her. He just wished he could be surer of his welcome there. She was smiling a bit in spite of her obvious concern about the old sister catching her talking to him.

He peered at Carlyn over the pillowcases flapping on the line. "I need to talk to you."

After he said it, he had no idea what to say next. He did need to talk to her, but not for any reason he could tell her. So many things clamored to fly out of his mouth. *You don't have to stay here. Let me help you. Let me protect you. Let me love you.*

He reined in his thoughts. Why would she believe he could do anything for her when he couldn't even keep her dog corralled?

She took another quick look around. "Sister Edna won't like it, but I must talk to you too." His heart lifted and then fell when she went on. "About Asher."

He jumped in front of her words. "That's what I came to tell you. He got away from Mrs. Snowden. I haven't been able to find him."

"I know." She reached through the clothes on the line to touch his arm.

He wanted to capture her hand and never let it go, but he had no right. Her gesture was innocent, without the meaning he wanted it to have. "You know? How?"

"He found me here." Instead of the smile he might have expected about that, she looked worried.

"So where is he?" Mitchell looked around. "The Shakers didn't harm him, did they?"

"Oh, no." She looked truly surprised by his question. "The Shakers are too kind to hurt Asher."

Mitchell felt a surge of hope at how she spoke of the Shakers as apart from herself. She hadn't completely gone over to their ways as yet. "Where is he then? I can't imagine him being far from you unless he was forced to be."

"He's in the West Family barn. We found him under the corncrib last night. He'd been shot."

"Shot?" Mitchell frowned. "Is he hurt bad?"

"His back leg is damaged, but the brother caring for him thinks it will heal."

"Who shot him?"

"I don't know." She pushed a stray lock of hair back under her Shaker cap. "I have to wonder if he ran afoul of Curt Whitlow."

"Have you seen Curt?" Mitchell asked. "Since you saw him with Brother Henry."

When she hesitated, Mitchell pushed her for an answer. "He hasn't been home and Mrs. Whitlow is worried."

"I haven't seen him." She looked across the pasture toward the woods. "I did glimpse a horse and rider yesterday out in the woods, but I'm almost certain it wasn't Curt."

Mitchell kept his eyes on her face. "Did any of those with you get a better look?"

"No one was with me." She unpinned one of the pillowcases, folded it and carefully placed it in the basket at her feet.

"You were alone? That might have been dangerous, Carlyn." Her given name escaped his lips before he could stop it.

She wouldn't meet his eyes as she took down another pillowcase. "I was often alone at my house, but here with the Shakers, it is difficult to have even a moment to oneself without others near enough to hear your every breath." She sighed and waved her hand to indicate the women around them. "Like now."

He didn't take his eyes off her. It didn't matter who was listening. Only that she was. "But there you had your dog to protect you."

"And my gun," she murmured.

"What happened to your gun?"

"The Shakers took it when I came into the village. They said such is not allowed here. Everything is peace. No need for weapons." She concentrated on laying the pillowcase exactly so in the basket. She looked up at Mitchell. "I am not sure they are right, but I came to no harm in the woods or last night when I waited with Asher for the morning light."

"You were out in the night? Don't you realize that whoever set the fire could still be lurking around the village ready to cause more trouble?" He wanted to grab her shoulders and make her look straight at him. "What were you thinking?"

"That Asher was hurt." She reached to unpin another pillowcase.

Mitchell pulled in a slow breath. He couldn't let his emotions cloud his thinking. She was right. She had not been harmed. "You need to tell me exactly what happened yesterday."

"I already told you. I took a walk so I could be alone for a while. Sister Edna was very unhappy with me for neglecting my duties, as she will be again when she sees me talking to you instead of efficiently gathering in the clothes. She is near despair in teaching me the Shaker way."

That news didn't make Mitchell unhappy. "All right. So you went into the woods to be alone. You saw someone on a horse but don't think it was Whitlow." He waited until she nodded. "But what of last night? What had you out in the middle of the night to find Asher when you didn't even know he'd gotten away from me?"

"It is a story too long to tell."

Mitchell crossed his arms and leveled his eyes on her. "Long or not, I'm not leaving until I hear it. I've got all day."

"But I have work to do." She jerked the last pillowcase off the line, dropped it in the basket without bothering to fold it as she had the others, and bent to pick up the basket.

Mitchell leaned down and put his hand on the basket to keep her from leaving. "Story first. Until I know who set the fire and why, I need to know about anything unusual happening around here. And a young sister wandering around in the dark is definitely unusual here in Harmony Hill."

"Not so unusual." She let go of the basket and straightened up. "I've been told such happens from time to time. A Shaker sister and brother succumb to temptation and sneak away as Sister Berdine and Brother Payton did last night. But they heard a dog whimpering, and Sister Berdine came back to tell me. She knew I had a dog before I came here."

"Then what?"

"I coaxed him out from under the corncrib, and he was bleeding. Brother Payton said to take him to Brother Willis at first light. So that's what I did." She looked to the west sadly. "But they will not let me go see him now. So many rules." Her eyes came back to Mitchell. "Will you go get him and take him home?"

"Do you still trust me to keep him? After what happened?"

"He likes you. In time, he will get used to being with you." She touched his hand lightly like the kiss of a butterfly. "Please."

It was on the tip of his tongue to tell her that she could get used to being with him too, but she'd given no sign she would welcome such words from him. She wanted him to take care of her dog. Mitchell held in his disappointment.

"All right. If he's able, I'll take him with me." Mitchell was rewarded with a full smile.

"Will you come back by here? So I can see him."

"Only if you make me a promise in return."

She looked leery of agreeing. "What promise?"

"That you won't go out alone at night until I catch whoever caused the fire."

"First Sister Edna wants me to promise that and now you," Carlyn said.

"Sister Edna?"

"Yea, she made me give my word I would not leave the sleeping room without waking her. I am not to do that anyway." Carlyn's smile came back. "But she knows I am prone to ignore the rules if they don't suit me. As now, talking to you." Her smile disappeared. "She has not been herself. Something is bothering her."

"About the fire?" The old sister had seemed to guard her answers the day he'd questioned Carlyn in Elder Derron's office.

"Perhaps. The fire did upset her."

"If she has information or even suspicions, she should tell me. Evading the truth is as bad as lying."

"Sister Edna wouldn't lie." Carlyn looked truly shocked. "She says a Believer must confess every sin and I have no doubt she does so."

"But it might not be her sin, but someone else's. She could be protecting someone."

"Who? She would have no reason to protect Curt Whitlow, and he was the one arguing with Brother Henry." Carlyn ran her fingers along the clothesline between them.

"I don't know, but I intend to find out." He barely kept from reaching for her hand. "After I see about Asher."

"Thank you, Sheriff Brodie." She bent to pick up her basket again and this time he didn't stop her.

"My given name is Mitchell." He kept his eyes on her face even as he felt the color rising in his own.

"Mitchell." She almost whispered his name, but she said it. Her cheeks pinked to match his as she lowered her eyes to the basket of clothes she held. "I must go. Sister Edna already has much to forgive in my behavior."

"Where is she? I need to find out if what's bothering her has to do with the fire."

"Please don't." Carlyn looked up, alarmed.

"If she knows something about the fire, she has to tell me."

"I suppose so, but don't let her know I said anything to you. She's ready to lock me away somewhere now."

"She wouldn't do that, would she?" Mitchell frowned.

"I don't think so, but she would be upset to know I spoke of her to you."

"I won't mention you."

"Thank you." She looked relieved as she turned toward the washhouse. She looked over her shoulder at him. "I will watch for you to come back by."

The West Family barn was easy to find. When Mitchell went inside, the dog barked, but only once. A greeting. Not a warning. Asher flapped his tail in the straw and struggled to his feet when he saw Mitchell.

"Easy, boy." Mitchell stepped inside the stall to kneel down by the dog. He pushed him down on the old blanket that must have been put there for him. His back leg was bandaged, but Asher didn't seem to be chewing on the wrap.

"He's a smart dog, that one." A Shaker brother came and leaned against the bottom stall door. He was tall and wiry with hands and face browned by the sun and wrinkled by the years. "He appears to know you. That girl what brought him over this morn acted like he was hers."

"He is, but she says she can't keep him here."

"Yea. Against the rules, but I keep waiting for Mother Ann to inspire the Ministry to change that. I've met many dogs that would make fine Shakers."

Mitchell stood to face the man. "I'm Sheriff Mitchell Brodie."

"Brother Willis Hayes." The man nodded at Mitchell but didn't make any move to shake hands. "So the girl gave you the dog?"

"She did, but he tracked her down here." Mitchell let his gaze slide back to the dog.

"Got hisself shot on the way." Brother Willis leaned on

the half door. "I picked out the buckshot and lathered him with our healing ointment. In a couple of weeks, he'll be back on all four. Might carry a limp."

"Who shot him?"

"No way to know that. But whoever it was must not have had a clear shot. That is, if they aimed to kill the dog. Could be they were merely trying to scare it off."

"From Harmony Hill?"

"Nay, no Believer would shoot at a stray dog. The poor fellow must have encountered someone from the world before he got to our village."

"When do you think he was shot?" The dog's wound probably didn't have anything to do with the fire, but then if there was a prime suspect for shooting Asher, it had to be Curt Whitlow, who seemed to have disappeared.

"No longer ago than yesterday. The young sister found him in the night." Brother Willis shook his head. "When she should have been in her bed. Bad things can happen in the dark."

"So they can," Mitchell said.

"Yea." Brother Willis pulled on his chin. "Those of the world refuse to allow us to live here in peace."

"You're thinking about the fire."

"Yea." A horse nickered in one of the stalls, and Brother Willis looked toward the sound. "It does not surprise me Brother Henry died trying to save his horses. I would be ready to do the same. The horse is a faithful servant."

"But the fire was intentionally set."

"Of that, there is no doubt." Brother Willis looked grim.

There were doubts about other things. Like whether Brother Henry was an intended victim or an accidental one. "Did you see Brother Henry's body?"

"Yea."

"He was badly burned. Are you sure it was him?"

"Who else could it be?" Brother Willis frowned. "It was his barn. And he is gone. Why would you ask such a question?"

"It's my job to ask questions and stop those who might cause trouble."

"Trouble can best be stopped by those of the world not coming among us stirring up things best left alone." The Shaker's face stiffened. It was plain he was including Mitchell in those of the world.

"But a man died."

"Every man has a time to die. Such is the Lord's plan."

"I doubt the Lord planned Brother Henry to be in the fire."

"The ways of the Lord are far above the understanding of man. It is best for us to accept what has happened and not linger in regret." Brother Willis shook his head with a look of pity spreading across his face. "That is hard for one of the world to understand, but if you would open your heart to our Mother Ann's teachings, then you would see. She taught us that if we take all sorrow out of life, we take away all richness, depth, and tenderness. Sorrow is the furnace that melts selfish hearts together in love."

"I still have a job to do," Mitchell said.

"Then you should go back to the world to do it and leave us in peace."

The dog whined, hearing the tension between them. Mitchell was wasting his breath arguing with the Shaker man, so he turned his attention back to Asher. "Should I take him with me today?"

"That would not be wise. Unless you have a wagon and someone to hold the dog to be sure he couldn't jump out and make his injury worse." Brother Willis opened the bottom door to the stall and stepped in beside Mitchell. He bent down to run a hand over the dog's back. "Better he stays here. Such a good dog will be no trouble."

"If you think that best." Mitchell knew the Shaker man was right, but he hated leaving Asher. Brother Willis followed Mitchell out of the stall.

When Asher whimpered, Mitchell looked back at him. The Shaker put his hand on Mitchell's shoulder. "Worry not. Elder Marcus has assured me the Ministry will allow me to care for the dog since we have a duty to be kind to animals. When the dog is well enough, we will bring him to you in the town."

Asher howled when Mitchell went on out of the barn. The lonesome sound made him want to turn back and take the dog, but Asher was better off there under the Shaker's care. If only Mitchell could believe the same was true for Asher's mistress. Something wasn't right here in the Shaker village, but whatever it was, none of the Shakers wanted to talk about it.

That included Elder Derron, who was waiting beside Mitchell's horse. The man stood straight and stiff and offered no greeting.

"Is something wrong, Elder?" Mitchell asked.

"Yea." The man twisted his hands together, and then pulled them apart to jerk on the corners of his jacket. "I've been asked to inform you the Ministry feels it would be best if you did not return to Harmony Hill. It is upsetting to our sisters to have you questioning them."

Mitchell studied the man's face. A little tic twitched his cheek. Mitchell let the silence build between them for a moment. "I would not want to upset anyone here in your village, especially your sisters, but I do need to talk to Sister Edna again. She may know something about the fire."

"She does not," Elder Derron said flatly. "You waste time here. Yours and ours. Those who set the fire are of the world. You will not find them here at Harmony Hill."

"Are you sure of that?"

"Yea, very sure." The elder buttoned his coat and then unbuttoned it. He played his fingers around the brim of his hat before he settled it farther down on his head. "Good day, Sheriff Brodie. We will send for you if you are needed."

Mitchell started to tell the elder he couldn't kick a sheriff out of his own county. But there were times to argue and times to step back and wait for another day to wage battle. With the elder watching him, he had little choice but to ride out of the village with no opportunity to go past the wash-house to keep his promise to Carlyn.

But he'd be back. And somehow, someday, he was going to leave this village with Carlyn riding on his horse behind him. That was a promise he was making to himself and one he would keep.

Asher's howls followed him out of the village.

31

Carlyn tarried gathering in the clothes as long as she could. When she heard Asher howling, she wanted to desert her clothesbasket and run to the West Family barn.

She might have dared it except Sister Edna was watching her. The sister wasn't working with the clothes. She wasn't working on anything, unless watching was considered work. Perhaps in the Shaker village, it was. Sister Edna appeared in the shadow of the washhouse shortly after Sheriff Brodie left. Every time Carlyn glanced her way, Sister Edna's eyes were fastened on her. With the old Sister Edna glare. The one that meant every rule had to be strictly obeyed.

If only Carlyn could understand why so many rules were necessary. Union, Sister Edna told her. Unity of spirit. But Carlyn could not imagine ever having unity of spirit with Sister Edna, even at the times when she surprised Carlyn with a gentler manner. That manner was nowhere in evidence now.

She must have found out about Carlyn talking to the sheriff. To Mitchell. Carlyn smiled as she unpinned two socks from the line and rolled one inside the other. It had been good calling him by his given name and hearing her name on his lips. That sign of friendship made Carlyn believe she could depend on him to do what he said he would do.

Yet the afternoon slipped past without his return. Her shoulders drooped as she carried in the last basket of clothes, and she could hardly push one foot in front of the other. She'd lost too much sleep. That was all. Her weariness had nothing to do with the sheriff not keeping his word.

"Is something wrong, Sister Carlyn?" Sister Edna stepped up beside her.

"Yea. I am very tired. May I retire to the sleeping room and skip the evening meal?"

"You have skipped too many meals of late, Sister. You must keep a uniform schedule of nourishment and rest to keep your body strong and able."

"I will be stronger tomorrow."

"And readier to apply yourself to the Shaker way?" Sister Edna did not seem to expect an answer. That was just as well, for Carlyn had none to give. "That is, unless you must witness a sister's descent into sin or dally with sin yourself by entertaining those of the world."

Carlyn didn't pretend not to know what Sister Edna meant. "I did not seek out the sheriff. He came to tell me he had lost my dog."

"The dog that you had to sneak out of our house to find in the night?"

"Yea. The one I could not leave wounded without finding him help. Brother Payton assured me you Shakers are ever kind to animals."

"Our former brother should have stayed in his retiring

313

room as well. Allowing himself to be lured into sin after so many faithful years. He will find no peace with that Delilah."

Sister Edna glared at Carlyn as though daring her to defend Sister Berdine. For once, Carlyn managed to stay silent as she stared down at the basket of clothes. It would not do for Sister Edna to glimpse the happiness Carlyn felt at the thought of Sister Berdine finding the love she had so long desired. As Carlyn's mother had been prone to say, the Lord could work in mysterious ways his wonders to perform. Was he also working wonders for her?

"It would be best if we did not speak of those who have deserted their calling and fallen by the wayside." Sister Edna heaved out a long breath. "If you do not change your thinking, the same can happen to you. It is not good to encourage the attention of those of the world. I fear you are putting your feet on a slippery path, my sister, when you stand and talk with the sheriff."

"I asked him to go see about Asher." When the lines between Sister Edna's eyes deepened, Carlyn added. "My dog. Remember, I told you the sheriff took in my dog when I found out he would not be allowed to stay with me here." Carlyn looked back toward the road. "He said he'd come back by here so I'd know about Asher."

"It is beyond my understanding how you can worry so about a dog." Sister Edna shook her head. "You should care for your sisters with the same fullness of heart."

"Yea, my sisters are very kind to me, but Asher was a faithful companion to me. I cannot help worrying about him."

"You have no need to worry. The dog is yet here where

Brother Willis can care for it, but Sheriff Brodie was asked to leave and not return to our village. One of the brethren will take him the dog when it has sufficiently healed."

"But what of the fire and Brother Henry's death? Is that not a matter for the law?"

A shadow passed over Sister Edna's face, but then her frown returned, fiercer than ever. "It is time to put that sorrow behind us and consider what is best for the Society."

"But—"

"No more argument. For your own good, you must give up worldly thinking and become a proper Believer novitiate. You will be safe here and find happiness once you abide by the rules. It is my duty to make sure that happens, and I take the duties assigned to me by the Ministry very seriously." The bell rang, signaling the end of the workday.

"Yea." Carlyn had no strength to disagree. "If only I can rest."

"You will rest at the assigned times, the same as all your sisters, and then you will eat the evening meal. After that we are to take part in a Union Meeting."

"A Union Meeting?"

"I've told you about them. A time to converse with our brothers. Five brothers and five sisters."

"Can I not wait until another night?"

"Nay. Eldress Lilith has told me to bring you." There was no give on Sister Edna's face.

"Why would she do that?"

Sister Edna's stern look gave way to concern for just a moment. Then her eyes tightened as she straightened her bonnet. "It is not our place to question the elders and eldresses. Only to do as they ask. Mother Ann directs the Ministry and the

Ministry directs the elders. It is as it must be. For the unity of our Society."

Carlyn fell asleep during rest time. Sister Alice shook her awake when it was time to go to the eating room. There Sister Edna had to touch Carlyn's shoulder to remind her to rise from prayers before the meal. She managed to swallow the few spoonfuls of food she dipped out on her plate. Then in a daze, she followed Sister Edna to the other side of the house to one of the brethren's rooms for the Union Meeting.

Sister Edna stopped her before they reached the door. Her eyes darted to the side as though to be sure no one was near. Even so, she kept her voice low. "Since you are new to our Society, it will be best if you listen and stay quiet."

"Yea," Carlyn murmured. "But what if I cannot stay awake?"

"Worry not. I will poke you should you nod off." Sister Edna did not smile as she led the way into the room.

The brethren were already seated facing the sisters. Carlyn and Sister Edna were the last to arrive. Sister Mamie and Sister Adele smiled at them, and Eldress Lilith nodded solemnly as they took the empty chairs. Of the men, she knew only Elder Derron. The brother who sat directly across from her looked very young and as out of place as Carlyn felt. That mattered not. She merely had to make it through the hour and then to bed. She was too tired to even think of sneaking away to see Asher.

Carlyn sat up as straight as she could and struggled to stay awake. They talked of new songs to learn and how much applesauce might be sold on the trading trips. Elder Derron spoke at length about what was selling and not selling since he handled much of the commerce of the family. One of the brethren, an older man named Jackson, reported on the hay harvest and the corn not yet picked.

The talk was easy, as though they were sharing time in a parlor on a Sunday afternoon until one of the brothers—Brother Marvin, if Carlyn remembered his name correctly—brought up the barn. "Has the sheriff found those who burned our barn? I saw him riding through the village today."

His words were better than a poke to keep Carlyn awake. The ease fled the room to be replaced by an odd tenseness.

Elder Derron finally answered, "Yea, he was here, but he was looking in the wrong place. Those responsible won't be found in our village."

"They were here once," Brother Marvin said.

"In the night," Eldress Lilith spoke up.

"Yea, such men use the cover of night to hide their sinful ways," Elder Derron said.

Sister Adele, a tiny slip of a woman who appeared to be even older than Sister Edna, let out a gasp. "You don't think they'll come back, do you? They could burn us in our beds."

"Calm yourself, Sister Adele." Sister Edna spoke up in a strident voice. "No need to have the vapors. That would not be becoming for a Believer."

"Nor would being burned to a crisp in our beds." Sister Adele crossed her arms and glared at Sister Edna.

"Here, here." Eldress Lilith clapped her hands as though bringing order to a room of unruly children. "We must focus on pleasant things, my sisters and brothers. You will make our young converts have unhappy dreams."

"One looks to be near dreaming already." Elder Derron leaned forward in his chair toward Carlyn. "Did you not sleep well, Sister Carlyn?"

She peeked out of the sides of her eyes toward Sister Edna, who sat stiff in her chair, her eyes straight ahead. Carlyn kept her answer short. "Nay, not last night."

"And you talked to Sheriff Brodie, I've been told." Elder Derron didn't let his eyes stray from Carlyn.

If the air was tense before, now it was crackling. Carlyn waited for Eldress Lilith to clap her hands again and move the conversation back to better topics, but she did not seem as ready to call down the elder as the sisters. Carlyn moistened her lips and wondered what answer would give her the least trouble.

"Yea, I did." Sometimes simple truth was the best way.

"And did he ask about the fire?"

"Nay. We spoke of my dog. Not the fire."

"You mean the dog now being cared for by Brother Willis because he was injured." He leaned back in his chair and tilted it a bit off the floor.

"Yea. Someone shot him."

"Who?" Elder Derron dropped his chair back to the floor with a loud thump.

"I cannot say." She was beginning to feel as though she were on trial.

Elder Derron leaned toward her. "That man, the one you saw in the village before the fire. What did you say his name was?"

"Curt Whitlow. You told the sheriff you knew him." She stared straight at the elder. She didn't dare look toward Sister Edna, who would surely be turning pale because of Carlyn's lack of diffidence.

"Yea, so I do. Sister Edna claims the sight of him frightened you that day you saw him talking to Brother Henry."

"He had given me problems before I came here."

318

"What sort of problems?" The elder was insistent.

"What difference does that make?" Sister Edna spoke up. "That was before our sister joined with us. Part of the sufferings of the world. Now she is with us. One of our sisters."

"Yea," Eldress Lilith agreed. "I cannot see the purpose of your questions, Elder Derron, when we are supposed to be having a pleasant visit."

The elder held up his hands and leaned back in his chair again. "I was simply going to ask if she thought Curt Whitlow might have shot the dog."

"Then that is what you should have asked without traveling around the world to do so," Eldress Lilith said.

"What does it matter anyway?" Brother Marvin said. "It is a sorrowful shame to be so wicked to shoot a dog, but I doubt those of the world consider it a crime. The crime was the fire that killed our Brother Henry. That is what we need to consider."

Sister Edna fixed a hard look on Brother Marvin. "What we need to consider is peace and unity among us."

"Yea," Eldress Lilith said. "Let us appeal to Mother Ann to bring peace to our midst and close our meeting with a song. Sister Mamie, lead us in something to unify our spirits."

"Yea." Sister Mamie thought a moment and then began to sing. "When cheer fills the hearts of my friends, and brethren and sisters are kind."

The others joined their voices to hers. Carlyn had never heard the song so she simply did as Sister Edna had earlier ordered. Listened.

> What joy to my bosom it sends, what peace to my
> troubled mind.

To know that my dear gospel kin have love and affec-
tion for me,
My spirit from sorrow does win and causes dejection
to flee.

With that, the meeting was over. Carlyn was so eager to
go to bed she didn't notice Sister Edna wasn't behind her
until she got to their sleeping room. But it wasn't her duty to
watch Sister Edna. Sister Edna's duty was to watch Carlyn.
This night she could watch her sleep. Even so, Carlyn was
relieved when Sister Edna came into the room, as though by
some strange upheaval of circumstance, she had to feel as
responsible for Sister Edna as the older sister was compelled
to feel for her.

Along with the other sisters, Carlyn knelt to silently say
her evening prayers. *Thank thee, Lord, for the day. Protect
us through the night. Give us blessings on the morrow. In
Thy holy name I pray.*

That was the first prayer her mother had taught her. Simple. Complete. Quick. She needed quick tonight. Others
were still on their knees, including Sister Edna, when Carlyn
slipped under her bedcover.

She had thought she would sleep like the dead, but instead she kept jerking awake with her heart pounding in her
ears, unsure if whatever noise she'd heard was in her restless
dreams or in the room. Beside her, Sister Marie slept soundly.
All around the room, the sound of in and out breathing indicated all was well. She drew in a breath and shut her eyes.
Then the door slid open and closed. A furtive sound. Surely
the same as it must have sounded the night before when she
had followed Sister Berdine outside.

Carlyn sat up in the bed. Moonlight filtered through the window to show no bed looked empty unless pillows had been stuffed under covers. She looked toward Sister Edna's bed nearest the door. The covers were folded back neatly and the bed empty.

A call of nature perhaps. But they had a chamber pot so that trips to the privy were not necessary in the dark of the night.

She swung her feet over the side of the bed and listened intently. Was that voices she heard? There shouldn't be voices. Especially not angry voices.

She had promised not to go out of the room without telling Sister Edna, but she wasn't there to tell. She could wake one of the others, but if it turned out to be nothing, she would have done naught but steal her sister's sleeping time. It must only be an echo of a dream making her think she was hearing an argument. But she would not rest easy until she found out.

Without bothering to put on shoes, she tiptoed out of the room. In the hallway, the voices over her head weren't loud enough for her to make out words, but she heard no peace in the sound. At each end of the hall, steep stairways led up to the third floor. She headed toward the sisters' stairs. The third floor had no sleeping rooms, only chests built into the attic walls for storing extra clothing and essentials. And places to watch.

But no one would be watching at this time of the night. She should go back to the sleeping room and pull the covers over her head. If it was Sister Edna meeting someone for whatever reason, she would not welcome Carlyn's interference. Even so, Carlyn kept moving toward the staircase as silently as a willow leaf on the wind.

A shriek sent chills up Carlyn's back. A terrible crash followed. She ran then, her bare feet skimming the wood floor.

Sister Edna lay crumpled at the bottom of the steep stairs in a pool of moonlight coming from the window at the end of hall. Not in her nightgown as Carlyn was, but dressed as though ready for morning even though it must be hours before dawn.

"Sister Edna." Carlyn stooped down next to her, thankful to note her chest rising and falling. She touched her face and the sister's eyelids flew open wide.

She clutched Carlyn's hand. "It's not safe. He's . . ." Her eyes widened.

"Who?"

"Him." She moaned then and turned loose of Carlyn's hand to touch her bonnet. "My head." Her eyes seemed to stop seeing even before they closed.

"Sister Edna!" The woman gave no response. Carlyn touched her chest. It was still rising and falling.

Brothers and sisters, aroused by the noise of Sister Edna's fall, ran toward them from both sides of the house. They stopped in a circle around Sister Edna and Carlyn.

"Is she dead?" one of the sisters asked, dread in her voice.

"Nay. She yet breathes," Carlyn said.

Then Elder Derron pushed to the front of the Shakers. He was panting a bit. "What happened here?"

"She must have fallen down the steps," Carlyn said.

"Did she fall?" His eyes bored into Carlyn. "Or did you push her? Tell the truth, Sister."

32

"I would never do such a thing." Carlyn stared up at him. "I found her here at the bottom of the stairs."

"Yea, that is what you say, but your retiring room is far down the hall. Yet you were here first." Elder Derron's voice was harsh, his face accusing. She could hardly believe he was the same man who seemed so calm and in control behind his desk at the Trustee House.

One of the brethren stepped forward with a lamp. Carlyn put her hand up to shield her eyes from the light that shone down on her. They seemed more intent on accusing her than in helping Sister Edna.

"Please, she's hurt." Carlyn looked down at Sister Edna.

"That we can see, but we must know what happened," Elder Derron demanded.

Carlyn tamped down on her irritation. "Something woke me, and when Sister Edna was not in her bed, it seemed strange. I had never wakened in the night to find her bed empty."

"But there were times she found your bed empty, were there not?"

The lamp cast dark shadows on the wall behind the Shakers encircling her. Grim shadows. Carlyn straightened her shoulders. She refused to let them intimidate her. "I am innocent of any wrong here and only guilty of concern for my sister." Carlyn appealed to the sisters who seemed afraid to step past Elder Derron. "Please send someone to fetch your doctor. Sister Edna said her head hurt."

"She spoke?" Elder Derron sounded surprised.

"Yea, before she passed out."

"What did she say?" the elder demanded.

"What matters that?" Eldress Lilith pushed past him to kneel by Sister Edna. "Oh, dear Mother Ann, please help our faithful sister." She whispered the words as a prayer, then reached to touch Carlyn's arm. "Fear not, Sister. One of the brethren has gone for Brother Benjamin. His medical skill may bring our sister back to awareness so she can tell us what happened."

"Yea, I will pray so." Carlyn looked at Eldress Lilith, who let her eyes slide back to Sister Edna as though she wasn't sure Carlyn meant what she said.

"It would be better for you to tell the truth, Sister," Elder Derron said. "Perhaps you did not mean for her to fall."

"I would not hurt her. I don't care how difficult she is to please." Carlyn got to her feet to face the Shaker elder.

"Many hard things have happened in our family since you came among us. Carrying a gun, I am told." Elder Derron emphasized those last words. "And now this. I feel it best, for our safety and yours, to lock you in the vagrant house until we can summon the sheriff in the morning."

324

Carlyn's heart pounded in her ears. They couldn't think she had caused Sister Edna's fall, but then someone may have. She had heard angry voices. And Sister Edna had said he was there. "I am innocent. I would not hurt Sister Edna, but she said she saw someone. A man. Perhaps he is still here." She looked across Sister Edna toward the stairs.

Nobody moved.

"Sister Edna also often spoke of your loose attachment to the truth," Elder Derron said. "Is that not true, Eldress Lilith?"

"Yea, it was a concern to Sister Edna." Eldress Lilith did not look up as she continued to stroke Sister Edna's arms.

"Then you are in agreement, Eldress, that we must confine this sister until we can determine what happened here this night." Elder Derron sounded like it was already settled.

"Yea, that might be best," the eldress agreed.

"Best?" Carlyn stooped down beside Eldress Lilith. "You cannot mean to lock me up somewhere. I have done nothing wrong."

"If that is true, you have no reason to worry." The eldress finally looked at Carlyn. "The house we keep for those wayfarers who pass through our village in need of a bed is clean and warm." For a moment her eyes reflected kindness, but then the unyielding look was back. "You must do as the elder says. For your own security as well as ours."

Carlyn stood up. She wanted to run, but there was no escape. She took a deep breath. The eldress was right. She had no reason to worry. She had done no wrong, and when Sister Edna came to her senses she would not accuse Carlyn falsely. If she regained her faculties.

Eldress Lilith kept her voice calm as she took charge and

issued orders to those standing around her. "Sister Alice, accompany Sister Carlyn back to your room and stay with her while she dresses. The rest of you, return to your beds. I will wait here for Brother Benjamin to come."

Carlyn had no choice except to follow Sister Alice back to their sleeping room where she stood in the middle of the room, at a loss for what to do next. Sister Alice held clothes out to her. Carlyn stared at them a moment, but then pulled her gown off and took the offered dress and underskirt.

"We know you would not intend to hurt Sister Edna," Sister Alice assured Carlyn as she picked up the discarded gown and folded it neatly.

Carlyn paused in adjusting the dress to look at Sister Alice. "You can't think I pushed her?"

"Nay, we know you would not," Sister Marie spoke up beside them.

"Yea, it will all come clear in the morning light," Sister Alice said. "You have nothing to worry about here among us."

If only she could believe that was true. Instead, too many things had gone wrong at Harmony Hill while she had been there. Elder Derron was right about that, at least. The Shaker bell that had seemed her answer weeks ago had perhaps been a warning instead. Now they were going to lock her away, but come morning, she would collect her dog and leave the village to find another way.

With prayer. Her mother's voice tickled through her mind. *Always with prayer.*

Like a condemned person, Carlyn followed Elder Derron through the night to a small house at the edge of the village. The light from the lantern he carried wavered with each step and added to the surreal feel of the moment. It would have been better to walk with only the moonlight guiding their steps. Sister Alice and Sister Marie walked behind Carlyn.

At the house, Sister Alice lit a taper from the lantern flame and assured Carlyn once more that all would be well come morning. Sister Marie wept and hugged her. Elder Derron pointed the two sisters outside and, without a word, shut the door. The lock turned and Carlyn was alone.

She stared at the door and only barely kept from crossing over to try the handle. She took a deep breath. She was not afraid of being alone. In the last few weeks with the Shakers, she had sometimes wished for such silence. But it was disturbing to be falsely accused and locked up.

The truth would come out. She had no reason to feel doom settling heavily on her shoulders. Shadows from the candle flame flickered on the walls as though mocking her. She reached to extinguish it but hesitated. She would have no way to relight it. Was she so bereft of courage that she feared shadows?

Pray. That is the best way to find courage for whatever must be borne.

"But I have prayed," Carlyn whispered. "Over and over. And the answers seem few."

Pray anyway.

"Dear Lord." She shut her eyes. At least she could pray for Sister Edna. "Let Sister Edna come back to health. Give the Shaker doctor skill." It seemed odd praying aloud after all the silent Shaker prayers, but at the same time, the spoken words seemed necessary. "Yea, though I walk through the valley of the shadow of death, I will fear no evil. But I am afraid, Lord. Forgive me, but I am afraid."

The sheriff would believe her. Mitchell. Even if he had to arrest her, he would believe her. With that thought, she breathed easier. He would be there after the sun rose. He would help her. The Lord had given her a friend.

She left the candle burning. It might gutter out before morning, but if it did, she would face the darkness then. She had no idea what time it was. She paced around the small room that held a narrow bed and a table with a chair. A broom hung on a peg next to the door. She tried to push up the one window, but it would not budge. Nailed shut from the outside.

Her heart raced in a spasm of panic. She shut her eyes and blew out a long breath. She would not think about being locked in. She would only think about the morning when Mitchell would come.

She looked at the bed but could not lie down. Instead she sat in the chair and wished for her mother's Bible. But whether she had the Bible or not, she did have the verses her mother had helped her store in her heart for just such lonely times. Scraps of those verses rose in her mind. *For God so loved the world. The Lord is my shepherd. O God, thou art my God; early will I seek thee. Hear my voice, O God, in my prayer.*

The Scripture calmed her and she nodded off. The sound of the key turning in the lock brought her instantly awake. It was still dark. Sister Edna must have awakened and assured Eldress Lilith of Carlyn's innocence.

The doorknob turned, but slowly, almost furtively. Carlyn's heart started pounding again.

"Who's there?" She hated the way her voice quavered.

There was no answer as the door was pushed open. The

draft extinguished the candle but not before Carlyn recognized Elder Derron. Her knees went weak with relief. Relief that was short-lived.

He held his hand out to her. "Come, Sister. It is not safe here. Sister Edna was right. The man is here and he knows where you are."

"What man?" Carlyn stayed where she was. The elder sounded odd.

"Whitlow. You are right to fear him. He has evil intent against you. Against us all." The timbre of Elder Derron's voice went up, pushing fear into the room.

"Curt Whitlow is here?"

The elder's face was shadowed by his hat. "Yea. Mother Ann warned me in a vision of what must be done." He motioned for her again. "Hurry. While there is yet time."

Her heart pounding, she followed him out into the night. She didn't know why her feet were so hesitant. Elder Derron was with her. Curt wouldn't bother her with him beside her. Even so, the dark seemed to reach toward her, warning her of unseen dangers. It would be good to be back inside with the sisters around her.

The elder rushed her along the pathway. Disoriented by the night, she didn't realize at first that they were going away from the village instead of toward the Gathering Family House. When the rock pathway gave way to dirt, she slowed her steps. "Where are we going?"

"Somewhere safe." He looked back at her.

She stopped walking. "But this is the wrong direction."

"Nay. This is the way we must go." He grasped her arm. "Mother Ann has revealed to me what must be done."

"Your Mother Ann may be wrong."

"Nay, that cannot be. Mother Ann has shown me how to protect our Society."

"We should go back to the village." She tried to pull free, but he gripped her tighter.

"Nay, the danger is real. I have been warned that it is so. Those wishing to do evil have been seen near the houses. They might even now be lurking in the darkness around us." He tugged her forward. "It is my duty to make sure all is safe. To see to you. There is no turning back."

She looked behind her. The village seemed even farther away and the shadows darker. Curt could be hiding in one of those shadows waiting for her, and here, this far from all the Shakers, no one would hear her if she cried for help. No one but Elder Derron, who appeared to be unhinged by the night's happenings. Unhinged or not, it might be best to stay beside him. She stopped pulling against him and continued down the path with him. He did not let go of her arm.

The farther they went, the more it felt wrong, but what choice did she have? She knew what Curt was capable of doing. Elder Derron only wanted peace. Even if he was seeing visions, he would not harm her.

He pointed toward a root cellar. "Whitlow will not bother you here." He pulled her down some stone steps and opened a wooden door.

"Nay." Carlyn dug in her feet. "I will hide here in the shadows."

The elder breathed out a long sigh. "Sister Edna warned me that you continually rebelled against her instructions. Such a rebellious spirit does not become a Believer." He grasped her arm tighter until his fingers were bruising her arm. "You must do as you are told."

"I am not a Shaker believer."

"Yea, not all can be so blessed." Elder Derron leaned closer to her. "It is very dark. Come. Here's a lantern by the door." The handle of the lantern screeched metal on metal when he picked it up.

"Light it first so that we can see." She needed light.

"Nay. Best to wait until we're inside to light the match. Such a flare of light out here could draw the wrong eyes and increase the danger. Mother Ann has revealed to me that I must take the light into the darkness in order for all to be well."

When Carlyn still hesitated, he went on. "I promise there are no spiders or snakes."

If only she could see his face, but she could not. Nor could she pull her arm free of his iron grip. He tugged her into the root cellar and pulled the door shut behind them, closing out the scant light the moon had afforded them.

"You won't be found here." At last he turned loose of her arm. "Stand still while I light the lantern. You wouldn't want to fall over something."

Her heart pounded up in her ears as she rubbed her arm. She had been in root cellars many times, but never in the pitch black of night. She pulled in a breath to calm herself. A bad smell assaulted her nose. A dead mouse perhaps. The elder had not promised no mice.

He was fiddling with the lantern. When he struck the match, the flare blinded Carlyn for a second. Then the lantern light played on the earthen walls and revealed the source of the unpleasant odor. Curt Whitlow slumped against one of the walls. Though his eyes were open, the light did not bother him.

Carlyn ran for the door, but Elder Derron stepped in front of her. A moment ago, she had wanted to see his face, but now the sight of it terrified her. His eyes were focused on a spot beyond Carlyn as though seeing spirits.

"Mother Ann is merciful." His voice was as chilling as the damp, cold feel of death.

33

"Dear God," Carlyn whispered. Then no more words would come.

"Prayers are good, but a proper Believer speaks them silently." The elder's eyes came back to her. "That is as the Bible instructs. To go into your prayer closet." He looked around. "This can be your prayer closet. A wonderful place for prayer. I daresay even Mr. Whitlow said a few prayers in his time here." He gestured toward the body.

Carlyn kept her eyes on the elder. If she could distract him, she might get past him to the door. He did not seem to have a weapon. Then again, Curt was dead. Very dead.

"You killed him." Carlyn's voice sounded hoarse.

The man looked surprised. "Nay. That is not so."

"But he's dead."

"Oh yes, quite dead. But not by my hand. Mother Ann punished him for bringing trouble to our village. She was ready with her help since she knows I was merely trying to increase the Society's land holdings when I was enticed into

Mr. Whitlow's nefarious dealings. She is ever ready with her protection. First Brother Henry, poor soul, and then Mr. Whitlow."

"You killed Brother Henry too." Trembles swept up and down Carlyn until she could barely stand.

Elder Derron frowned. "Nay. How can you think I would kill Brother Henry?"

"If you set the fire, you caused him to die."

"You accuse me wrongly. I would never intentionally harm my brother. Even if he did threaten to report to the Ministry my errors in judgment." Elder Derron wrinkled his brow in bewilderment. "Poor Brother Henry was excitable. He no doubt was troubled with such panicked feelings when the barn began to burn. He was dedicated to his duty of caring for his horses. He would not have left any behind without trying to save them."

"You knew that, so you set the fire." Carlyn understood panicked feelings. Her heart was thumping in her ears.

"Nay, Sister. Stop and think. It is against a Believer's spiritual core to destroy anything. Certainly not a well-built barn or our good horses. Those of the world have no such qualms as they follow the devil's lead. But Mother Ann can defeat the devil. She took that evil and used it to protect our Society." He shifted his feet and the shadow the lantern cast on the wall behind him grew more menacing.

She couldn't worry about shadows. It was the man making the shadows she had to fear. He was insane, but if she could keep him talking, she might find a way to escape. "Your Mother Ann protected you by letting Brother Henry die?"

"What is death to a Believer except a step across a divide into a better realm? A place where all is peace and perfection.

Try as we might here at Harmony Hill, the world continues to sneak into our midst and bring trouble." His face went dark. He waved his hand toward Curt's body. "Like him." Then he turned his eyes back toward Carlyn. "Like you."

"Nay. I wish you no trouble."

"But you have caused trouble. You are the reason Sister Edna was watching me."

"Sister Edna was a watcher long before I came to Harmony Hill."

"Yea, but she did not watch me until you spied Brother Henry and Mr. Whitlow arguing." He narrowed his eyes on her until they were little more than slits. "What did she tell you when you found her? Did she say someone pushed her?"

"Nay." Carlyn pretended not to suspect him. "Do you think someone did?"

"Perhaps you."

"You know I did not."

"True. It is too bad you chose this night to become concerned for your sister. Because of you, I had to go all the way to the far end of the house to the other stairway and could not be sure what Sister Edna might have told you in her anguish."

"I told you what she said. That he was there."

"So you did." He breathed out a long sigh. "If not for you with your ready ears, no one would doubt that poor Sister Edna tripped over her own skirt tail. Which perhaps she did. Those steps are very narrow and steep. It would be so easy to fall." A strange smile slid across his face. "Especially if Mother Ann was displeased with our sister's refusal to stop poking into affairs that had naught to do with her. Mother Ann may have seen the need to protect us."

"If you have done no wrong, why do you need protection?"

"Not me. Us." He moved the lantern and the shadows seemed to dance with evil intent. But his voice stayed level and calm. "I have ever labored to be the perfect Believer. I willingly shouldered the burden of dealing with those of the world. The Ministry trusts me completely. Much harm would come to our Society if that trust was broken by those who do not know our ways. Mother Ann would never allow that."

"I thought your Mother Ann hated evil. That's why you have so many songs about chasing away the devil." Carlyn considered doing one of the stomping dances right then in hopes it would chase Elder Derron away.

"Yea, you begin to understand. At first, I wondered if I should confess my trouble with Mr. Whitlow and resign my position. But then Brother Henry died in the fire, and Mother Ann whispered in my ear that all would be well if I continued to be open to her leadership."

"Surely she would not sanction murder."

"Murder is a harsh word and one you use erroneously." His frown deepened. "No one has been murdered. Rather we have been gifted with an unfortunate series of events. Brother Henry perishing in the fire. Sister Edna tripping on the stairs in her haste to return to her sleeping room."

"What about him?" Carlyn motioned toward Curt's body without actually looking that way. "He is dead."

"That he is." The elder nodded his head a bit. "I plan to give him a proper burial before the sun rises. The earth awaits him."

"But you killed him. That's murder."

"Nay, Sister. I merely locked him here to give him time to

see the advantage of not bringing a claim against the Society for money he thought was owed to him. It had to be done. He was threatening to take possession of some of our best crop land. Mother Ann couldn't allow that."

"He's still dead."

"Not from my hand. Perhaps Mother Ann loosed demons on him in the night." He looked toward Curt's body.

She turned her mind away from the thought of demons. "How long was he here?"

"Not that long. Plus, I supplied him sustenance. I am not a fiend."

She couldn't believe she was feeling sorry for Curt, but she was. Locked in this dark place. Where it appeared the elder meant to lock her. She had to make him see that what he was doing was wrong and not part of a holy vision.

"Of course you aren't." She kept her voice soft. "You treat everyone with kindness. That's the Shaker way. To do good to all you meet. Sister Edna taught me that."

"Yea, but sometimes one has to consider the greater good. Mother Ann has revealed thus to me." He set the lantern down on a flat rock beside the door. "I must begin. The night is fleeing." He picked up a shovel that was propped against the wall.

"I can help." Carlyn tried to sound strong. "I can dig." She remembered hearing the sound of a shovel striking rock the night before.

"Digging graves is not sisters' work." He turned toward the door.

"Please. You can't leave me in here with him." She could not keep the panic out of her voice.

"He cannot hurt you now, Sister." His voice was almost

kindly as he looked over his shoulder at her. "He has gone beyond."

She ran for the door then.

He threw out his arm and knocked her to the floor. He stared down at her. "You cannot leave. Not until Mother Ann says you may."

She scooted back from him and scrambled to her feet. "What happens until then?" Her voice trembled, her courage gone.

"Nothing for you to fret about. Nor is there reason for you to worry about Mr. Whitlow. As I said, he is quite dead, but if it will make you feel better . . ." He set the shovel down and picked up something else.

Carlyn's breath caught in her throat when she saw the gun. "Dear God," she whispered again. It seemed only right that her last words be a plea to the Lord.

He held the gun up so she could see it better. "Do you recognize it?" He didn't wait for her to answer. "Yours, of course. The one you carried to Harmony Hill."

He turned and took careful aim at Curt's body. Carlyn squeezed her eyes shut and covered her ears as the shot reverberated in the root cellar. When the sound died away, the silence seemed almost as deafening.

Carlyn pushed words out into the dead air. "Why did you do that?"

"It seemed wise. That way if they do find Mr. Whitlow's grave and proceed to dig him up as I'm sure our good sheriff would demand be done, they will note the cause of death a gunshot to the chest. With your gun that you ineptly hid near his grave." He sounded almost cheerful. "It will all add up then and everybody will know what happened. He accosted you again and you shot him. Very simple."

"But no one will believe that." She had to convince him that his plan was flawed. "Why would I bury him and not go for help?"

"Because you were afraid. It will all be plain, I assure you, especially when you are not there to point out such discrepancies in the evidence. People believe what they see."

"Where will I be?" Carlyn could barely speak the words.

"That is up to Mother Ann, but a better place, I am certain." He sounded as if he were talking about nothing more troubling than the traders not selling all their jars of applesauce.

"What if I won't go?"

"But you will. Obedience to Mother Ann is necessary. Hands to work. Heart to God."

"Yea, Sister Edna has often told me that. But she also told me a true Believer must make confession of all wrongs."

"Yea, indeed. If there are wrongs, there is need for confession."

"So you confess your sins."

He inclined his head slightly. "I have always done so. It is required."

"Then you will confess this."

"This?" He sounded puzzled. "What is not wrong, what is done for the good of the Society, that must be done in secret and not for the praise of man. Mother Ann will reward me."

Carlyn frantically tried to think of something, anything that might give the elder pause. "But she won't reward you for being alone with a woman."

"Your female attributes do not tempt me. I have long been comfortable carrying the cross of celibacy." He waved the gun barrel toward her. "Now I must finish my duty. Turn around."

"No."

"You must do as I say."

"No." If she was going to die, she would not make it easy for him.

"I am not going to hurt you. Merely restrain you for a time while I remove Mr. Whitlow's body from your presence. You do want me to do that, don't you?"

"Yes." Carlyn backed away from him. "You don't have to restrain me. I won't try to escape."

He blew out a breath and set the gun down next to the door. "You do have a loose attachment to truth, Sister." With single-minded purpose, he grabbed her arms.

She screamed and kicked, but he paid her blows no notice. He pushed her back against the wall and pinned her there while he efficiently wrapped a rope around her wrists and tied her to some kind of brace attached to the wall. She yanked on it when he backed away from her, but she couldn't jerk free.

Elder Derron watched her for a moment. "That will only tighten the knots. If you stay calm, you may be able to loosen them with work."

Carlyn stopped pulling on the rope.

"See, you can learn to listen to wisdom." He smiled as though pleased. "Now, I must be about my work."

He blew out the lantern before he opened the door. The moon pushed a ghostly light into the cellar. After he set the gun and shovel outside, he grabbed Curt's arms. Carlyn closed her eyes, but she couldn't shut out the sound of Curt's body sliding across the dirt floor. The elder grunted with the effort of dragging the body.

"I could help you if you untie me." She couldn't just stand there and not try something.

The elder's only answer was an odd sound that might have been a laugh. She opened her eyes then. The body was gone and the elder leaned against the doorframe to catch his breath. At last he straightened up and looked toward her. "Remember, Sister Carlyn. Engaged in thy duty, fear no danger. We both have our duties."

"What is my duty?" Carlyn asked.

"To see what the darkness holds for you, of course. Perhaps Mother Ann will send you angels. I will pray such for you." With that he turned away and closed the door.

The black clamped down on her like a suffocating blanket. She pulled in a shuddering breath. They would not look for her until sunrise. She wondered if she would be able to hear the rising bell here underground. Or if anyone would hear her if she screamed. It would be useless to scream now even though she felt a scream rising within her.

Pray instead.

"But I have been praying. Every day. And now I'm going to die here in this dark place." Carlyn felt a surge of anger. "So my prayers have meant nothing."

Pray anyway. Surrender your will and pray with all your heart. Remember nothing can separate you from the love of God.

She grabbed on to that thought. She was not alone. The Lord was there with her. *Yea though I walk through the valley of the shadow of death, thou art with me.* Life or death, he was there. Nothing, not angels, nor principalities, nor powers, nor things present, nor things to come, nor height, nor depth, nor any other creature could keep her from the love of God. She let that promise Paul had recorded in Romans run through her mind.

341

"Dear Lord, help me," she whispered. "I am afraid."

Fear thou not, for I am with thee.

Her heart began to slow its pounding. She was still afraid, but she could think past the panic grabbing her breath. She was not yet dead. Where there was breath, there was hope. She twisted her fingers and picked at the knots binding her wrists. At last, she loosened the rope enough to pull her hands free. She felt her way around the wall to the door where she beat and kicked against it to no avail. He had made sure she couldn't open it.

Still, he had claimed to bring Curt water and food. Might he not do the same for her? She would listen for him and be ready to slip past him when he opened the door.

A sliver of moonlight came through a crack in the wood. Carlyn touched it. Somehow that tiny bit of light gave her hope. Even if the elder didn't return, someone would find her. Mitchell would not give up looking until he knew what had happened. He was that kind of sheriff. That kind of man.

34

Mitchell couldn't sleep. He shifted to one side and then the other until his sheets were in a tangle. With his every move, the bedsprings creaked and groaned until he expected Mrs. Snowden to bang on his door and tell him to be still. She didn't put up with boarders disturbing her sleep or that of her other boarders.

Elder Derron's words ordering him out of the village kept sounding in his head. He should have ignored the man. He should have gone back by the washhouse and kept his promise to Carlyn.

The elder couldn't have stopped him. The road through the village was a public road. Mitchell could have ridden in whatever direction he chose. Besides, he had the right to go wherever needed to uphold the law. But the man wasn't breaking the law. He was merely telling Mitchell to leave and not bother the members of the Shaker society.

Carlyn hadn't acted as though Mitchell was bothering her. She seemed eager to talk to him, even if it had only been about Asher. Mitchell didn't care. Not as long as she talked to him. The dog was keeping the door open. But then the Shakers had slammed it shut. It wasn't going to be easy finding a way to see her again, but he would. Somehow, he would.

He gave up on sleeping and walked as quietly as possible to the window. Not the least sign of dawn was showing in the eastern sky. Instead, moonlight traced shadows on the street below. As far as he could tell, he was the only person awake in the whole town. Tail up, a cat slinked out of the shadows on the hunt for mice.

Mitchell had the crawly feeling inside him that he needed to be on the hunt too. Something wasn't right. He didn't know what, but something wasn't right. He'd had the same kind of nervous feeling on nights before battles. A feeling that he needed to be ready. Even when there was no way to be ready for the kinds of things that awaited a soldier in combat. Except perhaps to die. Mitchell had prayed on those nights. The only way he knew to be ready.

But the war was over now. No battles awaited him at sunrise. But something was wrong.

A cloud slid over the moon and darkened the street. Down below him in the common room, Mrs. Snowden's clock counted out two strikes. The darkest hour of the night. He leaned his forehead against the window glass. Perhaps he should pray the way he had while he was staring up at the sky and waiting for the cannons to start firing at dawn. He knew what to pray then. For courage. For another day of life. To see Hilda again.

Funny how a man could fool himself about love. He hadn't seen Hilda again. And even though his pride was injured, his heart survived with little more than a bruise. Was he fooling himself again with the way he felt about Carlyn? Falling in love with a woman faithful to the union of marriage even in the absence of a husband.

Was it that very faithfulness that pulled him to her? Yet he wanted to take the man's place in her heart. No, that wasn't true. He wanted his own place. And whether he was a deluded idiot or not, he wanted Carlyn Kearney in his life. She was already in his heart, and this time if he was a loser in love, his heart was going to be more than bruised.

He breathed out a long sigh. His father used to tell him he liked doing everything the hard way. Now here he was, letting hope build up in his heart for the love of a woman who was not only married to a memory, but living with the Shakers where marriage was considered a sin. Maybe he should simply take a vow of celibacy himself. But he couldn't quite give up that dream of a little house with children running out to greet him at the end of the day. His children.

He had time. He could wait. For Carlyn. She didn't appear to be embracing the Shaker thinking. She had gone there for a roof over her head and food to eat. He could give her that, even if she didn't want to share his roof or put her feet under his table.

The moon came out from behind the cloud and spilled its silvery light on the street below again. The cat appeared out of the shadows, its prey in its mouth.

He turned away from the window and lay back down, but it was useless to close his eyes. Something was wrong, and until he figured out what that was, sleep wasn't going to be possible.

Like counting sheep, he went through the possible problems.

Curt Whitlow missing. The man was probably living it up in a nearby town.

Bank robbers. Nobody had tried to rob the bank since he'd been sheriff.

Florence. He was going to have to tell Mrs. Snowden to look elsewhere for a match for her niece.

Asher. Who had shot him and why?

Sister Edna. What did she know about the fire?

Elder Derron. What had made him so ready to chase Mitchell out of the Shaker town?

Carlyn.

He paused on her name. That's where the real worry was poking him. Something was wrong. He sensed it. Was she running away in the middle of the night the way the other sister had? And where was that other sister now? Would she have answers for him? Not answers about the fire and Brother Henry's death, but answers about Carlyn.

He wanted to get up again and pace around the room, but he made himself lie still. If he was awake to hear the clock strike again, he'd get dressed and sneak out of the house. Better to walk the streets than to lie there worrying about what he didn't know.

⸻

The silence pounded against her ears. Carlyn listened with her whole being, but there was nothing. Not even the scurry of a mouse. At least she thought it too late in the season for snakes. Better not to think about snakes. Better not to think at all. Just to be ready.

The trouble was, even if the elder did come back, he would be ready too. He knew she could untie her hands. He had

346

intended for her to untie her hands. What accident might he be planning for her? There were no stairs to fall down here. No fire to transport her to heaven. Just darkness and despair. Especially when the sliver of moonlight went away. A cloud must have drifted in front of the moon.

How long would it take her to die here? Or lose her mind? That would surely happen first. A person needed light. *God is light, and in him is no darkness at all*. The Bible verse popped into her head. She believed that. She could cling to that, to the Lord's light. Live or die, his light would be there for her.

She sank down to the floor and leaned against the wooden door. She shivered as the damp chill of the earth soaked through her dress. She shook it off. She could stand the chill. She'd been cold plenty of times. She needed to think about the Lord's light. It didn't matter what the time of day. It didn't matter whether one was in the bowels of the earth or the top of the highest tree. The Lord was the same. *In him is no darkness at all*.

No darkness. Another verse tickled her memory. Something about the Lord being an ever present help in trouble? She was certainly in trouble. She didn't want to die. She leaned her head over on her knees. Ambrose hadn't wanted to die either. He had wanted to come home to her and father those children they had dreamed of having. He was such a good man. A man who had shown her that God was light and not darkness. Her mother had tried, but always her father's condemning shadow had darkened her mother's message.

Away from her father, she had been able to see and embrace the joy of Ambrose's belief. She had surrendered some of that joy and stepped back into darkness when Ambrose didn't come home. But Ambrose hadn't given up on the joy of his belief. He had written her a letter of love. A letter of release. Find love, he'd told her. Have children. Live a full life. And now it looked as if that would never happen.

What about Mitchell? The sheriff's face as he'd looked talking to her the day before came to mind. She liked talking to him. She liked thinking about him as a friend. She liked thinking that maybe he was thinking of her as more than a friend. In time, she could return his feelings. If there was time.

Sister Edna had only just the day before shook her finger at Carlyn and quoted one of her Mother Ann's sayings about time when she thought Carlyn wasn't working efficiently enough. "Mother Ann says you must not waste one moment of time, for you have none to spare. For none of us know when our spirit is going to be called home. None of us. Brother Henry proved that."

Now it might be true for both Sister Edna and Carlyn. Better to drift away in a sleep like Sister Edna than to stare at death in the darkness.

The sliver of moonlight pushed through the crack in the door again. The sight of it awoke hope in Carlyn. She didn't have to sit there and feel doomed. She could do something. If nothing else, she could try to carve out a bigger hole in the door to let in more moonlight. If she could find a tool.

She ran her hand gingerly over the floor around her. Nothing but hard-packed dirt. Next she stood and felt along the wall next to the door. The wall was shored up by stones stacked one on another. She pulled on one of the rocks that jabbed out from the wall. It wiggled up and down. If she jerked out the rock, would that weaken the wall and maybe bring the earth down on top of her?

She could imagine Elder Derron returning to find her

suffocated under the dirt and thanking his Mother Ann for ridding him of one more problem.

"She wouldn't do that," Carlyn muttered and kept working on the rock. While she didn't believe in Mother Ann the way one needed to in order to be a proper Shaker, she had read the books Sister Edna had given her about the woman. Ann Lee warred against dirt and against what she considered worldly sins, but she also wrote many things about sharing with the poor and helping others.

She would not help Elder Derron murder people, however accidental he wanted to believe the deaths were. Instead, if she were able to send angels, they would be catching Sister Edna before she fell. Or leading the horses out of the fire along with Brother Henry. She wouldn't send demons, as Elder Derron had suggested.

The hair rose on the back of Carlyn's neck and she couldn't keep from looking behind her even though she knew no one was there. The darkness was no longer total. Her eyes had adjusted and she could make out the shape of rounded walls. She tried to remember what she had seen before the elder took away the lantern, but she had been too frightened by the sight of Curt's body.

Remembering that brought back to mind demons. She pulled in a breath to steady her nerves. There were no demons. Or angels either there in the dark cellar. She was alone. But it might be good to imagine angels. Shaker angels, if there were such a thing. Whirling and singing. Even stomping like the Shakers to chase away the threat of demons.

Carlyn stomped her foot so hard that her teeth clattered, but it did little except make her realize how very alone she was. She turned back to the wall to prize on the rock, but she couldn't pull it out of the wall. There had to be something she could use if she had the courage to keep feeling in the dark spaces. She ran her hand along the wall, shrieking and jerking back when she touched something slimy. She rubbed her hand on her dress and pulled in a shaky breath. Nothing but a worm of some sort.

Maybe if she sang the way she'd imagined the angels doing, she wouldn't be as afraid. One of her mother's favorite hymns came to mind.

"God moves in a mysterious way His wonders to perform." Her voice sounded thin, as though the dark was swallowing up her words before they could reach her ears. She pushed her voice out stronger on another line she remembered from the song. "You fearful saints, fresh courage take."

Fresh courage. Dear Lord, that was what she needed. That and an axe to chop through the door.

Her foot bumped into something and she barely held in another shriek. But whatever it was rolled away from her. Not a rock. It had moved too easily. She stooped down and felt around until her hand touched something. A canning jar. She pushed away the thought that Elder Derron might have brought water in it for Curt. It made no difference who had touched it last.

She retraced her steps to the rock jutting out of the wall and smashed the jar against it. The glass pieces showered down around her feet. She still held the mouth of the jar, now with jagged edges protruding from it. She gingerly felt around on the floor for the biggest shard of glass, then went back to the door.

The jar top could be her weapon when the elder returned. If he returned. He might leave her fate to his Mother Ann.

The Shakers wouldn't look for her. He would tell them that she had run away in the night. They would believe him. Even Sister Edna might believe him, should she regain consciousness. She would be glad not to have to accuse the elder.

It could be she might not remember what happened. Carlyn's little brother had fallen from a horse once and hit his head. He didn't recall even getting on the horse. He kept saying he'd fallen in the creek.

Carlyn wrapped the glass shard in a piece of cloth torn from her apron. With care, she scraped the glass against the wood next to the crack between the boards. The wood surrendered only a few splinters to her effort. But she kept on.

How long did it take a person to die without food or water? Days? Weeks? If she could make the hole big enough, perhaps she could yell if somebody passed by. She kept scraping at the wood.

Somebody would come. But would it be Ambrose to show her the way to heaven? Or Mitchell to offer her a new life here?

She wanted that new life. She shut her eyes and pulled up Mitchell's face. She wouldn't give up. She had to believe that neither would Mitchell. Not until he found her.

35

Mitchell was pulling on his trousers before the last chime of three finished sounding in the room below him. He didn't know what he could do in the middle of the night, but he couldn't stay in bed another second. After he strapped on his gun, he picked up his boots to go down the stairs in sock feet. No need waking the whole house.

Out on the porch, he dropped down on the steps to pull on the boots. The October air had a nip to it that warned of frost. If only the other warning that had kept him awake was as easy to decipher.

The moon slipped down toward the horizon on its way to the other side of the world as he walked through the town. Nothing was out of the ordinary with all the businesses shuttered for the night. The only light he noted was over the hardware store. The Harleys who lived there had a new baby. Even the saloon at the far end of town was dark.

Down the side street, nothing stirred at Curt Whitlow's house. No way for Mitchell to know if the man was home.

Mitchell went back out to walk the length of Main Street again. But it wasn't this town that had him awake in the wee morning hours. It was the Shaker town. And Carlyn.

He stopped in front of Billy's Barbershop. The man might know about the couple who had run away from Harmony Hill, but Billy wouldn't be there for hours. Mitchell couldn't wait that long. He'd go to the source. Demand to see Carlyn.

And if she looked like something was wrong, he would tell her straight out to come away with him. She could have his room at Mrs. Snowden's and he would bunk at the sheriff's office until she got news about her husband. He could wait. It would be better to wait. To be sure his feelings for her weren't just some wish-on-a-star dream. To give her the chance to decide if she could ever feel anything for him.

He stared up at the stars overhead, glittering brightly now that the moon was gone. A great place to send wishes. Or better yet, prayers.

"Lord, is it wrong to want her away from those people? To think I'm better for her than them?"

His only answer was the twinkle of the stars and the bay of a hound chasing through the woods to the south of town.

She didn't belong with the Shakers. He was sure of that. He even thought she knew that, but she believed she had no other way. He could offer her another way. Sister Edna and Elder Derron couldn't stop him.

The eastern horizon showed the first faint pink trace of dawn as he rode into the village. No Shakers were stirring, but they would be soon.

Mitchell tied his horse in front of the Trustee House and walked through the village. Everything appeared as peaceful here as it had in town. Could be his feeling of something wrong was simply due to his unsettled feelings about Carlyn. He stopped and stared up at the house where she would be sleeping. He imagined her peering out the window to see him there and then slipping down the stairs to come out to him.

He shook away the unlikely thought and made his way around the house to where the Shakers had already cleaned away the refuse from the burned barn. As Mitchell turned back toward the Trustee House to wait for the village to come awake, he spotted a man far down the path. Mitchell stepped behind a tree and waited. If someone had come back to make more trouble for the Shakers, he'd catch them in the act this time.

He fingered the butt of his gun, but didn't pull it out. It could simply be a vagrant passing through the village. But no. When the figure drew closer, it was a Shaker.

The man hurried through the gray dawn light, peering not only behind him from time to time, but up at the building tops as well. He was obviously worried someone might be watching. Mitchell scanned the area. He expected to see a sister also stealing back to her house after an illicit rendez-vous, but no one else was in sight.

Then the man drew closer, and Mitchell was surprised to recognize Elder Derron. The last man he expected to be sneaking about the village.

Mitchell started to stay hidden next to the tree, but he needed to confront the elder sooner or later. Best to get it over with. Besides, the man was acting decidedly nervous. If the elder had come upon another threat to their village, he'd be glad to see Mitchell.

But he wasn't. Instead, at the sight of Mitchell, the man stopped in his tracks, a look of something very near panic on his face. Mitchell had seen the same look on other men's faces right before they turned tail to run from the law.

"Elder Derron, is something wrong?" Mitchell spoke before the man could flee.

The elder recovered his composure. "Sheriff, you startled me."

"Sorry, I should have called out to you." Mitchell stepped closer to the man. The beads of sweat sliding down the elder's face didn't fit with the cool morning.

"Yea, that might have been best." The elder pulled out his handkerchief to dab at his forehead. "You caught me coming back from the bathhouse. It is good to start the day fresh. Our Mother Ann teaches that good spirits can't live where there is dirt."

"I see," Mitchell said.

The elder moistened his lips. "Did the eldress send for you?"

"I came to talk to your Sister Edna."

"Yea, of course. But you have to realize she may be out of her head for some time."

"Out of her head?"

"Yea, such a tragedy that she hit her head when she fell. Or perhaps when she was pushed." The elder sounded more like himself. "We locked the girl in the vagrant house. Since it seems she was the cause of Sister Edna's fall."

"The girl?" Mitchell narrowed his eyes on the man. "What girl?"

"Why, Sister Carlyn, of course. Didn't they tell you that when they came after you? There has been naught but trouble since she came among us. Men of the world sneaking about our village. The fire. Now, poor Sister Edna. Everybody knew Sister Carlyn had an uneasy relationship with her Shaker guide, but we would have never suspected such a tragic ending."

"Sister Edna told you the girl pushed her?" Mitchell watched the man closely. Something sounded a little too eager in the man's telling of what happened.

"Didn't she tell you the same?" The elder pulled his hat brim down lower on his head and kept his eyes away from Mitchell's face.

"I just got here." He could pretend to know more than he did only so long. "I haven't questioned her yet, but I think I should talk to the girl first. Hear her story."

"Very well, if you think that best," Elder Derron said. "I'll show you the way. But you can't allow her claims of innocence to sway you in your duty. It is quite plain she is responsible for Sister Edna's fall."

"Did someone see her push Sister Edna?"

"Nay, but she is nevertheless responsible. Mother Ann has assured me of that."

"Mother Ann?" Mitchell gave him a hard look. The woman who founded the Shakers had been dead for decades.

"Yea, I hear doubt in your voice, but though our mother has passed on from this earthly realm, she continues to lead us through visits of the spirit." The Shaker stepped off the pathway to walk around Mitchell. It was as if he needed to keep his distance. "Follow me. You will see."

Mitchell was definitely seeing that something wasn't quite right with the elder. Mitchell studied the man's back. He kept his shoulders very straight and no longer looked around as he had before Mitchell stopped him. In spite of what he said about coming from the bathhouse, his pants were far from clean and his shoes had dirt caked on them. Strange that he hadn't cleaned his shoes since he seemed so bothered by dirt.

"Have you been digging this morning?" Mitchell asked.

The elder's shoulders jerked as though Mitchell had struck him with the words. "Nay." He shot a glance back at Mitchell. "Why would you think that?" He spoke a little too quickly, almost tripping over his words.

"Your shoes."

He looked down but kept walking. "Oh. Yesterday I spent time in a garden. I will have to confess that I forgot to properly clean my shoes before I put them on this morn."

"I'm surprised you found any mud even in the garden. It's been dry for a while."

"Dirt can cling to one's shoes whether there is rain or not when the ground is properly tilled." He spoke without looking back. "The house is just up ahead."

The rising bell began to ring and once more the elder jumped. He had to have heard that bell thousands of times in his years at the Shaker village, yet the dongs seemed to unnerve him this day.

At the small house, the door was slightly ajar.

"Oh, dear heavenly Mother, she's gone." The elder reached for the doorknob with shaking hands.

"How do you know she's gone?"

"The door is no longer locked. She knew her guilt. She will be gone." He pulled the door open wider and moved aside to let Mitchell go in.

Carlyn was not there. Nothing looked touched except for a burned down candle. "Are you sure she was ever here?" Mitchell stepped back outside to where the elder waited.

"Yea, I locked her inside myself."

The lock showed no sign of being forced open. The bad feeling that had kept Mitchell from sleep grew stronger. "Who has a key besides you?"

"The only key is kept at the Trustee House. On a hook inside the cupboard in the front room so it will be available when needed. We do not turn vagrants away, but neither do we want them wandering about our village in the night hours. We must keep our sisters safe."

"Did you put the key back there last night?" Mitchell looked at the grass around the door. The ground was too dry to show tracks.

"Nay, it was after midnight and it seemed reasonable to leave the key at the Gathering Family House so that one of the sisters could carry the girl her morning meal."

"Did you entrust the key to someone for safekeeping?" Whoever had that key must have let Carlyn out of the vagrant house and would know where she was.

"Things were very frenzied with Sister Edna being carried to the infirmary and the peace of the house in upheaval." The elder shoved a hand in his jacket pocket and pulled it back out. "The key could be anywhere now."

Mitchell didn't know why Elder Derron avoided giving a straight answer, but he was sure the man knew exactly what he'd done with the key. The elder was a man who paid attention to details. "I didn't ask who had the key now. I asked where you left the key after you locked the door here."

"Why does that matter? She's gone. And good riddance." The elder's voice rose as he slammed the door of the house shut. "She was nothing but trouble from the day she showed up here, carrying a gun and with that dog. Now that dog is keeping Brother Willis from his proper duties. Nothing but trouble."

Mitchell had never seen Elder Derron so animated. Or so strange, but Mitchell couldn't worry about the elder. He had to find Carlyn, and the dog might be the answer. Carlyn wouldn't leave the village without him. "Is the dog still here?"

"How would I know? I have nothing to do with dogs. No proper Shaker does."

"Then we better go see."

"Go if you want, but I am too busy to look for dogs." Elder Derron's voice was still too loud. "I must clean my shoes and be ready for my morning duties."

"Your duties can wait. You need to come with me."

"Nay." The elder glared at Mitchell. "I have to clean my shoes."

"Elder Derron." A young brother ran down the path toward them. "I've been looking all over for you."

"You have found me now. Here with the sheriff." Elder Derron's greeting was curt. "What say you?"

The young Shaker gave Mitchell a sideways look, but he didn't allow his curiosity to distract him. "Eldress Lilith insists you must come right away to help with Sister Edna."

"Why does she need the elder?" Mitchell asked.

"Sister Edna is distraught and keeps calling for Elder Derron." The boy shifted his eyes from Mitchell to the elder. "Eldress Lilith hopes the sight of you will calm the sister, Elder. She says they can barely keep her restrained."

"She is awake?" Elder Derron's voice was faint, almost as if he were talking to himself. "Mother Ann allowed her to wake?"

"Come," the Shaker boy said. "Eldress Lilith will be

unhappy that I have been so long finding you. She's in the infirmary."

"I know where she is." Elder Derron's voice was firm again. "I cannot go there with dirt on my shoes. Tell the eldress I must clean my shoes."

"If you come, I will clean your shoes," the boy said.

"Nay, I must do it myself." Elder Derron turned and ran across the road.

Mitchell considered going after him, but it would be better to question the eldress. She might know where Carlyn was.

"The eldress is not going to be pleased." The boy blew out a breath. "But if you come with me, she may be less upset. After I found Elder Derron, I was to ride into town for you."

"Is Sister Carlyn there with her?"

"Who?" the boy asked, then answered his own question. "Oh, you mean the sister they locked up here last night. Is she in there now?" He peered toward the house.

"No."

"Then I guess I better tell the eldress that too." He turned and started toward the stone building in the center of the village.

Mitchell caught up with him. "Did you think Elder Derron was acting oddly?"

"All the elders are odd," the boy said. "You stay here long enough, you are going to be odd. I don't plan to stay that long." He glanced over at Mitchell. "I would just as soon you didn't tell anybody that. I wouldn't want them getting all upset. I plan to take off without having to hear them crying woe and telling me I'm on a slippery slope to eternal damnation."

"I doubt I'll have need to mention it."

"Good." The boy looked back over his shoulder to where Elder Derron had disappeared into the shadows. "But you are right. Elder Derron was acting stranger than usual. But if he said he had to clean his shoes, then he had to clean his shoes. These people make war against dirt."

36

Carlyn awoke with her head against the door and the shard of glass in her lap. Daylight pushed though the crack in the door that she might have made a fraction of an inch larger with all her gouging. When the moonlight had been blotted out by the dark hours before dawn, despair had overtaken her and she had whispered into the black air pressing in on her. "I am in my grave."

Pray anyway. Her mother's words echoed in her mind. So very slowly she whispered the Twenty-Third Psalm. How often had she heard her father read that at funerals? *Surely goodness and mercy shall follow me all the days of my life, and I will dwell in the house of the Lord forever.* That was where Ambrose was. Joyful in the house of the Lord. It was a house she wanted to dwell in someday, but not yet.

What would her mother pray? Carlyn shut her eyes as one of her mother's oft-spoken prayers echoed in her memory.

For trials, I give thee thanks, for such hard times make us depend more on thee. I thank thee for love, for without it we are but sounding cymbals. I covet thy watchcare over these, my children. And I pray for the morrow, that thou will give us another day to try to serve thee better. May we dwell in thy hope, O Lord.

"I pray the same. I need hope, Lord, that Mitchell will find me," Carlyn whispered. It didn't seem wrong to reach for Mitchell. A friend the Lord had put into her life. A man she might yet love if she were delivered from this tomb. She shut her eyes and his face was in her mind. He would find her. The Lord was giving her that hope. With that thought, an unexpected peace settled over her and she had dozed off.

When she heard the Shaker bell, the sound was so faint she wondered how far from the center of the village this cellar was. But the night before, she had heard the clank of a shovel when Elder Derron must have been digging Curt's grave somewhere near here. Would he come back tonight to dig hers? She shook away the thought. It was only the heavy door that muffled the ringing of the bell.

She would wait and pray and rejoice in the light pushing through the crack in the door to prove the Lord had gifted her with another day. She picked up the shard of glass and began whittling at the door again. Hands to work. Heart to God. She could embrace that Shaker teaching. Diligently, she continued to work with her hands while prayers without words rose from her heart.

⁓

When Sister Edna saw Mitchell, she tried to sit up and reach for him. Two Shaker women murmured calming words and kept her from rising.

"Don't upset yourself, Sister. Brother Benjamin says you should lie still and rest," Eldress Lilith said.

"You don't understand." Sister Edna pushed at their hands. "I must get her help. He means her harm."

"Who?" Mitchell asked.

She fell back on the bed, her face as pale as the white case on her pillow. "Sister Carlyn. I was wrong to not tell."

"Tell what?"

"About him." She shut her eyes. For a second, Mitchell thought she might have lost consciousness, but then she muttered, "Elder Derron."

The eldress leaned near Mitchell to speak close to his ear. "Sheriff, the poor sister is out of her head. Speaking such. Elder Derron would harm no one." She looked around at the young Shaker who had explained why the elder hadn't come with them. "Even now cleaning his shoes so that he wouldn't bring dirt into our presence."

Sister Edna must have heard at least some of what the eldress said. "There is dirt only Mother Ann can clean away." Her voice was weak.

"Brother Benjamin gave her a draught to calm her. He assures us that it is not uncommon to be agitated after such an injury and to fail to remember what happened," Eldress Lilith said.

Once more Sister Edna tried to get up. "Nay, he means her harm. She is in danger."

"Ease yourself, Sister." Eldress Lilith gently pushed her back down on the bed. "The young sister is quite safe here in the village."

"Nay, you must find her posthaste, Sheriff." Sister Edna focused her eyes on Mitchell. "I fear I will have her blood on my hands if you do not stop him."

"I will stop him." Mitchell made the promise to calm the woman, but inside he felt anything but calm or sure.

The eldress followed Mitchell back out into the hallway. She was unbelieving when Mitchell told her Carlyn was no longer in the vagrant house. "Elder Derron locked her there. He has the only key."

"He says he left it here."

"I did not see the key, but if he says he left it here, I am sure he did." She didn't quite hide the doubt in her eyes. "I will ask him where he left it when he comes and then see which of our sisters felt sorrow for Sister Carlyn and released her."

Mitchell leveled his eyes on the woman. "I don't think you can count on him showing up here."

Eldress Lilith's distress grew more evident. "You have to be wrong. Sister Edna has to be wrong."

"Elder Derron was not himself when I saw him."

She wrung her hands together. "But where did he go?"

"That I don't know, but I intend to find out."

"You have to be wrong," she repeated, more as if her own ears needed to hear it than to convince Mitchell. "Elder Derron is a good and faithful Believer. He would never harm one of his sisters."

"I hope you are right."

"I am." Eldress Lilith squared her shoulders. "If Sister Carlyn has left the vagrant house, it is to return to the world. She never fit into our Society here. It was only a matter of time before she deserted her calling here."

Mitchell didn't argue with her. "Send someone after Elder Derron. Whether he has done what Sister Edna says or not, he needs to tell what he knows."

"Yea, I will have Brother Lyle find him." She inclined her head in agreement. "Will you wait for him here, Sheriff?"

"No. I need to find your missing sister."

"Then you best look in the world." She turned on her heel and went back into the sickroom.

Hope and worry fought a war in Mitchell's head as he walked to the other end of the village. Had Carlyn run away as the eldress suggested? Had he lost her before he could even offer her his love?

Frantic barks told Mitchell Carlyn wasn't at the barn even before he went inside. Asher was up on three feet, staring intently at the stall door as though he could force it open.

"The dog is restless." Brother Willis came up behind Mitchell. "He must be in pain. I brought him a draught to dull his senses."

"No." Mitchell held up his hand to block the Shaker. "I need him with all his senses alert to find his owner."

"Do you speak of the young sister?" Brother Willis frowned. "Isn't she about her duties?"

"There was trouble at the Gathering Family House in the night."

"Trouble she caused?"

"Some have accused her, but the only sure thing is that she is missing this morning."

Brother Willis gave a disgusted snort. "If she is gone, she will have run back to the world. Probably enticed one of our young brothers to go with her."

"She wouldn't have gone without Asher." Mitchell stooped down beside the dog. "He found her here. He might be able to track her down now."

"Take my word. She will be long gone by now."

366

"Perhaps, but I must look."

"Yea, I suppose it is your duty." Brother Willis handed Mitchell a rope. "It would be best if the dog did not get his bandage wet."

Mitchell looped the rope around the dog's neck. Asher whined as though telling Mitchell to hurry. Once out of the barn, the dog gingerly put his injured paw down and strained against the rope.

"Easy boy," Mitchell told him even as he too wanted to break out in a run. But it would be better to stay calm.

At the vagrant house, Asher sniffed all around it and sat down as though to wait for Carlyn to come back.

"She's not here, Asher. You have to follow her trail." Mitchell pointed away from the house.

The dog whined, but made no move to get up. Mitchell studied the buildings and trees in every direction. He saw nothing to indicate which way Carlyn might have gone from here. Nothing.

Then just as he had earlier that morning, the young Shaker, Brother Lyle, was running down the path. The boy's face was red and his eyes wide.

"Sheriff Brodie. Eldress Lilith sent me for you. We found Elder Derron."

"And the girl?"

"Nay. Only the elder." Brother Lyle rushed out the next words. "He's dead."

"Dead?" Mitchell stared at the young Shaker. "Are you sure?"

"Yea, very sure."

Mitchell had no choice except to go with Brother Lyle, but Asher would not. When the dog refused to budge, Mitchell picked him up and shut him inside the vagrant house.

The dog's barks followed them as they hurried to the Trustee House where the Shaker doctor bent over Elder Derron's body on the floor in his office. Brother Benjamin looked up when they came in. "Fetch Elder Marcus, Brother Lyle."

The young Shaker was out the door before Brother Benjamin finished speaking. The doctor shook his head. "Death is not easy for the young to view."

Mitchell looked at Elder Derron, his face contorted in death. "What happened?"

"Sin would be my first guess." Brother Benjamin looked to be in his middle years. His gentle face was creased with concern.

"Are you saying he was murdered?"

"'Twould be better for him were that so, but nay, this was his own sin." The man stood and pointed toward the desk. "He wrote some last words and then drank that bottle of poison."

"Where did he get it?" Mitchell picked up the bottle. Arsenic.

"Perhaps from the tannery. Such is needed for curing the leather, but it matters little where he got it. He must have been tormented to commit such a sin."

"Do you know why he might be tormented? Did he write anything about the girl?"

"The girl?" Brother Benjamin's forehead wrinkled in a frown.

"Sister Carlyn."

"The one Sister Edna is fearful for? Eldress Lilith says they locked her in the vagrant house. That Elder Derron insisted." The doctor's frown deepened.

"So he did, and now she is gone and he's dead by his own hand." Mitchell looked down at the elder's body.

"Surely you can't think Elder Derron did her harm."

"Sister Edna thinks it possible." Fear that it might be true stabbed Mitchell's heart. "You said he wrote something."

"Yea, there on the desk. But nothing about Sister Carlyn. Only Mother Ann."

Mitchell went to the desk and read the elder's last words, written in neat script.

> *I faithfully performed my duty as revealed to me by Mother Ann. Even this. Yea, even this. In her sight, I am without blemish.*

"Deluded thinking." Brother Benjamin stepped closer to peer down at the elder's words. "A sorrow. We will have to labor many songs to bring peace back to Harmony Hill after the events of the last week."

Mitchell didn't care about the Shakers' peace at that moment. He only wanted to find Carlyn. Alive. He was wasting time here. If the elder had answers, he could no longer tell them. He took one last look at the man's body and could not help noting his shoes. They were scrubbed clean.

37

When Carlyn heard the dog, she knew, without doubt, it was Asher. But he sounded so far away.

Despair lurked in the dark dankness of the cellar behind her, but she kept her eyes on the bit of light forcing its way through the crack in the door. She needed hope. Asher might be nearer than he sounded. The heavy door had muffled the dongs of the rising bell. She couldn't be that far from the village.

She tried to think about how long she had followed Elder Derron blindly through the night. It was all such a blur. Her fright. Her misplaced trust. If only she had run the other way when she first wondered about the direction they were going.

She stood up and rammed her shoulder against the door. The door barely shook. It was useless. Just as whittling out the crack in the door was useless. She couldn't escape through a crack no bigger than a pencil.

But she could peek out at the world. She leaned down to put her eye to the small opening. All she could see were the stone steps down to the cellar door splashed in sunlight.

If only she could feel that sunshine on her face and be free from this place before the shadows returned with the night.

She wouldn't think about that. She couldn't think about that. Instead she sank back down on the floor beside the door and cupped her hands around the light coming through the crack as though she could gather it up to save for later. A gift from the Lord to keep her from losing hope.

Mitchell would come. He'd open the door and bring her back out into the light. She had to believe that.

She heard the barks again. Asher had tracked her to the Shaker village. He might do the same now. She listened with every inch of her being, but the sound seemed so faint.

Carlyn put her ear flat against the crack. If she could hear him, he might hear her and find the cellar. Then others might notice his barks. But what if the one to notice was Elder Derron? Would his unbalanced visions tell him to silence the dog? Silence her?

She had to take the chance. She couldn't bear another night of darkness.

She put her mouth close to the crack and attempted to whistle. Her mouth was so dry it took three tries before she managed to make a sound. Then she put her ear next to the hole again. Asher heard her. His barks changed, became high-pitched, but no nearer. He must be trapped and as helpless to open the door to freedom as she was.

"Dear Lord, let someone turn him loose," she whispered. Then she picked up the broken top of the jar and took up position beside the door. If Elder Derron had heard her whistle and came to silence her, she would be ready.

When Mitchell came out of the Trustee House and heard Asher's frantic barking, he pushed past the two Shakers coming up the steps. Brother Lyle called to him, but he didn't even look back as he ran toward the vagrant house.

The dog leaped out the moment Mitchell opened the door and landed on his wounded leg with a piteous yelp. He struggled up on three legs and looked around at Mitchell.

"Easy, boy." Mitchell stroked the dog's back. Suddenly the dog perked up his ears again. "What do you hear?" Mitchell held his head up to listen, but he heard nothing but the normal sounds of the day.

The dog limped away from Mitchell down the pathway. He looked back and barked as though to tell Mitchell to follow. Then he tried to run, but fell again. He scrambled back to his feet, but stood trembling, panting. Ears flat against his head, he sat down and raised his nose in a mournful howl. The sound pierced Mitchell. It couldn't be too late.

"Come on, boy. You can do it."

A Shaker man came across the road. "Where are you trying to take the dog?" he asked. Then before Mitchell could answer, the man looked down the path. "Nothing down that way except an old home place, but the cabin's long gone. We used the logs for a barn years ago."

"Are you sure nothing's there now?" Mitchell asked.

"Naught but an old cellar. Not used for anything these days. Could have fallen in by now."

"How far?"

The man pointed. "See those walnut trees yonder? You used to be able to see a dirt path along about there."

"Show me," Mitchell said.

The Shaker looked past Mitchell toward the village. "I have duties."

"Your first duty is to help me find one of your sisters who is missing. And this dog, her dog, thinks she went that way."

"Unlikely, but I will show you the path." He looked back at the dog and pulled out his handkerchief. He ripped it into three strips and tied them together. "Slip this under the dog's belly to keep the weight off that sore leg."

Asher whined and began walking again with Mitchell holding him up.

The Shaker nodded approval before striding in front of them, obviously eager to be finished with the interruption to his duties. When he stopped to point out the path, he said, "Looks as if someone's been passing this way. Can't imagine why."

His heart pounding, Mitchell could barely keep from pushing past the Shaker, but he let the man lead the way. Then the man pointed again. "There's a graveyard over there. And look at that. For all the world, it looks like a new grave."

Please, Lord. The words came unbidden to Mitchell's mind. He couldn't be too late. He forced himself to turn toward the fresh grave and remembered the dirt on Elder Derron's shoes. The Shaker man headed toward the graveyard, but when Mitchell moved to follow him, Asher refused to go. Instead he pulled against Mitchell and barked. Then Mitchell heard it too. A whistle. Not a bird. A person's whistle. Carlyn whistling for Asher.

He turned back toward the old cellar and ran with the dog. He could hear her now, calling to Asher. Calling to him. He couldn't lift the heavy wooden bar away from the door fast enough. She exploded out of the cellar into his arms.

"I knew you would come. I knew you wouldn't give up until you found me."

Asher tried to nose between them, but Mitchell kept holding her. He never wanted to turn her loose ever again. She twisted away from him to reach down to the dog. She laughed. "The Lord gave me a dog."

"And a sheriff." Mitchell kept one arm around her and she seemed happy with that.

She kept her hand on Asher's head, but looked back at Mitchell. "And a sheriff."

Tears filled his eyes. "I love you, Carlyn. Let me take you away from here."

She blinked as though the light was still too strong or perhaps his words too sudden. But he couldn't hold them back.

"I—" she started, but he jumped in front of whatever she was about to say. He couldn't bear to hear her refusal. Not now when he'd just been given the gift of seeing her alive and whole.

"Don't say no." He rushed out his words. "I know we can't marry. Not until you know about your husband. But you aren't a Shaker. Let me find you a better place and then maybe someday you'll be ready for a place with me."

She put her fingers over his lips. "Shh. Give me time. Let me feel the sunshine. I've been in the dark too long."

He picked her up then and carried her up the stone steps to the brightest spot of sunlight he could see. She put her arms around his neck and laid her head on his shoulder. Asher limped after them, obviously wishing Mitchell out of his way, but at least not nipping his ankles. Mitchell stopped walking but continued to hold her.

After a moment, she raised her head. "I can walk, you know."

"I know." He gently set her on her feet, but kept his arms around her. "I want to kiss you. Would one kiss be wrong?"

"Nay." She shook her head then with a frown and changed the Shaker word. "I mean no. A kiss will prove I am yet alive." She lifted her face toward his.

Her lips were even sweeter than he imagined. Whatever happened, whether she ever said yes, at least he had this moment with her in his arms.

38

Carlyn pulled away from Mitchell and whirled around, lifting her face to the sun while every inch of her tingled with joy. She laughed then, thinking of how she had finally learned to dance like a Shaker. Perhaps joy fell down on them in their worship and filled their heart, just as her heart was filling. With life. With hope. With the promise of tomorrow.

Then a shadow fell across her. When she looked around and saw the Shaker, she froze. With the sun behind the man, she couldn't see his face, but who else would it be but Elder Derron? Sensing her fear, Asher growled.

"What's wrong?" Mitchell had his arm around her again.

"It's him." She pointed. Mitchell wouldn't know to suspect him until it might be too late. The elder might have her gun and force them both back in the cellar. "He locked me in there."

"Nay, Sister. I would not do such a thing." The man stepped closer.

Relief swept through Carlyn. It wasn't the elder, but another Shaker. "I thought you were Elder Derron."

"Surely you have no reason to fear him either," the Shaker man said. "But I was right about the grave. Someone has been buried there."

"Curt Whitlow," Carlyn said. "Elder Derron buried him last night. He was in the cellar."

"Are you saying the elder killed Curt Whitlow?" Mitchell asked.

"Nay, that could not be so," the Shaker said. "The elder is a man of peace. You must be overwrought, Sister."

Carlyn looked from the Shaker to Mitchell. "He said he didn't kill him, that Curt died while locked away in the cellar." She looked back at the Shaker. "He claimed not to know why except that your Mother Ann must be helping him, that perhaps she sent demons. But then he shot him."

"Nay, Mother Ann sends us love, not demons." The Shaker recoiled from her words. "Your story does not make sense, Sister."

"Why did he shoot him?" Even Mitchell sounded a little skeptical.

"So if the grave was found, people would think I killed him. He had my gun." Carlyn was relieved Mitchell kept his arm around her.

"You should not make up such dreadful stories, my sister." The Shaker sounded so disapproving that Asher growled at him again.

"She's not making up anything." Mitchell stared down the man. "If she said he did it, then he did. We may never know why."

"That can be easily solved. We will ask him." The Shaker turned back toward the main village.

"He'll lie. You can't believe him." Carlyn twisted around to look up at Mitchell. He had to believe her.

Mitchell touched her cheek. "You don't have to worry about him now. He has to face his Maker with those lies."

"He's dead?" Carlyn couldn't stop trembling.

The Shaker man whipped around to stare first at Mitchell, then the gun he wore. "How?"

"I didn't shoot him, if that's what you're thinking. His own demons got to him first." Mitchell tightened his arm around Carlyn and looked down at her. "When he heard Sister Edna had come to and was talking, he took his own life."

"I do not believe you," the Shaker said. "Not Elder Derron. He would not commit such a sin. One that cannot be forgiven."

"Believe me or not, evil has been afoot here in your village and the elder succumbed to it." Mitchell's voice changed as he gave the man orders. "Tell your elders that I will need some men to dig up Whitlow's body and a wagon to carry it back to town. His family will want to give him a proper burial."

Carlyn felt a wave of sorrow for Curt's widow. A widow like her.

After the man left, Mitchell tightened his arm around Carlyn's waist. "I'll take you back to one of the Shaker houses. You'll have to wait for me there while I take care of things here."

"Elder Derron is really dead?"

"Yes."

"So much death. Perhaps my coming here did bring them misfortune as he said." She was suddenly so tired.

"He brought the misfortune on himself by wrong actions. You had nothing to do with it."

"But if I hadn't seen Curt and Brother Henry arguing, perhaps none of this would have happened." Carlyn stared down at the ground.

"The barn would have still burned. I doubt Elder Derron lit that fire."

"He said not. He claimed his Mother Ann was protecting him by allowing Brother Henry to die in the fire so he couldn't tell anyone about the trouble the elder was in with Curt. Everything else grew from that."

"Nothing about it was your fault, Carlyn. Nothing."

"Not all would say that is true."

"Sister Edna would. She demanded I find you."

Carlyn felt a smile coming back awake inside her. "She is demanding, but I should go see her. To thank her. Who would have ever thought I might owe my life to Sister Edna and a dog." She reached down and laid her hand on Asher's head.

"Don't forget the sheriff."

She looked back up at him then. "I could never forget the sheriff." The smile slid out on her face.

"Then will you leave here with me?" He turned her toward the Shaker village and kept her close to him while they walked. "Let me find you a place?"

She liked it there in this place beside him. She looked back at Asher limping along behind them. "There has to be room for Asher."

"No worries there." Mitchell glanced back at the dog too. "Mrs. Snowden has been beside herself ever since he got away from her at the boardinghouse. He has a way of worming into your affections."

"That he does."

Mitchell's arm tensed a little around her. "Do you think I might ever gain some of your affections?"

"You already have." Carlyn felt her cheeks warm.

"Then can there be hope of someday for us?"

His voice sounded so tentative, so unsure, that she couldn't keep from smiling up at him. "There's always hope, Mitchell." She stopped and turned to look up at him. "When you asked before, I wasn't going to say no. But I need time. Time to properly mourn Ambrose."

"So you believe he's gone now?"

"I know. I got a letter from a woman in the South who took him in after he was wounded in one of the battles. She buried him."

"I'm sorry."

And because he looked as if he really meant it, her heart warmed toward him even more. "He was a good man and I loved him very much."

"I know." He stared down into her eyes as though he could see to her heart. Perhaps he did as he went on. "But the heart has room for many loves."

"Yes. Yes, it does." Then she brazenly tiptoed up and put her lips against his there in the middle of the Shaker village with the sun shining down on them.

Epilogue

The sun was shining. The day was perfect. The night before, Carlyn had taken off her black mourning dress and hung it in the back of the wardrobe in her room at Mrs. Snowden's. Now Asher swept his tail back and forth across the floor when she pulled the yellow dress out, as if he knew the sight of that dress meant everything was changing for them.

The dress was ordinary with few frills or ruffles, but it was the color of sunshine. The minute she laid eyes on the bolt of cloth at Hopkin's Dry Goods Store a month ago she'd known that it would become the dress she would wear to begin her new life. With the sheriff. With Mitchell.

He had courted her with sweet patience and deliberate diligence after she came away from the Shaker village with him. The very sight of him now warmed her, like the sun was overhead and shining straight down on her.

In the kitchen, Mrs. Snowden was baking a cake big enough

for the whole town. At noon, Pastor Rory would stand in front of them in the parlor downstairs and read the words to tie Carlyn and Mitchell together till death parted them.

Carlyn opened her mother's Bible and touched Ambrose's letter stored there next to Psalm 23. She didn't have to read his words. They were written on her heart and she imagined him smiling down on her. He would be glad she'd found a man like Mitchell to father the children they had once dreamed of having together.

Below her, she heard Berdine come in the boardinghouse and call a greeting to Mrs. Snowden. Berdine was only weeks from delivering her first child. The first of half a dozen at least, she assured Carlyn.

Carlyn closed the Bible and ran her hand over the cover. Then she pulled the yellow dress over her head, smoothed the skirt down over her petticoats, and quickly fastened the buttons.

She took a last look around the room that had been her home for months. She would not be sleeping there this night. Mitchell had found them a house on the edge of town and had been spending every free moment building a picket fence around the yard. A place for Asher, he said, but she knew they were both seeing children playing with Asher in the sunshine.

Everything was good. She looked over at her mother's Bible again and her mother's voice whispered in her head.

Pray anyway.

And so she did. With a glad and thankful heart.

Acknowledgments

It has been good to return to my Harmony Hill Shaker village and walk those Shaker paths again. Without the encouragement of my editor, Lonnie Hull DuPont, I might never have discovered so many stories in that village. Lonnie is one of those people who are fun to work with and get to know. I love it when she starts hitting those exclamation marks!! So thanks, Lonnie.

On in the editing process, Barb Barnes makes sure I don't get carried away with pet words and run-on sentences that make readers dizzy. She keeps my characters on task and me too. Barb, you've made me a better writer. Thanks to Lindsay Davis too who is always ready to help whatever the need. A big thanks to the whole publishing team at Revell Books for putting my story in a great package and getting it in front of readers.

And of course I can never thank my agent, Wendy Lawton, enough. She encourages me and prays for me and laughs with me.

Here at home, I am blessed to have a wonderful family who support me and read my stories. You're the best.

Last of all I thank the Lord for giving me stories to share with you, and for you, my reading friends. I appreciate how you have been willing to travel with me from Rosey Corner to Hollyhill to Harmony Hill or wherever my imagination might take us. Who knows where we might go next? But wherever it is, I hope we'll all remember Carlyn's mother's advice to "pray anyway" no matter our circumstances.

Ann H. Gabhart is the bestselling author of more than twenty novels for adults and young adults. *Angel Sister*, Ann's first Rosey Corner book, was a nominee for inspirational novel of 2011 by *RT Book Reviews* magazine. Her Shaker novel, *The Outsider*, was a Christian Book Awards finalist in the fiction category. She lives on a farm not far from where she was born in rural Kentucky. She and her husband are blessed with three children, three in-law children, and nine grand-children. Ann loves reading books, watching her grandkids grow up, and walking with her dog, Oscar.

Ann enjoys connecting with readers on her Facebook page, www.facebook.com/anngabhart, where you can peek over her shoulder for her "Sunday mornings coming down," see bits of Shaker history on "Shaker Wednesdays" or laugh with her on "Friday smiles" day. Then, come visit Ann at One Writer's Journal, www.annhgabhart.blogspot.com. You never know what might show up there. Find out more at www.annhgabhart.com.

Meet

ANN H. GABHART

at

AnnHGabhart.com

Be the First to Learn about New Releases,
Read Her Blog, and Sign Up for Her Newsletter

Connect with Ann at

 Ann H Gabhart

AnnHGabhart

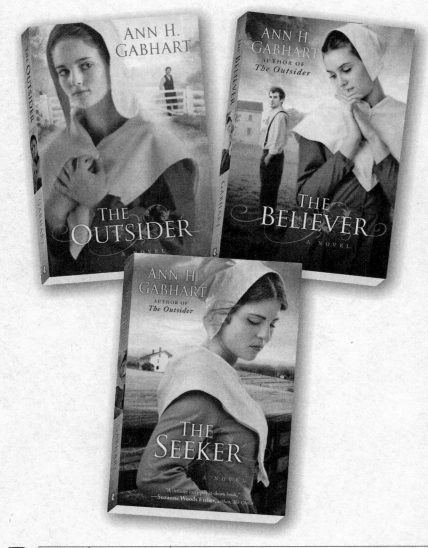

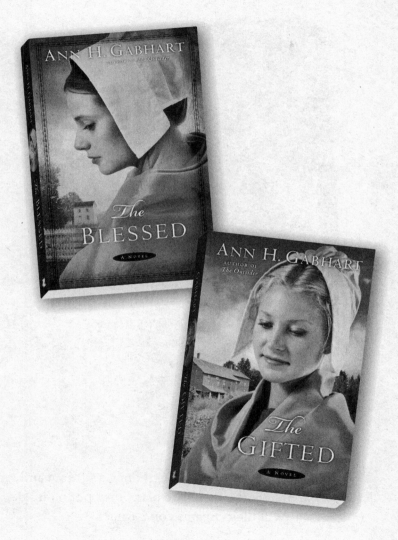

"Masterfully storytelling blends with a written love story about sisters everywhere."

—*Publishers Weekly*

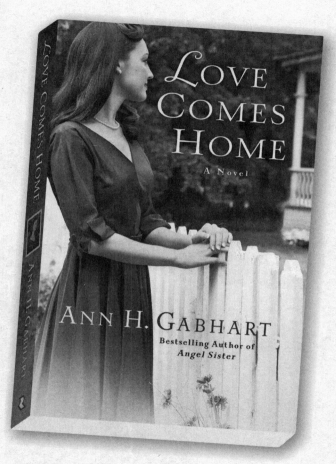

WWII is over, the boys are coming home, and Kate and her sisters are ready to pursue the plans they put on hold. Will their dreams come true?

Revell

a division of Baker Publishing Group
www.RevellBooks.com

Available wherever books and ebooks are sold.

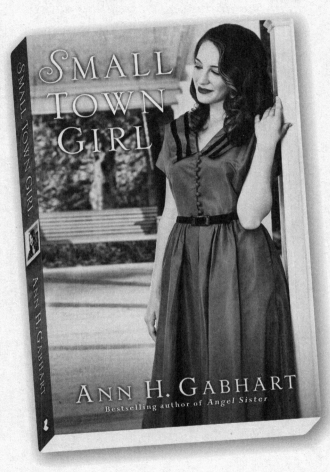

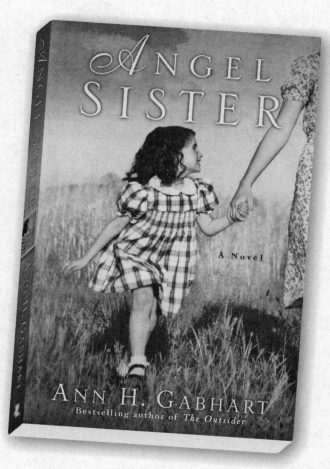

Nothing Will Be the Same after the Summer of 1964...

Hollyhill, Kentucky, seems to be well insulated from the turbulent world beyond its quiet streets. Life-changing events rarely happen here, and when they do, they are few and far between. But for Jocie Brooke and her family, they happen all at once.

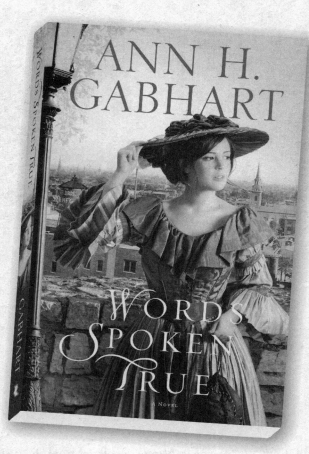

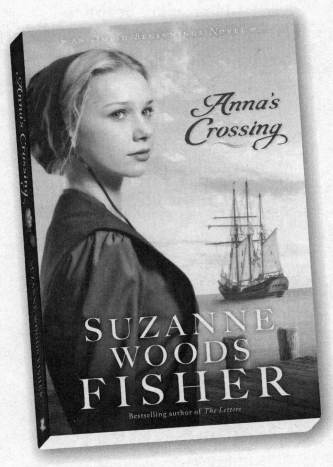

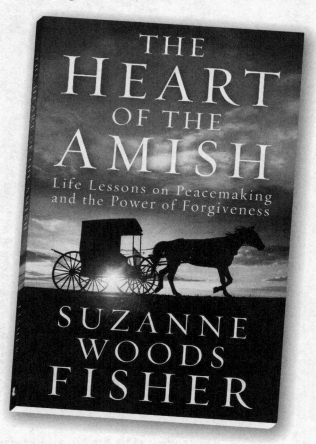